Praise for *The Shadow House*

'A thrilling novel with a fantastic setting and a plot
that unfolds with a devastating resolution'
Kayte Nunn, author of *The Silk House*
and *The Botanist's Daughter*

'With an air of menace from the first lines, *The Shadow
House* is a haunting mystery set in a creepy Australian
eco-village. Atmospheric and eerie, I flew through it!'
Allie Reynolds, author of *Shiver*

'A smart and twisty thriller, with each beat
of the plot timed to perfection'
Kate Mildenhall, author of *Skylarking* and *The Mother Fault*

'Vivid, tense and troubling. Anna Downes transports readers to
a world where everyone has a secret and no one can be trusted'
Candice Fox, author of *The Chase* and *Gathering Dark*

Anna Downes grew up in Sheffield, UK. She studied drama at Manchester before winning a place at the Royal Academy of Dramatic Art and moving to London to pursue an acting career that included credits in *EastEnders*, *Casualty*, *Holby City* and *Dalziel and Pascoe*, as well as a long-running stage production of *The Dresser* in London's West End.

Anna's bestselling debut novel, *The Safe Place*, was published simultaneously in Australia, the US and the UK in mid-2020. *The Shadow House* is her keenly anticipated second book.

Anna now lives on the Central Coast with her husband and two children.

# THE
# SHADOW
# HOUSE

## ANNA
## DOWNES

HODDER

First published in Great Britain in 2022 by Hodder & Stoughton
An Hachette UK company
First published in Australia in 2021 by Affirm Press

This paperback edition published in 2022

1

Map illustration by George Saad

A CIP catalogue record for this title is available from the British Library

Paperback ISBN 978 1 529 37512 1

Printed and bound in Great Britain by Clays Ltd, Elcograf S.p.A.

Hodder & Stoughton policy is to use papers that are natural, renewable
and recyclable products and made from wood grown in sustainable
forests. The logging and manufacturing processes are expected to
conform to the environmental regulations of the country of origin.

Hodder & Stoughton Ltd
Carmelite House
50 Victoria Embankment
London EC4Y 0DZ

www.hodder.co.uk

*For Grandad Ken*

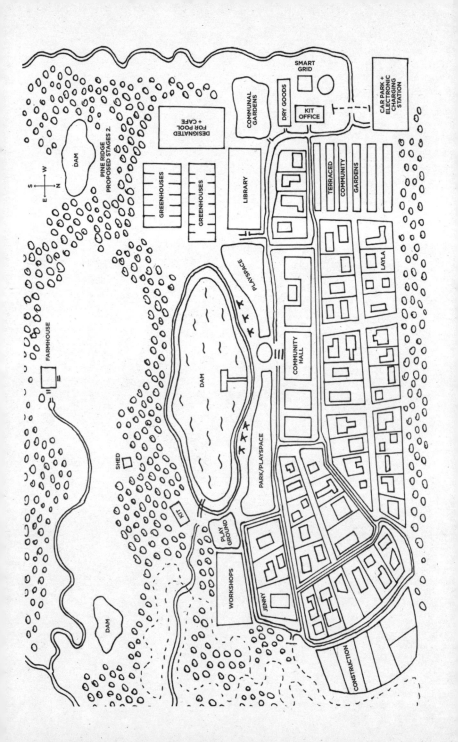

# PROLOGUE

The bones come first. A gift, but nothing wanted. Next, a doll: a likeness, a promise. And the blood marks the choice. It finds a face, and then you know.

*Help. I need help.* That's what he said; I remember it clearly.

Voices in the night, and footsteps, soft and slow on a carpet of green, on the grassy path that goes up to the blue sky and the diamond moon and the place where the birds fly north. That's where it happened.

A noise ... No, two noises, one after the other. First quiet, then loud. Oh, there was so much blood. I didn't know what to do; I didn't know how to help.

I remember all of it – only then I forget.

The rules, though; I won't forget those. Listen to me carefully, repeat after me: bones, doll, blood. That's how it goes. Things arrive, and then ... a magic trick. Here one minute, gone the next. No one knows where he went. No one except the birds. They know. They saw everything.

It wasn't his fault. It couldn't be stopped.

Things arrive, and then they take you.

# ALEX

## 1

'Okay, kids.' I brought the car to a stop and peered out the windscreen. 'I think this is it. We're here.'

Neither child replied. Glancing at each of their sleeping faces in turn – Ollie beside me in the front, Kara in the back – I felt a pang of anticlimax. The first time I'd seen Pine Ridge it had taken my breath away, and I'd been looking forward to seeing their expressions as we drove in. Well, Ollie's expression anyway. At eight months old, Kara couldn't yet tell animal from vegetable so I wasn't likely to get a reaction from her, but I'd been certain my fourteen-year-old son would be impressed. Instead, he was snoring. Headphones on, head lolling awkwardly to one side, drool glistening in the corner of his mouth.

'Kids,' I said again, a little louder. As if in response, Ollie's phone lit up in his lap, buzzing softly with a notification. I glared at it, tempted to pick it up and hurl it straight into the nearest bin.

Instead, I checked the house number and street name again. Definitely the right address, and the description matched. A split-level at the far end of the village, the last in a row of four. White walls, blue roof, two balconies and a timber staircase at the side. No one was waiting to greet us, though – which seemed strange until I remembered that I hadn't given an arrival time when I'd emailed a few days earlier. I'd had no idea when or even if we'd be able to get away, so I'd told them I'd have to play it by ear. *No problem!* had been the cheerful reply. *Just pop into the office when you get here, and we'll show you around.* But the office had been empty when I'd passed, so I'd carried on driving along the narrow main road to our allocated unit, following the directions I'd been given. There was no rush; eventually either someone would find us or we would find them.

I took a breath. The car was cramped and had that family-road-trip smell: feet and Happy Meals. Our belongings were packed around us so tightly I'd half-expected the windows to burst. Storage cartons, loose shoes and books, jumbo flexi tubs bought in a hurry from Kmart and stuffed with our dirty laundry: I'd crammed them Tetris-style into every inch of available space. An expert job, if I did say so myself. But if there was anything I did well, it was packing up and moving on.

I rolled my window down and a fresh breeze pushed its way into the car, mussing my hair like a drunk uncle and bringing with it the sweet, earthy scent of resin. A tingle of excitement skipped across my skin: *I live here now.*

I looked over at Ollie again, ducking my head a little to see under the peak of his cap. It was one of those gorgeous Australian November days – not too hot or sticky, just perfectly pleasant – but my son was bundled up in his usual sloppy green hoodie. It needed a wash; the orange circle on the front bore a tomato sauce stain the size of a fifty-cent piece.

'What's wrong with you?' he said, suddenly opening one eye. 'Why do you keep staring at me?'

'Oh. Sorry. You're awake.'

'What?' My son held one of his headphones away from his ear and tinny music escaped from the padded speakers: a thrum of bass overlaid by a single screeching note like an air raid siren.

'I said, you're awake.'

'Um, obviously.' He pushed his cap back and tugged his headphones down around his neck. 'Why are we stopped?'

'Because we're here. We've arrived.'

Ollie shrugged and picked up his phone. Checking the notifications, he moved his thumbs rapidly over the screen. *Tap-scroll-tap-tap-scroll.*

'Don't you want to get out and take a look around?'

With his eyes still glued to the screen, Ollie opened the car door and got out. Quickly checking on Kara – still asleep – I did the same. I could smell orange jasmine, lilly pilly, lemon myrtle and just a touch of sea salt. No car fumes, no bitumen, no overflowing wheelie bins. I inhaled and my lungs felt fresh and clean.

Ollie turned in a slow circle, surveying his new surroundings. Although it was just two hours from the guts of Sydney and only fifty kilometres north-east of the Central Coast's suburban sprawl, Pine Ridge ecovillage could not have felt more remote. Nestled high up in the hills and built on former farmland, it seemed completely cut off from the chaos of the city. No skull-shatteringly loud roadworks, reckless P-platers screeching their tyres or the constant ECG *blip-blip-blip* of pedestrian crossings. From the middle of the two-hundred-acre site, all you could hear were birds, bees and the hush of the wind.

The sense of peace was exaggerated by the shape of the valley – shallow and round, like a dish – and the flat stretch of water that lay at the bottom like an enormous blue puddle. The surrounding trees acted as natural soundproofing, muffling what little noise there was until the quiet felt almost artificial. The beauty of the village, too, seemed unreal. The Lego-spill of buildings from the top of the ridge to the valley floor reminded me of those European towns featured on jigsaw puzzles and postcards – Positano, Cinque Terre, Santorini – and their proximity to the dam made me think of the tranquil lakeside settlements I'd visited while backpacking in my late teens: Bled, Hallstatt, Seyðisfjörður, San Marcos La Laguna.

Ollie, however, was unmoved.

I jangled my keys while I waited for his verdict. My adrenaline levels were still high from the quick exit, the fast drive. Both hands on the wheel, one eye on the rear-view mirror. Dry mouth, cracked lips, nailbeds bloody and stinging after weeks of nervous chewing.

I watched my son's face, desperately wanting – *needing* – him to like it as much as I did. Driving down from the ridge just moments ago, I'd been so confident. How could you *not* love the seclusion, the sense of absolute safety? The road that wound away from the freeway and down into a lush tangle of eucalypts, the turquoise sparkle of the dam, and the way the land held the houses like a pair of cupped hands. It was perfect. But now, seeing the isolation through my son's eyes, the colours of Pine Ridge took on a darker hue.

In some areas, the village was still under construction. The roads were powdery, marked with dirty tyre tracks and clumps of earth. Mud-spattered concrete mixers sat next to freshly poured slabs and elaborate timber frames, and dotted around the periphery was evidence of the old farm the village had been built over: abandoned trailers, coils of rusty wire, stacks of discarded piping. Rickety old sheds slouched in corners like sulky children.

But, judging by the pace at which the development had grown since I'd first seen it, that would all get cleared up soon enough. Thrown away or burned. Paved over, smoothed back, polished up and transformed into something better. Out with the old, in with the new. I liked that sentiment. Clearly, there was no room for the past in a place like Pine Ridge. Or that was my hope anyway.

'I cannot believe,' Ollie said eventually, in the disdainful tone of voice he reserved especially for me, 'that you're making me move to a hippie commune.'

'It's not a commune. It's an ecovillage.'

'Whatever.' He went back to his phone. 'It's a dump.'

I sighed, deflated. 'Why don't we go on up and take a look around?'

We climbed the six wide steps that led up to the house. On either side, terraced retaining walls had been topped with grevillea, bottlebrush and other low-maintenance shrubs, giving the garden a slightly wild and unkempt feel.

'Why couldn't you just have grounded me or something?' said Ollie behind me. 'That's what all the other parents have done. No one else is getting pulled out of school and shipped off to the middle of nowhere.'

At the top of the steps, I studied the windows, looking for signs of life. 'This isn't your punishment, Oliver. Try to think of it as an experiment. The lease is only three months. If after that we decide we don't like it, we can leave.'

'Like we always do.'

'Not always.'

'Yes, always.'

'And you *are* grounded.'

'What?'

'Until further notice. *That's* your punishment.'

His jaw fell open.

'Sorry, mate,' I said. 'Your actions, your consequences.'

'But I didn't even *do* anything!' He stared at me, outraged. 'I already told you—'

'I know what you told me, and I don't want to hear it again, not right now. We can talk about it later.'

He scowled for a moment longer before returning to his phone, face blank, jaw set, neck bent forward at an alarming right angle.

I tried the front door, but it was locked. I knocked, but there was no answer. I took a step back, studying the first-floor windows. The house, like many of its neighbours, was built on a steeply raked block, and from what I could see, the two levels had separate access. The upper connected to the road behind while the lower – a smaller, self-contained version of the more spacious upstairs – opened onto the road in front.

'Why only three months?' Ollie's sharp question came out of nowhere.

'What do you mean?'

'Just seems random, that's all. Like, isn't it usually six months? Or twelve?'

'This place works a little differently,' I said. 'They only want permanent residents, because they're trying to grow the community, so you get three months to decide if you want to invest – like, try before you buy. And if you don't want to commit by then, you have to move on.'

'So, what happens if we want to stay?'

'Well, we could build.' I walked around the side of the house to where a paved patio had been set into the lawn. The wooden staircase I'd glimpsed from the road led up to a small balcony on the first floor. 'They have a scheme here called "collaborative living", where you put your name on a list, they match you with people you might like to live with, and then you all buy a block of land together.'

'Huh,' said Ollie.

'You split the cost of the land but build your own separate houses, which makes it half the normal market price.' I looked back at the lower level windows. The whole place seemed deserted. 'I don't think anyone's here. Should I go upstairs, do you think? Or head back to the office?'

Ollie ignored my questions. 'I don't get it. You want us to buy a house with strangers?'

'Not a house, a block of land. The individual house, once we built it, would be ours. You could help design it. Doesn't that sound exciting?'

'No, it sounds mental.'

I wandered back around to the front of the house.

Ollie followed me. 'Why would we buy anything with people we've never met?'

'Well, obviously we'd meet them first. That's the point of the temporary lease; it's like a trial run. Gives us time to get to know people, see if we like them.'

*And see if they like us*, I added silently.

'What if no one wants to live with us?' said Ollie, as if reading my mind.

I shrugged. 'Then we leave.'

'Right.' He pulled his cap down over his eyes. 'Of course we do.'

'Oh, come on,' I said. 'Don't be grumpy. Look at the view!' I spread my arms wide, gesturing to the forest on our left, the houses to the right, and the undeveloped land on the other side of the valley. Rainwater tanks sat in terraced gardens and solar panels reflected the sun. Butterflies and bees orbited nasturtiums and geraniums, and directly in front of us, just visible over the top of the neighbouring houses, the dam reached out to a rising hill and bright green grass stippled with shade. In an empty paddock, a single old farm building stood prettily like a scene from a painting: white weatherboard, a gabled roof and a wraparound veranda.

'Isn't it beautiful?' I breathed.

'It's shit,' came Ollie's blunt reply. 'Where are the people? Where are the shops, the cafes, the surf clubs? Where is the *surf*?'

I pointed out a volleyball net strung up between two poles, and an adventure playground under bright orange shade sails. Barbecue stations, picnic tables and a swimming jetty that stretched out over the glittering surface of the dam. The freshly paved roads, I said, were perfect for bike and scooter riding. 'It's like a holiday park, don't you think?'

With a mere toss of his head, my son made it clear that he did not. 'Can I have the car keys?' he muttered. 'I need to charge my phone.'

His dismissal hurt. I dug in my pocket and passed him the keys. As I watched him trudge back down to the road, I spotted something on the top step. A brown cardboard mailing box sitting in the shade of an overgrown shrub, half-hidden by flowers and leaves. I crouched down to take a closer look: was it meant for me?

The package was unmarked – no name, no address – and unsealed. Curious, I pulled back one of the flaps, revealing feathers and a tiny scaled claw. A single beady eye. And glistening pink lumps.

'Oh, god.' I jumped away from the box. Was that … a *dead bird*? I went back to check. 'Ugh, gross.' Definitely a bird. Definitely dead, squashed and mangled, like it had been gutted by a cat or a fox. Some of its feathers had been torn out and tiny bones were sticking out of a gash in its flesh. The inside of the box was smeared with a dark, oily-looking substance.

What the hell was a dead bird doing on the doorstep? Surely the rental properties were checked and cleaned before new tenants moved in?

Then I heard a noise. A swishing, crackling sound coming from somewhere nearby. It sounded like footsteps moving through long grass. I got to my feet. Turning in a slow circle, I gazed up at the house, my eyes travelling the walls to the upper level, the windows and the overhanging eaves. I looked at the neighbouring houses and into the forest, but as far as I could see, no one else was around.

I glanced down at my car to where Ollie was sitting in the front passenger seat with the door open, his headphones back over his ears. He already hated the place; smashed animal corpses wouldn't improve his opinion. I picked up the box and walked around the side of the house. Finding a bin at the back, I lifted the lid, threw the box inside and immediately felt better.

But as I returned to the front of the house, I was gripped by a wave of panic so intense that I had to lean against the wall to stop my head from spinning. Was I doing the right thing, moving to Pine Ridge? The cumulative weight of my decisions threatened to crush me: all the things I could have done but hadn't, all the things I'd done but shouldn't have. Every choice suddenly seemed like the wrong one.

My heart raced, my stomach churned. *All your fault. Shitty mother.*

Closing my eyes, I tried to calm my thoughts but heard Stuart's voice instead. *Go on, run. Go ahead and try. I'll find you.*

I sucked in a breath and let it out slowly. *Get. It. Together. Your children need you.*

Right on cue, I heard my daughter stir, her soft kitten noises floating through the open car window. My breasts tingled as my milk came down in response – nearly time for another feed – and as Kara's cries increased in volume, my own words to Ollie echoed in my head: *Your actions, your consequences.* Briefly I considered opening my mouth and wailing along with her.

But, no, everything would be fine. Better than that, it would be great. I had already done the hard part and now I would make us a new life. We would be okay.

I opened my eyes and thought about the glorious distance between me and Sydney, the gigantic spread of national park with its creeks and cliffs, rainforest and swollen rivers. I looked at the hills, the trees, the water, and all those shiny new homes. Above them all was the sky, big and bright and full of potential.

*Breathe in.*

*Breathe out.*

*It will be fine.*

There was nothing better than a fresh start.

# ALEX

## 2

Just as I was soothing Kara and wondering what to do next, we met our first neighbour: a thin woman wearing a long linen dress and a yellow headscarf who came hurrying along the road from the direction of the gates. 'Hello,' she said, offering her hand for me to shake. 'You must be our new arrivals. I'm Jenny, I live upstairs.'

'Alex,' I said, grasping her palm. 'Lovely to meet you. Thanks for letting us move in at such short notice.'

'My pleasure. And no need to thank me – I mean, I suppose I'm technically the landlady, but we don't really think of each other in those terms here. The land belongs to everyone.' She chuckled self-consciously. 'So where are you from? Is that an accent I can hear?'

'Yes, I grew up in England but I've been in Australia now for almost as many years. We've just moved from Sydney.'

'Ah, Pine Ridge will be quite the change for you, then. Here's the key. Sorry I wasn't around when you arrived; I only popped out for ten minutes. Did you find the place okay? Can I help you with anything?'

I liked Jenny immediately. Despite her gaunt face and skinny frame, she had a lively, infectious energy.

'Well, hello there, sweetie,' she said, tickling Kara under the chin and making her giggle. 'Aren't you precious?' She even got a smile out of Ollie, which, at that point, felt like a small miracle.

Jenny kept Kara entertained while Ollie and I dragged our life from the car like guts from a fish, chatting cheerfully as we hauled it all up the steps. She was so kind and eager to please that I couldn't bring myself to mention the dead bird in the box; I didn't want to get off on the wrong foot by complaining.

Fortunately, I couldn't find fault with anything else. The unit itself was delightful. The living area held a sofa, rug, coffee table and small TV. Light spilled in through two good-sized windows and a set of sliding glass doors led to a small entertaining deck. The kitchen was light and airy, with a brand new electric oven and subway-tiled walls, and a bowl of yellow lemons had been placed on the timber-topped island bench, bright as a holiday in Spain. It was so cute I could've cried.

Jenny showed us where everything was and how it worked, and then just as she was leaving, a man appeared in the doorway carrying a bottle of wine and a brown paper bag.

'Ah, Kit,' Jenny said. 'Good, I was just about to call down to the office. Alex, have you met our founder?'

'Yes, of course.' I gave Kit a friendly wave.

'Alex!' said Kit, enthusiastically. 'So glad you made it.'

My stomach flipped. I'd forgotten how attractive he was. Tanned skin, a light beard and dark hair tied back in a man bun. A fit-looking physique pleasantly showcased in a muscle T and cut-off shorts. A smile as white and clean as a bedsheet drying in the sun.

Kit Vestey and I had met just once, by accident, outside a Bondi yoga studio several months earlier. Kara and I had been leaving our very first (and last, as it turned out) Mums and Bubs yoga class and we'd both been cranky: she'd missed a nap, and I was pissed off with all the rich-ass 'mumpreneurs' who were so much bendier than me and whose children were so much more compliant than mine. Kara had spent the whole class wriggling away from me and side-eyeing all the other infants as if to say, *Designer nappies? Headbands? These are not my people* – which, quite frankly, had been fair enough.

Despite my mood, however, I'd said hi to the guy handing out fliers in the lobby, because the way he'd smiled at me made me think I knew him. He asked me how I'd enjoyed my class, which seemed like confirmation that we knew each other, so we stood there for a while, chatting about yoga like old pals – and then he handed me a flier. *Pine Ridge*, it said. *Create the life you want.*

I realised then that, in fact, he was a total stranger, and I'd made the mistake of engaging with a street salesman. I started to make my excuses, but the feeling of déjà vu was so strong that I found myself lingering as he made his pitch. *Community, sustainability, great for the planet, affordable housing, blah blah.* 'It's not really my thing,' I said in the end, 'but it was nice to meet you.'

Days later, the name Pine Ridge was still stuck in my head, as was the guy's warm smile. I kept thinking about the flier I'd tucked into my handbag.

And then one day, when things had got really bad, I went for a drive. Ollie had left for school, Stu had left for work. Kara hadn't slept in what felt like months, so I was at a pretty low ebb. I'd just intended to drive around the block to get her to sleep, but for some reason I kept going, edging further and further out of the city, until I ended up on the freeway. I drove and drove, near stoned with exhaustion, wondering if perhaps I'd finally gone round the bend and would end up somewhere near Cape York ... and then I saw an exit coming up, a slip road snaking off to the side, little white arrows on the tarmac pointing the way. My brain said, *Turn here.* So I did. Twenty minutes later, I saw the sign and realised my subconscious had driven me all the way to Pine Ridge.

I parked. Took a look around. And promptly fell in love. The rolling hills, the forest, the colour and the light ... *I'm home*, I remembered thinking, before telling myself to snap out of it and mainline some caffeine in case I started hallucinating.

I didn't stay long that day, and I didn't see Kit. I spoke briefly to a woman who assumed I was lost (when I didn't correct her, she gave me directions back to the freeway), and then I drove home. I told myself I'd put Pine Ridge in my back pocket, save it for a rainy day. And when the rain finally – and inevitably – fell, I made a call. Fortunately, Kit seemed happy for me to pay the three months' rent upfront and in cash when I arrived.

At the time, it'd felt like the best idea in the world. But now, standing in my new kitchen, the whole thing felt very rushed and I questioned myself all over again.

'Well,' said Jenny, 'if you two already know each other, I'll get out of your way. Alex, it was lovely to meet you. Have fun unpacking, and if you need anything, just ask.' Giving me a quick pat on the arm, she disappeared out the door, leaving me alone with Kit.

'Fast work,' he said, stepping inside the unit and nodding at all our boxes and bags. 'Looks like you've got your roots down already.'

'Not our first rodeo,' I said. 'And Jenny helped. She's very nice.'

'I'm sorry, I should've been here, too. I honestly don't know where the day has gone. Can I bribe you into forgiving me?' He handed me the wine: a buttery-gold white with a handwritten label. 'A little welcome gift, homemade by one of our residents. And this is bread and cheese.' He put the paper bag on the kitchen bench. 'I thought you might be hungry after your journey.'

'Thank you.' An embarrassing blush crept up my neck. Looks-wise, Kit wasn't especially remarkable: average height and build, brown eyes, thick eyebrows and sharp lines that ran down each side of his mouth when he smiled. But he had some major charisma going on, and something about him made it hard to look away, like when a painting draws your attention but you can't articulate why.

There was an awkward pause I didn't know how to fill. I became painfully aware that I was a mess: dirty hair, no make-up, denim shorts and an unflattering T-shirt I'd thrown on in the dark that morning. I hadn't even showered yet. Kit, by contrast, looked fresh, clean and confident. His T-shirt, I noticed, bore a swirling eye-like symbol below the words *What's your truth?* I almost laughed. *My truth? Oh, honey, you don't want to know.*

I cleared my throat. 'Sorry, I should introduce you to the kids. This is Kara.' I bent down to lift my daughter from the floor where she'd been rolling around on her mat, safely hemmed in by boxes, holding her toes and babbling to herself. She clung to me and shoved her whole hand in her mouth.

Kit gave her a wave. 'Ah, she's beautiful.'

I smiled at her proudly. 'She knows it, too.'

Kara removed her hand from her mouth and blew a spit bubble. 'Bah bah,' she said, and banged her hands together like she'd just performed a magic trick.

'My son Ollie's around here somewhere, too. I'll go find him.'

'No, it's alright, let him settle in,' Kit said. 'Can I help you bring anything else up from the car?'

'No, I think we're all done.'

'In that case,' said Kit, 'why don't I show you around the village? I've just about got enough time to give you the grand tour.'

Stuffing Kara in her pram and forcibly dragging Ollie with me, I followed Kit around Pine Ridge, oohing and aahing at all the special features. We walked back to the main gate and started with the site office, a cleverly renovated shipping container set in its own little garden. Through the glass wall at one end, I could see a long tidy desk, and two chairs set up in front of large computer screens. 'That's where I spend most of my time,' said Kit. 'If you have any problems or questions, you can usually find me in there.'

Next to the office was a long shed with a mechanical code-lock on the door and a sign that said *Food Store*. Behind that was a stretch of lush garden, bursting with colour, and even further beyond, a long row of curved greenhouses covered with plastic sheeting. 'There were fourteen originally,' Kit said, 'but only one or two were still in use when we bought the land. The plastic had all blown off and the beds were overgrown, but they had heaps of potential. We've got nine of them back up and working now.'

In the centre of the village overlooking the dam was a community hall, a gym and a small cafe run by a volunteer. 'We've got plans to build a bigger one over by the greenhouses,' Kit explained, 'along with a pool and a wellness centre.'

There was a tool library, from which any resident could borrow any DIY instrument imaginable, and an actual library, well stocked with new titles. Kit also showed us two different playgrounds. 'We try to give the kids as much to do as possible to get them off their screens and outside. Although they really don't need much encouragement. They seem to want to be outdoors all the time, even when the weather's crap.' A brand-new climbing wall and a skate ramp, he said, were on their way.

We carried on past more houses, more gardens and a third playground. The village was anything but busy, but now I could see what I'd missed from the position of our unit: a quiet but constant buzz of low-level activity. Parents with small children playing on the shores of the dam; work-from-homers taking coffee breaks on their balconies; retirees in hats and gardening gloves, kneeling in dirt, ripping weeds from the soil. Everyone smiled and waved as we strolled past.

We stopped for a moment in the shade of a tree. Kara mewled

in her pram. It was hot and she was getting hungry.

'As you can see, there's still a lot to do,' Kit said. 'The stormwater drainage on the top road went in last week, and that round house – you see the one over there with the cob walls? That's finished now, too. We're looking at renovating some of the old farm buildings next.' His eyes lit up as he described plans for a backpacker hostel, a woodwork studio and a gift shop.

I raised my eyebrows. 'Gift shop?'

'I know, I know.' Kit laughed and shrugged his shoulders. 'But we need the income.'

Beside me, Ollie sighed loudly. *Can we go*? he mouthed as soon as he had my attention. *I'm bored.* Kara, the little co-conspirator, kicked her legs and whined. I shot them both a stern look and held a finger up: *Just one more minute.* I was tired and irritable too, having spent most of the night awake, anxiously composing last-minute to-do lists and obsessively googling the endless ways in which my baby could die in an unfamiliar environment (exposed power points, choking hazards, germs, looping electrical cords, unsecured cupboards, sharp corners, unexpected pans of boiling hot water, cranky neighbours with potentially aggressive dogs; the list went on and on).

'There are hiking trails through the forest,' said Kit, oblivious to our silent family conference. 'Just look for the signposts. And the dam is safe for swimming so feel free to take a dip whenever you like.'

'Great,' I said, trying to stay engaged. 'The water looks beautiful. The whole place is beautiful.'

Kit smiled. 'Thanks. We like it.'

'How long has it taken to build?'

'So far? About six years.'

'And before that it was just farmland?'

'Yep. As far as the eye can see.'

'What kind?'

'A flower farm. Quite a big operation, too – or it was, back in the day. You can still see parts of it. Some sheds, the greenhouses. And the paddocks over on the far side of the dam are still more or less as we found them.'

My eyes skimmed across the dam and up the undeveloped hill. 'Will you build over there, too?'

'That's the plan.'

'What's that over there?' I pointed at the abandoned building I'd seen earlier, the one that looked like a painting. Single storey and elevated on stumps, with wide eaves and a plantation-style balustrade.

Kit followed my gaze. 'That's the old farmhouse, where the family used to live.'

'It's so pretty.' I flashed back to one of my favourite childhood storybooks, about a little girl who lived in a big white house with a neat picket fence and had grand country adventures. I remembered tracing the illustrations with my fingertips, desperate to live between the pages.

'It is nice,' Kit agreed. 'Or it was. It needs a *lot* of work. Occasionally we talk about renovating it but … I don't know, we might just knock it down. No one wants to live there anyway.'

'Why?'

'Oh, it's silly, but the house has a bit of a history. The farmers who used to live there lost a child; their son went missing. Most people round here reckon he just ran away, but some say there was more to it, and now there's this local rumour that the house is haunted or whatever.' He laughed again. 'No one believes it, obviously, but you know how these things stick. Everyone here just gives it a wide berth.'

'Huh,' I said, reaching into the pram to tickle Kara, who giggled with delight. 'A haunted ecovillage. Now that's one I haven't heard before.'

Kit laughed, too. 'No, well, we like to think we're unique around here.'

Ollie rolled his eyes and gave me another pointed look. Ignoring him, I smiled politely at an older couple making their way home from a swim in the dam: wet hair, bare feet, damp towels wrapped around their bodies. They waved and Kit beckoned them over to introduce us. They started chatting about something or other, and I tuned out. Turning around to check on my kids, I saw that Ollie had his phone out again.

'Hey,' I hissed. 'Can you pay attention, please?'

'To what?' he muttered. 'No one's saying anything interesting.'

I fought to stay calm. I understood things had been tough for him lately, and he was struggling with the move, but since we'd arrived he'd done nothing but pout and complain.

My eyes fell on his phone. 'Who are you texting?'

'No one.'

'Ollie?'

'I'm not texting.'

'So then what *are* you doing?'

'None of your business.'

I bit my lip and tried to keep my voice level. 'Is it Stuart?'

'Nup.'

'You haven't told him, have you?'

Ollie sighed. 'And what if I do?'

I hesitated. How much did Ollie know? How much should I tell him? *As little as possible* was the obvious answer. 'It's just … it's better if he doesn't know where we are.'

'Uh-huh.' My son regarded me coolly. 'Might've been good to figure that out before you had a baby with him, hey?' He tossed a contemptuous look into Kara's pram.

I couldn't think of a response. *Ollie, 1: Mum, 0.*

I let it slide and returned my attention to Kit and the retirees but couldn't find a way back into their conversation. I waited politely for them to finish, gazing over at the beautiful storybook farmhouse. There was, I realised, a dark shape on the veranda just behind one of the posts. Was someone up there? I waited for the shape to move. But the longer I looked, the more I suspected it was just a shadow cast by a tree, or perhaps something left leaning against the balustrade. I shielded my eyes from the sun, straining to see more clearly.

'Seriously, Mum, can we get out of here now?' Ollie said, loudly enough for Kit to hear. 'I am so done.'

I was mortified. '*Oliver.*'

He scowled at me, and a spiteful, unforgivable thought flashed through my mind: *Lucky farmers. If my son disappeared, I might not mind so much.*

# RENEE

## 3

'Ivory? Ivor-eee. Where are you?'

Bending down to peer underneath an empty metal trolley, Renee Kellerman puckered her chapped lips and made a series of squeaky kissing noises.

'Ivor-eeee. Come on out now, puss, it's breakfast time.'

Like all the other places she'd looked, the space under the trolley was empty of everything but dust balls and dried leaves. No flash of white fur, no flicking tail or pink tongue. She straightened up and, placing her hands on her hips, looked around the wrapping room. *Where the heck is that cat?*

Just beyond the doorway, Michael stood conducting the morning meeting under the tin roof of the big shed. Eleven team members huddled around him in a ragged circle, rubbing their bleary eyes and shuffling their feet.

Twenty years ago, when she'd first moved to the farm as a newlywed, mornings had been like one big party: a crowd of people milling around, chatting, laughing, rehashing the previous night's footy or arguing over whose turn it was to help out with the weekend market run. Renee would scurry around like a waitress, handing out hot coffee and bacon and egg rolls, and generally making sure that everyone was adequately prepared for the day ahead. Making breakfast for over twenty people had added an extra hour to her daily schedule, but she didn't mind. The backslapping and banter, she'd quickly discovered, were as much a part of the morning routine as the rising of the sun itself.

But then came the drought. For almost a decade, crippling conditions had seen the team cut down to a third of its original number and the merry babble of voices reduced to a low, solemn hum. It had taken Renee just ten minutes to brew the coffee, and another five to butter the toast. No more banter, no more bacon and eggs; the drought had taken them, along with all their profits.

*Never mind*, she thought, glancing up at the bulbous grey sky. *It's all over now.* The last six months had seen unprecedented rainfall and the next six at least looked set to stay wet, so even though they weren't quite back to full strength yet, she knew they weren't far off. Michael had worked hard to keep the business afloat and his efforts had paid off; re-expansion had already started and the bacon was back. As surely the cat would be, once she got bored of chasing skinks.

Before she left the shed Renee checked the coolroom, sliding open the door and securing it with the latch. She stuck her head inside. There was a small chance Ivory had been locked in there overnight; it wasn't like the poor thing could heed the same incessant safety warnings Renee doled out to Gabriel every day of his life. *Never let that freezer door close behind you; always put the latch on so it doesn't slide shut. Never go down to the dam at night. Never play with chemicals. Never go into the farm sheds or play with the equipment. Never stick your fingers into the conveyor belt while it's running. Never put your hand into a small space without first checking for spiders. Never run around in long grass.* Her fears were not unfounded. A young boy had fallen into a sinkhole a few years ago. A local girl had been bitten by a snake. Cautionary tales, everlasting fuel for a mother's fire.

It was only after Renee had married a farmer that she'd had any idea of how dangerous the job was. A century ago the most you had to worry about was getting jabbed by a pitchfork, maybe run over by your horses. Now the hazards included grain bin suffocation, tractor rollovers, fume exposure, livestock accidents, electrocution, limbs snagged and captured by machinery. Every day was a dance with death.

She frowned. It was true that a flower farm didn't have as many risks as an agricultural station, but when you laid out the risks, it was a small miracle both the cat and her son had survived thus far. Fortunately, they were both such home-loving creatures, so unlikely to wander too far from the soft furnishings and sunbeams of the house, that neither had come to any harm – but just because nothing had happened *yet* didn't mean that nothing would.

A thorough search between the trolleys turned up nothing but unswept corners and eventually Renee had to concede that the coolroom was empty. She checked her watch: 7.20am. The school bus would be arriving soon. Time to get back to the house. Shivering, she swept her eyes around the coolroom one last time. Then, with a final desultory call – *'Ivor-eeee'* – she made her way back to the door, lifted the latch and dragged the heavy silver panel back into place.

Renee was too late to see her son off. As she drove the buggy up the hill, she could just make him out in the far distance, a lanky silhouette sloping away up the lane. He was almost certainly too far away to hear her, but she called out anyway, leaning from the buggy and waving, and the futility of the gesture seemed briefly poignant. For years now, she'd felt as though all he'd done was travel further and further away from her.

She went back to the house, finished up the morning chores and joined the pickers in the greenhouses. Filling the buggy with buckets of water, she followed behind as first the lilies were gathered, then the freesias and finally the dahlias. She collected each bunch of flowers with a nod of satisfaction; their output might not be as significant as it once was, but the product was still topnotch. The farm would bounce back to its former glory, she was sure of it.

When all the buckets were full, Renee drove the buggy up to the shed to unload. She packed the flowers neatly into the trolleys and moved them into the coolroom, then refilled the buckets with fresh water, reloaded the buggy and started again.

Later on, while the rest of the crew emptied out the plundered greenhouses and moved on to raking and planting, Renee took the car and went shopping. In busier times, she had ordered their groceries to be delivered in bulk and direct to the farm. While this had been more convenient than going to the shops herself, it had also meant that she hardly ever set foot off the property. Farming was a full-time job in the most literal sense: it was twenty-four hours a day, seven days a week, no holidays, no breaks. During the quiet years of the drought, the ninety-minute round trip to the nearest shopping centre had seemed like a treat, one that she allowed herself even as the farm grew busier again. She would take her time, wandering through the aisles and running her fingers along the shelves, picking up jars of jam and selecting the juiciest cuts of meat, making sure to buy local where possible. She might taste a few cheese samples, stop somewhere for a coffee, or even pause for a while in the IGA and entertain the idea of testing out a new brand of laundry detergent. The whole trip felt like trying on a different life for size, and she always returned to the farm in a better mood.

Today, though, as she drove back in through the gate and steered the car over the bumpy gravel driveway, she had a feeling that something was off. She parked in her usual spot, got out and looked around, her skin prickling unpleasantly – but as far as she could see, nothing was noticeably strange or different. Except …

Something was rustling in the trees behind the house. An animal? They got deer in the woods sometimes. She stood still in the middle of the driveway, listening. But then, almost as abruptly as it had started, the rustling stopped.

Leaving the groceries in the boot of the Jeep, Renee climbed the porch steps and pushed open the screen door.

'Hello?'

Her voice echoed through the house and bounced off the surfaces. Her watch now read 4.30pm. Gabriel's beaten-up black

Adidas had been thrown in their usual spot on the shoe rack and his schoolbag lay discarded on the mat, but Michael's work boots were still missing; he wouldn't be home for another half-hour yet. Nothing was out of the ordinary, so why did she feel so uneasy?

She shot a look down the hall, thinking for the thousandth time that they absolutely *had* to redecorate. Having been handed down through generations, the house was a mix of decorative styles, exemplified here by Renee's dainty tulip-style lamp on Michael's grandfather's ugly hardwood console table, and her gorgeous floral wallpaper, forever marred by an apparently non-negotiable display of antique farm tools: hay hooks, pitchforks and a hand-forged brush axe, all intended to evoke the sweat and satisfaction that come with an honest day's work, but which actually just brought to mind a torture chamber.

Halfway to the kitchen, Gabriel's bedroom door was shut but, as always, it radiated energy, a sort of *hum*. You could practically see the gloom seeping out from the edges. She moved towards it, letting the screen door shut behind her. 'Gabe? You here?'

There was a short pause, and then a muffled affirmative grunt.

'Everything okay?'

'Yup.'

'You need anything?'

'Nup.'

Silence.

Renee stepped right up to the bedroom door and placed her

fingers on the handle. 'Is it alright if I come in?'

She waited. No reply.

Renee took a few deep breaths, raised her eyes to the ceiling then tried again. 'Gabriel? I'm coming in, okay?'

No answer.

She opened the door.

The sudden flurry of movement made her jump. Gabriel was sitting upright at his desk in front of his giant gaming rig, headphones on, one hand on the hurriedly closed lid of his laptop. A thick spiral-bound pad of paper was balanced over his knees.

Renee froze. 'Oh,' she stammered, her face flooding with heat. 'Oh. Sorry. I, um, I knocked, but—'

'Mum, get out!' Gabriel said, his voice strangled.

Renee stood paralysed in the doorway. She took in the sight of her son: his chest so inwardly curved it was almost hollow; long legs jutting out under the table like overstretched pieces of elastic, swamped in loose tracksuit pants. His sallow skin was riddled with acne, his hair so oily it appeared to be wet. The room smelled sour, like morning breath. She tried not to grimace. He made her think of frogs, of cave-dwelling creatures who never saw the light of day.

Then her eyes fell on Gabriel's arm, the one holding the pad in his lap. Just below the elbow was a dark row of red marks. Cuts. Four of them, jagged and red. The surrounding skin was swollen and shiny.

Renee gasped. 'What ...?' Instinctively, she went to touch him, but before she could get close Gabriel jumped up, tucking his arm behind his back. The swivel chair spun around between them like a fairground ride.

'Gabe? What's going on? What happened?'

Gabriel tugged his sleeve down and regarded her with hooded eyes. He blinked once. Twice. 'The cat,' he muttered. 'The cat scratched me.'

Renee hesitated, a multitude of responses occurring to her at once: *Ivory? Are you sure? When? How? Are you okay? Where is she? Have you cleaned it? Do you need me to look at it, dress it? We should—*

But Gabriel was already in motion, hurrying forward and ushering her out of the room.

'Wait—' she said, stumbling backwards. Then the door shut, and she found herself once more on the other side, alone and confused, her ears ringing painfully in the swollen silence.

Later that night, after Michael had returned home and dinner had been cooked, served and eaten, Renee took out the rubbish. Still fretting over the scratches on Gabe's arm and the whereabouts of the cat, she didn't see the cardboard box on the front porch until she was almost on top of it.

She assumed at first that it'd been left by one of the workers: a borrowed tool, perhaps, used and returned, or a cake baked by somebody's wife as a gift. Maybe it was another of Gabriel's regular online orders – though if that were the case, wouldn't the package be addressed and sealed instead of flapping open like that?

She reached for it but stopped right before her fingers touched the lid. There was something on the lower left-hand corner ... a picture, a logo? She looked more closely. It was a stain. A big, dark, spreading stain. Ink, or paint.

Renee frowned. The stain, she realised, was leaking through the cardboard onto the wooden panels of the porch. Whatever was inside the box was wet.

'Michael,' she called. A fly landed on her nose; she flinched and batted it away with her hand. *'Michael!'*

But she was already reaching for the flaps, peering inside, gasping and recoiling at the sight of matted white fur, mangled flesh and oozing blood.

As her eyes traced the lifeless outline of her beloved Ivory, the cat who'd kept her company for over nine years, she began to tremble. When she reached the place where the cat's head should've been, she screamed.

# ALEX

## 4

At first, we lived out of suitcases. The move had exhausted me even more than I'd thought, and I was still so jacked with anxiety that I couldn't bring myself to unpack in case we had to run again. But on the third day, once I'd relaxed a little, I opened a couple of boxes and put a few things away. And then once I started I couldn't stop.

Sweat rolled down my back and my shoulders burned as I charged around the unit with armfuls of clothes and piles of towels, scattering our belongings in an attempt to make the place my own. In between nappy changes and breastfeeds, I opened crates and unzipped bags, running through a mental checklist as I took stock of our stuff. Laptop, check. Charger, check. Breast pump, nappies, bottles, soft toys. Shoes, make-up, underwear, nursing pads. The good saucepan, the sharp knives. I'd forgotten my favourite coffee mug and a couple of baby blankets, but otherwise we seemed to have everything.

I saved the most important bag for last, an old Sportsgirl duffle in which I'd shoved my two most important possessions: a large Tupperware container, and a picture frame made from paddle-pop sticks.

I took the bag into the laundry and quietly closed the door

behind me. Taking out the container, I popped the lid and checked the contents. Once I was satisfied that everything was still there, I wrapped up the container in a bin liner and shoved it to the very back of the cupboard under the sink, tucking it behind a value box of detergent. When that didn't seem enough, I arranged a stack of sponges and cloths around the detergent as well.

Back in my bedroom, I placed the picture frame front and centre on my chest of drawers.

'Well, thank Christ you didn't forget that piece of crap,' said Ollie, sauntering past the doorway on his way to the toilet.

'Shhh,' I hissed, pointing at the travel cot where Kara was taking a nap.

He ignored me. 'You sure you've got all the other essentials? Tie-dyed T-shirt? Hempseed oil? DIY kombucha kit?'

'Keep your voice down.' I crept from my room and closed the door. 'And it's not crap, it's beautiful.'

Ollie had made the frame at day care, back when I was the axis on which his world spun. Sure, the green glitter had faded and some of the sticky gems had fallen off, but it had been a Mother's Day gift and I'd treasured it ever since; wherever we went, it came with us. It currently held a photo of Ollie cradling Kara on the day she was born – the only hard-copy family photo I had.

'What's with the shitty attitude, anyway?' I added. 'And when are you going to unpack your stuff?'

The bathroom door banged shut and I swore under my breath. In addition to stubborn and uncooperative, my son was being aggressively antisocial. Having very quickly realised that confining him to the house was more likely to hurt me than him, I'd gone back on my decision to ground him and suggested he go exploring. Of course, that meant Ollie spent all morning lying on the couch in his undies, playing on his phone with the volume turned up in a blatant effort to piss me off.

Aware that he needed space, I left him to it, focusing instead on feathering my new nest, and for a while I felt fine. We hadn't brought any furniture with us, but luckily the unit came furnished with all the essentials and what few items we *had* brought seemed to fit perfectly, as if we'd always been there. The place was now looking pretty good. But it was hot – the delightful spring weather had intensified to a soupy humidity overnight, and the ceiling fans just weren't cutting it – and I was tired. Unsettled by the move and plagued by new teeth, Kara had tossed, turned and grizzled from dusk till dawn, and what little sleep I'd managed had been ruined by vivid dreams of ungodly noises coming from the woods and dead birds falling from the sky.

Calls came through at all hours, day and night. Texts arrived, one after the other, landing on the screen like little bombs. I deleted them all, ignored my voicemail, but kept my phone close, unable to turn it off. I had no intention of responding to the messages – but a small, pathetic part of me, inured to the adrenaline and drama, was perversely glad to see them.

The toilet flushed and Ollie emerged from the bathroom. I watched, bristling, as he returned to the sofa and flopped back into the teenager-shaped dent he'd made in the cushions.

'Hey,' I called. 'Phone away now, please.'

'What?'

'You've been on it all morning. It's time for a break.'

'In a minute.'

'No, now. Come on, I need your help.'

Ollie ignored me. *Ping. Ping. Ping.* Nothing got under my skin quite like that sound – despite the fact that my own phone was vibrating in my pocket with a stream of notifications.

I stormed through the hall and into the living room. 'Put. Your. Phone. Down. Now. Please.'

From the travel cot in my bedroom, I heard a soft cry. *Shit.* Kara was waking up.

'Turn it off,' I said, 'or, I swear to god, I'm going to lose it.'

'So what else is new?'

I glared at him.

'What?' he snapped. 'What do you want?'

'Seriously?' My voice rose a few octaves. 'What I want is some help. Maybe a little *enthusiasm* for a change.'

Behind me, Kara's grizzling was turning into an intense wail.

'Enthusiasm?' Ollie threw his phone down and sat up. 'You want enthusiasm? About moving *here*? Okay, cool, here we go then. Oh, Mum, thank you so much for dragging me away from my home to this half-built dump in the middle of nowhere. Oh, I'm just so happy to be here! I just can't wait to die of boredom, or from eating too many lentils or whatever. Let's all go and make dreamcatchers and then dance around a maypole. This is my absolute dream life, and you're the best mum in the whole entire world!'

'Don't get smart,' I said. 'It's lovely here.'

'It's a fucking hole.'

'You watch your mouth.'

'No, it's literally a hole, in the actual ground. I feel like I'm in a crater. And there's nothing to do. Like, *nothing*. No shops, no clubs, no buses, no anything!'

'Well, that's kind of the point, that's why we're here.'

'No, it's why *you're* here.'

Kara let out an ear-splitting shriek.

Pinching the bridge of my nose, I took a deep breath. 'Ollie, listen. I know things have been rough lately, and I know you don't fully understand what's going on, but sometimes you just have to trust me.'

'Trust you?' Ollie echoed. 'Trust *you?*'

Kara screeched again, loud as a feral animal. On the sofa, Ollie's phone lit up. *Ping. Ping. Ping.* I pressed my fingers to my forehead. There was so much noise.

'You know what?' said Ollie, standing up and pushing past me. 'I'm out of here.'

'Hey,' I said, striding after him. 'Don't you *dare* walk away from me, we are not done here. And turn your bloody phone off, I can't hear myself think.'

He shrugged me off. I saw red. I snatched at his T-shirt and heard the *snick-snick-snick* of cotton stitches coming loose. I froze. In my hand, I held a fistful of material; I'd ripped my son's shirt almost clean off his body. We both stared at the hole I'd made – and then Ollie laughed out loud, which made me want to laugh, because the whole thing was kind of hilarious, a

38

game gone too far, like when he was small and he'd ask me to play dinosaurs and I'd put just that little bit too much effort into perfecting my roars. But then Kara let out her very best howl, the one that attacked your skull like a jackhammer, and Ollie's expression switched back to enraged.

'For fuck's sake, Kara,' he yelled in the direction of my bedroom. '*SHUT THE FUCK UP!*'

I was stunned. My son's face was flushed with rage – teeth bared, eyes bulging, fists clenched at his sides – and in that moment, he looked like a fully grown man. A man I was desperately trying to escape.

'Okay,' I said, as soon as I could speak. 'Get out of my sight.'

He didn't move.

'I mean it, Oliver, go cool off. I don't care where, just *go*. And don't you ever speak to her like that again. She is a baby, and your sister.'

Still, Ollie didn't move. The simmering potential of his body filled the room and I found myself tensing up, waiting, preparing …

In the end, though, he backed down.

'Half-sister,' he said, quietly. And then he stormed into his room and slammed the door.


An hour later, I ran out of jobs. I'd hoped we might all go for a walk together and explore the parts of the village we hadn't yet seen, but Ollie hadn't come out of his room and I was still fuming, so I pulled on my runners, strapped Kara into her baby

39

carrier and set out to walk off my rage.

Turning left outside the house then left again at the edge of the forest, I walked uphill, looping around the topmost residential sections. Kara sucked her fists and kicked her little feet with excitement while I stickybeaked at the other homes, most of which had large decks, lush vegetable gardens and bright, gleaming exteriors. My favourites were the Tiny Houses, which reminded me of fortune-teller wagons or lavishly designed garden sheds. They seemed far too small to comfortably accommodate even a single person, but a few sneaky peeks through windows revealed surprisingly roomy spaces fitted with fully equipped kitchens, bathrooms and loft-style bedrooms with ladder access.

When I'd seen all the houses, I circled back and went looking for the forest trails Kit had mentioned. At the edge of the tree line just past our house, I found the first signpost and followed it along a path that led uphill again, this time all the way to the ridge then back down to the valley floor. Hanging from my chest, Kara stared with wide-eyed wonder at the tall eucalypts, dangling creepers and huge muddy arboreal termite nests. I stared too, fully expecting poisonous snakes to slither out from the bushes or spiders to drop from the canopy. A city girl at heart, I was suspicious of most noises and flinched constantly; the ticks, mosquitos and leeches of Australia were a world away from the benign ants, slugs and earthworms I'd grown up with in England, and I still wasn't used to them.

Kara stuck out her arms and gripped my fingers as we walked, and I calmed us both by pointing out all the different trees in a singsong voice. There were brown ones, their slick branches like muscular arms, red ones with gaping knotholes, and silver ones streaked with yellow and copper as if someone had dabbed at their trunks with a paintbrush. *Look, there's a bird's nest! Look, there's a cobweb!* And then, as I reached out to show her the zigzag tracks on a scribbly gum, tracing the moth grub's journey through the layers with my finger, I noticed a different kind of marking. Crude lines cut deliberately into the bark.

I went closer to take a look, expecting a name or a love heart. *Ruby luvs Lachlan 4eva* or some such cuteness. But instead I saw three sides of a square topped with an arrow, like a house with a roof. Inside the shape were three smaller symbols arranged in a triangle, but the carver hadn't been precise enough and I couldn't make out what they were.

A little further along the path I saw the mark scratched into the trunk of another tree. Then I saw it again, and again, always that same house shape with the three pictures inside. I didn't know what it meant but it gave me the chills.

And then I heard a noise behind me. I jumped about a foot in the air and, in one instinctive and ungainly move, wrapped my arms around Kara and scampered up the path, anticipating a slithered pursuit. But when I turned around, there were no scales, no fangs, just Kit Vestey standing on the path in a black singlet and running shorts.

'Alex,' he said, his mouth round with surprise. 'Sorry, I didn't see you there … are you alright?'

'I'm fine.' I paused to catch my breath. 'Just startled, I guess.'

'Sorry.' A smile tugged at the corners of his mouth. 'I was

miles away and going too fast. Not as fast as you, though. Wow, what did you think was coming, a mountain lion?'

I tried to laugh it off. 'Obviously. They're pretty common round here, right?'

'Positively rampant. Good to know your reflexes are in fine working order, though.' He waved at Kara. 'Hey there, little one.' She kicked out her legs and smacked her lips in response.

'It's lovely in here,' I said, nodding vaguely at the trees. 'Much bigger than I expected, and so peaceful.'

'I know, I love it,' Kit said, wiping sweat from his brow. 'I try and do a loop of the trails every day. There are more over on the other side, behind the dam. You should check them out. Do you run?'

'Absolutely not.' I shook my head, all too aware of how the baby carrier squeezed my tummy fat down until it oozed like toothpaste over the waistband of my shorts. I patted Kara on her velvety head. She reached up and grabbed a handful of my hair. 'Not with this one hanging off me, anyway.'

'Ah, no, of course.'

'She weighs a ton these days.' Wincing, I prised the strands from her chubby fists. 'Actually, speaking of, it's probably time for us to head home.'

Kit nodded. 'Good call. Mind if I walk with you?'

'Sure, of course.'

The forest didn't seem so sinister with someone else around. We set off back down the trail, settling into an easy conversation, leaving the snakes, spiders and tree carvings to their own creepy business. I chattered almost nonstop to hide the fact that Kit's presence made me nervous; my head knew much better but, faced with a decent-looking guy with a kind smile, my heart was an idiot every time. The beads of sweat on his skin, the freckles on his shoulders, the heat that seemed to roll off him in waves … just the nearness of him gave me tingles.

I pushed the feeling away. No good could come of it. My fool heart could sit back down; I had to be on Team Head this time.

Kit asked polite questions about the kids, how Ollie was settling in and whether or not I'd thought about schools for the following year. I'd answered with the truth, that Ollie had struggled socially at his last school, so I would let him skip the final few weeks of term and think about enrolling him somewhere new in January. I might even homeschool; how hard could it be? *Pretty fucking hard*, I secretly suspected. Kara would want to be *on* me twenty-four seven, I would be distracted and Ollie would be bored. His frustration would escalate as my patience ran dry. He would ignore my repeated efforts to police his screen time, spending his days gaming, scrolling listlessly through YouTube and eating his way through the contents of the fridge – and I would let him, to ease my guilt.

Fortunately, I now had the food part of that scenario covered. We'd had a constant stream of visitors the previous afternoon, Pine Ridge residents welcoming us with locally produced milk and eggs, honey and jam, apples and onions. Some had even brought home-cooked dishes: veggie lasagne, mushroom stroganoff and a steaming ratatouille. I'd opened the door to a salt-speckled family of five, the kind of people you'd find travelling around Australia in a campervan; two artsy-looking women and their daughter; an elderly man with cotton-wool hair; and a softly spoken couple called Paul and Simon who owned a fat blonde Pug called Al (the only names that stuck in my head, for obvious reasons). I was especially happy to meet a sweet dark-haired woman around my age, a fellow single mum who thrust a homemade carrot cake into my hands and introduced herself as Layla. 'Welcome to Pine Ridge,' she said in a folksy voice. 'We're so happy to have you here.'

In all honesty, I hadn't known what to expect from an ecovillage (privately, I'd assumed the same as Ollie: that it would be full of yoga fanatics and tree-huggers) but both the diversity of people and the immediate sense of community were surprising. I hadn't felt so unconditionally welcomed or accepted since my backpacking days of hostels, bus stations and beach bars. I said as much to Kit and it seemed to make him happy.

I then asked him where he'd gone to school and how he grew up, but his answers were short and vague. 'All over the place, really. Sydney mostly, but also Europe and the States. It's actually a lot more boring than it sounds. What about you, have you seen much of the world?'

I told him a few travel stories, which led to bucket lists, which somehow led to favourite movies, and I found myself passionately dissecting the underrated genius of Dwayne 'The Rock' Johnson. Kara babbled along with me, punctuating my anecdotes with little gasps and squeals. Then, in an attempt to demonstrate some intelligence, I asked him how it was that he'd founded an entire ecovillage. 'It's hard to believe you did it all yourself,' I said. *You're so young*, I almost added, but quickly realised that such a comment would only serve to highlight how old I was in comparison. There had to be ten years between us at least.

'I didn't do it *all* myself,' Kit replied. 'There was a whole group of us. Just friends at first, people I met on the activist circuit. But once we found the land and blocked out the rough plans, we got serious. We met with investors, architects, builders, city officials, local council – god, the meetings went on forever. Then we got the green light, and it was on. We had to plant crops, install a wastewater treatment system, construct a wetland, pass tests, meet criteria. Not a one-person job at all.'

'I can imagine.' I couldn't help but smile. Kit lit up when he talked about Pine Ridge; it was nice to see someone so passionate about their job. 'Sounds like a lot of work.'

Kit shrugged. 'Weirdly, the work itself is the easy part. Things are more chilled when there's stuff to *do*; it's the bits in between that are challenging. The decision-making, the endless discussion. The tension can get a little out of hand sometimes, but we're figuring it out. And it's all worth it. I knew as soon as I saw the land that it would be perfect.'

I had to agree. Despite Ollie's negativity and my own second-guessing, I was hopeful that Pine Ridge would be the place for us. Natural beauty. Community. Isolation. Protection. Obscurity. And once the wellness centre, cafe and pool were up and running, there might even be some opportunity for work.

Our pace naturally slowed as we made our way out of the trees and reached the edge of the village, and I found myself wishing we could carry on, perhaps for hours, just walking and talking beneath the cornflower-blue sky. I had a strange sense that Kit was an old friend, that I'd known him for years – and as we approached our unit I almost asked, *Where do I know you from?* But just as I turned, the question on my lips, my phone buzzed in my pocket. Once, twice, three times.

Surreptitiously, I checked the screen. My stomach dropped. Stuart.

Kit carried on chatting, but I couldn't think. The buzzing continued – four times, five – and I became so distracted that Kit asked if there was anything wrong. Eventually I used Kara as an excuse. 'Sorry,' I said. 'I'm watching the clock. Parenting 101: you don't monkey with naptime.'

I climbed the steps to my front door with shaky legs.

'Hey, Alex,' Kit called from the road below. 'I forgot to tell you. On Thursdays everyone gets together at the greenhouses for dinner. Come down around five and bring a dish.'

*Buzz. Buzz. Buzz.*

I smiled and gave him a thumbs-up. And then, with my guts churning and my heart in my mouth, I went inside and closed the door firmly behind me.

I read Stuart's messages while feeding Kara some puree, spooning sweet potato into her mouth with one hand, scrolling through hate mail with the other. The good news was that he still didn't seem to know where we were. The bad news was that he was getting more and more frustrated.

*Bitch*

*Fuck you*

*Watch your back slut I will find you*

*I will fucking bury you and your freeloading dropkick youtuber of a son fucking no hoper*

That last message was confusing, as well as offensive. I read it again. What did 'youtuber' mean? Was it meant to be an insult? Ollie wasn't an actual YouTuber; if he were, I would know about it ... wouldn't I?

When Kara was finished eating, I hitched her onto my hip and went to my son's room.

'Ollie?' I knocked softly on his door but there was no reply. I pushed it open to find an empty room and a scribbled note on his bed. *Gone skating.*

*Fine*, I thought. At least he was now getting out of the house.

After I put Kara down for her nap, I checked Ollie's Facebook page, knowing I probably wouldn't find anything. 'Facebook is for old people,' I'd once heard him say. He used it occasionally to access games and other websites but preferred Snapchat and Instagram. Those accounts were private, though, which meant I couldn't see his activity without getting into his phone: an impossible task, like stealing gold from a dragon but trickier and more terrifying.

His Facebook profile was the same as ever: no new posts, tags or check-ins – but, in the Photos section, I found a video. It had been posted just over three weeks ago, via YouTube. Without thinking twice, I clicked.

Ollie was standing in his old bedroom in Stuart's house. He'd tried to disguise it by covering the back wall with a bedsheet, but I could see the corkboard poking out and the edge of his RL Grime poster. He'd dragged his desk into the middle of the room and was sitting behind it, holding a large cardboard box with a fold-over lid. He was wearing blue surgical gloves.

He introduced himself, then explained how he'd purchased a 'mystery box' from the dark web using bitcoin. 'I literally have no idea what's inside,' he said, 'so I'm a little nervous to find out.'

His voice was weird; he'd affected a faux-American accent.

'Right,' he said, 'I'm opening the box. It has a small tear in one side, but otherwise it's undamaged. Okay, I've got it open, I'm going in … ew, the whole box reeks.' He waved his hand in front of his nose. 'Okay, okay, oh my god, wait a minute. There's something in here. I can't quite make it out, but it looks like a bag? It is, it's a lunch bag.'

He pulled out a pink lunch bag with a picture of a butterfly on the front. 'Oh, yuck, it stinks. I don't know why, but it does.' He unzipped it. 'There's, like, this *smell* coming from inside it. And look at these stains.' The bag was streaked with a rusty red substance. 'Is there anything inside it? Yeah, I think there is.' He peered inside, then his eyes returned to the camera. 'Guys. This looks bad.'

Reaching into the bag, he pulled out a small yellow T-shirt with a unicorn motif. The T-shirt was grubby and stained with the same rusty marks as the lunch bag. He also pulled out a ball of twine. A USB stick. A mobile phone. A roll of black bin liners. And a small plastic bag of white powder.

I pressed my fingertips into the corners of my eyes. What

had I just watched? What was going on? Trying to understand my son these days felt like opening a door to a pitch-black room and peering around inside. Where the problems had once been more or less simple (toilet training, temper tantrums, unexpected questions about death), they were now so far out of left field I couldn't keep up. It was, of course, all my fault. I'd been so busy with the move, so distracted by Kara and the logistics of leaving Stuart that Ollie had been left largely unsupervised.

*Fuck.*

It was just one problem after the next, like the Hydra's heads. You chopped off one and two more sprouted immediately in its place.

# ALEX

## 5

Outside, the sun had passed its highest point and was now on the downslide to the ridge, passing behind tiger stripes of cloud and painting them pale gold. Sloshing a glass of the wine Kit had brought, I sat on the bottom step and breathed in a lungful of sticky-sweet afternoon air. The cicadas were loud, a noisy chorus of lovesick men, as were the village kids returning from school, but underneath it all I could hear the familiar clatter and roll of a skateboard. Ollie hadn't gone far, then.

I sipped the wine – a little vinegary but drinkable – and watched the clouds for a bit, then I checked the mailbox just for something to do. It held a single piece of brown Kraft paper, torn from a roll and folded once; junk mail, I assumed, or a community round robin. But when I opened it up I found the house-shaped box I'd seen in the woods, drawn with what looked like a black Sharpie.

Putting my glass down, I smoothed out the paper. The three symbols were clearer here than they had been on the trees: the one at the apex looked like a wishbone, and the two at the bottom were a stick figure and what might've been a teardrop.

I glanced around. There were people about – a neighbour

pegging out laundry, a boy riding his bike – but no one was lurking nearby, watching me. I looked back at the piece of paper. What did it mean? And why was it in my mailbox?

'Hey,' I called as the boy on the bike pedalled towards me. 'Hey, kid, can you help me with something, please?'

The boy slowed and eyed me suspiciously. He was about six or seven with matted hair and bare feet. His T-shirt showed a picture of the Earth; the slogan said, *There is no Planet B.*

'Can you tell me what this is?' I held out the piece of paper and tapped the drawing.

The boy craned his neck. When he saw the mark, he stiffened. Shot me a look from beneath his floppy fringe. He looked nervous.

'Someone put it in my mailbox,' I said, 'and I don't know what it means. Can you tell me?'

'It's a house,' said the boy. There was a gap in his front teeth where the top two had fallen out.

'And what's inside the house?'

The boy looked down at the drawing then quickly away again. 'Things,' he said.

'Okay. What kind of things?' When he didn't reply, I pointed at the first of the symbols, the one that looked like a wishbone. 'What's this one?'

The boy's eyes bounced from me to the drawing and back again. He scratched his nose. 'A bone,' he said eventually.

'Hmm. Thought so. And this?' I pointed to the stick figure in the bottom left corner.

'A doll.'

I nodded and tapped the third symbol. 'This one is a teardrop, right? Or rain?'

'No,' said the boy. 'That's blood.'

'Blood?' Despite the heat, I shivered. 'Is it a puzzle or a game? Like, a scavenger hunt or something?'

The boy squinted at me.

'It's okay, you're not in trouble.' I gave him a reassuring smile. 'I'm just new here and I need help figuring it out.'

The boy looked up at me and sighed. 'It's the witch,' he said. 'It's like … it's her sign.'

'Witch?' Whatever I'd been expecting him to say, it wasn't that. 'What do you mean?'

'So, um, there's this witch in the woods?' The boy mumbled. I had to bend down low to hear him. 'And these monsters? And they take kids? But before they do, they, like, bring things to your house.'

I raised an eyebrow. 'A witch that takes kids, huh? Sounds like fun.'

'It's true.' The boy jabbed a finger at the paper in my hand. 'She brings the *things*. So, bones first. Like, something dead. An animal or a fish or something. Then she brings you a doll. It's supposed to look like you. And then she makes blood come out of your walls, and the blood finds a photo of the person the witch wants, and then that's how you know who she's going to take next.' He looked at me expectantly.

I blinked. 'O-kay.'

'Can I go now?'

'Sure. Thanks for helping me out.'

''S okay.'

I stood back as if to let the boy pass, but he didn't move.

'Is this your house?' he said.

I nodded.

'It probably means she's coming here next.'

'What?'

'The drawing in your mailbox.'

I laughed. 'Okay, cool. Thanks for the advice.'

The boy shrugged. 'It happened before. Up there.' The boy twisted on his bicycle seat and pointed across the valley to where the lone farmhouse stood, bleach-white in the blazing sun.

Kit's words came back to me. *The house has a bit of a history.*

'How do you know?' I said. My words accidentally came out sneery, as if *I* was the child, and the boy sighed as if he agreed.

'Everyone knows,' he said. He placed his foot back on the pedal.

'Wait, what do you mean?'

The bike started to move.

'Hey,' I said. 'Wait a sec. What happened, exactly?'

The boy stood up on his pedals as if he couldn't get away from me fast enough. 'The witch,' he called out over his shoulder as he picked up speed. 'The witch took the farmers' kid.'

And then he rounded the corner with a *tring* of his bell and I couldn't see him anymore.

# RENEE

## 6

Right after they put Ivory in the ground, Renee Kellerman saw a snake.

Not a real one. Just a picture, hovering in the air. It was normal. Sometimes she experienced emotions through a sort of projective synaesthesia: she saw images as she felt things. Physical pain, for example, was a rusty bear trap, its jaws snapping shut in the blink of an eye. Fear was an ice fishing hole, perfectly round and bottomless. And, apparently, heartbreak was a thick snake in a constriction coil, tightening slowly around its prey.

As Michael stuck the blade of his shovel into the ground, digging up spadeful after spadeful of wet earth and tipping it into the hole, Renee saw that snake, all wound up like a noose knot. And the more dirt that went in, the clearer she saw it. The scales. The bulging muscle. The crushed, pulpy mess at its centre. She cried silently the whole time, her tears mixing with the drizzle that fell as if in sympathy.

Michael continued to dig. Each clump of earth hit the plastic bag with a dull thud. When the plastic was all covered up, the falling dirt made no sound at all. And then Ivory was gone, swallowed up, claimed by the soil.

'Why would someone *do* something like that?' she said when he finished.

Michael smoothed the hole over with the end of the shovel. 'I don't know.'

At his feet, his beloved black labrador, Ebony, waited patiently for instructions. Her tongue was hanging out of her mouth; her eyes were bright and alert. Renee suddenly wanted to kick her, the slobbery, selfish animal. Why had she survived whatever it was that Ivory had not?

Michael stuck the spade into the soil one last time and leaned on the handle. He wiped his brow with his sleeve. 'Right,' he said. 'That's done, then.'

Renee sniffed. 'Yes.'

Michael blinked, then looked up at the sky. 'I'd better be getting on,' he said. 'Before it really starts coming down. There's a lot to do. The tulips ...'

Renee pulled her raincoat more tightly around her body and swept the tears from her cheeks. She had things to do, too.

She was on the veranda, banging the mud from her gumboots by the back door, when she heard the voices. She stopped mid-stamp and listened: a soft murmur of conversation was coming from inside the house – but who could it be? Not Michael: she'd just left him down at the greenhouses. Had Gabriel invited *friends* over? Surely not.

Slipping off her boots and shoving them upside down on the rack, she nudged the door open and peered through the gap into the kitchen. It was empty. So was the adjoining living room. The voices, so hushed they were almost whispers, seemed to be coming from the hall.

'Hello?' she called.

The voices stopped, as if the house had suddenly swallowed them. The hairs on the back of Renee's neck stood up.

Then someone called out. 'Ren? Is that you?'

Renee let all her breath out in one go as she recognised the voice. Shrugging off her jacket, she padded across the tiles in her socks and peered around the corner into the hallway to find her parents, April and Frank, standing outside Gabriel's bedroom door with their arms folded.

'Ah, *there* you are,' April said, a little sourly.

'And there *you* are,' replied Renee, 'apparently.' She waited for an explanation. When none came, she added: 'You gave me a shock.'

'I can't imagine why.' Behind her glasses, April's eyes were round with bemusement, as if the house was hers and Renee was the one who had turned up unannounced.

Sighing, Renee tried again. 'What are you doing back here?'

'Waiting for you,' said Frank, grimly.

'And trying to have a chat with our grandson.' April unfolded her arms and walked forward, presenting her cheek to be kissed. 'But, evidently, he's *busy*.'

Renee embraced her mother, holding her breath to prevent April's cloying perfume from getting stuck in her throat.

'Weren't you expecting us?' said April. 'I said to Frank, I said, she's forgotten. Didn't I, Frank?'

Renee froze. *Crap. What was the date?* She glanced down at her soil-smeared T-shirt. 'I hadn't forgotten,' she said, trying unsuccessfully to cover her blunder. 'I just got caught up. We're flat out these days.' With her cheeks flushing pink, she ushered them through the kitchen and into the living room. 'Let me just get changed and I'll make you a nice cuppa.'

Frank shook his head. 'Already had one.'

'Made it ourselves,' April added.

'Right, well, I'll put out some snacks, then. Here, sit down, make yourselves comfortable, I'll be back in a tick. Dinner won't be long.'

In the shower, Renee gave herself several mental kicks; tonight had been in the calendar for weeks. Racing through a list of meal options, she realised with a sinking heart that nothing she'd bought would go down well. Steak was too chewy for Frank's dentures, curry too spicy for April's delicate stomach, and so on. She sighed. Visits from her parents were hard enough even when she *was* organised.

'Your latch is broken,' said Frank, as she hurried back to the living room wearing clean clothes and smelling of soap.

'Sorry?'

'The latch on the front door. The lock doesn't click in properly. You have to give it a real push before it engages.'

'Oh, really? I'll get Michael to have a look.' Renee swept her gaze around the room, checking for flaws, anticipating more criticism. There were a few dishes in the sink, and a full laundry basket dumped on one of the sofas, but other than that it wasn't too bad.

'The whole place smells of smoke,' said Frank. 'Who's smoking?'

'No one's smoking, Dad. They're just burning some old frames down in the south paddock.'

'I didn't think burning waste materials was legal.'

'It's just wooden frames, Dad. Nothing to worry about.'

*Chicken*, she thought, closing the windows with a sigh. *A nice chicken salad, garlic bread, with ice-cream and strawberries for dessert.* Surely, neither of them could find fault with that?


'Bloody quarantine services called earlier,' said Michael, grabbing a slice of garlic bread from the basket and tearing off a hunk with his teeth. 'Because *they* didn't do a proper job on that tulip delivery, *I've* got to gas them all over again – at my own expense.' He chewed loudly, with an open mouth. April and Frank averted their eyes.

'Salad, Dad?' Renee spooned dressed leaves onto her father's plate. Michael and her parents had always been a tricky combination, best managed with good food and a hefty pinch of salt. With their ramrod-straight backs, well-practised sanctimony and starched Sunday Best, April and Frank irritated the heck out of Michael. And with his plaid shirts, sun-bleached hair and callused hands, Michael intimidated April and Frank. After many years of simmering tension, the pretence of mutual respect had been all but dropped; only Renee still seemed to have the stamina for it. *They're family*, she insisted whenever Michael got fired up. *And we don't have much of that left.* That evening, however, even she was feeling the strain.

She'd done her best to lighten the mood but April and Frank had remained prickly – and then Michael had blown in from the paddock like a hurricane, Ebony at his side, and the atmosphere had nosedived from there. He stomped around the house, banging doors and bellyaching and generally putting everyone around him on edge. He'd even gone so far as to call Frank's car a 'piece of shit', which had prompted Frank to make ill-considered comments about the 'shabby' state of the farm. Thankfully, Renee managed to quickly diffuse the situation with some alcohol and a few well-placed questions about April's blood-thinning meds and Frank's dodgy knee, subjects of which her parents never seemed to tire.

'Shouldn't we wait for Gabriel?' said April, when everyone's plates were full. 'Assuming, of course, that he's joining us?'

'I'm not sure what he's doing,' Renee lied. She knew full well her son wouldn't be joining them for dinner that night. He hadn't eaten with them for months. 'I don't think he's feeling well. It's okay, I'll keep something warm for him.'

Frank pursed his lips and threw a glance at his wife.

April caught the look like a ball. 'You should let us take him to church,' she said.

'That's not necessary,' said Michael, sticking his fork into a piece of chicken.

April ignored him. 'That boy needs help, Renee.'

Renee literally bit her tongue, catching the tip between her teeth and applying pressure.

'Those screens are poisoning his mind,' April continued.

'How can he think, focus, reflect? He needs peace and quiet at his age, not filth and flashing lights.'

Michael grunted. 'What he needs is to leave that room. Help out around here once in a while.'

'How is he doing at school?' April said. 'Does he have any friends?'

'He has his own ways of socialising,' said Renee, unable to help herself.

'You call what he does on that machine socialising?' Frank stared at her, the skin around his eyes as blue and papery as an elephant's.

Renee looked away. *Yes. No. Maybe.* Kids nowadays met up online instead of in parks; their playgrounds were virtual instead of grassy. And wasn't that better? At least Gabe was at home, where she could keep an eye on him – and she'd read somewhere that computer geeks were *in*, that people with tech talent were *cool* these days. She couldn't explain that to her parents, though.

In truth, she had no idea what Gabe was doing on his computer, but she did know that getting angry wouldn't help. And didn't he deserve the benefit of the doubt? He could be doing something wonderful in there. Perhaps one day he'd emerge from his room and announce that he'd just discovered a cure for cancer or invented time travel. Half the world's tech geniuses were socially reclusive. Renee would've bet her last dollar that most Nobel Prize winners had produced their best work alone in their bedrooms while wearing unwashed tracksuit pants.

Frank put down his cutlery. 'He should be eating with the family,' he said, pushing back his chair and heading for the hallway. 'I'll go and talk to him.'

'Don't bother, mate,' Michael called after him. 'There's no point.'

'I wouldn't be so sure about that,' said April. 'Frank can be quite persuasive when he wants to be.'

Renee said nothing. 'Persuasive' wasn't the word she'd use. 'Obdurate' would be more accurate. According to her father, the world worked in a certain way – *Frank's* way – and he would not hear otherwise.

'Speaking of church, did I tell you they just finished renovating the hall?' April said, barrelling through the tension. 'It's lovely. Very modern. A local dance teacher is renting it on Saturday mornings.'

Renee feigned polite interest.

'Sue is trying to convince me to go. She says salsa is great for her back, though I cannot understand how. She's having a dreadful time with her arthritis. I suspect she needs a new doctor. Her GP has *no* idea.'

Renee tuned out. While April expounded on the inadequate GP, she pushed her food around her plate, focusing instead on her father's muffled voice in the hallway. From the corner of her eye, she could just about see him standing once again outside Gabe's room, one hand on the frame, speaking softly through the half-open door.

'I saw your neighbour the other day,' said April, tapping Renee lightly on the arm. 'At the fruit shop. What's his name again? The one who lives over the back there.'

Renee frowned. 'Dom Hassop?'

'Dominic, yes. Delightful young man.'

Michael snorted into his beer. 'He's not that young.'

'He looked thin, I thought,' April said, ignoring him. 'Has he lost a lot of weight?'

Renee shrugged. 'Maybe. I heard he's going through a nasty divorce, but I don't know the details. We don't see much of the Hassops anymore.'

'Really? I thought you were quite close with them. What's his mother's name? Tess?'

'Bess.'

'That's right. Lovely woman. Haven't seen them for years. Are they well?'

'No idea,' Michael said, taking another swig of beer.

'Michael and Dom's fathers were friends, back in the day,' said Renee, eager to hurry the topic along. 'But we've all grown apart now. Everyone's so busy.'

'Hmm,' said April. 'Shame. As I remember, they were very nice.'

Renee quashed a rising pang of guilt. It *was* a shame. For years, Dom and his father had helped out around the place; Len Kellerman had treated them like family and Renee had looked forward to seeing them. Both were a welcome change from Len's straight talk and his relentless work ethic, which over the years had gone from admirable in Renee's eyes to overbearing and sometimes downright insane. Even after both patriarchs had passed away and the sons had assumed their respective roles, Dom would still come over to lend a hand and visit his 'buddy' Gabe; Bess would bring a cake and Renee would serve tea on the veranda. And when it was all hands on deck, Renee would often drop young Gabriel at the Hassop farm during the day so Bess could babysit while Renee pitched in.

But for some reason Renee had never really understood, Michael had never seemed to like Dom much; he was always sniping at him, putting him down. The visits became less frequent. Dom met and married a woman who very quickly fell pregnant with twins – and then Bess got sick, and the social calls stopped altogether. It was sad, really. Renee knew she should've made more of an effort. Bess's health had deteriorated fast, and the twins wouldn't have been easy. And now Dom was coping with a divorce …

'I really ought to look in on them sometime,' she said quietly. 'I'm sure Dom could do with some support.'

'Yeah, right,' sneered Michael. 'Good old Dom needs *heaps* of support.' He banged his beer bottle on the table and froth spilled over the top. 'You know he left one of his trailers blocking that access road this morning, even though I've told him enough times that it's *our* right of way? Couldn't even get the truck out this morning, set me back hours. And he has the cheek to come to *me* and complain about a bloody bonfire! Reckons I'm burning plastic. You'll pollute the water, he says, you'll poison my orchard. Bloody drama queen. One of these days I'm gonna knock the bloke out with a mallet.'

'I'm just saying,' said Renee, her voice level, 'that he'd be doing it tough right now. He always adored Rachel.'

'Well, she obviously didn't think much of him, did she? Otherwise she wouldn't be doing a runner.' He let out another gassy belch as if that proved his point.

Renee studied her husband. His face, already lined and ruddy from decades of days spent working in the Australian sun, was so crumpled and flushed that his freckles had all but disappeared. The tip of his nose was peeling, the skin as dry and white as ash. He looked like a volcano on the brink of eruption. He used to be so funny, so full of life, a real larrikin. Back when they were dating, he used to bring her huge bouquets of flowers and treat her to secluded sunset picnics. Down the pub, he was known for his boisterous behaviour and rowdy jokes, his ability to sink schooners at lightning speed – but alone with her, he was different. Tender and thoughtful. He used to make her feel special. Now, he just made her feel queasy.

She dropped her gaze, looking instead at her embroidered tablecloth, the vase of lilies on the counter, the dirt-spattered windows she'd been meaning to clean and the cushion near the log-burner that, heartbreakingly, was still covered in cat hair.

Somewhere behind her, a door closed softly. Footsteps sounded in the hallway and Renee turned hopefully in her seat – but Frank had returned alone.

'What did Gabriel say?' asked April. 'Is he coming to eat?'

Frank sat down and retrieved his fork from his plate. 'No,' he said, curtly. 'No, he is not.'

Across the table, Michael shoved another piece of garlic bread into his mouth. 'Told ya,' he said. 'No bloody point.'

'I don't know why you won't let me take Gabriel to church,'

April said later, as they finished dessert. 'His soul is quite clearly in turmoil.'

'Oh, jeez,' muttered Michael, tossing his spoon into his bowl and leaning back in his chair. 'Here we go again.' On the floor, Ebony lifted her head, watching him.

'I would've thought you'd be grateful for the help,' said April, exchanging another look with Frank.

'We're dealing with it, Mum,' said Renee, standing up to clear the plates. 'Just let us handle it our own way.'

'And what way is that, exactly?' Frank waded in. His voice was mild, but Renee could hear the steel beneath. 'Because I'm not seeing much evidence of strategy. Or discipline.'

'Does he *ever* come out of that room?' said April. 'Is he even eating properly?'

'Of course he is.' Fumbling with the cutlery, Renee dropped a spoon and it clattered to the floor.

Ebony let out a bark. 'Shh, girl,' said Michael, giving the dog a reassuring pat on the head.

Renee stooped to pick up the spoon then took the plates to the sink. 'I told you, he's just not feeling well tonight. He'll eat when he's ready.'

Frank sighed. April pressed her mouth into a thin line.

Michael pushed back his chair and stood up. 'Well, it's getting late,' he said. 'You'll probably want to head off soon, won't you, Frank?'

'*We* think,' said April to Renee, ignoring Michael completely, 'that if you won't let us take him to church then you should at least let us pray. Right now.'

Michael threw up his hands and stomped over to the back door with Ebony at his heels, her tail wagging furiously. *Where are you going?* Renee mouthed at him, but he ignored her.

At the table, April and Frank closed their eyes and held hands. 'Father,' April intoned. 'We thank you for our many blessings.'

Renee let the plates tumble into the sink with a clatter and turned on the hot water.

'We pray today for our angel, Gabriel. May his heart be filled with the love of Christ. Help him see the light.'

Shoving his feet into his work boots, Michael grabbed his jacket and opened the door, ushering in a gust of cool evening air. Ebony slipped swiftly through the gap as if she were fleeing the scene of a crime.

'Deliver him from the demons of this world,' said April, her eyes still closed, 'and break the devil's grip.'

In the open doorway, Michael turned back and gave Renee a look she couldn't quite read. Disgust? Derision? Regret? He opened his mouth to say something, but then seemed to think better of it. Instead, he followed his dog out into the night and slammed the door shut behind him.

Renee inhaled slowly, then let her breath out in a rush. She wanted to lie down. No, she wanted to climb right out of herself and disappear, shed her skin like a snake and leave it crumpled on the floor like a pair of old pyjamas.

Turning back to the sink, she plunged her hands under the scalding faucet.

# ALEX

## 7

Kara woke up from her nap grouchy and miserable. I held her close and sang her favourite songs, but she wouldn't stop grizzling. 'Poor baby,' I crooned. 'Those teeth are really giving you grief, hey?' She snuggled into me, whimpering.

I nuzzled her back, thinking of the boy on the bike and the note in my mailbox.

I remembered making up stories like that when I was a kid. There'd been an old fungus-covered tree stump in our primary school playground, and we'd all believed for years that if you touched the tree you'd catch the fungus like a disease. I'd had nightmares of mushrooms bulging under my skin like boils. But something the kid said had spooked me. *She brings things*, he'd said. *Something dead.* It made me think of the box I'd found on the doorstep, the bird corpse inside.

Of course, I had enough worries without buying into a children's story. While I breastfed Kara, I watched Ollie's video again. Then I googled *dark web mystery box*. The results showed a surprising number of recent news reports, some from major outlets, with headings like *Dangerous Craze Goes Viral* and *Unboxing Trend Takes Disturbing Turn*. And under the videos tab, I found clips with captions like *The scariest thing I ever saw.*

*Warning, disturbing content.* Recordings of other teens, mostly boys, all feverishly unpacking boxes ordered from the dark web, pulling out everything from used clothes and sinister-looking photographs to animal skulls and even a bloodied screwdriver. I scrolled through the list, checking each screen grab ... and then there he was. My baby boy, standing tall and skinny in the shirt I'd bought him for his last birthday. The title of Ollie's clip read *Dark Web Box Goes Horribly Wrong.*

Nausea roiled in my gut and I broke out in a sweat.

Clicking on the link at the bottom of the video, I discovered that he'd set up his own channel. There were three other videos. *Warning: scary content.* Astonishingly, he had thousands of subscribers and even a Patreon page. The videos had almost a million views each.

Gently lifting a milk-drunk Kara onto my shoulder, I carried her to Ollie's room. He still hadn't come home; if he didn't show up soon, I'd have to go and look for him. Pushing open the door, I wrinkled my nose at the potent smell of adolescence. We'd only just arrived; how was it already so strong? Where had the sweet, sleepy, crumpled-pyjama scent of his younger years gone?

The room was a mess – the curtains were drawn, the bed unmade, and he still hadn't unpacked – but I saw no evidence of clandestine filmmaking. Kara laid her head on my shoulder and sucked her fingers. I patted her little bottom and turned in a circle, accidentally stepping on Ollie's favourite green-and-orange hoodie. I nudged it aside with my foot. It was tempting to tidy up, but Ollie hated me going in his room and we'd already fought enough for one day.

And then Kara straightened in my arms, cooed and reached out for something behind me. 'Buh,' she said, banging excitedly on my shoulder.

My heart sank. I turned to find Ollie standing in the open doorway. 'Hi,' I said.

'What are you doing in here?' he said. 'Why are you creeping around in my room?'

'I wasn't creeping.'

'You've got no right to go through my shit, it's none of your business.'

'Well, actually, mate, your *shit* is very much my business. You make it my business when you plaster yourself all over the internet, when you order illegal items and have them delivered to my house.'

'Illegal? What are you talking about?'

'I've seen the videos, Ollie. The dark web? Are you kidding me? That's where paedophiles and hitmen hang out! And, I swear to god, if you're messing around with drugs at your age, I—'

'It's not ... There weren't any drugs.'

'What was that powder, then?'

He didn't answer.

'Honestly, Ollie, I gave you the benefit of the doubt with all that stuff at school. I believed you when you said you weren't involved, but now what am I supposed to think?'

He dropped his gaze.

Kara wriggled in my arms. I cleared a space for her on the floor and put her down, keeping half an eye on her in case she swallowed something radioactive. 'Where did you get them?'

'Get what?'

I wanted to shake him by the shoulders. 'The *boxes*.'

Ollie hesitated. 'I bought them.'

'Obviously. But who from?'

'Dunno.'

'What do you mean, you don't know? You obviously communicated with someone. You gave them money – probably *my* money – and an address. Who? A company, an individual?'

'I don't know, okay?'

I chewed my lip. I didn't know much about the dark web, but I did know that the point of it was total anonymity. He probably had no idea what he'd got himself into. 'Listen,' I said, trying and failing to keep my anger in check. 'I get that things have been hard for you lately, but I would've thought that given what happened at school, you'd have more sense than to, to' – I paused, trying to articulate exactly what I thought he'd done – 'make things any *fucking worse*.'

Ollie stared at me. On the floor, Kara rolled onto her side and patted me on the knee.

I shook my head and heaved another sigh. 'I just don't know what to *do* with you anymore.'

My son narrowed his eyes. 'Are you scared?'

'What?'

'Are you?' His face was blank, his voice flat. 'I don't know where the boxes come from. Anyone could've sent them. But whoever it is knows where we live. I had one sent here. We could all be killed in our beds tonight.'

I gaped at him. 'Stop it.'

'Someone could be hiding under our beds, behind the curtains, in the wardrobe. They might jump out while you're brushing your hair and slit your throat.'

'I said *stop.*' I knew I should say something clever, something that proved that I was in control, but my mind seemed to have blown a fuse.

Ollie gave me a faux-sweet smile. And then, in a move that was now as old as time, turned on his heel and stormed out of the house.

Half an hour later, he still hadn't come back. I started to worry. *He'll be fine*, I told myself. *Pine Ridge is small, there are people everywhere, let him cool off.*

I distracted myself by playing with Kara. I cleaned the bathroom, played with Kara some more, then tried to put her to bed. But as soon as she saw her cot, she screamed for what felt like a year and I couldn't get her to stop. She wouldn't take her dummy, wouldn't feed, wouldn't be comforted; she seemed to be under the impression that I was trying to skin her alive, not lull her to sleep. As I waltzed her around the kitchen, I knocked a plate off the counter, which smashed on the tiles and sliced the top of my foot open, so by the time Ollie returned – safe and well, of course – my rage had shot to the next level.

I didn't hear what Ollie said as he walked in the door, but I assumed it to be awful, so I snarled at him. He, of course, snarled back, and the whole circus started up again. He called me hysterical, so I confiscated his devices. Ollie clenched his fists and spat through his teeth while I stomped around the unit, picking up anything that could possibly connect to the internet and shoving it all into one of the topmost kitchen cupboards: a futile act, given Ollie was now taller than me by at least an inch.

The symbolism, however, was not lost on him. 'One week,' I shouted, brandishing my index finger like a dagger. He kicked the wall and burst into tears, triggering a sickening wave of mum-guilt. I reached for him – but then Kara upped her own game; she was a tiny dictator and volume was her weapon of mass destruction.

At some point during all of this, I glanced at the clock. *Shit.* No one had eaten. No wonder we were all apoplectic. I started tearing around the kitchen with Kara wailing on my hip, flinging open cupboard doors with my free hand and slamming pans onto the stove, attempting to both prepare the dinner and punish it for being yet another thing I had to do for someone else. Ollie disappeared into his room, and, despite having readymade meals from the neighbours in the fridge, I was determined to make the most elaborate dinner ever conceived, so that Ollie would feel *terrible* about treating his poor hard-working mother so atrociously.

But my fireworks display of martyrdom only served to upset Kara even more – and then it was *really* late and she still hadn't had a wash, so I hauled her to the bathroom, peeling off her clothes and pulling off her nappy, at which point I understood the smelly and very unpleasant reason she'd been so cranky.

Sinking onto the tiles, I whispered heartfelt apologies while smearing Sudocrem over her angry red skin, kissing her pearly toes and crying a river of regret.

That night, Kara woke up roughly every forty minutes. She cried and cried, and I paced the room, rocking her, soothing her, cursing her, pleading with her, anything that might make it all stop. I was so hot, so sweaty. The claustrophobia of being needed all the time was choking me.

Of course, whenever she did pass out, I was so wired from the crying that I couldn't sleep. Desperate for comfort, I turned to the internet. I dialled down the brightness on my screen to its lowest level, covered my head with a sheet and entered the late-night chat groups. I searched for all the usual hashtags: #3amfeedingclub, #twilightdairy, #sleepdeprivedbutstillalive. I scrolled through the posts, craving camaraderie – but the comments only fed my irritation.

*It's hard but hang in there.*

*It goes so fast, enjoy it while you can.*

*You're a superwoman!*

*You've got this, girl.*

I itched to reply with expletives. These women didn't understand how I felt. If they did, they wouldn't be writing peppy shit like that. Instead, they'd be writing *Fuuuuuck meeee I want to diiiieee.*

Around 3am, I started drinking. I pulled a bottle of vodka from my secret stash at the back of my wardrobe, gulping back way more than I'd intended. It didn't help. I just felt sick and disorientated. I got up to go to the toilet and cracked my head on the doorframe. In the hallway, a flat line of light spilled from the bottom of Ollie's door. Maybe he'd fallen asleep with the light on. Maybe he was still awake. Why and how did teenagers willingly choose to stay up all night? It didn't make sense. I would've done anything, literally *anything*, for a full night's sleep.

Feeling my way back to bed, I climbed between the sheets as quietly as I could, but Kara heard me. She howled and I picked her up. She wriggled and shoved me away. Our bodies bumped together in the dark like rubber rings. The bottle of vodka, on the other hand, behaved perfectly. It waited quietly and patiently on my bedside table like a loyal friend. I screwed off the cap and took swig after swig.

*Please, please, baby. Please stop crying.*

In eight months, I hadn't slept for more than two or three hours in a row. There was a physical gap in my body where sleep should be – and a dragging, aching sensation, like grief. It dimly occurred to me that it hadn't been like this with Ollie. It was tough, sure, but never *this* hard. He'd been a deep sleeper, an enthusiastic eater and my tiny best friend. As old as ten, he would climb onto my lap and ask for a snuggle. But things changed shortly after he turned eleven. He clammed up, got angry, became shifty and secretive. And then suddenly it was like we were speaking entirely different languages. I'd say something and he'd look baffled. Then he'd reply, and it would be my turn to be confused. Being around him became like hosting a foreign exchange student, but without the pleasantries. Or an end date.

Kara's crying was like nails scraping the marrow from my

bones. I got up and pulled the travel cot flush against my bed. I placed Kara inside and lay back down, draping my arm over the side of the mattress to pat her.

I'd drunk way too much. The bed wobbled beneath me like a poorly made raft on a raging ocean. A black wave sucked me up, and I teetered on its spumy crest before freefalling down the other side. Too scared to move, I lay staring at the ceiling, convinced I could hear screams coming from the forest outside.

Kara tugged on my hand. Her little fingernails scratched at my palm and I wrapped my fingers around hers until it was impossible to know who was clinging to who.

I closed my eyes and dreamed of violence.

Of Ollie, standing motionless over Kara's cot.

Of stick dolls, dead birds and pictures carved on trees. A glowing white house on a steep green hill. And a grey-haired witch, standing in a forest with her arms raised high.

# ALEX

## 8

The next day, Ollie still wasn't speaking to me. I waved a selection of different olive branches but none of them worked, and by 4.30pm he was still stubbornly refusing to communicate, gluing himself instead to the sofa and the extreme sports channel.

I was changing Kara's nappy on the floor, quietly seething at the noise level, when there was a knock at the door.

'Hell-ooo?' said a voice. 'Anyone home?' The door opened and Jenny appeared, wearing another brightly coloured headscarf.

'Hi,' I said, fixing Kara's nappy into place and sitting up. 'Come in, Jenny, how are you?'

Kara rolled over to see what was happening.

'I hope I'm not disturbing?' A sunbeam crossed her face and made her look tired: her cheekbones seemed sharper, her eye sockets even more hollow than when we'd last spoken.

'Not at all, we were just finishing up.' A screech of tyres and a loud crash rang out from the TV screen. 'Ollie, can you turn that down, please?'

Grudgingly, he knocked the volume down one level.

'I love what you've done with the place.' Jenny stepped further into the unit and gazed around. 'Very cosy.'

'Thanks. It's starting to feel like home, anyway.' Scooping Kara up and onto my hip, I crossed to the kitchen bench and offered her a chunk of ready-peeled banana. She snatched it out of my hand and began chomping on it like she'd been starved for weeks.

'My goodness, your girl likes her food, doesn't she?'

'Some days yes, some days no. Today is very much a yes day.' Kara inhaled the banana and reached out for more. 'Look at her, she's an animal.'

Jenny smiled. 'No, she's adorable. Listen, I've had this old TV sitting in my spare room for a while now and it never gets used. I was wondering if you or Ollie might want it?'

'What?' said Ollie, jumping off the sofa. 'A TV? How big is it?'

I gave him a look. 'That's very kind of you, Jenny, but—'

'I'll take it,' he said, literally putting his hand up. 'For my room, Mum. Please?'

I sighed. I was reluctant to add yet another screen into the mix – but on the other hand it would be nice not to have Ollie dominating the lounge all the time. 'Are you sure you don't want it?' I said to Jenny.

'Like I said, it's just gathering dust.'

'*Pleeeeaase?*' Ollie begged.

I rolled my eyes. 'Okay, fine.'

'Yes!' Ollie pumped a fist in the air. 'I'll go clear some space.'

'What do you say, Oliver?' I called as he disappeared into his room.

'Thanks, Jenny, you're the best,' he called back as the door swung shut.

'Well, that's settled, then,' said Jenny, whose smile was so wide it transformed her whole face. 'Also, Kit asked me to call in on my way to the greenhouse and remind you all about the meet.'

'The what?'

'Dinner tonight. Down at the greenhouses? We do it every Thursday. Kit said he mentioned it.'

'Oh!' I slapped a hand to my forehead; I'd completely forgotten. 'Yes, he did but I – he told me to bring a dish and I haven't made anything, so ...'

'That's okay,' said Jenny. 'No one will mind. Just throw on a pair of shoes and come on down.'

'Um ... okay, well, I'll have to freshen up a bit. And probably bribe Ollie into coming.' I smiled wryly. 'He's not my biggest fan right now, we had a fight.'

'Oh dear.' Jenny watched me feed Kara another piece of banana. 'It must be hard work raising those two on your own. I hope I'm not speaking out of turn here, but if you ever need a babysitter, or even just someone to talk to, I'd be happy to help.'

I hesitated. It was a generous thing to say, but it put me on edge. Was I so obviously battling? My gut reaction was to make my capability clear. *I don't need anyone, thanks, I'm doing just fine.* But my need to prove I could do everything myself had got me into trouble before. Well-meaning colleagues, thoughtful friends; I'd pushed them away because sometimes the sting of vulnerability hurt more than the struggle itself.

I forced a smile. 'Well, that's nice of you. I could certainly do with some tips!'

'Tips?' Jenny laughed. 'Oh no, sweetheart, you don't want advice from a lonely dinosaur like me. I'm retired, I have no kids, no partner, and I don't understand computers. I don't even have a mobile phone, can you believe that? But I do have time, and you're always welcome to that.'

It was clearly meant as a joke, so I smiled, but her comments struck me as sad. Did she really have no one in her life?

'Anyway.' Jenny shrugged her bony shoulders. 'You know where to find me. Look, I'll leave you to it; come on down to the greenhouses whenever you're ready, we'd love to see you.'

As I watched her go, it occurred to me that maybe her offer hadn't been purely selfless. Maybe Jenny needed the company. Maybe I should invite her in for tea sometime. It wouldn't hurt me to accept a little help, and it certainly felt nice to know that there was someone nearby looking out for us. Like a neighbourhood watch.

'Hey, Jenny?'

She turned back.

'You haven't seen anyone hanging around here lately, have you?'

'What do you mean?'

'I don't know, just ...' *A dark-web delivery guy. A furious ex. A witch.* 'Anyone unfamiliar, walking around the village?'

Jenny frowned. 'I don't think so. No other new arrivals, if that's what you mean. Why?'

I shrugged. 'It's okay, it doesn't matter.'

She tilted her head, her face full of concern. 'Everything alright?'

'Sure,' I said, breezily. 'Everything's fine. And thank you for checking in. It really means a lot.'

'No problem. That's what friends are for.'

'You ready, Ollie?' I called, spraying on some perfume. 'Come on, we don't want to be late.' I checked my appearance in the mirror. I looked tired, but my hair was brushed, I'd put on some lipstick and my clothes bore minimal food stains. Not too bad.

'What are we doing again?' Ollie asked as we walked along the road towards the greenhouses. Five minutes earlier, I'd caved and given him his phone back; in return he'd put on one of his 'good' T-shirts and agreed to come with me to dinner.

'Meeting and greeting. I think.' Kara looked up at me from her pram, thoroughly unimpressed with the bow I'd stuck in her hair.

'You *think*?'

'Apparently on Thursdays everyone has dinner at the greenhouses. Odd place to eat, but, you know, when in Rome.'

'Aren't we a bit overdressed for a greenhouse?'

'I don't know.' I shrugged. 'It's dinner.'

'Why can't we just eat at home by ourselves?'

'Stop, it'll be fun.'

It was another beautiful golden-hued afternoon, warm enough for a spaghetti strap dress and my favourite leather slingbacks. For some reason, I'd imagined that dinner in a greenhouse would be like a garden-themed wedding: loaded trestle tables, fairy lights and sangria served in mason jars. When we arrived, though, it was clear that Ollie's instinct had been right – this was not dinner as the city knew it.

There *was* a trestle table, but it had been piled irreverently with foil-covered bake trays and cling-wrapped bowls. And not another red lip or rouged cheek in sight. Everyone was wearing shorts and singlets, rubber thongs and crocs, and they were all covered in mud. 'Oh my god,' I breathed, and almost turned the pram around.

'Hey, you're here!' said Kit, approaching in boardies and a light blue muscle T. Between his broad shoulders, golden tan and the watering can in his hand, he looked like a male model on location. 'Hello again, miss,' he said to Kara, then nodded warmly to Ollie. 'Hey, mate.'

'Hi,' Ollie mumbled, his eyes on the ground.

'You look nice,' he said to me. 'We might need to get you a couple of aprons, though. Messy stuff, this gardening.'

My cheeks burned. I felt like the lone guest at a costume party who hadn't got the memo.

'Here, take this.' He held out the watering can. 'I'll be back in a sec with aprons and gloves, and you can get stuck in.' He bounded away.

At my side, Ollie radiated disdain.

'See,' I said, holding up the watering can. 'Told you. Fun.'

Thursday afternoons, as it turned out, were all about community food production. Villagers brought their kids and pitched in to prepare seedlings, or spread mulch, or lay down new dripper lines before digging in to a potluck dinner: tortilla wraps and coleslaw, tabouleh and bean salads, zucchini slice and

81

grilled corn cobs. Depending on their age and level of enthusiasm, the kids would either lend a hand or jump on dirt mounds while munching on tomatoes picked straight from the vine.

The vibe was extremely friendly; I waved and said hello to the few people I'd already met: Jenny; Paul and Simon and their dog, Al; the two artsy women, the surfy family of five, and the retirees I'd met with Kit my first day. Names went in one ear and out the other, but no one seemed to mind. In fact, I was surprised how much effort people made to ensure I was included. I was given a trowel and a pair of gloves, and soon I was kneeling in the dirt, elbow deep in mulch and having a surprisingly nice time.

And though there were no twinkly lights or vine arbours, the greenhouse turned out to be the perfect place for an alfresco supper. The setting sun provided a honey-gold glow, and everywhere I looked there were flowers: a snowy white delphinium in with the radishes. A perfect lily, sprouting between the peas. Roses, lisianthus and gloriously full dahlias, all growing unexpectedly among the herbs and veggies. The advantage of building on a former flower farm, I supposed.

When Kara got bored of sitting in the pram, I pulled her out and plopped her at my feet, where she immediately set about trying to shovel as much soil into her mouth as possible. 'No, don't eat that!' I cried, scooping her away from a vegetable patch mulched, apparently, with chicken poo. She gazed up at me, gurgling with contentment. Ollie, however, was not as easily convinced. He stood next to me with his arms folded, refusing to join in.

'Come on,' I said, selecting a trowel. 'It's only mud.'

'I am *not* kneeling down in *that*,' he hissed.

'Oliver,' I said, standing up. 'Can you please stop being such a—'

'Sorry to interrupt,' said Kit at my shoulder. There was a teenager standing next to him; a girl with blue hair and square-rimmed glasses. 'Just wanted to introduce you to someone. This is Violet. Violet, this is Alex and Oliver.'

Ollie and I immediately dropped our battle stances. 'Hey,' Ollie said, sticking out his hand for the girl to shake and I baulked. His grin was sort of ... *wolfish*. When had he started to look at girls like that?

Violet, it turned out, was the older daughter of Layla, the single mum who'd dropped round with a carrot cake on our first afternoon. She was around Ollie's age, maybe a little older (fifteen or sixteen at a guess, but it was hard to tell with girls) and wore a glittering stud in her right nostril. Behind her glasses, black kohl lines flicked from the corner of each eye. She was, I thought with mild dismay, extremely cool.

'A few of us are hanging out over there if you want to join us,' she said, nodding to a spot on the road where teens were riding bikes and skateboards. 'Unless' – she shot a pained look at the vegetables – 'you'd rather stay here?'

'Oh, no,' said Ollie, quickly. 'Nope. Definitely not. I'll come.' And off he went.

Layla herself then appeared and reintroduced herself. Like me, she was new to Pine Ridge and had recently separated from her partner; she and her two girls were also on the collaborative living list and looking to buy land. 'Violet has really struggled with the move,' she confided, kneeling down in the dirt and helping me discourage Kara from eating more poo. 'But she's at that age. You know, hates me, hates everything. We fight roughly 200 per cent of the time.'

'Thank god,' I said. 'I thought it was just me.'

'Believe me, it's not. Living here is helping, though. And luckily my younger daughter isn't quite so fiery.' She nodded at a meek-looking girl with a sharp fringe sitting on a plastic crate a short distance away, her head in a book. 'Isn't it funny how two people can be raised in exactly the same way but turn out so different? Violet is a beast, but Amy is so shy, so sensitive. It's all I can do to get her to say hello to anyone.' She sat up on her haunches. 'Hey, sweetheart,' she called. 'Wouldn't you rather go on up to the road and hang out with the other kids?'

Amy shrugged, then went back to her book.

Layla shook her head indulgently. 'Bless her, she's still my baby. Not literally, thank Christ! I couldn't handle an actual baby right now, not on top of teenager mayhem. I don't know *how* you're doing it.'

I made a big mental note to make friends with this woman.

'You guys,' Layla called to a group digging for potatoes. 'Come and meet Alex, she just moved in.'

I met an environmental scientist from Iceland, a botanist from Cairns and an architect from Melbourne. I talked to couples who'd fancied a sea change, singles who wanted to live 'alone but together'. Kids were pointed out and names were thrown around. Jesse. Naz. Remy. Will. Phoebe. Felix. Taylor. I looked for the kid on the bike who'd told me the spooky witch story but couldn't see him; there were just too many people. Everyone smiled and waved. *Welcome, welcome, welcome.*

Best of all, I discovered parents just like me. Dads with bags under their eyes, mums with egg on their shirts. *Hallelujah.* Two of these mums, Shannon and Mariko, had absorbed Layla into their regular meet-ups for coffee or lunch while their kids ran around, and right away I knew that they were my kind of girls. They demonstrated their zero interest in small talk by skipping right over it and instead diving happily into haemorrhoids, sleep deprivation and postnatal hair loss. When they invited me to join them at Layla's place for their next 'mum hang', I accepted so fast it made them laugh.

There were a few people who weren't so friendly – which, I supposed, was to be expected for a community of that size. There were always one or two rotten apples. One resident in particular seemed particularly stand-offish, a dark-haired woman called Maggie whose face was dominated by horsey teeth, a square jaw and a permanent frown. Instead of greeting me warmly like the others, Maggie said a terse hello then beat a hasty retreat as if I might be carrying something contagious. *Never mind*, I thought, as I was introduced to a doctor from the Northern Beaches. *You can't please everyone.*

A little later, though, as I stood with Shannon and Mariko at a workbench, cutting hessian sacks into strips to cover the newly turned beds, I found myself feeling restless. I couldn't focus, and my eyes kept wandering around the room as if I'd lost something. At first, I couldn't figure out the problem – I could see both my kids; my phone and keys were in the pram – but then I realised with a plummeting heart that my subconscious was looking for Kit. Somehow and without my knowing it, my attention had hitched itself to his movements. Even as I chatted and smiled and ate and worked, a small part of me was keeping track of where he was and what he was doing – and it seemed I wasn't the only one.

Looking around, I began to understand just how central Kit was to the Pine Ridge community. As he moved through the greenhouse, people turned their heads towards him the way sunflowers chase the sun, especially the women. My stomach churned as I watched him chatting to Layla by the food table (big smile, firm eye contact, a hand that momentarily covered her whole shoulder), and the depth of my attraction hit me like a sack of wet sand.

*Shit.* I was doing it again: projecting my neediness onto the first person who made me feel special. But I wasn't special at all; this was just the way Kit treated everyone. Or worse, the way he treated new arrivals. The attention he'd given me, the forest walk, it was probably all just part of the sell. *We need the income*, he'd said. And what were new residents if not that?

I decided it might be time to go. I laid my scissors on the workbench and looked down to where Kara had been playing at my feet just seconds before.

'You okay?' Mariko asked.

'Yeah, I'm fine, I just …' I ducked my head to look under the bench. She'd been right there, playing with a plastic pot. 'Have you seen Kara?'

'She went thataway,' someone called merrily, pointing down

the neat lines of earth with a gloved hand.

I looked and spotted the soles of my daughter's chubby feet as she crawled slowly but steadily towards a row of freshly planted strawberries. 'Whoops, thank you!' I called back, giving chase. 'Kara, stop!' I reached her just as she grabbed one of the plants and pulled it right out of the ground. 'No, honey, that's not for you.' She giggled as I brushed the dirt off her hands and knees.

'Do you mind?' said a harsh voice.

I turned, startled. It was the unfriendly woman with the horsey teeth, Maggie.

'We only just put those in,' she said.

'I know, I'm so sorry. She's just curious. I'll put it back.'

The woman scowled at me. 'No, leave it. Just keep your rug rats under control. It's a greenhouse, not day care.' Then, turning away, she muttered something that sounded a lot like 'city princess'.

I bristled. 'Excuse me?'

Maggie turned back and eyeballed me. 'You people are all tourists. You swan in here, have yourselves a little holiday, but this is our life, our *work*. This land is special and ought to be treated as such.'

The confrontation was unexpected, and a hot flush of mortification crept up my neck. 'Oh. Okay ... sorry, I didn't—'

And then Kit was at my side, bounding into the exchange like an overexcited puppy. 'Hey, Alex, I see you met Maggie!'

In an instant, Maggie's face transformed. The frown disappeared and was replaced by an adoring smile.

'Maggie's one of our very first Pine Ridgers,' said Kit,

wrapping an arm around the woman's shoulders and giving her a squeeze. 'A very important person to know. This place is as much hers as it is mine.'

'Clearly,' I said, flashing a fake smile. I did *not* like her.

'I was just about to grab a bite,' said Kit, turning to me. 'Can I make you up a plate?'

I was hungry – I hadn't eaten a decent meal in what felt like weeks – but Maggie's comment had left a sour taste in my mouth. And I couldn't quite shake my earlier thought: that maybe Kit was not quite as sincere as I'd first thought him to be.

'No, thanks.' I bounced Kara on my hip, not quite able to meet Kit's eyes. 'I should probably get this monster home.'

'You sure? We've got homemade pizza.'

'Really, I'm fine.'

'Oh, you've got to try it, it's amazing.'

I felt Maggie watching me. *City princess.* 'I don't like pizza,' I lied.

'Hold up,' Kit grinned. 'Say that again. You don't like pizza? Are you crazy?'

My stomach churned. Stu's voice. *Have you lost your mind, Alex? Have you gone psycho? Calm the fuck down, you need to see a fucking doctor.*

'Not crazy,' I said, trying to keep my voice level. 'Just tired. Thanks for a lovely afternoon, Kit, you've all made me feel *very* welcome.'

I felt Maggie's eyes burning into me all the way back to the road.

# RENEE
## 9

'This GoPro makes an awesome tech gift,' said the perky young shop assistant, holding up something that looked like a smartphone dressed up as the Batmobile. 'It only came out this year. It's got everything from an improved lens and higher frame rate to a simpler interface and way more ports. Great for recording family holidays.'

Renee shook her head. 'Not really my son's thing,' she said. The sound of the shopping mall pulsed around her, a stark contrast to the silence of the farm. 'I need something more … computer related. But something new. Do you have anything really cutting edge?'

The shop assistant brushed a lock of curly hair from her eyes and gave her a blank look.

'He's a gamer,' Renee explained.

'Oh, I see,' said the assistant, her eyes widening. 'Well, then let me show you our consoles and accessories.' She led Renee over to a different area. 'Sony's new PlayStation wireless headphones are pretty exciting. The audio quality probably isn't the best on the market, but the surround sound adds depth to gameplay and the mic is great for in-game chat. Or what about the iPad 2? It has a front-facing camera and a faster A5 dual core processor, and it matches up nicely with some of the more popular games like *Ticket to Ride* and *Ascension*, if that's the kind of thing he's into?'

Renee stared at the endless array of bizarre objects, searching in vain for something Gabriel did not already have. When she saw the price tags, her jaw fell open.

'Or maybe a gift card?' said the shop assistant, hurriedly. 'Then your son can put it towards something he really wants.'

Renee smiled weakly. Last year had been just as challenging; in the end she'd gone for a pair of computer glasses with specially tinted lenses; the year before that had been the adjustable laptop stand. She'd been assured by other similarly chirpy store employees that they were good gifts. Gamers, they said, were notoriously hard to buy for; they were very particular about their hardware and often bought products directly online, so it was best to let him decide. But Renee couldn't stand the idea of just giving her son a piece of paper in an envelope. The magic of birthdays was in the rip of shiny paper and the sharp intake of breath when the wrapping was peeled back. So, every year she went to the same shop to choose yet another in a long line of 'bestselling' products that she hoped would knock Gabriel's socks off.

This year, though, Gabriel had done something he'd never done before; at least, not since he was a child. He'd given her a *list*. She'd nearly fallen over backwards with shock when she found the little scrap of paper sitting on the kitchen table. At first, she'd assumed it belonged to Michael – but upon examination, she recognised the spidery handwriting as Gabe's.

Pursing her lips, she held the list in her hand and squinted at the words. *Mini LED torch*, it said. *Phillips screwdriver. Cable ties. Tweezers. Grounding strap.*

Gabriel's passions had once been much less difficult to fathom. From an early age he'd shown an interest in art, and over time he'd developed a talent for drawing: portraits, still life, landscape, animals – he had a real eye for natural beauty. He'd never left his room back then, either, but at least the reasons had seemed somewhat more noble. The constant scratch of lead on paper, his head always bent over a sketchbook; Renee had told everyone who would listen that her son would be a famous artist one day. But as far as she knew, he hadn't picked up a pencil since he'd transferred his interest to computers a few years back.

She looked again at the items on the list. Machine maintenance tools, she guessed. Gabe had built his own gaming rig and the results were mindboggling: gunmetal grey cubes, circuit boards, colourful wires and flashing lights, all painstakingly fitted together to create something that actually worked. It was impressive ... but the new items he'd asked for were hardly 'gifts'. She couldn't imagine wrapping up these banalities and presenting them to him on his birthday. She wanted to find something *special*.

But a smarter, more rational part of her knew from experience that whenever she spent money on something expensive, it just disappeared into Gabe's room like a rock thrown into a deep, dark well. They never saw him enjoying anything, which pretty much defeated the point of the giving.

Then again, all she really wanted was to please her son. The distant memory of his smile was almost enough to bring her to her knees right there in the aisles of TechHeaven. And a part of her still hoped that, if she bought the right presents, he might one day share a little of their meaning with her. She wanted so much to understand him.

Oh, for the days when all he'd asked for were pencils and paper.

'I think,' Renee said, 'I'll just go for the camera thing. The GoPro. Nice and easy.'

'Great choice,' said the assistant, visibly relieved. 'I'm sure he'll love it.'

'Gabriel?' Michael's deep voice rang out from the hallway, followed by the sound of a fleshy fist pounding on a door. 'Gabriel, open this door right now.'

In the kitchen, Renee positioned the GoPro in the centre of a thick sheet of wrapping paper. She brought the top and bottom edges together, securing them with a strip of Sellotape, then set about folding in the side sections.

'Gabriel!' Michael was getting louder.

Without saying a word, Renee turned the gift the right way up, carried it over to the dresser and stowed it in the cupboard. She'd learned over time that her husband was like a thunderstorm; you just had to wait until the black clouds passed. Unfortunately, his moods seemed to be getting darker and more intense with every passing year, and the gaps between them fewer and further between.

The doorknob rattled one last time, and then Michael came stamping down the hall. 'For shit's sake,' he muttered as he entered the kitchen. 'Since when has he had a lock on his door?'

'Lock?' Renee said. 'Are you sure?'

Michael went to the fridge for another beer. Twisting off the cap, he lifted the bottle to his lips and took a deep slug before answering. 'Pretty fucking sure.'

'Maybe the door is just stuck.' Checking the dresser for dust, she straightened the plates and gave the teacups a quick wipe with a napkin. 'Which reminds me – can you take a look at the front door? Dad said the latch isn't engaging properly.'

Ignoring her, Michael wiped his mouth and stared out of the kitchen window.

'Please, Michael, don't be too hard on him. He's upset about the cat.'

Michael snorted. 'The cat. Sure. Always some excuse.'

'We have to respect his needs.'

'The kid turns sixteen next week. What he *needs* is to grow the fuck up and help out around here.'

Renee gave up. She and Michael had played out this same row over and over again, often with Renee in tears and Michael speaking through clenched teeth. '*I've* been working on this place since I could walk,' Michael would say. 'It wasn't an option; my old man picked me up by the scruff of the neck and threw me in the greenhouse.' And Renee, shuddering at the memory of her brutal ex-military father-in-law, would reply gently that Gabriel just wasn't suited to the land and maybe they should be encouraging a career in some other field instead, perhaps something in an office. And then Michael would look at her like she'd just suggested Gabriel become a tap dancer, and Renee would get defensive, and they'd both start yelling. It was the same every time, a script they both knew by heart, and neither deviated from their lines.

Occasionally, Renee would have to admit that her husband was half right. Gabriel was getting older; he would have to find a job eventually. But he'd always been a bit *different* – and over the last few years he'd slowly become so reclusive, so resistant to life in general, that she now doubted he could dress himself for an interview, let alone get himself to one. If he barely left his room, couldn't hold a conversation, couldn't even eat in front of other people, and if he flat-out refused to see a doctor for help, then how could she ever expect him to do anything as comparatively complicated as work?

Taking another long slug of beer, Michael wandered over to the sink, where he stood and gazed out of the window.

Renee brushed a cobweb from the top corner of the dresser. Rubbing the sticky strands from her fingers, she studied her husband, taking in his mottled cheeks and rounded shoulders. His blue checked shirt, and the gaping hole at his belly where a button or two had popped off. The shadows under his eyes, almost as dark as Gabe's. It had been a difficult few years, there was no doubt about that – but she couldn't understand why he was quite so stressed. After the terrible strain of both the global financial crisis and the drought, things were finally looking hopeful. The rain was coming down and orders were going up.

The land was hydrated, and though the crop was still small, it was more beautiful than ever.

Renee watched as Michael finished off his second beer, threw the bottle in the bin, then poured himself a whisky. Shuffling back to the lounge area, he flipped on the sound system before collapsing onto the sofa. Ebony flopped onto the cushions and curled up next to him as the jangling opening bars of Paul McCartney's 'Fine Line' hurtled from the speakers.

As Paul sang merrily about recklessness, courage and choosing the right road, Renee walked slowly to the fridge and began pulling out ingredients for dinner. Just under the music, she could faintly make out another rhythm: the incessant tap of fingers on a keyboard coming from behind Gabriel's closed bedroom door.

On the sofa, Michael closed his eyes.

*It's a fine line,* warned Paul, *when your decision makes a difference. Get it wrong, you'll be making a big mistake.*

# ALEX
## 10

'Homeschooling is just so *hard*.' Layla reached for the platter, cut a fat slice of cheese and pressed it onto a cracker. 'I'm lucky that Amy is so good, but Violet never listens to me, I can't make her do anything. I don't even know where she *is* half the time.'

Tucked away at the back of the village and high up on the slope, Layla's unit was probably one of the best positioned in the whole of Pine Ridge. She had the upper floor of a split-level similar to Jenny's, with huge windows and stone benchtops and an enormous entertaining deck with a panoramic view right across the valley. The outdoor dining table was large enough for twelve but that afternoon it was just Layla, Shannon, Mariko and me; plus our kids, who, by some happy accident, were all occupied and quiet. Kara was under the table playing with measuring cups and saucepans, while Mariko's almost three-year-old son buried Lego in the planters. Amy was inside, sitting up at the kitchen bench diligently doing some art homework, and Shannon's six-year-old twin girls were in the communal garden out the front, playing on a wooden swing set. Violet and Ollie had rejected us all and taken their skateboards down to the cycle path that looped the dam. I could see them in the distance, wheeling around with two or three other teens, yelling out to one another and sucking on Layla's homemade ice-blocks.

'You know you don't have to do it, right?' said Mariko, dipping a tortilla chip into the guacamole bowl and popping it into her mouth. 'There's a perfectly good high school down the road.'

'I've heard it's good,' agreed Shannon. 'But I totally get why you'd rather have them here. It's such a delicate age.'

Layla pushed her plate aside and laid her head down on the table. 'Delicate, and impossible. I need a drink. Is it too early for a drink?'

'It's never too early,' said Mariko. 'What have you got? No, don't tell me. Stay there, I'll go rummage in your fridge.'

Despite my fuzzy head and fluttering nerves – I'd drunk myself to sleep again the previous night, lurching from one unpleasant dream to another – I couldn't help but smile. These women made such a refreshing change from the 'friends' I'd made in Sydney, mostly the wives of Stuart's business associates, whose tight, designer-clad bums and taut abs made me want to weep. My local mothers group had been no better; it was like they'd arrived home from the hospital to find all their muscular definition waiting for them on the doorstep, along with the night nanny and the private paediatrician. My reality had been so far removed from theirs that I might as well have been a different species. The Pine Ridge mums, on the other hand, were funny, honest and (homeschooling and greenhouse parties aside) *normal*.

'I think you're doing an amazing job, Layla,' I said, glancing over my shoulder and into the house where Amy was still hunched over her artwork. I pictured Ollie's usual pose: hunched over his phone. 'You've got the screen thing nailed anyway, which is more than I can say.'

Layla smiled and squeezed my arm. 'Thanks. I know I shouldn't complain. They're good kids, really.'

I had to agree. On the whole, all the Pine Ridge kids were eerily well behaved. Well, all except mine.

'Hey, Shan,' Mariko yelled from the kitchen. 'Can you bring me that knife from the table? And the strawberries? And maybe the watermelon too? I'm going to improvise a fruit punch.'

'Oh, Lord.' Shannon stood up. 'No good can come of this.' She carried the bowls of fruit into the kitchen, leaving me alone with Layla.

The morning was bright and warm. Lazy clouds drifted across the sky, casting patchy shadows and causing the light to change like someone was playing with a dimmer switch. Mixing in with the sound of Kara bashing on saucepans was the delicate chime of bellbirds and, from somewhere directly above us, the whistle-crack call of a whipbird.

'So, what are you doing about school next year, Alex?' Layla asked, stifling a yawn. 'Have you enrolled Ollie anywhere yet?'

I shook my head. 'Not yet. I was thinking of homeschooling too, actually, but now I'm not so sure.'

'Oh no, please don't let my whingeing put you off. I'm just having one of those days. It's actually very easy. A total walk in the park.'

I laughed. 'No, it's not you. I just don't know if it's right for us.' Translation: *there may be no faster or more efficient way to decimate what's left of my relationship with my son than to try being his teacher as well as his parent.*

We lapsed into a comfortable quiet, the silence punctuated only by the raucous laughter of kookaburras and the sound of Mariko dropping stuff in the kitchen.

Layla cut another slice of cheese. 'Where did you guys move from again?'

'Sydney.'

'I know, but which suburb?'

'We moved around. Last place we lived was south Bondi. Near Waverley Park.'

'Oh, nice. So, which school did Ollie go to, then? Was it Randwick? Or Rose Bay?'

I reached for a cracker. 'No, neither of those.'

'Reddam? Cranbrook?'

I chewed slowly, trying to think of a way to change the subject, but my brain was momentarily paralysed by the memory of Principal Tinsley's booming voice. *You'll be pleased to hear that we've decided on just a suspension,* he'd said, his fat hands clasped across his stomach. *Although I must emphasise the serious nature of the situation.*

'We lived in Clovelly,' said Layla. I could feel her watching me, her curiosity sharpening. 'Funny to think we lived so close.'

*It's just for the remainder of term. He can start afresh next year when this whole business has blown over.* I'd told him I thought a suspension was too harsh a consequence, that if the school kept it up they'd have no students left. *We have to take a hard line, Ms Ives,* the principal had replied, his eyes roaming disdainfully over my unwashed hair and spit-stained T-shirt. *Think of those poor girls. Imagine the humiliation.*

'Those private schools can be tough, can't they?' Layla pressed on. 'The fees are exorbitant.'

*I must say, it's very disappointing. Oliver was such a good kid when he arrived. Exemplary, even. But his behaviour has undergone such a major U-turn this year that we feel he would benefit from a short period of reflection.*

'And some of them are nothing short of toxic. I mean, I thought the Eastern Suburbs was a safe bet, but it seems none of us are safe anymore. You must've heard the stories?'

I nodded slowly. It wasn't just Ellenhurst High. The news was full of Sydney school scandals: muck-up day pranks gone wrong, hotness ratings lists, sexting, even a recent string of assaults. But somehow Ollie's school had copped some particularly brutal coverage and the media made an example of them – hence the overly stringent punishments.

'I think it's all about boundaries,' Layla said, 'especially when it comes to screen time. Some parents just don't know how to put them in place.'

I felt my palms start to sweat. *Perhaps you could spend some of that time encouraging your son to talk about his feelings. The teenage brain is extremely vulnerable, especially during times of great change, and too much time spent online can be extremely harmful. Here, I have a print-out somewhere.* Principal Tinsley had handed me a glossy leaflet entitled 'Screen Addiction and Internet Safety'. I was tempted to throw it in his face. Instead, I went several steps further and withdrew Ollie from school. *We're leaving*, I wrote in an email a few days later. *How's that for reflection?*

'Homeschooling is tough, but I think it's worthwhile,' Layla said, still watching me. 'No peer pressure to worry about, right?'

I wanted to tell her, I really did. She wasn't stupid; she knew I was holding back. But I needed friends, and I needed Pine Ridge. If Layla or anyone else found out what had happened at Ellenhurst, I might risk losing both.

'Okay, ladies,' said Mariko, returning from the kitchen with four glasses and a jug of something pink. 'Summer is served.'

'Oh my god.' Layla laughed. 'What is in that?'

Shannon grimaced. 'Best not to ask. Alex, are you having one?'

I declined, knowing that day drinking on top of night drinking would be a terrible idea.

'Ouch,' said Mariko, pouring three glasses of pink stuff. 'What happened to you last night?'

'What do you mean?'

'Well, it's Saturday and you're all clammy and trembly. Either you ate a bad kebab, or you had yourself some fun.'

'Oh, did you go *out*?' said Layla. 'I haven't been out in years. What's it like these days? Tell me everything. The drinks, the food, the dancing. I need details.'

I laughed. 'Don't be ridiculous. We're in the middle of nowhere, where would I go?'

'Were there boys?'

'Stop it.'

'Or maybe just one particular boy?' Shannon gave me a wink.

Mariko gasped and clapped her hands. 'Oh no you *didn't!*' she squealed.

'Didn't what? What are you talking about?'

'Don't be coy.' Shannon took a sip of her drink. 'There's something between you and Kit, isn't there?'

'What?' I felt my cheeks flush with heat. 'No!'

'Oh, come on,' said Layla, slyly. 'That boy can't keep his eyes off you.'

'Dude, you'd better move on that shit,' said Mariko. 'He is so hot it hurts.'

I shook my head vigorously, while my heart did a secret cartwheel. 'No, no, it was absolutely nothing like that *at all*. I just had a rough night. Couldn't sleep. You know how it is.' I nodded at Kara, who had grown bored of the saucepans and was now grabbing at my legs. I reached down and pulled her onto my lap.

'Oh, I know it well,' Layla said. 'The girls killed sleep for me. They're easy now they're older, they don't get up anymore, but I still struggle. I just lie awake worrying. I call it the night mind. You know, where you can't switch off?'

'Oh, yep.' Mariko nodded hard. 'You wait and wait for sleep to come but it never does, and your head is just like *ticktickticktickticktick.*' She twirled a finger at her temple: an endlessly spinning cog.

'But it's not just normal worries,' agreed Shannon. 'Everything is so much worse at night. It's like your brain mutates into something with teeth, and the littlest things become *huge.*'

'Exactly,' said Layla. 'And it never goes away.'

'Oh, don't say that,' wailed Mariko. 'It *has* to get better! I was so sleep deprived earlier this year that one night I went to the bathroom, except it wasn't the bathroom. I pulled down my undies in the living room and nearly weed on a chair.'

'I once cried so hard after a bad night that our neighbours called an ambulance,' said Layla lifting her glass as if in a toast. 'They thought I was dying.'

'So, what was the problem with the little madam anyway?' said Shannon, jerking a thumb at Kara, who was reaching for the cheese. I pushed the platter out of her reach. 'Is she teething?'

'They're always teething,' said Mariko. 'The teething never ends. Like, *never.*'

'Actually, the problem wasn't really baby-related.' I hesitated, unsure how much to say. On the one hand, I felt like I could tell my new friends anything and they would understand. *But.* There was always a *but.*

'I've just been having these bad dreams lately,' I said. 'And I know this sounds odd, but I keep hearing noises in the woods. Like, I don't know, shouting or something? And then there was this kid on the road the other day ...' I trailed off and forced a laugh. 'Look, you'll probably think I'm out of my mind, but I have to ask: do you know anything about, um ... a witch? In the woods?'

There was a pause. The girls exchanged a look. Then Layla sighed. 'So you heard, huh?'

Shannon shook her head slowly. 'I guess it was only a matter of time.'

'We should've told you sooner,' said Mariko.

A shiver trickled unpleasantly down my back of my neck. 'Told me what?'

'The only downside about living at Pine Ridge,' said Mariko, 'is that damn witch. Her and her gang of forest monsters. Pesky buggers. Better get used to them, though, they're a pretty permanent fixture round here.'

I looked at them each in turn, trying to read their faces.

'Look, as long as you don't bother her, she won't bother you.' Layla said, wide-eyed and solemn. 'Although, she does enjoy a sacrificial ritual, so if you get time you might want to slay a goat on an altar, just to keep her happy.'

There was a nauseating moment of silence. And then they all started laughing.

'Obviously, we're kidding,' Layla said.

'It's a little village joke,' said Mariko. 'We get a lot of possums and foxes at night. They make the strangest noises, and the kids all say it's the witch, just to scare each other.

'It's like a game. They dare each other to go into the woods and call to her, that kind of thing.'

'But it's just a bit of fun,' Layla said quickly, catching my expression. 'They know she's not real.'

Shannon shook her head. 'It's cute, but we don't encourage it.'

'Unless they haven't done their homework or whatever,' said Mariko. 'And then it's like, do it or the witch will get you!' She curled her hands into claws and drew her lips back over her teeth. '*Raaaaaahh!*'

My skin tightened. *The witch took the farmers' kid.*

'Oh, your face!' Shannon patted me on the back. 'You really must be tired if you believed that rubbish.'

*Crazy. Batshit. Fucking mental patient, you should be locked up.*

'Have a drink, Alex,' said Layla. 'It was just a joke.'

I made myself smile as if I thought it was funny.

By the time I left, the day was nearly done. The shadows were lengthening, and the sun was sinking behind the ridge as I pushed Kara's pram towards home. Passing Ollie on the road, I waved and signalled to him that I was leaving.

'Make sure you're home for dinner,' I called as he skidded to a stop next to Violet. He flipped up his board and caught it, making a show of rolling his eyes to demonstrate exactly how daggy and excruciating I was. Violet giggled, and the adoring look he gave her sent a small knife through my heart.

The other kids, I noticed, were keen to impress her too. Whether they were out riding or tossing a footy, they orbited her like little moons, keeping an eye out for opportunities to win her attention. She was just one of those girls, I realised: a natural queen bee who stuck out purely because she fitted in so well, who effortlessly transcended the social hierarchy because she'd inherited all the right genes and knew exactly what to do with them. It was a shame her younger sister hadn't been so lucky. It wasn't hard to imagine why Amy preferred the company of her mother; Violet's shadow would be a tough one to live in.

As she let out another peal of cool-girl laughter, I made a

mental note to watch her. I wanted so much for my son to make friends; I just had to make sure that it was with the right people this time.

I took the scenic route home, pushing Kara's pram on the cycle path that ran around the dam, singing mindless nursery rhymes to her as I went. The moon had risen, bathing everything in a silver light. The farmhouse shone white on the hill and I stopped to admire it; creepy history or not, I couldn't believe it hadn't yet been renovated. If Pine Ridge needed money, they couldn't go wrong with a lovingly restored, picturesque Airbnb. I wondered if they might consider selling it.

Suddenly a light flashed in one of the windows – a flat bluish glow, like the sweep of a torch. And then, just as quickly, the light was gone.

I stared, waiting for it to come back on, wondering if I'd imagined it … but the house remained still and dark.

And then Kara squawked – *Come on, Mum, what's the hold-up?* – and I dragged myself away, soothing her with more songs before she cracked it and started wailing.

When we reached our steps, I unclipped Kara from her seat and carried her on one hip while I dragged the pram up behind me with the other. I paused at the top to catch my breath, spots swimming in front of my eyes, then slid my key into the lock. As I did, Kara squealed in my arms and arched her back so far and so unexpectedly that I nearly dropped her; I stumbled, and my foot hit something. I looked down.

There was a box. Sitting against the wall next to the drainpipe. Brown cardboard. Unmarked and unsealed, exactly the same as the one before.

Furtively, I scanned the house, the garden, the road below. No one around. No noise, except the swish of the trees above my head and the railway-line song of the cicadas.

Unlocking the door, I took Kara inside and placed her down among her toys. Then I went back outside, picked up the box and brought it into the kitchen, closing the front door behind me. Holding my breath, I put it down on the counter and pulled back the flaps.

Inside was a sheet of bubble wrap. Tentatively, I lifted one corner and took a peek underneath. No feathers, no blood. Just a pile of sticks, and some lumps of material. Reaching in, I poked one of the lumps. It felt inanimate, so I picked it up.

It was a doll – of sorts. Two twigs pressed together into a cross shape and bound by gauze wrapped so thickly that it looked like a lumpy body, out of which the twigs stuck like two arms and a single spindly leg. A head had been made from a ball of wax and wrapped in the same way, so the doll appeared to be wearing a hood. Crude indentations in the wax formed a face: two eyes and a gaping mouth.

I stared at the sort-of doll and the sort-of doll stared right back. Was this one of Ollie's mystery boxes?

And then I remembered the boy on the bike. *Then she brings you a doll.* I looked again at the gauze. *It's supposed to look like you.* The material had been dyed dark green and had a bright orange circle painted on the front, just like Ollie's favourite hoodie.

On the floor, Kara whined and reached for me. Abandoning the box, I picked her up – and then I heard something. Laughter, and a shout from outside. The trundle of wheels and a bicycle bell.

Holding Kara tight, I went to the window and pressed my face to the glass. Dusk had already tipped over into night, but it was still light enough that I could see a group of kids at the edge of the forest. Ollie was with them, one foot on his skateboard; Violet, too. They were all standing in a huddle, staring into the trees. One of them yelled out, a single loud vowel – then they all turned around and took off again, careering back through the village, whooping and hollering as they went.

Kara wriggled and kicked her legs. Reaching out, she tapped the window with an open palm as if trying to show me something … and then I saw it. A figure at the edge of the forest, half-hidden in the tree line not far from where the kids had been.

I cupped my hand around my eyes, trying to see more clearly. It was an old woman. Skinny, pale clothes, grey hair. She was standing very still, staring after the kids, watching them disappear around the corner, just as I had been doing.

Suddenly, the old woman moved. Her head swivelled in my direction, and—

'Ow.' I jerked backwards and rubbed my eye: Kara had flung up a hand and whacked me right in the eyeball. I glared at her. 'What did you do that for?' Kara gazed at me, then gurgled and knocked her gums against my shoulder. 'Alright,' I said. 'I get it, you're hungry *and* tired. Just give me one more minute, okay?'

I turned back to the window, to the shadows in the forest, but all I could see were trees and darkness.

# RENEE

## 11

Renee dragged her palm across the fogged-up mirror and her reflection appeared in its wake. Leaning forward, she turned her head appraisingly from side to side. Her face was changing. All her features seemed to be travelling slowly downwards, drooping and dripping like candlewax towards her chin, neck, chest. She pulled at the sides of her face with her fingers, trying to scoop everything up and pat it back into place, but it was no use. Her cheeks, once plump and rosy, now hung like saddlebags, and the corners of her mouth turned down like a clown's. One of her eyes had definitely got smaller over time; the eyebrow had collapsed above it like a rotten bridge.

She squeezed toothpaste onto her brush. *Christ*, forty-four years and almost half of them spent on the farm. At least her teeth were still good. And although her hair was thinner than it used to be, it was still there, and still brown if you didn't count the greys. Which she both did and didn't, depending on the day.

Giving her reflection one last baleful look, she raised her toothbrush to her mouth – and stopped as she heard a thud … and then a faint creak.

'Michael?'

When he didn't reply, she put down her toothbrush, opened

the door of the ensuite and peered into the bedroom. Michael was already snoring, the whisky having yet again done its job.

She heard it again. *Thud. Creak. Shuffle.*

'Michael,' Renee hissed. He didn't even stir.

*There is no tiger*, she told herself sternly, repeating a phrase once given to her by a therapist. 'Try to remember,' the therapist had said, 'that the physical symptoms are caused by your body reacting inappropriately. The fight or flight response is designed to kick in during life or death situations: for example, a hungry tiger in the room. It is not designed for when a bulb has blown, or you're late for an appointment, or the baby is crying.' *Or when you're imagining noises in the house.*

Tightening the belt on her bathrobe, she crossed the bedroom and stepped out into the hall. Immediately opposite, Gabriel's door was shut. She listened again but heard nothing. Seconds passed. Minutes.

Outside, a wind swept in over the ridge, shaking the red gums and cabbage palms, swooping down on the house and crooning its way through the gaps in the timber cladding. Maybe that was what she'd heard. Just the wind. Or the dog.

'Ebony?' There was a pause, and then the unmistakable *tack-tack-tack* of paws on the floorboards. Ebony came trotting in from the living area and sniffed Renee's feet, her eyes focused and alert.

Renee reached down and scratched behind the dog's ears. 'Hey, Ebs,' she said. 'Was that you making a noise in there? You're not used to sleeping in the house, are you?' Ebony usually slept in the screened-in porch just off the laundry, but after what had happened to Ivory, Michael had brought her bed inside. Len would've had a fit. *Animals outside*, he used to growl. *They need to know their place.* 'Everything's okay. Go on, now. Off you go, back to bed.'

Ebony licked her lips repeatedly, a sign of agitation.

And then they both heard it. Footsteps outside, on the veranda.

Renee froze. Ebony turned her head sharply towards the front door, her tail flat. She sniffed the air and growled.

The night was still. *There is no tiger. Probably just possums in the bins again ...* Fighting a melodramatic urge to rip one of the farm tools off the wall and brandish it like a weapon, Renee switched on the outside light and went right up close to the glass. On the porch, a small shape hovered in the air. A bird? A giant moth? A piece of paper caught in a spider's web?

Another noise at her back: the rattle of a latch, the squeak of a hinge. She whirled around to see Gabriel's door crack open, just wide enough for Renee to glimpse two frightened eyes and an open mouth. 'Mum?' he said in a small voice. 'What's going on?'

'Everything's okay,' she said, repeating the line she'd given the dog. 'Nothing to worry about, go back to sleep.'

Ignoring her, Gabriel crept forward, his eyes on the object outside.

Hardly daring to breathe, Renee opened the door and peered out, flinching as a breeze eddied around her ankles.

'What is that?' whispered Gabriel.

Hanging above the front steps, dangling from the eaves by

111

a piece of string, was a doll. A Christmas angel, a tree-topper, complete with sparkly dress, wings and a halo.

The wind picked up and the doll spun in a circle. The string had been tied around its neck like a noose.

And then came a rush, like the whistle of a whip right before it cracks, followed by the sound of smashing glass and a series of wet *splats*.

Gabe yelled out and Renee jumped as Ebony dashed through her legs out the door, barking furiously. In between the barks, Renee heard a rhythmic *swish-crunch*; someone was running through grass and leaves, either towards the house or away.

'Michael!' she yelled, holding on to the doorframe with both hands.

He appeared in the hallway. 'What the ...?' he said, rubbing his sleep-creased eyes. 'What's happening?'

Ebony's barks became more frenzied – she was back inside the house – and both Michael and Renee started moving at once, following the sound, hurrying together down the hall, past the bathroom, into the kitchen and around the corner, where they skidded to a stop.

The living room was bleeding. The sofa, the walls, the family photographs on the side table, all spattered with red. Blood dripped down the window glass in thick rivulets. Two of the panes had broken, allowing the night air to roll uninvited through the jagged holes.

Renee covered her mouth with her hands.

*There is no tiger.*

Gabriel edged past her, his mouth hanging open.

*There is no tiger.*

Michael was already at the back door, fumbling with the lock, yanking it open, switching on the light, striding outside.

*There is no tiger.*

There wasn't a tiger. Of course there wasn't. But there was a lot of blood. The house was soaked in it.

# ALEX

## 12

Holding on to the sink in my bathroom, I turned on the tap and watched the water swirl down the plughole. Despite the two coffees I'd already sculled, I was so tired I could hardly stay upright. Maybe I needed to slap myself, pinch my skin, bite my lip till it bled; a nice hot cup of pain to start the day. It seemed to work in the movies. I whacked my cheek with an open palm. My face stung, but it didn't wake me up.

Sighing, I washed my hands, wincing at the sight of my nails, bitten to the quick. I kept flashing back to the kid on the road, the spooky story. My new mum friends laughing at me, making fun of my fear. Stuart's threats, the way his face twisted when he was angry.

I pressed my fingers to my temples; my head was pounding again. I considered taking a quick nap right there on the floor; curling up on the bathmat and drifting off, just for ten minutes. But every time I closed my eyes, I saw the horrible stick doll and its waxy face. The dead bird and its unseeing eye. The images swirled together with echoes of my now-recurring nightmares, until I could no longer distinguish dream from memory, memory from dream.

*Coffee. I need more coffee.*

Splashing some water on my face, I straightened up and got on with the day.

The meeting had already started when I arrived. The door banged when I pushed it open, causing countless pairs of eyes to swivel in my direction. Jostling the pram over the threshold, I edged my way inside and hovered by the wall, waiting for someone to tell me what to do next.

The Pine Ridge community hall was a single-storey gabled conversion, clad on the outside with black corrugated metal and decorated inside with white walls, concrete floors, bifold glass doors and ceiling fans that reminded me of wind turbines. In line with its intended function as the heart of the village, it occupied a central position overlooking the dam. The interior was open plan, just one enormous gleaming room with two subdivided spaces at each end: a kitchen to the right, and a room on the left that had been filled with toys and soft play equipment and was used as an unofficial creche. The overall effect was stark and functional: this was a place for business.

I'd already seen the villagers en masse but, unlike at the greenhouses, the vibe here was static and serious. Black folding chairs had been arranged in a circle and every single seat held a Pine Ridge resident. At the back of the room stood a PA system and a whiteboard, next to which sat Kit, spine straight, feet planted firmly on the floor, microphone in hand. As soon as I saw him, I couldn't help it: my whole body hummed like a tuning fork.

He looked up. Our eyes met. I felt the blush creeping up my

neck before I could do anything to stop it.

Kit waved and gestured for me to join. 'Everyone, make room for Alex. Can someone get another chair?' After some shuffling and scraping, a gap appeared in the circle.

Parking the pram against the wall and locking it in place, I checked under the hood. Kara's little face was the picture of peace. Mine, on the other hand, felt swollen with fatigue – and, despite much teeth-brushing, I was pretty sure I stank of alcohol. The late-night vodka was becoming a habit.

As I joined the circle, I kept my head down and the meeting continued around me. I felt like everyone was staring. But when I finally glanced up, not one person was looking my way. The whole room was focused on Kit, who was congratulating everyone on a Greenpeace fundraiser they'd all apparently organised a few weeks ago.

'It's a great feeling to know that in supporting the fight against global deforestation, Pine Ridge is making a difference,' he said. 'Together, we raised a grand total of eight hundred dollars, which makes me very proud.'

Everyone clapped.

'Now, let's talk about plans for the wellness centre ...'

While he spoke, I took the opportunity to check out the crowd. Layla, Shannon and Mariko were there, their faces unusually sombre. Jenny in purple dungarees and matching headscarf. The retirees, the surfy parents, the botanist and the architect. Paul and Simon (no sign of Al). And horse-faced Maggie, sitting ramrod straight with her arms folded and her nostrils flaring.

After Kit finished speaking, two people I hadn't yet met stood up and delivered a ten-minute proposal on the development of a therapy space and day spa. I saw Maggie's eyes darken. A muscle twitched in her jaw.

'Does anyone have any objections to this proposal?' Kit asked when the presentation was over.

Several people, including Maggie, raised their hands with their fists clenched tight.

'Okay, I count six. So, on the count of three ... one, two, three.'

Everyone with a fist in the air lowered their arm and held out their hand, either palm down or palm up.

'Alright, four objections and two questions.'

Kit turned to Maggie, whose palm faced down, and handed her the microphone.

'I think expansion is a terrible idea,' she said, loudly. 'We're overcrowded as it is, and the original intention of the village is becoming diluted. I make no secret of it; I am opposed to further development, tourists and any more newcomers.' She flicked a pointed look in my direction.

I blinked.

Kit pressed his lips into a line. He looked like he was holding in a very big sigh.

Maggie stood up and passed the mike across the circle to the next person with their hand out. 'I agree,' said a man with dreadlocks. 'I moved here to get away from the rest of the world. I say we close the community, and keep it closed.'

Across the circle, I saw Mariko roll her eyes. Layla shook her head and flicked me a sympathetic look.

As two other residents voiced similar opinions, the tension in the room rose. I found myself shrinking further into my chair as the meeting dragged on. Eventually, though, Kit was forced to wrap things up.

'I'm mindful of time,' he said, wearily. 'So I suggest we appoint a small group to work out further evaluation criteria, details of which will be shared at the next meeting. Now, let's move on to something a little more cheerful: our annual summer solstice party on the twenty-second, and the Pine Ridge Christmas lunch. Maggie, would you like to kick us off?' Kit smiled stiffly and passed her the microphone.

'Thank you, Kit,' said Maggie, standing up and accepting the mike as if it were a bouquet of flowers. 'I've got a few surprises in store for this year's solstice: a special theme and gifts for everyone. Although, I have to say the credit for the idea should really go to our beautiful Pine Ridge kids.' She beamed around the room. 'I find their creativity so inspiring. If only we adults had even half their imagination, half their belief, the world would be a better place.'

I wanted to vomit. She might as well have broken into song: that cheesy Whitney one about children being the future.

'We're less than two weeks away now,' she said. 'So there's no time to waste. Let's confirm jobs. We're going to need plenty of volunteers.'

When the meeting was over, sign-up sheets were tacked to the wall. While everyone around me stood and began writing their names down, I hurried back to the pram, determined to leave before anyone could talk to me. Unfortunately, Kara woke up screaming and I had no choice but to feed her there and then. I lifted her from her pram and took her to a corner to attempt a breastfeed.

*Christmas*, I thought miserably. I hadn't even begun to get organised.

Village chat floated around me.

'What about prawns this year?'

'Who's going to dress up as Santa?'

'How are you getting on with the winter wonderland theme?'

'We've already made heaps of fake snow, we just need snowmen and reindeer.'

I sat there thinking, *fake snow? It'll be thirty-five degrees!* I would never get used to hot Christmases; nothing about them made sense. Instead of frosted windows, log fires, mulled wine and twinkly lights, Australia had salads and seafood, tinnies and pool floaties. The shopping-centre Santas all looked dangerously dehydrated. Every year felt more and more like a practical joke.

'I know!' said someone. 'We can get the kids to make icicle decorations and hang them from the roof!'

I looked away, cringing into Kara's hair, and I realised I wasn't the only person hiding out, avoiding conversation. Over on the other side of the room, Layla's daughter Amy sat alone on a chair with a book in her hands. Her head was bowed, her fringe falling in her face. Perhaps it was just because she was so small for her age (if I had to guess, I'd have said more like

119

ten than thirteen), but she looked extremely fragile. *Poor kid*, I thought. *Doesn't she have any friends?*

Amy looked up, meeting my gaze head-on, and I had the distinct impression she'd been waiting for me to notice her. I smiled, but she didn't smile back. I tilted my head quizzically. Amy continued to eyeball me. Her expression was intense, almost pleading. She looked like she was trying to tell me something. And then my view was blocked by Violet suddenly appearing in front of her sister. Bending down, Violet whispered something in Amy's ear. Amy's face fell. Slowly, she stood up and shuffled away with her head down. The small, lonely shape of her made me feel sad.

'Well, that was awkward,' said Layla, striding over with Mariko and Shannon in tow.

'She's a nightmare, that woman,' said Shannon. 'Always ready with a spanner to throw.'

'Just because she was here first, she thinks she owns the joint,' Mariko huffed. 'If she hates other people that much, she should just go live in a cave. She'd be much happier, I'm sure.'

I smiled. 'It's okay, I'm sure she means well.'

'You don't have to be nice, everyone knows Maggie is awful,' said Layla.

'And totally not our friend,' Mariko added. 'We've already told her she can't play with us.'

'Good to know,' I said, laughing. 'Hey, Layla, is Amy okay? I think she and Violet might have had a row or something. She was just sitting over there a minute ago looking pretty upset.'

'Oh, jeez,' Layla sighed. 'Where did they go, did you see?

Never mind, I'll go find them. Ugh, there's always something. See you girls later.'

'Yeah, I gotta run, too.' Shannon checked her watch. 'Why don't you stop by later, Alex? I've got heaps of old baby clothes, some of them might fit Kara. We'll go through the bag, maybe pour ourselves a cheeky sundowner.'

I beamed. 'Sounds good.'

After finally managing to successfully feed Kara, I readjusted my top and lifted her onto my shoulder. The atmosphere felt less hostile than it had before. I wasn't *unwelcome*. Maggie would just have to get used to me. I still had plenty of time left on my lease; at some point I would muster the courage to ask Layla if she'd like to collaborate, she would almost certainly say yes, and then I would become as much a permanent fixture at Pine Ridge as the witch and her monsters. (See, I could make village jokes, too.)

Patting Kara on the back, I stood up and wandered over to one of the sign-up sheets. *Food Prep.* Sure, why not? I was handy enough in the kitchen. I imagined happy smells and bubbling pots, Bublé playing on the stereo. Not quite real Christmas, but close enough.

Grabbing a pencil, I jotted my name down. And I didn't even care when, seconds later, Maggie elbowed past me and, with three brutal strokes of her own pencil, scratched out her name on the *Food Prep* list and signed up for *Decorations* instead.

# ALEX
## 13

As I wheeled Kara out of the community hall, I spotted Ollie and Violet with the usual gang, loitering on the road with their bikes and skateboards. They looked shifty; but then groups of teens always looked suspicious to me. It was the chimp-like movement they retained from early childhood paired with their growing bulk. They needed to move to expend energy, but their bodies had become long, wide and hefty; they still wanted to run and climb and show off, but they were too big for the playground. Watching them was an exercise in anticipation, like winding a jack-in-the-box and waiting for the surprise.

'You'll never be that big, will you, baby?' I whispered to Kara, clicking her straps into place. 'Promise me you won't.' She raised her eyebrows and squealed, slapping her thighs in emphasis. I interpreted the squeal as her solemn oath and kissed her on the cheek.

'Alex.'

I turned around. Kit was striding over the gravel towards me, squinting against the sun. My spine fizzed a little. How was he *doing* that?

'Listen,' he said when he reached me. 'I'm so sorry about what happened in there. It wasn't an attack on you personally, it was just Maggie being Maggie. You okay?' His brow wrinkled adorably with concern.

'It's fine. I won't expect any pitchforks at my door.'

Kit laughed. 'No, please don't.'

A breeze purled around us, lifting the hairs on my arms and tickling the back of my neck. 'The meeting was interesting. What was with the hand signals? Spontaneous game of Rock Paper Scissors?'

Kit laughed. 'I guess it does look a bit bizarre if you're not used to it. It's just a way to make sure that everyone's voice is heard.'

'Like the conch in *Lord of the Flies*?'

'Kind of. Less symbolic, though.'

'And more effective.'

'You'd hope.' He grinned and my stomach flipped. 'I'll walk you through it properly at some point, so you can join in and have your say.'

Blushing, I looked away, towards the kids on the road. They were now bunched up in a huddle, looking at something Violet was holding in her hand. She was smiling; Ollie was laughing. *Us against the world.* I felt a pang of nostalgia. At fourteen, my friends had been my whole universe. It had been a long time since I'd felt that kind of freedom.

'I was just about to take my paddleboard down there,' Kit said, assuming incorrectly that I was looking at the water. 'I've got a spare one if you'd like to join me?'

I looked up sharply. 'Paddleboarding?'

'Yes.'

'With you?'

'With me.' His gaze was steady, his meaning clear. 'We could maybe grab some lunch after?'

I didn't know what to say. I wanted to. God, I wanted to. 'That sounds lovely, but I can't. Sorry. It's Kara, I have to—'

'Hey, Alex,' Layla said, jogging up behind us and tapping me on the shoulder. 'Amy's not feeling the best so I'm taking the girls home to watch a movie. Would Ollie like to come?' She looked from me to Kit and back again. 'Oh, sorry, am I interrupting something?'

'No, not at all,' I said. 'Really, it's fine, I was just heading home.'

'Actually,' said Kit. 'I was just asking Alex if she'd like to come paddleboarding with me.'

Layla raised one eyebrow. 'Oh, were you now?'

'But I have Kara,' I said quickly, 'and she'll be hungry again soon, so I ought to get home.'

'No, don't be silly, you two should go!' Layla waved her arms, shooing us away. 'I'll take Kara. She and Ollie can both come back to my place. You take a break, have some fun.'

I baulked. 'That's very kind of you, but I couldn't.'

'Of course you could! Honestly, an hour or two won't hurt. Do you have expressed milk? Formula? Preferred solids? When was her last change?'

I shook my head, insisting that I couldn't possibly impose, but Layla was adamant: Kara would be fine, it would be a pleasure to help out, easy-peasy: just hand over the food and the nappy bag, and the rest was simple.

'Come on, Alex,' she said after my fourth refusal. 'It quite literally takes a village. Go on, take a break.'

I looked at my daughter, calm and content in her pram. She would be okay; it might actually do her some good to spend a little time away from me.

*Just do it. Take the help.*

'Sure,' I said, joy sparking in my belly. 'Okay. Thank you.'

After I'd briefly explained Kara's routine and promised I'd be no longer than an hour or two, I jogged home to get my swimmers, passing Ollie and his mates on the way. They were still huddled, but their attention was now fixed on the other side of the valley. In the centre of the group, her hair flashing azure in the sun, Violet pointed to the paddock above the dam and all the other kids turned their heads as one. In my hurry, I only vaguely registered that they were all staring in the direction of the farmhouse.

# RENEE
## 14

Renee woke on the couch with a wet sponge in her hand. She was sitting upright as if she'd been watching TV, her head hanging to the left, her chin slick with drool. Her dreams clung to her like cobwebs.

*... running through the trees, but not running, legs aren't working, just spinning uselessly, brushing the forest floor, need to go faster ...*

She moved and a sharp pain shot up the side of her neck. Straightening up, she shuffled to the edge of the seat and looked down. The sponge had left a wet mark on her skirt and there was a bucket on the floor, full of pink water.

*... a deafening sound, a horrific rumbling, the pines are falling one by one, something is coming, something monstrous ...*

She put the sponge in the bucket. Rubbing her eyes, she listened to the whir of the oven and the dull thump of Michael's boots on the veranda outside. The windowpanes that had not been broken and covered with sheets of plywood were smeared with pink suds.

*... out of the woods, down the hill to the dam, my baby, my angel, sitting alone by the water, faster, go faster, legs spinning, have to get there, have to save him, but ...*

From somewhere in the house came a gentle but insistent

tapping. The sound of a door opening and closing. Outside, the dog barked twice. Renee frowned. She'd been doing something, but what?

... *a giant red wave, roaring, pouring, crashing down the hill, the house goes down like it's made of paper* ...

Cleaning. That's what she'd been doing. Scrubbing the walls, the upholstery, the ruined family photographs, trying to wash out the blood.

No, not blood. It looked like blood, but it wasn't. It was paint. Dark red. Convincing. Someone had thrown a rock that had smashed the window, followed by balloons filled with burgundy paint. The sofa looked like a butchered animal. And poor Gabe, he'd seen it. He'd seen everything.

Another sound. A clatter in the hallway, a murmur of voices.

Renee's heart rate picked up. The clock on the wall, the hands, surely they were wrong? She'd only sat down to rest for a moment, she'd just closed her eyes for two seconds ...

She shot off the sofa. The walls were still marked with paint, the sofa still wet. Gabe's school photos, the family portrait, lay face-down on the side table, utterly ruined, and she hadn't yet iced the cake.

'Renee? Hell-ooo?'

Naturally, April and Frank had arrived early. Frank was all starched linen and pressed lines in a white shirt and stiff blue jeans; April had paired a purple chenille sweater with a jade green scarf that matched the frames of her glasses. In her hands, she carried a gift wrapped in shiny paper and a bottle of red wine.

Ebony came scampering in after them, pawing at their clothes, her tongue hanging out of her mouth. 'Down!' yelped April immediately. 'Ugh, ridiculous animal.' Ebony slunk away.

'Michael is washing the side of your house,' Frank said, as if this might be news to Renee. 'You're not repainting again, are you?'

'Why is there a Christmas angel hanging on the porch?' April said, almost simultaneously. 'Isn't July a little early for decorations?'

Renee swallowed. The tree-topper. In all the chaos, she'd forgotten to cut it down. 'It's not a decoration,' she sighed, accepting both the wine and the gift from her mother. 'There was ... an incident.' She led them into the living room.

April looked around, her eyes widening, her jaw falling.

Frank went straight for the windows. 'What on earth happened?' he said, touching the plywood.

'Nothing much,' said Renee, heading back to the kitchen and setting the gifts down on the bench. 'Some idiot thought it'd be fun to throw paint at our house.'

'What? Why?'

'Oh, who knows? Just local kids, I'm sure.'

April, quite rightly, raised an eyebrow. There *were* no local kids, not really; the farms were all too spread out. 'Have you reported it?'

Fetching three glasses from a cupboard, Renee opened the bottle and poured the wine. 'Not yet. We didn't want to spoil today.' Not strictly true. Renee had wanted to call the police, but Michael had said no. *No point making a fuss. I'll deal with it.*

They would call later, he insisted, after lunch.

'You took photographs, though?' said Frank, narrowing his eyes. 'The insurance company will ask for photographs.'

'Of course we did.' That wasn't true, either. Michael had dragged out the hose before Renee had even moved. He'd turned on the tap and hosed down half the house, leaving just a powder pink stain on the white cladding. He'd gone straight back out there this morning to scrub at the window frames, the fretwork and the light fittings, but the paint job for which they'd paid a fortune only the previous year was wrecked.

'The sofa,' said April sadly, her hand at her mouth. 'Oh, the antique rug.'

'Never mind, worse things happen at sea.' Moving on autopilot, Renee glided to the airing cupboard for a pile of sheets, which she draped over the furniture to cover the marks. 'There, that's better. Let's not give it another thought, not today.'

'Where is Gabriel?' April said. 'Still in his room, I expect.'

'He's just getting dressed.'

Renee handed out the wine and they all sipped in silence, looking anywhere but at each other.

Eventually, Frank ambled out the back door to go and give Michael a 'hand', which really meant standing behind Michael and pointing out all the spots he'd missed, and Renee went to check on the lamb. Sliding her hand back into the mitt, she opened the oven door and heat blasted her face.

'Listen, Ren,' said April, following her. 'Do you think that maybe ...'

'What?'

'Well.' April put down her wineglass and lowered her voice. 'Do you think that perhaps Gabriel … you know.'

'No, I don't know.' Renee banged the oven door closed.

'Well, *this*.' April shrugged and gestured at the mess. 'The angel on the porch, the cat …'

'Mum, if you're suggesting that Gabe might have something to do with those things—'

'No, of course I'm not.'

'—because he was standing with me when the paint was thrown, and he would never have hurt Ivory, not ever. He loved that cat.'

'No, Ren.' April was standing close enough that Renee could see the tiny hairs on her upper lip, and the sharp line of her lipstick. 'I don't mean to suggest that he did any of it himself. I just wonder … well, your father and I were talking the other day and—'

There was a knock at the door.

Both women frowned.

'Who's that?' said April.

'I'm not sure.' But then Renee remembered: in a fit of guilt last week, she'd called the Hassops and asked them to lunch. *What a stupid idea*, she thought, pulling off the oven mitt and tossing it back onto the counter. *Whatever was I thinking?*

She'd been thinking that Dom and his mother Bess might appreciate an invitation, they might like to see Gabe all grown up, they might serve as buffers and dissolve the inevitable tension. April's prayers and Frank's criticism would be replaced by light-hearted small talk and references to the 'good old days'.

But when Renee opened the door and saw her neighbours on the doorstep, waiting politely with gifts in their hands, she felt nothing but sadness. It had been too long. It would be awkward. *This was a mistake.*

'Hello, Bess,' she said. 'Hi Dom. It's lovely to see you, thank you for coming.'

'Thank *you* for having us,' said Dom with a gentle smile. 'Good to see you. It's been a while.'

'It certainly has. I'm so sorry that I … that we haven't—'

'Please.' Dom held up a hand. 'No need for apologies.'

'But I should've …'

'Water under the bridge.'

Beside him, Bess smiled.

Hope rose in Renee's heart; perhaps it wouldn't be so bad. It really was lovely to see them. She took their coats. 'Come on in. Let me get you a drink.'

Dom took Bess's arm and guided her gently through the hall and into the kitchen. 'Mmm,' he said. 'Something smells good.'

'Dominic,' said April, gliding forward in a cloud of perfume. 'My goodness, it's been a long time. You look well.'

Renee cringed at the lie. Dom didn't look well at all. The years had ravaged his former boyish good looks and his face was now lined and pallid. Bess, too, had aged a great deal in a short space of time; she seemed to have shrunk since Renee had last seen her. Her skin appeared unsure what to do with the lack of her, and there wasn't much going on behind the eyes. Dom was now probably caring for her full time, and with a divorce on his hands as well … Renee winced – another guilty twinge – and made a mental note not to mention Rachel or the girls.

'How's Rachel?' asked April. 'And the girls? Last time I saw them they were barely walking.'

'Oh,' said Dom, his face visibly falling. 'They're doing okay. But, you know, the separation – sorry, the *divorce* – has been tough on us all.'

'I can only imagine.' April patted him on the arm. 'What's the custody arrangement?'

'Um.' Dom flinched. 'The, uh, decision hasn't been made yet.'

'And are you sleeping?'

'Well, I have a good doctor, if that's what you—'

'Of course.' April gave his arm a squeeze. 'If there's ever anything I can do for you, if you need to talk, just say the word.'

'Thank you,' said Dom, in a way that suggested he would be doing no such thing.

'And Bess …' April turned to Dom's mother. 'How wonderful to see you, too.'

Bess looked startled, as if she'd just arrived by time machine and was trying to figure out what year it was.

Renee tried to catch Dom's eye – *How's she doing?* – but he was already wandering away into the living room. 'The house looks great,' he said, then stopped. 'Oh dear. What happened here, then?'

Renee balled her hands into fists. The floor was swept, the dining table set with the best china, and a vase of dahlias stood on the kitchen counter. There were presents and wine and very soon the cake would be iced. If you didn't look at the windows or the walls or the sofa or the rug, you might think that everything was fine. Better than fine: perfect. So why did everyone keep looking?

'Nothing,' she said. 'Just a little accident. What can I get you to drink?'

But April was already swooping in, entering the conversation like an actor who'd been waiting in the wings for their cue. 'Terrible, isn't it,' she said. 'Happened overnight, and they have no idea who did it. And they haven't even called the police yet, which I think is a mistake – but then again, you never know how helpful the authorities will be. My friend Denise was robbed the other week, someone broke into her house while she was out shopping, and the police did nothing. No evidence of a crime, they said, because technically nothing was taken, but Denise said …'

Renee tuned out. The day was slowly but surely slipping from her grasp. April was droning on and on, Dom was frowning as if April were speaking a foreign language, and poor Bess was staring around the room as if she thought the furniture might sprout wings and fly away.

In an attempt to regain control, Renee went back to the kitchen to arrange cubes of cheese and cabanossi on a plate. Then she removed the bowl of icing from the fridge and spread it over the cake with a butter knife, taking her time to smooth the whole thing into a perfect creamy column. When the spongey surface was completely covered, she hurried down the hall and knocked lightly on Gabriel's door.

'Are you ready, love? Everyone's here, and lunch is almost done.'

He didn't answer.

'I've made your favourite.'

Nothing.

*Don't do this*, Renee thought. *Please, not today.* She rattled the handle, but the door was locked. 'Gabe?'

'Alright, I heard you,' came a low muffled reply.

She waited, her insides trembling, but the door remained closed.

Back in the living room, Michael was standing by the dining table, swigging a beer and clapping a stone-faced Dom on the back with a soapy hand. 'Hate to say it, mate,' he was saying, 'but I never liked your Rachel. Always suspected she might do a runner. She'll probably get the kids, but the women always do – and, to be honest, it might not be such a bad thing. All that space, all that time to yourself ... I'd chew me own arm off for a bit of that sometimes, you know? I'd kill for a bit of peace and quiet.'

April was still talking to, or rather *at*, Bess, appraising the stains on the sofa as though reviewing an art exhibition. She'd tugged back the sheets so the whole place once again looked like a crime scene; the only thing missing was a chalk outline. 'Dead as a doornail,' she said. 'In a cardboard box. And headless. *Headless!* Can you believe it? Who would do that to a cat?'

Bess had picked up one of Gabriel's ruined school photos and was cradling the broken frame, shaking her head at the smashed glass and the smeared picture within. Her eyes were as round as saucers, her sinewy body small and vulnerable next to April, who looked grotesque in comparison, her make-up too thick and parody-bold, her hand gestures too wild.

'I said, that's evil, didn't I, Frank? There's no two ways about it, that's the devil's work.'

Frank stood by the window with his arms behind his back, nodding along with his wife.

To Renee's horror, Bess too began to nod. *Yes. Yes. The devil, oh yes.*

And Renee just stood there in the doorway watching it all unfold, thinking, *This? This is my son's sixteenth birthday party?*

Oblivious, April leaned closer to Bess. 'Did I tell you I found a Christmas angel hanging above the door when I arrived? Hung from a noose, it was. And just look at that picture.' She nodded at the photograph in Bess's hands. 'I mean, the message couldn't be clearer, could it? The *angel Gabriel*. I'm telling you now, that boy is in danger. His soul is in trouble, Bess, I can just feel it.'

'*Mum.*'

'Yes, dear?'

Renee jerked her head in the direction of the hall. 'A word, please?'

'I was only expressing an opinion,' April said once they were out of earshot.

'Well, don't,' Renee whispered. 'Please, not today.'

'Fine, fine.' She spread her hands in a show of innocence. 'I'm just saying, the devil has claws. I'd hate for him to sink them into my grandson.'

'So, where's the man himself?' said Dom, as Renee refreshed everyone's drinks. 'Sixteen is a big deal. Seems like only yesterday he was five years old.'

Renee smiled. 'Time flies, hey?'

'I can't wait to see the little legend.'

'Don't get your hopes up, mate,' Michael muttered, now on his third beer. 'Kid spends more time in that room than the Pope spends in the Vatican. Haven't seen him since 2006. Forgotten what he looks like.'

'He won't be long,' said Renee. 'He's still getting dressed.'

'What has he got in there,' Michael said, 'a team of stylists?' Slamming his bottle on the table, he stalked to the bathroom.

'Everything alright, Ren?' Dom said, careful to keep his voice down. 'Something going on with Gabe?'

'Everything's fine,' she said, heading back to the kitchen.

Dom followed. 'Renee?'

At the stove, she picked up the oven mitt then put it back down again, her eyes stinging with rising tears. 'Honestly, Dom. Michael's right – I've tried everything, but Gabe won't leave that room. It's all I can do to get him to go to school. I'm so worried about him.'

Dom patted her on the back. 'Mind if I try?'

Renee pressed her fingers to her eyes. 'Be my guest.'

Ten minutes later, lunch was on the table. April showed Bess to her seat while Frank poured himself a Scotch. Michael claimed his usual chair at the head of the table, picking off a fat chunk of lamb from the pot with his fingers and passing it to Ebony before anyone else had been served. Renee handed out napkins and poured more wine, trying not to look at her son's empty chair—

'Well, look who decided to put in an appearance,' said Michael in an odd tone of voice.

Startled, Renee followed his gaze. 'Oh,' she gasped, and nearly dropped her glass.

Gabe was hovering in the doorway with Dom at his side, wearing a navy blue collared shirt and smart black jeans; he'd even brushed his hair. Renee couldn't believe it. By some miracle, Dom had succeeded in persuading her son from his room.

'Oh, darling!' She rushed to him, her heart bursting, and wrapped him up in a hug. 'Happy birthday! Oh, you look so handsome. Here, come and sit down, I've made your favourite. Lamb shanks with mashed potato.'

Ushering Gabriel to his seat, she looked back over her shoulder at Dom. *Thank you*, she mouthed. Hanging back near the door with his hands in his pockets, Dom smiled and shrugged. *No big deal.*

Renee beamed. She fussed around Gabriel, piling food onto his plate and fetching his gifts while April and Frank fired a rapid round of questions as if pressed for time: *how are you, how's school, are you still drawing, who are your friends these days?*

At the end of the table, though, Michael looked thunderous. 'How was the journey from your bedroom to the table, your Highness?' he sneered. 'Not too stressful, I hope?'

'Give him a break, mate,' muttered Dom, taking a seat at the table.

A vein throbbed in Michael's forehead. 'A break?' He stabbed a piece of lamb with his fork. '*I'm* the one who needs a fucking break.'

'Michael,' Renee warned.

'What? I work myself to the bone every goddamn day and no one says shit; this one sits down to eat and gets a round of applause. It's outrageous.'

There was an awful silence. Gabriel seemed to shrink in his chair, folding over as if winded.

'Give it a rest, Mike.' Dom was still, his voice dangerously low, his lips white. 'It's the kid's birthday.'

Michael and Dom stared at each other for what felt like a long time.

'You know what?' Michael said at last. 'I just remembered. I already ate.' He pushed back his chair and stood up. 'Happy bloody birthday, mate.' Striding to the back door, he pushed it open and disappeared outside.

No one said anything for several seconds.

Renee's cheeks burned. Then she forced her lips back and bared her teeth in a smile. 'Come on, everyone,' she said. 'Dig in before it gets cold.'

# ALEX

## 15

Steadying the board on the water, I clambered on and pushed off from the shore, paddling on my knees to get my balance. Then I put my hands down, positioned my feet and stood up.

Sunlight refracted beneath me; above, the sky blazed blue. The stillness was unreal. All I could hear was the water, the wind, the frogs and the birds. No one was clinging to me, no one needed me. I felt light, as though I were made of gossamer and the air could pass straight through my body. I dipped my paddle, pushing the board forward, and my reluctant abdominals engaged with the movement.

Somewhere behind me, Kit was catching up. Glancing over my shoulder, I saw his rapid approach, his movements fluid and comfortable, his muscles rippling under boardshorts and a rashie. In contrast, I felt out of place and awkward. At nearly nine months post-partum, my body was still not my body. I was unfit and, even though I'd worn my most sensible black one-piece instead of – god forbid – a bikini, I was unused to displaying so much skin outside of my own bathroom. I both wanted and did not want him to see me; the situation was at once thrilling and horrifying. I pushed harder, propelling myself over the water.

'Does yours have a motor or something?' he said, eventually

drawing level with me. 'If I'd known this was going to be such a workout, I might not have asked you along.'

I smiled and dug in my paddle, slowing down and subtly changing direction. *Don't get too close.* 'So, what's a summer solstice party, then?'

Kit shrugged a little self-consciously. 'Ah, it's just a thing we do every year. Silly but fun. We do the whole snow and ice thing at Christmas, Santa's sleigh, the reindeer, all that good wintery stuff. But three or four days before that, when the solstice hits, we celebrate summer.'

The tail ends of our boards bumped together, and I stiffened as my board rocked beneath me.

'We set up dinner outside, string up some lights, play some music. Maggie does a theme, like costumes or decorations or gifts. She organises most of it, actually.'

'Really? Maggie doesn't strike me as much of a party girl.' The nose of my board veered away from his and the strip of water between us widened.

'Oh, yeah, she loves it. Celebrations are her thing. Kirtan, Agnihotra, bunya pine festivals, Beltane, she does it all.'

'I literally have no idea what any of those words mean,' I said, paddling frantically to correct my path.

Kit laughed. 'I didn't either before I met Maggie. Okay, let me see if I can get this right ... so, Kirtan is Indian call-and-response storytelling. Agnihotra is an Ayurvedic purifying rite, and Beltane is the Gaelic May Day celebration. Boom. How's that for general knowledge?'

'You'd be handy in a pub quiz.'

'Some might say unbeatable.'

'And the pine festival thing?'

'An Indigenous tradition based on the harvesting of nuts from the bunya pines. You see those tall trees over there?' He pointed across the dam to our left, where dark green points rose from the canopy like drops of icing on a cake. 'Their cones are the size of soccer balls.'

'Wow.'

'Uh-huh, yep.' He puffed out his chest and raised one eyebrow in a cartoonish smoulder. 'Pretty impressive, right?'

'If you like facts about balls.'

'And do you?'

'Not so much.'

'Ah, rats. Thought for sure that would've won you over.'

We laughed, and the tension dissipated.

'Anyway, it's all a good excuse for a party. And Maggie's nice enough when you get to know her.'

'Hmm.' I dipped my paddle into the water again and pulled up a string of green weed. 'I'll take your word for it.'

Kit laughed again. 'Alright, fine, she can be hard work. But, to be fair, it's not just her. Some residents are hell-bent on cutting themselves off. Close the village, disconnect the wi-fi, really go off-grid. And I get it, I do. The world is scary right now, there are some truly awful people in it.' He paused and, fleetingly, his expression became pained. 'I understand the impetus to hide, much more than they think. But it's not practical; it's not reasonable.' Another big smile. 'It's fine, they'll all come around eventually.'

We lapsed into an easy quiet, drifting in parallel, our paddles rising and falling with a natural rhythm. I focused on my balance, hyper-aware of Kit's presence beside me. The air between us felt charged, like an atmosphere that might burn me if I crossed it.

I cleared my throat. 'So you grew up overseas, huh? That must've been interesting.'

'Nah, not really. More fun for my parents than for me. But you, you've been everywhere. Your travels sound infinitely more exciting than mine.'

'Oh, I don't know about that. I definitely haven't been everywhere. And I haven't been anywhere exciting for a long time. Just the Sydney school run. Midwife clinics. Supermarkets, afternoon tea.'

'Right.' Kit was quiet for a moment. 'So about that … what's your deal at the moment?'

'My "deal"?'

'No, sorry, I just mean … like, what's your, ah, *situation*?'

'Oh.' I dropped my gaze and watched a school of tiny fish darting and milling in the water beneath me. How to tell my tale of woe?

'It's alright,' Kit said, after an awkward stretch of silence. 'You don't have to talk about it if you're not comfortable.'

'It's not that.' And it wasn't. A part of me felt *very* comfortable with Kit, more comfortable than I wanted to admit. It was as if we'd already told each other all our stories. But I also knew I should be careful. Pump the brakes, keep the drawbridge up. 'Sorry, I just don't share stuff about myself very easily.'

'That's okay,' he said. 'Neither do I.'

That was true. I realised that I barely knew a single detail about his life.

We paddled for a few more moments, our strokes growing more and more languid. Inside, I battled with myself. To trust or not to trust. In the end, I figured I could afford to share just a little. Maybe then Kit would do the same.

'I was born in England,' I began, keeping my eyes on the board. 'My family are all still over there. I came to Australia when I was twenty, backpacking with my boyfriend at the time. We both loved it here, got jobs, settled down, played house. I worked as a nanny; he was a builder. After a couple of years, we both got permanent residency. And then we got pregnant.'

I took a breath, momentarily reliving the anxiety, the panic.

'It was an accident. But I thought, why not? I love him, he loves me, we're happy, we have money, it's all good. I believed in destiny back then, so … anyway, my boyfriend seemed pleased at first, but then one day I woke up and he'd gone. Just like that. Just packed his stuff, got on a plane and left.'

I felt rather than saw Kit looking at me. 'Wow,' he said.

'Savage, right? I don't even know where he went. Not back to England, I don't think, but who knows?' I paused, waiting for the knot in my throat to ease. Even fifteen years later, it still hurt. 'By that point I was quite far along, too far for an abortion. But I like to think I would've kept it anyway.' I swallowed. '*Him*. Ollie.'

We reached the far shore of the dam. Silently and easily, we turned our boards around and set off back in the other direction.

'How did you manage it?'

'I had friends, and a very kind boss. She was amazing, actually. She was my immigration sponsor, helped me upgrade my qualifications after Ollie was born. No idea what I would've done without her. She moved to Canada a few years later; still emails to see how we're going.' I forced myself to smile. 'Ollie and I were a little team. We moved around a lot. Different towns, different schools, different jobs.'

They were good memories. Port Stephens. Port Campbell. Fremantle. The Great Barrier Reef. Just me, the road and my tiny best friend.

'I like moving. It's kind of my thing. But then one day Ollie said he was tired of travelling around. He was nine, I think? Maybe ten. We were in Sydney at the time, so that was where we stayed.'

'Why didn't you go back to England?' Kit dug in his paddle and slowed down to match my pace. 'If you don't mind me asking?'

'I, um …' I never knew how to answer this question. 'I … My dad … is not a nice guy. He never hurt me – not physically, anyway. But my mum … well, let's just say it wasn't a great way to grow up.'

'I'm so sorry.'

'Yeah. It got rough sometimes. At home, I mean. When I was little, I built forts in my room and hid. Lay down, pretended I was dead. I always kept a packed suitcase under my bed, drew up these elaborate escape plans. I had this picture on my wall of the perfect house with the perfect family and told myself that one day I would go there.'

I could still see it in my mind, could recall every detail. White picket fence, wraparound veranda, roof like a wide-brimmed hat. Just like the farmhouse on the hill. I glanced up at the paddock, but from this angle the house was obscured by trees.

'I thought it was normal. I thought that's how everyone lived: on a knife's edge, ready to go. When I finally realised it *wasn't* normal, I got angry. With my mum, mostly. I just didn't understand how she could've let it carry on. Why didn't she just leave? I didn't get it.'

I took a breath. Steadied myself. 'She's still there. In England. With him. I have a brother but he's a lot like my dad.'

Kit nodded. 'Are you still in touch?'

'Not really. They came out once, not long after I'd had Ollie. It was painful. Nothing had changed.' I said the word 'painful' in much the same way as you might describe standstill traffic on the freeway: ugh, *painful*, eye roll. But, in reality, the pain of that visit had been the most excruciating of my life. The sight of my mum leaving, checking her bags at Kingsford Smith Airport and disappearing meekly through security with barely a backward glance, had left a mark on me so significant it was a wonder people couldn't see it on my skin. I knew I couldn't reasonably have expected her to stay – after all, I had been the one who'd moved away. But watching her go had ripped my heart right out.

*Don't leave me. Please stay.* She hadn't.

'And Kara?' Kit said. 'At what point did the stork drop her on your doorstep?'

145

My heart twisted.

*Crazy bitch. You're insane. You need medical help.*

'Ah, that's a tale for another time.' I dug my paddle into the water and sped up. 'So, what about you?'

Kit cleared his throat. 'Me?'

'Yeah, you. I've showed you mine, now you show me yours.'

'Ohhh.' Kit raised his eyebrows and gave me a dazzling smile. 'Well, if that's the game we're playing ...'

But he didn't say anything else, and I felt a prickle of irritation. *Great listener, but terrible sharer*, I thought. *Red flag.*

Turning away, I looked across the dam towards the village. I wondered what Kara was doing, whether she missed me—

And then I saw it.

The shape. The shadow.

The old woman from the woods, grey and still, standing in the shade of a tree, one hand on the trunk, her long hair whipping across her face. Close enough for me to see the specifics of her clothes: a mint-green raincoat over what appeared to be a nightgown.

My scalp prickled. My pulse sped up.

The woman on the shore shimmered like a mirage, her edges blurring and bleeding into the background. She looked at me and raised her arm.

And then I felt my board tipping, tilting, sliding out from under me. I staggered, throwing my hands out, trying to stop myself from falling, falling, falling ...

*Slap.*

My body hit the water, all arms and legs, and I was in,

146

weightless, the water snapping over my head with a *whooomp*. Bubbles, white noise, pressure in my ears.

I bobbed back to the surface, heavy and humiliated. Grabbing my board, I hoisted myself back on.

Somewhere to my left, Kit was calling me. 'Alex? Are you alright?' His voice sounded like it was coming from very far away.

'Did you see that?' I gasped, flopping around like a seal.

'See what?'

'The person on the ...' Pushing my sodden hair from my eyes, I looked back at the shore – but the grey-haired woman had vanished. I knelt on my board and blocked the glare of the sun with my hand, scanning the circumference of the dam.

'What's up? What are you looking for?'

*Insane. You've lost your mind.*

I shook my head. 'Nothing.'

'You sure?'

'Yeah, I ... I thought I saw something but ... I guess I didn't.'

Kit looked as if he was about to say something else, but then seemed to change his mind. 'Come on,' he said. 'Let's head back. Give me a hand with the boards?'


I hadn't realised how heavy the paddleboards were until I carried mine in from the water.

'Woah,' I said. 'How did you get both of these down here by yourself?'

'With difficulty,' Kit said, laughing. 'No, kidding, it wasn't too bad. I don't live far.' He pointed to a building just visible beyond a cluster of gum trees.

We gathered up our towels from the bank and dried ourselves off, then heaved the boards across the grass and through the trees. Kit's house was L-shaped and startlingly modern. Situated in its own clearing and clad entirely with caramel-coloured wood, it blended perfectly with the forest itself: an architecturally innovative gingerbread cottage.

'Oh, wow,' I said, stopping to rest several metres from the front steps. 'It's gorgeous.'

'Thanks. I sort of designed it myself, with a bit of help, obviously. Got time to come and have a look?'

He led the way around the side to a neat lawn and a large deck. We hauled the boards up onto the timber, then Kit opened a set of sliding doors and I followed him into an extremely tidy living area with a comfortable-looking sofa, a stocked bookshelf and a wood-burner. A guitar leaned on a stand in one corner, a large plant spread its leaves in another. The kitchen was at the back: new appliances, simple cabinetry, clean surfaces. No fuss, no clutter.

Kit went straight to the fridge. I hung back at the door, wary of leaving a trail of wet, sandy footprints.

'Beer?'

I shook my head, but then changed my mind. 'Actually, go on then, yes, please.' My accidental swim had woken me up a bit, but my mouth was still dry, my head still fuzzy. A beer was exactly what I needed.

Kit returned from the kitchen with two frosty bottles, and

we cracked the twisty tops together. Then he took out his phone, tapped the screen, and music began to play from a hidden source, a gentle chiming melody with a husky female voice.

'Cheers,' he said. 'To a good day.'

'A good day.' *Clink.* I drank deeply, three long glugs, then a yawn took me by surprise. 'Sorry,' I said, my eyes watering. 'Bit tired.'

'That's alright,' Kit said. 'Big move, new house, two kids. I'd be tired, too.'

I nodded and, briefly, the room spun. 'Whoops,' I said, reaching for the back of the sofa.

'You alright?' said Kit, stepping forward. 'Do you need to sit down?'

'I'm fine.' I reddened. 'Well, not *fine* fine. I've got a lot going on right now. But it's all good, I'll be okay.'

'Maybe take a load off anyway,' he said. 'Just in case.'

We sat on the sofa and I sank into the cushions. It might've been the sun or the beer or the spontaneous exercise, but I suddenly felt incredibly weary, as if the weight of the last few days – weeks, *months* – had just dropped from a great height and landed on my head.

'Anything you want to talk about?'

He was just being nice, I knew that. It wasn't a real offer. But even though Kit hadn't reciprocated, talking on the dam had felt so good. No one had listened like that in years.

'Probably not a good idea,' I said. 'If I start, I might not stop.'

Kit shrugged. 'I've got time.'

I narrowed my eyes. 'How about *you* tell *me* something first.'

'What do you mean?'

'Anything. Where did you go to school? What's your family like?'

Kit took a sip of his beer. 'Okay. Well, I didn't get on with my parents. Living with them was hard. Not in the same way you describe living with yours, but still difficult. I don't speak to them anymore.'

'Why not?'

He sighed. Opened his mouth, then closed it again. 'Sorry,' he said eventually. 'I don't think I really want to talk about that. Do you mind if I tell you something else, something different?'

I shrugged. 'Go for it.'

He dropped his gaze into his lap. When he looked up again, I noticed his eyes were a deep shade of blue-grey, like glimpses of stormy ocean waves.

'Some time ago,' he said, 'before Pine Ridge, I was in a very bad place. I had no direction, no motivation. I felt sad and unhappy almost all of the time. And then one day, I almost drove my car off a bridge.'

I felt myself take a sharp breath. *Didn't see that coming.*

'I'd stopped in the city. I could see the bridge, I knew where the gap was – and I was sitting there in the middle of the day, with the engine running and my foot on the pedal, just ready to go. And then this person walked past, this woman. Someone else followed, and then another person, and another. And suddenly – it was so weird – there were hundreds of them. Old people and babies and schoolkids and families, all carrying signs and shouting. I thought at first I was in trouble, I thought they were angry – but they weren't, not exactly. I got out of the car and joined them, and the atmosphere ... it was electric. Everyone was so energised, so full of hope. I'd never felt anything more powerful in my life.

'Turned out,' Kit said, 'I'd inadvertently parked right next to the meeting point for a climate change protest. By the time I got back to my car, I felt different. I know it sounds dramatic, but that protest saved my life. And it sparked the very first idea for Pine Ridge.' He gave me a wry smile. 'I haven't tried to drive off a bridge since.'

I studied him, unsure how to react. It was a big deal, sharing a story like that, and I could tell the emotion behind it was real. But there was something a little *off* about what he'd said, something I couldn't put my finger on. He was definitely holding back. Not lying, exactly – more like choosing to leave things out.

'Your turn,' he said.

I decided to adopt the same game plan: share only what felt comfortable and leave out the rest.

'Shortly after Ollie and I decided to stay in Sydney,' I said, picking at the label on my beer bottle, 'I met someone. I was lost without the road, and lonely. Ollie was at school all day and I couldn't find my feet, so Stuart felt like the answer. He was charismatic, popular. He owned a couple of restaurants and was always surrounded by people; he gave me money, a home, a car. He took care of everything. I thought he was giving me what I wanted: the happy family, the fairytale. But I moved too fast. I was in too deep before I realised what I'd done.' I shuddered,

151

ashamed of how willingly I'd relinquished the reins of my life. 'He hurt me. Many times.'

For a long while, I'd lived in a kind of trance. I allowed myself to be swept along and ignored the warning signs. The first time the sex got that little bit too rough. When he locked me in the house and took my keys. All the times he said he didn't want me to work, that he was 'traditional' and wanted to be the 'provider', that it was best if he gave me a cash allowance. The first time he told me I was crazy, and the first time I questioned my own judgement. *Maybe I am losing my mind.* 'Cunt,' he once yelled at me, rolling in at 3am, pinning me to the bed and breathing heavily into my ear.

'Then I found out I was pregnant again.' I drank, three large gulps. The beer fizzed in my throat. 'Once again, I convinced myself it was a good thing: everyone had problems, a baby would surely fix ours. And for a while things did get better. But then they got worse. Much worse. And then Ollie got into trouble at school.'

One day, when I'd been figuring out how to conceal the bruises on my upper arms and ribs, I got a call from Ollie's school to say that police were investigating allegations that male students had been distributing explicit images of their female classmates. They'd uploaded the images to a file-sharing platform and then passed the link around. The girls were shockingly young.

'The school confirmed that Ollie wasn't directly involved,' I said, 'but he got caught with the link on his phone – which to me was just as bad. He hadn't reported it, hadn't told anyone, just passed it on like it was nothing. I got angry and made a fuss, told the school they were incompetent. But really I was mad at myself. The whole thing was my fault, because of what I'd made Ollie live with. Because of the example I'd set.'

In hitching our family's wagon to Stuart's, I realised, I'd desensitised my son. I'd taught him first-hand that women were to be disrespected. Disregarded. That treating them like shit was normal.

'After I spoke to the principal, I went home to speak to Ollie. I found him playing some video game with Stu. They were both sitting on the couch in exactly the same position, both with the same gormless expression on their face, and I just thought, *Okay, shit, I'm raising another one.*'

I drank again, forcing the beer down past the knot in my throat and into my stomach. 'A couple of days after that, I woke in the night to hear Kara crying. I got up, went to her room, and Stuart was in there. Just standing over her cot, watching her cry. He'd been out drinking, and there was this look on his face …' I tipped the bottle and drained it. 'I knew then that I hadn't just put myself in danger, that all three of us were at risk. So I ran. Took the kids and left.'

'You're incredibly brave,' Kit said, after a moment of quiet. 'It takes a lot of courage to do something like that.'

I stared at the empty bottle in my lap. I didn't think of myself as courageous. How was it brave to have watched my father belittle and control my mother for years, and then fail to recognise the very same pattern unfolding in my own life? No, if I'd had courage, I would've left much sooner. If I'd been brave, I would never have moved in with him in the first place, would never have forced my son to do the same. I'd never have given up my job, my friends – and I wouldn't have stayed silent after the first night Stuart put his hand around my throat and held me against the wall.

But I did all of those things because, somehow, they made sense. They felt more normal, more reasonable than any of the alternatives. Right up until they didn't.

And then, *I* did something to *him*.

But I decided not to tell Kit about that. Better he believed I was brave.

The sofa moved underneath me as Kit got up and fetched two more beers from the fridge. 'Ollie's lucky to have a mum like you,' he said. 'Someone who really cares.'

I shook my head. 'I always thought I'd be better at it than I am. I thought I'd be a cool mum, happy to talk about drugs and sex and the best-slash-worst ways to sneak out of your bedroom window at night to go see a band. But it's a different world now. I don't know what I'm doing.'

Kit passed me a new beer.

'This screen stuff is killing me,' I continued. 'I didn't grow up with technology, I don't know it like he does. It's like he's this alien, speaking a language that I don't, growing up in a completely different universe, and yet I'm supposed to guide him through it.'

'I can only imagine how hard it must be,' Kit said. 'But, you know, you're probably not saying anything that your parents didn't say. Or their parents.'

'What do you mean?'

'Well, maybe tech isn't entirely to blame. It's not *that* scary.'

'You sure about that?' I thought about the dark web. 'It seems pretty terrifying to me.'

'Sure, but only as terrifying as anything else. The internet is just life with a megaphone. Everything that's online can also be found offline. It's all the same thing; the online version is just louder and shinier.'

'And more accessible. And more addictive.'

'There is that. But if it wasn't tech, it'd be something else.'

'Uh-huh.' I took a long swig of beer. 'Let's chat again when you have kids, see if you still say the same.'

'Sorry.' He smiled. 'That was a bit high-horsey of me. I'm just saying that the screen stuff doesn't have to be so frightening.'

*Well, you would say that; you're just a child yourself.*

The thought took me by surprise. I studied Kit's face, looking for crow's feet, scars, the telltale signs of gravity. *How old are you?* He studied me right back. I suddenly became very aware of how long I'd been talking and how much I'd said.

There was a beat, a shiver of anticipation, like the pause between a bolt of lightning and the inevitable roll of thunder.

And then Kit moved closer to me. Put his hand on mine. He was so close, I could see the detail in his eyes, the flecks of brown among the blue. They reminded me of the dam, of refracted sunlight and concealed depths.

'Alex,' he said. 'I just want you to know ...'

Closer, closer. He smelled of sunscreen and coconut shampoo. I could feel his breath against my skin. His features

155

began to blur.

'… that if you were mine, I'd never hurt you.'

Closer still. Just inches between us.

'I would always protect you. I'd do anything to keep you safe, make you happy.'

He placed his hand on my cheek. His thumb brushed my jaw; his fingers found their way to the back of my neck. He tilted his head, his eyes on mine, seeking permission, *Is this okay, can I, are we …*

His lips touched mine, and it was like sliding into a warm bath, jumping off a cliff and flying, all at once. He smelled like holidays. He tasted of electricity. He was comfort and danger; a sharp bite, and a delicious slow burn.

I sank deep, lay back and left the world behind. Couldn't get close enough. The coconut scent of him, hot breath on my neck, salt on my tongue. Intoxicating and terrifying, all at once.

An urgent stretch of fabric, the pop of a button, his hands on my hipbones.

And then …

*Rough palms on my back. My face in the mattress. Pressure. Pain. The blue bloom of a bruise.*

I jerked away and sat up.

Kit froze. So did I.

'I'm sorry,' I whispered, hanging my head.

'No, *I'm* sorry. Wow, I'm … I shouldn't have—'

'It's fine.'

'It's not.'

'No, it really is, I just … I don't think I'm …'

'I know.'

'I'm not—'

'I know. I understand.'

'Really?'

'Of course. *Of course.* Whatever you feel comfortable with, whenever you're ready.'

I looked at my beer. 'I should go.' I put the bottle on the floor and stood up.

Kit stood with me. We looked at each other for a moment and my heart did a slow pirouette. *Fuck it. Just kiss me.* I dropped my gaze. 'Can I use your bathroom?'

Kit laughed. 'And there's the bucket of cold water I needed.'

Heat rushed to my cheeks. 'I think we both needed it.'

Stepping back, he pointed at a hallway to the left of the kitchen. 'Third door on the right.'

'Thanks.'

I walked away, my footsteps too loud in the silence.

The hall was, like the rest of the house, neat and clean. White walls. Full-height windows, minimal furniture. Stylish but bland. No photos or clues as to who Kit was deep down, or what his tastes might be. Was it always this pristine, I wondered? Or had he tidied up especially for me, knowing how the afternoon would play out? The music, the beer, the confession ... had it all just been one big orchestration? I passed an open door and glimpsed a bed. The sight of his sheets made me breathless.

Finding the bathroom, I slipped inside and locked the door. Standing in front of the mirror, I stared at my mussed hair and the rising flush of stubble burn around my lips. What was I doing? I'd shared too much too quickly. *Stupid, stupid.* What had happened to keeping my guard up?

I pulled my phone from my pocket. After first checking there were no panicked messages from Layla – *Kara's fallen down a well; she's choking, vomiting, I've called an ambulance* – I googled Kit's name, kicking myself for not having thought to stalk him earlier … but there was nothing to stalk. No social media accounts, no blog posts or interviews, nothing on LinkedIn or Wikipedia. He was on the Pine Ridge website, of course, and I found a handful of news articles referencing his work as an ecovillage founder, but there was absolutely nothing personal. No school history, no ex-girlfriends, very few images. It was as if, prior to the development of Pine Ridge, Kit Vestey hadn't existed.

I looked back at my flushed reflection. *Shit.* Thanks to my traitor heart and motormouth, Kit now knew a hell of a lot about me – but I knew next to nothing about him.

# ALEX

## 16

Over the next few days, my unease only seemed to grow.

I tried to think calmly, rationally. *You're just exhausted,* I told myself again. *It's the night mind, like the girls said. Tickticktickticktick.* I kept busy with meetings and party prep, volunteering for Games and Entertainment as well as Food Prep; I avoided being alone with Kit by taking Kara on baby play dates and helping out at the greenhouses. The distractions helped, but I was still plagued by black clouds of worry. I kept hearing odd noises, both outside and inside the house. I felt watched, somehow: a constant crawl just under my skin. And then one afternoon, when Kara and I were returning home from a walk, as I pushed open the front door of our unit and walked inside, the feeling intensified.

Once, many years ago, after dropping Ollie at day care I'd hurried out into the car park and accidentally got into a car belonging to another mum. I'd opened the door, sat down in the driver's seat and tried to fit my key into the ignition before I realised that the car was not mine. It looked like mine, from the model and colour right down to the handbag on the passenger seat and the lip gloss in the cupholder – but the bag was a different style, the gloss a different brand. The disorientation had made me feel seasick, as though everything around me was suddenly liquid instead of solid. Walking into our unit that day was a lot like that, except my house was still my house; the room was the same, the furniture and belongings all definitely mine. And yet somehow they were not.

I looked around, trying to pinpoint the problem. I stared at the fridge. Was it just me, or were the magnets muddled, the photos out of place? The books on the shelf looked odd, too, like they'd been swapped around. The cushions on the sofa seemed to be arranged differently, and there was a 2-inch gap between the sofa and the wall. Didn't it usually stand right up against it?

'Ollie?' I called, not expecting a reply; he'd gone to Violet's and wasn't likely to return before dinner. The unit was empty.

Shaking my head as if to physically shift the brain fog, I set about putting Kara down for her nap. But in my bedroom, I had the same sense that things weren't quite how I'd left them. Nothing was obviously wrong, but nothing was quite right either. And then I realised that my photo frame, my sparkly paddle-pop treasure, was missing from my bedside table. Frowning, I had a look to check that it hadn't fallen off but couldn't see it on the floor.

A memory – many memories – surfaced of hunting for keys, earrings, my wallet, notes from school, things I'd put down only moments before and which had seemed to vanish into thin air, things I later found in unlikely places: on top of the cistern, behind a plant, under the couch. Stuart's false innocence, his practised routine. *I have no idea what you did with it. Not my job to keep track of your shit. You must have put it there and forgotten. You're crazy. You've lost the plot.*

My skin prickled. I pulled out my phone. I realised I hadn't heard from Stuart in a few days. What did that mean?

Dragging my focus back to Kara, I put her down in her cot and patted her gently. Once she was settled, I closed my bedroom door as quietly as I could and tiptoed down the hall to the laundry. Opening the cupboard under the sink, I moved the detergent aside, opened up the bin liner and checked the Tupperware container. Only when I was sure that it was still there (and, except for what I'd already used, still full) did I allow myself a deep breath.


That night Kara slept better than she had in months, but I couldn't relax. I lay awake for hours, my night mind running wild. I thought about the bland white walls of Kit's house and the colour of his eyes. Long grey hair, the *tring* of a bicycle bell, and deep lines sliced into the bark of trees. I studied the corners of the room, half-expecting a slow seep of liquid, a black trickle running from ceiling to floor. Rolling over, I buried my face in the pillow.

And then I heard something.

A whimper.

And then a soft rustle, like two dry surfaces sliding against one another, coming not from the forest but from somewhere within the unit.

Sitting up, I reached for my phone: 2.41am.

*Rustle-hiss.*

I pushed back the sheets and my feet hit the carpet like lumps of clay.

*Rustle-hiss.*

I checked on Kara: fast asleep in her cot. Then I grabbed a water glass from my bedside table, the only possible weapon within reach. Tiptoeing to the door, I opened it just a crack.

'Ollie?' I whispered.

My heartbeat throbbed in my ears.

I stepped out into the hall. The noises became louder but more confusing; they sounded like they were all around me, coming from the walls and the floor.

'Ollie? Is that you?'

The whimper became a moan.

I turned to face my son's bedroom door. It was closed. No light shone around the edges. Tiptoeing over the carpet, I reached for the handle and opened the door.

Ollie was alone in his bed, twisted up in the sheets, curled into a tight ball with his back to me. I looked around. The walls were clean and normal. No seeping liquid, no torrent of blood. No witch.

'Ollie,' I whispered, creeping closer. 'Ollie, are you alright?'

One of his legs twitched. I placed my hand on his shoulder and gently pulled it towards me, rolling him over. His face was wet, his eyes scrunched closed. The noise he was making reminded me of Kara's sleep sounds: soft involuntary sighs, too delicate for words.

'Shhhhhh,' I said, stroking his hair. 'It's okay. I'm here, I'm with you. It's just a bad dream.'

He stilled at my touch, just as he had when he'd been young. His face relaxed but he didn't wake up. I kissed his brow, smoothed his hair away. My baby boy.

*Click.*

The door had closed behind me.

I whipped around, but no one was there.

*Rustle-hiss.*

Pulse hammering, I got up off the bed and crept out of Ollie's room, closing the door softly behind me. I peered around the corner into the living area and allowed my eyes to adjust to the dark. Everything was flat and grey, like a photocopy. I took stock of the ordinary: sofa, armchair, coffee table, TV. The kitchen, too, was still. Stove, kettle, sink. No one there, nothing unusual. Just shadows.

And a squat cube-shaped object on the counter.

I crept forward, spine tingling.

A box sat next to the fruit bowl. The same as the others.

*Oh shit oh shit oh shit oh shit.*

I went to the knife block and grabbed the biggest, sharpest blade. I held it in my fist, scanning the corners of the rooms and the windows, taking snatches of air through my nose. The fridge hummed. The clock ticked.

When finally I dared to move, I braced myself and pulled the flaps open with my free hand … but the single object inside was small and simple.

A square made from lolly sticks. Green glitter, sticky gems. My paddle-pop frame – but its contents different, changed. Kara's tiny face still looked out at me, but Ollie's had disappeared. Obliterated by a thick substance, a red so dark it was almost black.

*Rustle-hiss.*

I spun around, the knife in my hand – the room was empty, but something was moving. On the side table next to the armchair, a book lay open. The pages were turning by themselves. I inched closer. An unexpected breeze brushed my goosebumped skin – I looked up and saw the back sliding door standing wide open.

And next to the door, the living room wall was smeared with red.

# RENEE
## 17

Renee was dreaming again, not about running through forests or great waves of blood, but about water. A constant drip, leaking from the ceiling and landing on her head.

*That's evil. That's the devil's work.*

Pressing a hand to her sternum, she turned onto her side and tried to push the dream away – but it followed her.

*Drip. Drip. Drip.*

She turned her head into the pillow and got a mouthful of it, soft and smothering. The material tasted sickly sweet: neroli and orange blossom.

*That boy is in danger.*

Two red eyes, two huge horns.

*The devil has claws.*

Four long cuts. Four sharp talons.

*I'd hate for him to sink them into my grandson.*

Renee sat up in a rush, throwing off the blanket with the last of the dream. She sat for a while on the edge of the bed, breathing hard. Her nightgown grew cold and, realising how damp it was, she looked up at the ceiling. No water, no leak. Just sweat.

She let her eyes roam in the darkness, skimming over the solid walls of her bedroom, the picture frames and the tongue-and-groove wall panelling. In between Michael's snores, she heard something else. A high-pitched whine, like a mosquito but much further away.

Renee stood up. Padded to the bedroom door and opened it. Across the hallway, pale light shone from under Gabriel's door. The whine started up again. It was coming from inside her son's room.

She stepped forward. Knocked softly.

'Gabe?' she whispered.

The noise stopped.

She knocked again but there was no reply. She tried the handle, but the door was stuck. *Not stuck. Locked. Again.*

'Gabe?' Renee pressed her ear against the wood and heard a faint sniff. The swish of bedsheets.

She tried the handle again, pushing her shoulder up against the door. It wouldn't budge.

'Gabriel, are you alright?'

She kept on turning the handle, pushing against the door. 'Gabe, please, I know you're awake. Let me in.'

Finally, there was a scuffle. Then the latch clicked, and the door cracked open.

Renee peered into the room, expecting to see Gabriel standing in front of her, or sitting at his desk. But he was in bed, sitting with the covers pulled right up to his neck.

'Oh, sweetheart,' she said. 'What is it?'

The room was dingy, the only light coming from the gaming rig. The monitor was on, the nebulous screensaver swirling and pulsing with purple and pink light. The thing next to it, the 'case' or the 'tower' or whatever it was called, was also lit up, the fluorescent tubes shining like glow sticks.

Goosebumps sprang up on Renee's arms, and she realised a breeze was coming through the window. 'What's that doing open?' she said. 'It's freezing out there tonight.'

She crossed the room and tugged the sash closed, then went back to the bed and sat on the edge of the mattress, trying to think of the right thing to say. She'd held her son's little body through ear infections and tummy bugs, comforted him when he'd lost his favourite cuddle toy at four years old. She'd cleaned up scrapes, wiped away tears, pressed bags of frozen peas to swelling bruises and cradled him on her lap. She'd always been the first person he would turn to, the first pair of eyes he would seek. *There*, she would say. *All better now. Mummy's got you.* These days, though, none of that worked.

'Are you still upset about your birthday?'

After Dom had somehow coaxed Gabe out for lunch, she'd been so happy. The day, it seemed, had been rescued. But then Michael caused a scene and the atmosphere fell flat. She did her best to resurrect it, but it wasn't long before Gabriel scuttled back behind his locked door. In the two weeks since, he'd somehow managed to retreat so far into himself it was as if he wasn't even there anymore.

'I'm so sorry that it didn't ... well, it wasn't quite the celebration I'd planned.'

But Gabriel didn't even seem to be aware she was speaking. She studied his face. Under the sheets, she realised, her son was shirtless and shivering.

'Sweetheart, what's wrong? Are you sick?' She reached for his forehead, but before her fingers could touch his skin Gabriel pulled away. He lurched backwards and as he did the blanket fell away, revealing his chest.

Renee gasped. Gabriel scrabbled at the sheets, but she grabbed hold of the other end and pulled. His naked torso was covered in dozens of new scratches. He looked like he'd been in a fight with a rake.

'Gabe ... oh my god, what happened?'

The lines were long and raised. His skin was smeared with dried blood. He snatched back the sheets and pulled them up to his neck.

'It's just a rash,' he said.

'A rash? Are you sure? Let me see.'

Gabriel flinched again. In the dark, his eyes looked flat and black. He was silent for what felt like hours. And then a tear slid down his cheek. 'There's something coming for me, isn't there?' he said.

Renee pressed her hand to her heart. 'What? No, of course not. What are you talking about?'

Gabriel swallowed thickly. His breath was shallow, faltering. 'All that stuff ... Ivory, the angel thing, the paint. It's about me, isn't it?'

Renee shook her head. 'No. Absolutely not, it's got nothing to do with you.'

'What is it, then?'

She bit her lip. 'It's just a ... I'm sure it's just ...' She trailed off, wishing she had the words.

'It is. Something's coming.' Gabriel curled up into a ball and covered his head with his arms. 'Don't let it get me. Mum. Please, don't let it in.'

# ALEX
## 18

By the time the sun rose, I'd been up for hours. As the temperature soared and the village began waking up, I sat in the kitchen with my phone in my hand, scrolling through old messages from Stuart.

In front of me on the island bench, the two packages sat side by side: the doll box that I'd dug out of the cupboard, and the one that had turned up overnight. The dead bird was long gone, taken away with the rest of the village rubbish.

Lifting my tired, stinging eyes, I gazed around the room. The wall was still wet from where I'd attacked the thick red smear with soap and hot water. I'd made enough Halloween costumes and patched up enough scrapes to know the difference between real blood and fake – but still, the sticky substance, slapped on with an open palm and wiped in a wide arc, was extremely unnerving. The substance, whatever it was, had come off for the most part, but there were still traces on the skirting board and the floor where the liquid had dripped and pooled in the cracks. My nailbeds were red rimmed too, even though I'd scrubbed them almost raw with a scouring brush. *Out, damned spot.*

The back door still stood open, allowing a soothing flow of morning noises. Birdsong, crickets and the occasional slam of a car door. Soft guitar music, floating through an open upstairs window along with the gentle rattle of crockery.

In the dark of night, I'd been convinced: the witch was on her way. But now the sun had risen, my rational brain had kicked into gear. There was *not* a malevolent supernatural being stalking the forest at night. I did not, could not, believe that. There were so many more likely explanations. Ollie, for one. He'd ordered dark-web mystery boxes for his YouTube videos; the resemblance of the contents to the Pine Ridge myth was just a coincidence.

Or Stuart. Maybe he knew someone in the village, or he'd had me followed. He'd found us and was toying with me. But why would he go to the effort of the boxes? Wouldn't he just skip straight to the part where he ripped me to shreds? Show up and strongarm me into the car? That was more his style.

I looked back at my phone. Stuart's calls and texts had been incessant since we'd left, a barrage of threats and abuse mixed in with declarations of feigned indifference – *I'm done with you, bitch, happy to see the back of you, take your kids and piss off, couldn't give a shit what happens to any of you.* Then, three days ago, they'd stopped abruptly. What did that mean?

I drummed my fingers on the lid of one of the boxes. I brought up my contacts and stared at Stuart's number. I dialled – then immediately hung up again.

'What's for breakfast?' Ollie stumbled into the kitchen and stuck his head in the fridge.

'Are these yours?' I said, ignoring his question.

Ollie blinked. 'What?'

I nodded at the boxes on the benchtop. 'Are they for you? Did you order them?'

He stared at the boxes. 'No.'

'You sure?'

'One hundred per cent.'

I took a deep breath and let it out slowly. 'Alright. Tell me again about the boxes in your videos. The truth this time. Where did they come from? What are they?'

Ollie looked as if his brain was running a million miles an hour. But then he seemed to sag. 'They're not anything,' he said, turning back to the fridge.

'What do you mean?'

'I mean they're not real, I made it all up.' He grabbed the milk and drank straight from the carton. Then he sniffed the air. 'Why does it smell like soap in here? Have you been cleaning?'

'You made what up?'

He wiped his mouth and shrugged. 'The mystery boxes are fake. I made them myself.'

'Fake?'

He nodded. 'Loads of people are doing it. It's like that unboxing thing everyone was into years ago, with the make-up and toys and games, except this is supposed to be from dark-web sellers. Like, stuff they needed to get rid of, or couldn't sell any other way? But it's all just staged.'

I frowned at him. 'The white powder, the lunch bag. You did all of that?'

'It wasn't hard. The powder was just cornflour. I found the lunch bag in a park, dressed it up a little.'

'But … why?'

'To get viewers. To make money.' He rolled his eyes. 'Look, it's not a big deal, alright? There were a few kids at school who were YouTubing. They were making heaps of cash through subscribers and ads and stuff. I just thought, like, okay, that doesn't look hard, I could do that. I thought we could use the money. It was pretty easy, I just copied one of their videos, filmed it on my phone, posted it and that was it. Everyone loved it so I made a couple more.'

'Wait, wait, wait.' I ran my hands over my face. 'So, what was all that stuff you said the other day? About the dark web, and not knowing who sent the boxes? You made that up, too?'

Ollie shrugged again.

'So you've never even been on the dark web?'

He looked down at his feet.

'Oliver,' I said. 'You said that whoever was sending those things knew where we lived. You said we could be killed in our beds, that our throats would be slit. Why would you do that?'

He mumbled something.

'What?'

'To scare you.'

I stared at him.

Heaving a sigh, he folded his arms and leaned against the counter. 'I'm sorry, okay? You freaked out so bad that I thought, fine, alright, if she thinks it's real I'll just tell her it's real. But it's not.' He looked at the boxes on the island bench. 'What *are* those anyway?'

How could I explain? I dropped my head into my hands.

'Doesn't matter.'

'I'm sorry,' Ollie said after a while. 'I didn't know the videos would upset you so much.'

Sighing, I kneaded my forehead with my fingers. 'How much money did you make, anyway?'

'Huh?'

'From the videos. You said you did it to get cash.'

Ollie spread his hands and pushed out his bottom lip. 'Couple of hundred dollars?'

'Not bad. What were you going to do with it?'

'Dunno.'

'Oh, come on. You must've had some kind of plan.'

He paused. 'Queensland,' he muttered.

'Sorry?'

'I thought we might go to Queensland, alright?'

'What? Why?'

'I just … I felt bad. We stayed in Sydney because of me, and then everything ended up shit. I wanted things to go back to the way they were when it was just us. I wanted to help us get away. From Stuart.' He looked away. 'And from Kara.'

'Kara?'

'Where is she anyway?'

I tilted my head towards the bedroom. 'Napping.'

'Well, she's annoying. She cries all the time.' His chin quivered. 'And you love her more than you love me.'

'What?' My mouth fell open. 'Oh, Ollie, no, that's not true at all. Of *course* I don't. I love you both the same.'

'Well, you shouldn't!' Ollie backed away, trapping himself

in the corner near the sink. 'I was here first. You should love *me* more.'

'Ollie, I ...' My heart. Oh, my heart. 'I had no idea you felt like that.'

'No, well, you wouldn't, would you?'

I stood up and walked around the bench, but he dodged me. I touched his arm and he winced.

'Ow.'

'What?'

He snatched his arm away from me. 'Nothing.'

'Ollie, what's wrong with you?' I grabbed his hand and pulled up the sleeve of his hoodie. There was a long gash on his forearm, running from the elbow halfway to the wrist.

'Oh, honey, what's this?'

'Leave me alone.'

'How did you do that?'

'I just came off my board yesterday, it's not a big deal.'

I reached for him, but he pulled away again and held his arm close to his chest.

'Stop fussing, will you?' he yelled. 'It's not like you care what I think or feel. You've always just done whatever *you* want to do, and I've just had to fit in. All that moving around ... I hated it. I mean, sometimes it was cool, but I could never make friends, not proper ones. No point, we were always just saying goodbye.'

My chest hurt. I remembered the point at which Ollie began to lose interest in socialising with other kids; he'd just shrug whenever I suggested he go and introduce himself. *Nah, I'll stay at home*, he'd say. *Watch a movie*. I just thought he was being a sulky teenager. *They all do that*, a fellow mum told me. *Get used to it.*

'But … what about Sydney? You made friends at school, right?'

'Uh-huh. And how do you think I did that?'

I shook my head, not understanding – but then it clicked. The file-sharing link, the YouTube videos. A lonely boy's guide to making friends.

My own eyes filled up. *I'm so sorry, buddy.* I wanted to hold him and make everything better. 'Here,' I said, reaching for him again, 'let me help you clean up that scratch.'

But Ollie threw up his hands. 'Can you stop? I'm not a baby, I don't need you to clean me up.'

We stared at each other. I didn't know what to say.

And then, from the corner of my eye, I caught movement on the patio. Someone was standing outside, listening through the open door.

'Hello?' I called. 'Is there someone there?'

I heard the scuff of a shoe and the soft awkward sound of a throat being cleared. And then Violet's beautiful blue head popped into view. 'I'm so sorry, Mrs Ives,' she said. 'I didn't mean to interrupt. I was just waiting for Ollie.'

'You're not interrupting,' Ollie said before I could open my mouth to correct her: *It's Ms Ives, thank you very much.* 'I'm coming right now.'

'Hang on,' I said, trying to claw back some authority. 'What's happening? Where are you going?'

'Fishing.'

*'Fishing?'*

'Hang on a sec, Vi, I'll just grab some toast. You got the rods?'

I looked Violet up and down. She was wearing a short white dress with spaghetti straps. 'You don't look like you're going fishing.'

Ollie sighed. 'Actually, I'm not hungry. Come on, Vi, let's go.'

'But, Ollie,' I said. 'Your arm …'

At the back door, Ollie spun around. 'Mum, leave it. I'm *fine*.' Giving me a hard stare, he disappeared into the sunshine.

Violet turned to follow, but at the last minute she turned back with an odd expression: a small smile, eyes flashing with something that looked like triumph. I couldn't work out what it meant.

I was still staring after them when my phone rang.

Edging to the corner of the benchtop where I'd left it, I peered uneasily at the screen. An unknown number. I let the call ring out, then waited. A minute or two later, the phone pinged with a notification: a voicemail. I hit play.

'Alex,' said a familiar female voice. 'It's Susan Parker from across the road?'

I frowned. My old neighbour in Bondi.

'Look, I haven't seen you around for a while, and I'm pretty sure you've moved on – at least, I *hope* you have – but I just wanted to give you a heads up that there's been some odd activity at your house, and … well, if you could call me back that would be great. It's about Stuart. There's just something I think you ought to know.'

# ALEX
## 19

Stuart was missing.

When I called Susan back, she told me that four nights ago, sometime around midnight, she'd heard two motorbikes pull up in front of our old house.

Peeking through the window, Susan had seen two figures dismount the bikes and head around to the back of the house. A few minutes later, she'd heard what sounded like breaking glass, so she hurried to her guest bedroom, which overlooked our garden. She'd seen flashes of torchlight inside – and then watched as Stuart opened a window, climbed over the rail of the upstairs balcony, dropped onto the lawn and ran off across the yard. 'He jumped the fence,' she said. 'Like a bloody racehorse.'

Assuming we were being robbed, she called the cops. But by the time they arrived, the thieves, or whoever they were, had gone. The attending officers told her they would investigate – but two days later, Stuart hadn't returned home, so she went back to the police. They seemed oddly cagey, though, so she phoned a friend whose husband was in the force.

'She told me,' said Susan, 'in confidence, of course, that Stuart is being investigated for money laundering. Apparently he's been mixed up with bikies for years but they couldn't get proof. And they probably won't get any now, either. Looks like he's ticked someone off and made a run for it. They're trying to track him down but the latest is that he somehow boarded a flight to Indonesia. Have you heard from him, Alex? Do you know where he is? And where on earth are *you*?'

I hung up. Sat down. Stood up again. Poured a wine.

*Jesus Christ*. Money laundering. *What the fuck?* But that meant … *Shit*.

I took the wine to the laundry, opened the cupboard under the sink and took out the Tupperware container from behind the detergent. Popping the lid, I ran my fingers over the bundles of crisp notes inside. About four months into our relationship, I'd gone into Stuart's study to find a stapler and found a huge hoard of cash in a drawer, stuffed inside a large envelope. Obviously I'd been surprised, but it also made a certain sense. Stuart was well off, his restaurants had done well, but for some reason I never could fathom he had a weird mistrust of banks. *I don't want the government knowing how much I have*, he used to say. *If they own your money, they own you.*

I hadn't mentioned the envelope to Stuart; I'd just put it back in the drawer and walked away. But I hadn't forgotten it. And then when I'd decided to leave, I'd taken it. Not the whole lot, but over half. A snap decision. Payback. *Hasta la vista, dickhead.* I'd emptied the envelope, replaced two thirds of the cash with folded newspaper, then wedged a few of the bundles back in so it looked untouched. Only then did I realise that all the notes were one hundred dollar bills. I'd never seen so much money; I'd had trouble finding a container large enough to fit it all in.

Driving away with it in my car had felt like the biggest win of my life. Except now it seemed like it hadn't belonged to him. Had he been safeguarding it? Or stealing it?

I swallowed a mouthful of Chardonnay so big it actually hurt going down. Thank fuck I'd got the kids out of there when I had.

*Okay, just breathe.*

Stuart didn't seem to know I'd taken the money. There was nothing in his messages to suggest he did, anyway. Maybe he hadn't noticed; maybe he'd underestimated me. Either way, if he didn't know then no one knew. There was no trail to lead anyone to me.

*Wait.*

Cogs turned slowly in my head and I felt a cold dread. If no one knew about the money, if Stuart was on the run and Ollie's videos weren't real, then what the fuck was happening at Pine Ridge? Where were the boxes coming from?

Gulping down more wine, I thought about the noises in the night, the grey-haired woman, the symbols in the woods and the little boy on the road – even the red smear on the wall. Only I had seen and heard those things. No one else could confirm they'd ever happened. I'd read stories about combat veterans so affected by PTSD that they became delusional; women whose minds were so ravaged after giving birth that they shattered like sheets of glass. What if I'd overheard some of the Pine Ridge kids talking and my sleep-deprived brain had cooked up a few hallucinations?

But …

*The witch took the farmers' kid.*

Kit had told me about the farmhouse. I definitely hadn't imagined that.

I put the Tupperware container back in its hiding place and returned to the kitchen to snatch up my phone. I discovered that the flower farm on which Pine Ridge had been built was called Kellerman & co. There were a few old listings on sydneymarkets. com.au, Localsearch and White Pages – nothing since 2012 – and an announcement on a New South Wales business awards website that Leonard Kellerman was named Flower Grower of the Year in 1991, 1993 and 1994. I found a local community newsletter from 1996 that confirmed Leonard's death and the passing of the business to his son, Michael. And in August 2011, a handful of news articles reported the disappearance of sixteen-year-old Gabriel Kellerman, son of Michael and Renee.

The pieces were short, though, and without much detail. All I could find out was that the boy did indeed vanish, but that the case was eventually closed. He ran away, they all said. One article mentioned in passing that the boy had been upset after the mysterious death of his cat; another said that the Kellermans had reported intruders on the property in the weeks preceding his disappearance. But no specifics were disclosed, and the reports stated emphatically that after a full investigation, the police had ruled out any foul play.

I put my phone down and poured more wine. Then, carrying my glass, I went to the front-facing window and gazed out across the valley.

Alone on the hill, backlit by the morning sun, the farmhouse returned my stare.

# RENEE
## 20

Renee steered the vacuum cleaner over the bedroom carpet, feeling utterly disconnected from her own body. Her hands belonged to someone else; her feet weren't quite attached. She was less a person, more a receptacle. A bucket of water, full to the brim.

Fat lines appeared then disappeared in the plush pile. Secret paths. Hidden ways. *Follow the yellow brick road.* Renee pictured herself throwing down the vacuum and walking away without even turning the damn thing off, heading off over the rainbow, never to return. Instead, she finished the job, switched off the vacuum at the wall and wound the power cable neatly back into place. The hum of the motor was replaced by rain drumming on the roof.

'Really, Renee,' April called from the bathroom. 'The state of your bathroom. I'm going to need a chisel to get the limescale off these taps.'

Renee closed her eyes, wishing for the umpteenth time that she hadn't accepted her mother's offer to help with the housework. *A little assistance isn't going to hurt*, Frank had said, firmly. *You won't even know I'm here*, April had chimed in. And Renee, tired and overwhelmed, had agreed. Now, though, the house felt too small, too loud; the more April cleaned, the less space there seemed to be.

'And don't even get me started on the grout. My goodness, I'll be here for weeks.'

*Dear god, I hope not.* Her parents had always been intense; it was one of the main reasons Renee had married so young, and for a long time after the wedding even phone calls had been too much. Eventually, with the help of some literal and figurative distance, a husband with a good sense of humour (where had *that* gone?) and a father-in-law with directly opposing world views, Renee had been able to let them back into her life on her own terms. But lately it felt like her carefully laid boundaries were blurring, and the old intensity was not just back but had mutated.

With her fingers still wrapped around the vacuum handle, Renee stood at the window and watched the water pound the roof of her car and drip from the trees. It collected in pools on the driveway and gushed from the gutters, rushing down to the dam and bursting its banks. It hadn't stopped for days now, and the incessant white noise was starting to itch, like a lining of coarse wool on the inside of her skull.

Pressing her forehead against the glass, she stared down to where the greenhouses were little more than ghostly outlines at the bottom of the field. Somewhere out there, she assumed, Michael was getting on with the jobs. Picking, wrapping, cooling. Ploughing, raking, planting. The greenhouse roofs needed reinforcing. The plastic sheeting on one had already ripped; if they didn't act quickly, it wouldn't be long before the sheer weight of the gathering water did the same to the rest.

She hadn't spoken to her husband in weeks, though; he could be anywhere. And quite frankly she couldn't care less about the greenhouses. She had more important things to think about.

A soft knock made her jump and she turned to find her mother in the doorway, a bright yellow rubber glove on each hand.

'Ren, love,' April said. 'I think the doctor's here.'


'Well, you can rule out anything bacterial or viral,' said the doctor in the kitchen afterwards. 'Those wounds have been self-inflicted.'

Renee threw a glance down the hallway to the porch where April was beating the dust from the welcome mat. 'Are you sure?'

'Well, he denies it, of course, but the lines are clearly demarcated from the surrounding skin, and the pattern is geometric. Not the kind of thing you see with a rash. And he's very cagey about them, which is a sure sign. There are the other red flags, too: moodiness, insomnia, even a possible eating disorder. If I were you, I'd be getting your son some psychiatric help as soon as possible.' The doctor rifled through her bag. 'And maybe limit his screen time. There's a direct link between technology and teenage depression.'

She issued a referral to a Sydney clinic and wrote out a prescription for a 'light' antidepressant. 'See how he goes with that, and I'll see him again in a month.'

Renee started to cry. 'I'm sorry,' she said. 'I just feel so useless.'

'I know it's difficult,' said the doctor, kindly. 'But self-harm is, sadly, quite common. Kids do dangerous things to put the world to the test.'

As soon as the doctor left, Renee called the clinic, but the earliest appointment wasn't until the following week. She marked the date in the calendar with a fat red pen, waves of worry roiling in her gut. At least she had a week to figure out the logistics of physically getting Gabriel there. Until then, she would keep him home from school. And she would stay with him. Because it wasn't just Gabriel; everything else was getting worse, too.

They'd buried the cat; Michael had successfully cleaned the red splashes off the house and painted over the stain, and they'd tried to move on. But Renee kept hearing footsteps outside the house at night, and the phone rang constantly. In fact, they'd received so many prank calls, they had to unplug their landline and screen all their mobile calls. The farm's website and Facebook page had both been hacked. Someone had posted photos with the Kellermans' heads photoshopped in: Nazi rallies, pornography and scenes of grotesque animal cruelty. They'd received so many alarmed responses from customers and clients that they'd had to delete their account and shut down the site.

Michael had called the police and spoken to an officer who suggested that they were being 'trolled'. The advice was to stay off the internet for a while. 'They can't do anything,' Michael explained impatiently when he eventually put the phone down. 'The Facebook stuff is impossible to trace, and we don't have evidence of any actual physical threat.'

'Are you joking? Our cat was killed,' Renee said.

Michael shrugged. 'She could've been hit by a car up on the

road. Maybe someone recognised her and brought her back.'

'Do you really think that?'

A silence fell between them.

'What did we do to deserve any of this?' Renee whispered. 'Why is it even happening?'

'Who the hell knows. There are some sick people out there. But, like the cops said, if we stay away from the internet and try not to react, they'll get bored eventually.'

Renee had wanted to scream. What if the internet didn't stay away from *them*? Everything they did now was online.

Sighing deeply, she went to the laundry and grabbed the basket, then set off back to the bedrooms to collect the dirty linen. In the hallway, she stopped.

April was outside Gabriel's door again, a cloth and a spray bottle of cleaning fluid at her feet. She was standing with her face pressed right up against the wood, eyes closed, mouth moving, one hand raised. She was murmuring something, but Renee couldn't make out the words.

'Mum?'

April stopped her muttering and opened her eyes. 'Yes?'

'What are you doing?'

April looked down at her feet, then up at the ceiling. She patted the door as if it were an old friend. 'Helping,' she said, mildly. 'I'm just helping.'

Then she picked up the cloth and the bottle and swept away to another part of the house.

'How are you going with the medication?' Renee sat on a chair next to her son's bed, stroking the oily hair from his head. 'Are you taking it?'

Gabriel didn't answer. He lay on his bed beside her, fully clothed in the same old shirt and tracksuit bottoms, his eyes closed.

In the six days since the doctor's visit, Renee had given him a little white tablet every night before bed. She couldn't be sure whether or not he was actually swallowing them, but he was already confined to his room, and forcing pills down his throat felt too much like prison. She consoled herself with the thought of their first clinic appointment, scheduled for the morning. The psychiatrist would be able to tell her what to do.

'You know we're going to see someone tomorrow, right? To help you get better?'

She'd thought about trying to trick him into getting in the car. *We're going for ice cream! Would you like to choose a new toy?* But it wouldn't work, not like it used to when he was younger. She'd just have to be honest and hope for the best. Worst case scenario, she'd call an ambulance.

'Would you like to talk to me a little bit before we go? Just so I can help when we speak to the new doctor?'

Gabriel didn't answer. His eyes were bloodshot, his body limp. It was like he just wasn't in there anymore.

Renee persisted. 'He's going to ask you questions about the … marks on your body. How you're feeling. It might be easier if you get used to saying things out loud.'

Blank stare. Slow blink.

'Gabriel, please tell me. Did you do those things to yourself? Or did someone else do it?'

Always the same questions, every day for the last week. He never gave her even a flicker of a reply.

'Was it someone you know? Someone close to you? A friend from school, or …' She couldn't go there, couldn't say it. Couldn't even think it.

For the first time, though, Gabriel shifted and the look he gave her shattered her heart.

'I'm scared,' he said, his voice cracking. 'Something's coming. Please, I don't want to be here anymore.'

Five minutes later, Renee had switched off every button, unplugged every cord and cable. She carried every last component of the gaming set-up out of his bedroom and into her own. Monitor, keyboard, mouse, speakers, case, headphones, webcam, USB sticks, toolkit, smartphone, laptop, even the GoPro she'd bought for his birthday: she put everything in sight on the top shelf of her wardrobe and pushed it to the very back. Gabriel's desk was completely clear of everything except pencils and paper. Tomorrow, she would take Gabe to the clinic. She would stay by his side. She would do everything it took.

And she would fit his door with a brand-new barrel bolt. On the outside. Just in case.


The next morning, Renee got up early, showered, dressed and made a big pot of coffee. Then she pulled some eggs from the fridge, a loaf of bread from the pantry, and for the first time in two weeks she made breakfast for the team. Then she warmed up the pastries she'd bought especially for Gabriel, put them on a tray with a glass of freshly squeezed juice and carried the whole lot to his bedroom. Today would be a *good* day. Today, everything would change. Finally, she would get some answers and Gabriel would get help.

Just as she was placing the tray down on the floor, the front door opened.

'Ren,' said Michael, standing in the doorway. Water dripped from the hood of his waterproof coat. The rain hadn't slowed overnight.

'Can you take your jacket off, please?' said Renee, knocking on Gabriel's door. 'You're getting the floor all wet.'

'Ren,' he said again.

Sliding the new bolt across the door, Renee realised that something about her husband's face was odd. He was *smiling*.

'I have some news,' he said.

'Okay,' she said, warily. 'Good news, I take it?'

'Yes,' said Michael. 'Very good.'

'Well, that's nice.' For a moment, she felt a glimmer of hope. They hadn't shared a smile in years. 'Can you just wait a second while I give Gabe his breakfast?' Without waiting for a reply, she picked up the tray from the floor, nudged the door with her hip and pushed her way inside.

When she saw the empty room, the tray slipped from her grasp.

Gabriel wasn't there.

# ALEX
## 21

The more I stared at the farmhouse, the closer I wanted to get. I had no idea what I expected to find, but I knew that I wouldn't get any closer to the truth without going up there and taking a look around.

Pasting a smile on my face, I knocked on Jenny's door. When she answered, though, I almost changed my mind. Caught unawares, my neighbour looked frail and forlorn.

'I'm so sorry,' I said, trying not to look at her head; her scarf had slipped a little to reveal a small patch of hairless scalp. 'Were you taking a nap? I can come back another time.' I wondered at the treatment she was receiving but couldn't bring myself to pry.

'No, it's fine, I was just resting.' She adjusted the scarf and smiled at Kara, sleep-soft on my hip. 'Hello, little one,' she said, her face lighting up. 'What a lovely surprise. To what do I owe the pleasure?'

'Well, I ...' A flush crept into my cheeks. 'I was just wondering ... you know that thing you said last week? About babysitting? I was thinking that if you're not busy – I mean, obviously feel free to say no if it isn't a good time, but I was hoping that ...'

Jenny beamed. 'Would you like me to watch Kara for you?'

'Yes. I mean … yes. I'd just really love to go for a run. She's already fed and changed, and I've got everything set up downstairs. Would you mind?'

'Of course!' Jenny clapped her hands together. 'Oh, I thought you'd never ask.'

'Thank you. I promise I won't be long.'

An hour or two, I'd decided, would give me more than enough time.

In the thick of the woods, gigantic red angophoras towered and twisted above me, their trunks knotted and gnarled like creatures in a Guillermo del Toro movie. Cabbage palms shimmied in the breeze; banksias bounced at head height. Long strips of paperbark littered the ground like scraps of fabric on a sewing room floor.

I strode quickly over the rutted ground, following the signs, sticking to the trails.

*Bones, doll, blood.*

*The witch took the farmers' son.*

That poor woman. If I lost Ollie like that, I would die. I thought about his quivering chin, the crack in his voice. *You love her more than you love me.*

I swallowed a lump in my throat. *That's not true. I love you both the same.*

Did I, though? I knew I should, but when Ollie was glowering at me or sulking or yelling 'Everything bad in my life is because of you,' perhaps I *did* love Kara more. My sweet tiny bundle of a baby girl; the way she clung to me, needed me, chose me above everyone else, every single time. The gorgeous, clean-slate smell of her. But then, on other days when Kara was screaming and I hadn't slept for a week and my body felt feeble, it was my smart, funny boy who I adored most. His independence, sense of humour and all our shared history. We had habits and routines; we'd moulded to each other long ago. And his hugs, when they came, were more precious for their scarcity.

When I got home, I told myself, we would talk it out. We would be fine. I just needed to sort this witch out first. Hysterical laughter bubbled in my throat – what had my life become? – but I swallowed it back down. The situation might be absurd, but it was happening and I had to deal with it. My kids were everything to me.

Clambering over rocks and stumbling on clumps of dried mud, I turned away from the path I'd been on the day I'd bumped into Kit, descending instead into the valley. The carvings were on the trees here, too. Some looked fresh, the lines revealing the soft pale wood beneath the hard casing of the bark, but some were decidedly older. At the bottom of the valley, I found a creek and, hopping over its stepping-stone crossing, began to climb up the bank on the other side. The path was less obvious here, less well trodden. It became skinny and then almost non-existent.

I pushed through long spiky leaves and emerald ferns, determined to make it to the top, and at last I broke free of the trees. The path opened onto a sloping paddock where the grass was patchy and the ground dry and untended. Shielding my eyes from the sun, I looked up to where the sun-bleached farmhouse stood at the top of the hill.

It was bigger than I'd thought – the roof stretched back further than it had been possible to see from down in the village – and prettier. But with the light shining from behind, it cast a long shadow over the grass: a dark rectangle with a pointed roof. I took a few uneasy steps towards it, thinking how much the shadow looked like the tree carvings ...

But then I noticed a much smaller building to my left, tucked into the bottom corner of the paddock. A weather-worn shed with corrugated walls and tin roof, leaning to one side like an elderly drunk, tucked so far into the tree line it was almost hidden from sight. Curious, I went to have a quick look.

Vines and brambles had crept up the outside walls of the shed, but the two small sliding windows were intact and the door seemed relatively new. I nudged it open, bracing myself for movement. Inside, the shed was dingy but empty. I could just about make out two rattan chairs in a corner, stacked one on top of the other, the seats torn and frayed. In another, a disused fridge and a sketchy-looking ladder. Bizarrely, there were three foam mattresses on the floor, arranged in what might've been a circle, each fitted with a sheet, as well as two plastic buckets, one lying on its side near the door and the other near the fridge. Scrunched-up chip packets littered the floor, and there was a sour, fungal smell, like a mixture of sweat, mushrooms and engine oil. The words 'Love Shack' had been spray-painted onto the back wall.

I shivered. Squatters, probably. Making a mental note to tell Kit, I backed out of the shed and closed the door with my foot.

The walk up the hill to the farmhouse was much more pleasant. With the rise of the ridge all around and the velvet roll of fields, the landscape was impossibly romantic. I felt like I was in *Country Style* magazine; all I needed was a white cotton smock and an enormous straw hat. The further up I went, the more lush and daisy-dotted the grass under my feet became. The air was fragrant and somehow made my lungs feel bigger than they were. Above my head, birds flew gracefully across a taut blue sky.

Up close, I could see that the once-white weatherboard cladding was streaked with watermarks, the paint peeling like sunburnt skin and the guttering coming loose in places. But the timber had held its shape, as had the wraparound balustrade. The fretwork around the eaves, too, was in good nick. Something about the light up here – the way the rays seemed to hit the walls dead on – gave the house an otherworldly sheen. I was reminded again of my favourite picture book and the house I'd fantasised about as a child. *One day*, I'd told myself over and over, *I will escape and live in a place like that.* Despite my grim reason for being there, a part of me felt victorious, like eight-year-old me had finally made it.

I took my time walking around and discovered that what I'd assumed to be the front facade was actually the side; the front door was situated to the left, set into the eastern wall. I changed direction and found a circular driveway, an ornate stone birdbath and a jacaranda tree in glorious full bloom. Four wooden stairs led to a porch and a front door flanked by stained-glass sidelights.

I climbed the steps and peered through one of the windows. I could just about make out a dark, empty room. Returning to the door, I tried the handle – and I was surprised when it swung open with a creak. I peeked inside and saw a long dusty hallway.

'Hello?' I called. My voiced bounced off the walls like a stone dropped into a well.

The house smelled musty but nowhere near as pungent as I'd anticipated. The walls were papered with what had once been a delicate floral print: bluebells or cornflowers. On the right was a row of empty coat hooks and, above them, a display of ugly, unpleasant-looking vintage farm tools.

Four doors led off from the hall, one on the right and three on the left. Behind the first on the left was a bare space that might've once been a guest room. The one on the right led to another empty but considerably larger room decorated with chintzy wallpaper and timber panelling. Only two items of furniture remained: a vast empty armoire standing against the far wall and, in the ensuite bathroom, a rainbow-edged mirror hanging above a dust-laden sink.

The second door on the left led to a third bedroom, still furnished with a single bed and what appeared to be a table or a desk. Both were covered with dustsheets. I had a look underneath; the bed still held its mattress, the desk still had its chair. Compared with the other barren rooms, this one might almost feel cosy – if it weren't for the locks. Two thick barrel-bolt latches had been fixed to the doorframe; one on the inside and one, strangely, on the outside.

The next door opened onto a main bathroom, unremarkable

except for the mesmerising black and white floor tiles. At the end of the hall I found a spacious kitchen, a dining area and a long living room with a fireplace.

A back door, also unlocked, led out onto the veranda. It was a bit raggedy; the paintwork was peeling out there too and some of the floor panels had rotted through. The view, though, was spectacular: a perfect panorama across the forest, dam and the whole of Pine Ridge.

I leaned against one of the posts. From this angle, the village looked quite different, the houses all facing the same way. The sweeping, tiered curve of the development actually reminded me of a concert hall or an amphitheatre, with the farmhouse as the main star, almost as if the village had been built to showcase its beauty.

And then I remembered something. Kit's grand tour on our first day, the way the farmhouse had commanded my attention. Captivated, I'd stared up and thought I'd seen …

I was standing in the exact place where the shadowy figure had been.

Chilled by the thought, I straightened up and moved to a different spot.

On my way back inside, I noticed a stain on the cladding, a faint pink splat, and tiny flecks of red stuck in the grain of the window frames. And then—

My breath got stuck under my ribs.

Down low on the wall, right where it met the floor, was a drawing.

*The* drawing.

The sign of the witch.

I stepped back, and it was as if more scuttled out from the woodwork like spiders, dozens of house-shaped boxes with symbols inside, scribbled in black ink above my head near the eaves, under the windowsills, on the balustrade posts, on the veranda floor, on the steps that led down to the grass.

I hurried back inside, my skin crawling, and let the screen door slam behind me. I studied the floors, the walls, the ceiling. Then I strode through the kitchen and looked back down the hall. No drawings, but something was definitely off. There were water stains on the ceiling and the paint was bulging in places, but for a house that had sat empty for six years, it was remarkably free of grime.

I crossed to the nearest window and looked down into the tracks. I swept my finger over the sill and checked the skirting boards. Where were the dead flies? Where were the cobwebs, the rat droppings? And then, in one corner, I saw a small plastic cockroach trap.

Someone, I realised with a jolt, was quietly taking care of the place; not so much that anyone would notice, but enough to keep it from falling into ruin.

I suddenly felt extremely uncomfortable, like I was being watched.

*Time to leave.*

Poking around had been a mistake. I'd found no clues at all, no photographs, no forwarding address laid conveniently on the kitchen bench …

*Wait.*

There *was* something in the kitchen. I'd missed it before, but just to the right of the stove, propped up against the tiled splashback, was a piece of paper.

I went closer. It was an envelope.

With my name on it.

*Alex Ives.*

'What the fuck …?'

I picked up the envelope and turned it over. It was sealed.

A feeling of dread spread slowly through my limbs. I turned and looked over my shoulder, around the room, hardly daring to breathe. It was like standing in a vacuum.

With my pulse thudding in my ears, I broke the envelope's seal and opened it. Inside was a single piece of white paper, folded just once. Written on the paper in slanted cursive were two lines.

*My son was taken.*

*Yours will be too.*

# ALEX
## 22

I ran out the back door, down the veranda steps, over the grass and back through the forest, clutching the note in my hand. When I made it out the other side, I was breathless and sweating.

Who had left me that note? Was it a warning or a threat? Did it refer to the farmers' missing son, Gabriel? In which case, had the Kellermans written it? Were they still around, living close by, maybe even wandering around in the woods and by the dam? What did Mrs Kellerman look like? Did she have long grey hair and own a pale raincoat?

Whatever the answer to those questions, I held on tight to one thing: I did *not* believe in witches. And nothing was going to hurt my boy. I'd put him in harm's way too many times already; from now on, I would do everything it took to keep him safe.

But as I emerged from the forest and hurried along the road, I thought about the dark, sticky picture frame and the blood-red smear on my wall, and every part of my body became tense. Sliding my phone out of my shorts pocket, I called Ollie. No answer. I texted him: *Hey mate, you okay?* Then I forked right at the workshop, away from my unit and towards the dam. I stood on the shore, scanning the banks.

*Please let him be there, please let me find him …*

It took me a few minutes, but eventually I spotted him, sitting on a rock in the shade of a tree, with a fishing rod in his hand. Violet sat by his side, her toes in the water, the hem of her white sundress blowing in the breeze. Flushing hot with relief, I stood in the shade of the tree and watched them, too far away to see their faces.

I texted him again: *???*

I saw him check his phone then put it away again without replying. He was ignoring me.

Resisting an overwhelming urge to rush over there and drag his ass home where I could be sure he was safe, I tried to think logically. My son was okay, I could see him, and panicking wasn't going to help. I had to remain calm and clear-headed if I was going to figure this shit out. Whether or not I had imagined certain things, whether or not the note in my hand had been left by the Kellermans, *something* had happened six years ago, possibly the same thing that was happening to me, and a boy had gone missing.

Changing direction, I jogged the short distance to Kit's house but, finding the windows dark and the door locked, I pivoted again, hurrying back around the dam to the office instead. The thought of confessing anything at all was painful – Kit would almost certainly laugh at me. But then again, he was the highest level of authority at Pine Ridge, he'd been there the longest, and if anyone should be able to provide some sort of explanation, it was him.

I jogged over the grass, past the playground and the

community hall, slowing only when the converted shipping container came into view. As I passed the dry goods store, I stopped for a moment to catch my breath. *Be calm*, I told myself. *Stay cool. Inhale, exhale.* When finally I felt like I had my nervous system back under control, I approached the office.

The curtains were drawn across the large picture window at the end and the sliding doors were closed. I knocked, but there was no answer. No lights, no movement. I tried the handle and, surprisingly, the door cracked open.

'Hello? Kit, are you here?'

Nothing. *Dammit.*

Slipping inside, I closed the door behind me. Kit's office, like his home, was small but clean and well ordered. Running the length of the back wall was a white benchtop with built-in drawers and three computer workstations. A tangle of cables snaking out from the wall, and a huge blinking black tower.

Directly above, succulents dripped from a shelf of the same length. The whole place smelled of new carpet and Kit's delicious citrusy cologne.

I folded my arms and chewed my bottom lip, trying to think where else Kit might be. I had to tell him about the note; and I needed him to help me find the Kellermans.

And then I had an idea. Casually, I wandered over to one of the workstations and tapped on the keyboard. The corresponding monitor sprang to life, but the screen was password protected. *Hmm.* Kit probably kept all business-related contact details on his phone or computer – but if I was lucky I might find some contracts or legal documents filed away somewhere, perhaps from the sale of the land? I opened a few drawers but found nothing interesting. Under a scramble of pens, charger cords and sticky notes, I unearthed a plastic document wallet stuffed full of paper, but it just turned out to be info sheets on environmentally abusive multinationals and protest fliers. *Throwing Away the Future*, it said. *How Corporate Giants Still Have It Wrong on Plastic Pollution 'Solutions'.* I tossed the whole lot back in the drawer.

I turned in a slow circle. *If I were a contract of sale, where would I be?* To my right was a small kitchenette and coffee machine; to my left, a coffee table and two armchairs. On the wall above the table was a large whiteboard, covered in writing. I stepped forward to take a closer look. In black and green erasable markers, someone had drawn a neat table with four columns and written the words COLLAB. LIVING across the top. The first column held a list of names. The second column contained a series of bullet-pointed information, the third was for addresses, and the fourth column held just a tick or a cross. I scanned the names column for *Kellerman* but couldn't find it. About halfway down, though, I found my own name. *Alexandra Ives (37).* And in smaller lettering beneath: *Oliver (14), Kara (BB).* There was my old address, the name of Ollie's school and the profession I'd supplied ('childcare educator'; I hadn't worked in over a year but had decided that 'stay-at-home mum' didn't strike a financially secure enough tone). In the third column on my row was Jenny's name and address, but the fourth column was blank; no tick, no cross. My fate had not yet been decided.

I found Layla's name, and Shannon's, plus many others that I didn't recognise. Some had a question mark where their temporary accommodation should've been, which suggested that they were new or hopeful residents. There were phone numbers, postal and email addresses, websites, jobs, places of work. I wondered if Maggie was aware of the sheer number of 'city folk' Kit had lined up.

Turning away, I rifled through a couple more drawers. I checked the photocopier, the printer tray and the cupboards in the kitchenette. In an alcove behind the kitchen, I found a storage cupboard full of stationery. Quickly checking the door, I rummaged through the shelves. There were notepads, pens, pencils, markers ... ink cartridges, stacks of paper ... Sellotape, white-out, staples, paperclips ... flash drives, spare chargers, extension leads ...

And on the very bottom shelf, I saw packing tape, scissors, Kraft paper and a fat roll of bubble wrap.

Kneeling down, I swept my hand along the shelf and pulled out a whole stack of flat-packed cardboard boxes. Medium-sized. Brown. Exactly the same as the ones that had turned up at my house.

I sat back on my haunches, my body pulsing. *It's a stationery cupboard*, I told myself. *Nothing unusual about postage materials kept there.* But I couldn't stop the chill that was spreading slowly through my chest like a hoarfrost.

And then I heard voices outside.

Jumping to my feet, I dashed back out into the main office space and saw Kit and Layla through the picture window, rounding the corner near the terraced veggie garden, heading towards the office.

*Shit.*

I probably had about half a second to get out before they got close enough to see the front door of the office. Without thinking twice, I snuck out and hurried around to the back of the shipping container, where I flattened my back against the wall and waited. Kit's and Layla's voices got closer. Then I heard the door open and close.

I let out a slow, shuddery sigh of relief. They hadn't seen me.

I was waiting for an opportunity to walk quietly away when I heard my name. 'It's not that I don't like Alex,' said Layla, her words drifting through an open window. 'I just don't know if collaborating is the right thing. For either of us, you know?'

I froze, one hand on the wall.

'But I thought you and Alex were getting along great,' Kit said. 'Violet and Ollie seem to be close, anyway. I assumed you'd both be keen.'

Whatever Layla said in response was covered by the scrape of a chair from inside, and a gust of wind in the trees above.

Then Kit spoke again. 'Okay, I hear what you're saying. But ...'

The trees rustled again. I missed the rest of the sentence, but then Layla jumped in over the top. 'No, no, no,' she said, loudly. 'Of course I would *never* judge on gossip. It's just that, honestly, I'm not sure I'd feel comfortable.'

My jaw fell open. *What?*

Checking that there was no one who might catch me listening, I inched around the corner, creeping closer to the door until I reached one of the windows. Slowly and carefully, I peered through the glass. Layla was standing nearest to me, her back turned, arms folded. Kit was over by the whiteboard, his hands in the pockets of his shorts.

'Look, she's obviously got problems,' Layla was saying. 'Sometimes I feel like she's just not in the room, you know? And her temper … I just don't want my girls living in close proximity to that kind of parenting. I don't want her yelling to be the last thing they hear before they go to sleep at night.'

I ducked back out of sight, my hand at my mouth.

'I mean, I don't want to cause trouble, but as far as I'm concerned the girls come first. And Amy's issues aside, I feel like Ollie's presence has been destabilising for Violet. Ever since he arrived, she's been acting up, pushing boundaries, staying up late on her phone. It's just not like her.'

*Destabilising*? I had to bite my hand to stop myself from speaking out loud. Ollie was no angel, I knew that – but neither was Violet. And her boundary pushing was not new behaviour. Layla had complained about it at the greenhouse party. Why was she lying now? And what 'issues' did Amy have?

'Have you discussed any of this with Alex?' Kit said. 'Does she know how you feel?'

'No,' Layla said, 'I don't want to make things awkward. I'd just rather take the idea off the table.'

'Alright,' said Kit, after a short pause. 'That's no problem at all. I'm sure I'll have no trouble matching Alex with someone else, she—'

'Oh, I wouldn't be so sure about that,' said Layla, cutting

in. 'From what I understand, I think most people feel the same way I do.'

I was stunned.

After several seconds of gaping like a fish, I crept away from the office, making sure I couldn't be seen from the windows. *Most people?* Did that include Shannon and Mariko? Had they all just been pretending this whole time? I knew that Maggie hated my guts, but everyone else had seemed friendly … how could I have misread things so badly? And how did Layla even know anything about my yelling? *Fuck.* Was I really such a shitty parent?

I walked faster, desperate to get back to my kids to prove to at least myself that I was a good mum, a loving mum, responsible, vigilant … but with every step my vision became blurrier and my heart heavier, until the events of that morning – my bloodied walls, the farmhouse, the note – seemed hazy and distant, like the rapidly fading memories of yet another bad dream.

# ALEX

## 23

I went home to do the only thing I could think of, the only thing I was any good at: pack my bags and run.

I pushed the door open to find Jenny in the kitchen with both my kids, a pot of yoghurt in one hand and a spoon in the other. Kara was in the highchair, gleefully slapping her palms on the tray and bouncing up and down in her seat; Ollie stood opposite, leaning against the stove with his arms folded. There was a dressing on his arm, and a first-aid kit stood open on the island bench. They were all laughing.

'Oh, Alex,' said Jenny when she saw me. 'Come watch this, it's the absolute cutest.' Holding a spoonful of yoghurt high over her head, she made exaggerated aeroplane noises and zoomed the spoon down to Kara's mouth. When Kara ate the yoghurt, both Jenny and Ollie shouted, 'Yay!' and clapped their hands. Kara burst into peals of adorable laughter and banged her own hands together with glee. Her smile shone a small light on my pitch-black mood.

'Oh my goodness,' I said, mustering some enthusiasm. 'I haven't seen her do that before. Well done, baby girl. Your first clap! So clever.'

'I'm not sure how much food is actually staying in her

mouth,' said Jenny, zooming the spoon again, 'but it sure is fun, isn't it, little one?' She and Ollie cheered, and Kara repeated her newly acquired party trick.

I watched, half-detached. The scene was a stark contrast to the one I'd endured early that morning, as if the universe was providing me with a helpful demonstration of what family life *should* look like. I snuck a glance at Ollie. Even he seemed different; sun-flushed and happy.

'How was the fishing?' I asked.

'Good.'

'And your arm?'

Ollie looked at the dressing on his forearm as if surprised to see it there. 'Fine. Jenny put some stuff on it.'

'Just some Betadine,' Jenny said, nodding at the open first-aid kit. 'I hope that's alright?'

'Of course.' My voice came out high and tight.

'It's a pretty bad cut. I was worried about infection.'

'Really, it's fine.'

'He says he came off his skateboard.'

'Yes, I know. I tried to clean it up myself this morning but apparently *my* first-aid skills weren't good enough.'

There was an awkward pause.

I didn't mean to sound ungrateful, I really didn't. I knew Jenny was just trying to be nice – but all I could hear was Layla's voice; all I could see was that note. And all I could think about was how long it would take me to leave Pine Ridge.

Once Jenny had gone back upstairs, I pulled down our suitcases from the top of my wardrobe, opened them up and started throwing things in. Clothes, shoes, toothpaste, books. Anything I could lay my hands on, in it went. But after twenty frenzied minutes, I stopped. Normally, packing made me happy. Usually, it gave me a sense of regained control, of freedom and possibility. But this time I just felt tired. Numb. On the bed, my floral print bag looked like an inappropriately vibrant coffin: bright pink on the outside, but with the sad remains of a life laid out inside. My body hurt, my eyes ached.

'Mum?'

I looked up to see Ollie standing in the doorway, leaning against the frame.

'I just want to say sorry. For this morning. I was out of line. I shouldn't have spoken to you like that.'

I blinked. 'Oh. Okay. That's very adult of you.'

He shrugged. 'I was being selfish.'

I hung my head, my heart cracking. 'No, *I'm* sorry. It was my fault. Everything is my fault.'

He crossed the room and I pulled him into a hug, wrapping my arms around his ever-expanding shoulders and breathing him in. Under all the deodorant and hormones, there was still a faint trace of crumpled pyjama.

I was still happily sniffing when Ollie pulled abruptly away and stared at the snarl of belongings on the bed. 'What are you doing?' he said.

'What?'

'Are you packing?'

'Um.'

'Are we leaving?'

'Well—'

'No.' He shook his head. 'Just ... no.'

I threw my hands up. 'I thought you'd be glad! You said Pine Ridge was a dump. You said the lentils would kill you.'

'Did I?'

'Yes!'

'Well, I changed my mind.'

'Really?'

'Well, not about the lentils, they're awful. But the rest of it's not too bad. The people are mostly cool, and Vi says that the school down the road is alright. She's going to ask if she can go next year.'

'School, huh?' I smiled wryly. 'Not keen for home education, then?'

'Hell no.'

'Well, I must say I'm shocked.' I looked at the half-packed bags on the bed. 'So you really want to stay?'

He shrugged. 'I don't especially want to go. And' – he blushed – 'I kind of told Vi I'd go to that solstice party with her, so ...'

There was a smudge of something on his cheek: mud or chocolate or Vegemite. Reflexively, I leaned over and rubbed it away with my thumb and he grimaced, just like he used to do when he was small. I considered his long frame, his coarse mop of hair. Time was so weird. When children are small, every single day lasts an eternity; the hours pass so slowly, it's like the clock is ticking backwards. But then one crazy day, you look up and your firstborn is closing on five foot six, has bumfluff on his chin and is going to parties with girls.

I took a breath, thinking. Ollie wanted to stay. And, before today, so had I. I'd chosen Pine Ridge because it was perfect for us, because I'd believed it was what the kids and I needed – and getting there had not been easy. I'd fought for our new life, at great personal risk, and it wasn't right that I should be bullied into giving it up. I was *done* with being manipulated. I was *done* with being pushed around.

Turning the floral suitcase upside down, I emptied the contents onto the bed.

'Okay, then,' I said, reaching up to ruffle my son's hair. 'We'll stay.'

# ALEX
## 24

A couple of days later, my phone rang during a food prep meeting in the community hall – a meeting that, following the decision I'd made, I felt I should attend in the spirit of making an effort.

I'd just settled Kara in the creche room and taken a seat in the circle when my pocket began to buzz rhythmically. I pressed my hand against it, wondering if anyone would notice if I slipped away … but when I looked up to find Kit watching me, I stayed put.

The air between us felt thick with energy, and he kept trying to catch my eye as if attempting to communicate telepathically. I kept my head bent and my gaze low, silent thoughts of cardboard boxes and packing tape mixing with memories of his breath on my neck, his hands on my skin …

Layla was there, too, sitting on the opposite side of the circle with her hands in her lap, a wan-looking Amy at her side. As far as I knew she had no idea I'd overheard her conversation with Kit at the office, but still awkwardness hung between us like a suspicious odour. I sat in my plastic chair, picking at my cuticles, my stomach feeling like a bag of smashed glass. What had happened to make her feel that way about Ollie and me?

What had she told people about us? I wanted so much not to care what others thought of me and my family. But I did, I really did.

Fortunately, the tension didn't seem to be affecting my kids. The surfy mum was running the creche room that day, and she had her hands full with babies and toddlers all making individual bids for freedom. Kara, however, was like a pig in poo. She'd seemed delighted to get rid of me, crawling to the soft play equipment the second I plonked her down and diving headfirst into the ball pit without even a backward glance. Hers was the only high-pitched screech I *couldn't* hear.

Over on the other side of the room near the kitchen, Ollie was making a gingerbread house with Violet – or, more accurately, Violet was making a gingerbread house while Ollie rolled pieces of dough into balls and flicked them across the table. They were listening to the same music, sharing earbuds, bobbing their heads to a beat only they could hear, their lips moving as they whispered the lyrics in unison. Every so often one of them would tap their foot or jab their finger repeatedly in the air, and the other would smile. I thought it was sweet – but Layla clearly disagreed. I snuck a glance and found her watching them closely, her arm wrapped protectively around Amy's narrow shoulders. It made me realise how quickly I'd decided that Layla was 'my kind of person' – but, as with Kit, I didn't really know much about her. Who was she when no one was looking, when all the doors were closed and the lights went out? What did she believe, deep beneath her skin; what stories did she tell herself? How did she interpret the world for her kids?

As the rest of the group chatted about butter beans, rhubarb crumble and potato bake, I grew more and more uncomfortable until I was second-guessing myself all over again: maybe I should've packed that bag after all.

In my pocket, my phone buzzed again. A voicemail.

I shifted impatiently in my seat, racking my brains for an excuse to leave so I could check my messages.

'So,' said Kit. 'We need someone to do a quick stocktake in the dry goods store and make a list of any ingredients we're missing. Volunteers?'

I put my hand up so fast I almost pulled a muscle.

After verifying that Kara was okay in the creche – absolutely fine, still zero interest in seeing me – I wandered over to the store, dialling into my voicemail as I went.

'Alex, hi.' A man's voice, cheerful and radio-smooth. 'Mark Oppenheimer here. Apologies for not returning your call sooner, it's been a hectic week. So, with regards to the Kellermans, I don't usually give out contact details, but given the situation I'm sure it'd be fine.'

In the spontaneously concocted message I'd left for the real-estate agent, I'd claimed to be a producer on *Who Do You Think You Are?* doing some research for an episode with the Hemsworth brothers. 'We suspect,' I'd gushed, 'that Mr Kellerman is very distantly related.' People would do anything for TV.

'Michael's a good bloke,' continued Mr Oppenheimer, 'and

his family's lived around here for generations, so I'm sure he'd love to help. And if there's anything at all we can do for the show – if you want to shoot a scene here at the office or maybe have a chat about the local area – you just let me know. I actually know a guy who went to school with Chris Hemsworth. Down in Melbourne. Might be helpful. Anyway, you can reach the Kellermans on …' He rattled off a phone number, twice. A landline, I noted, not a mobile. 'Best of luck. I'll give you a buzz later on, just to check in, see if we can do anything.'

I hung up and saved the message.

When I reached the store, I punched the code and let myself in. The yeasty smell of bulk grains enveloped me, pulling me into the cool, dry dark. Shelves reared up on either side, filled with sacks of flour, boxes of tea and jars of dried legumes.

Switching on the light, I grabbed a pen from the table behind the door and replayed Mark Oppenheimer's message, scribbling the number on my hand as I listened. Then I dialled. The phone rang once, twice, three times, four.

*Click.* A man picked up and cleared his throat. 'Yes?'

'Oh, hello. Is that Michael Kellerman?'

'Speaking.' His voice was crackly. I pictured a frail gentleman in his seventies. White hair, twinkly eyes, collared shirt under a cashmere sweater. His wife pottering around in the background making tea.

'I'm so sorry to bother you,' I said, 'but I was wondering if I might be able to speak to you about … that is, if you might have the time to …' I dried up. I hadn't thought this through; I didn't have the words to hand.

'You're not a journo, are you?' His voice had taken on a sharp edge, and I revised my mental picture. A thin man with grey stubble and turned-down mouth. A face ravaged by time, grief and paranoia.

'No, no, definitely not. I just – well, I live up at Pine Ridge, Mr Kellerman. You know the ecovillage that was built on your old farm? And I—'

'Ah, shit, what the *hell* do you want?'

I froze. The frail old gentleman had gone; the man on the other end of the line now had sunken cheeks, bad teeth and a comb-over.

'Just leave me alone, will ya?'

'But, Mr Kellerman,' I spluttered. 'I need to speak to you about your son.'

'Fuck off.' The line went dead.

I held the phone away from my ear and stared at it.

As I did, the door to the storeroom opened and someone walked in.

Maggie.

The atmosphere in the storeroom changed immediately. She froze when she saw me, her face changing from a neutral, bored expression to something active, something dynamic. Her jaw slid to one side, her nostrils flared, proverbial daggers flew from her eyes. God, she really hated me.

Unsure how to respond, I did as little as possible, and eventually Maggie pursed her lips and pushed past me to a shelf at the back, making a point of not thanking me when I pressed myself awkwardly against the flour to make room for her. She

215

slapped her hand down on a box of candles and pulled them from the shelf as if cross with them, deliberately imbuing her movements with hostility. *You're on my turf*, her body was saying. *I'm in charge here.* I rolled my eyes. Weren't we both too old for that crap?

Grabbing two more boxes of candles, she made to push past me again, but the parent in me bristled. If she wanted me to move, she would have to use her manners.

She glared at me. I glared back.

'Ex-*cuse* me,' she said at last.

'That's better,' I replied, and gave her a few inches.

We faced off again, neither of us prepared to back down. It was like a Western set in a wholefoods shop. Middle-aged *Mean Girls*.

I broke first. 'If you're trying to intimidate me,' I said, 'don't bother, because it won't work.'

'Intimidate you?' sneered Maggie. 'I have no idea what you're talking about.'

'Oh, my mistake. All this time you've been trying to make me feel *welcome*. Sorry, I must've misunderstood.'

'No,' she said, bluntly. 'You're *not* welcome.'

I opened my mouth, comeback at the ready, but then stopped. Was that what had been going on? The boxes, the symbols, even the note? Had Maggie been trying to scare me away? Was the whole village in on it? Perhaps it was how they got rid of 'undesirables': they fucked with your head so that you walked away first.

'I know what you've been doing,' I said, taking a gamble

– and just briefly, Maggie's face went slack. She looked guilty as hell, and now I had no doubt that she was hiding something.

But then she looked me right in the eyes, drew back her lips and bared her horsey teeth in what I assumed was meant to be a smile. 'You know,' she said, languidly, 'the problem with people like you is that you are so ... flat. One-dimensional, like a paper doll. You only see things one way. Whereas I' – she lifted her gaze to the roof of the store – 'I see everything. I hear everything.'

I made a face. 'O-*kaaay*. Well, maybe I see and hear more than you think I do.'

'Mmm.' Maggie shrugged and licked her lips like a kid eating an ice cream. 'Or maybe you just see what *I* want you to see.'

I thought about that. 'Um ... what?'

'Exactly.' Maggie laughed. 'You don't get it because you're not up here with me.'

I glanced at the ceiling, then down at the floor. When I looked back at Maggie, I noticed that her pupils were dilated. Her eyes were flat black dinner plates edged with gold. 'Right,' I said. 'So, is that code for "I'm really fucking high right now"?'

Maggie made a soft guttural sound in her throat, as if hacking up a fur ball. I was concerned until I realised she was laughing. Raising a hand, she unfurled a finger and waved it in front of my face. 'Open your mind, Little Red Riding Hood.'

I flinched – I thought she was about to tap me on the nose. But then she curled her hand into a fist, brought it to her lips and giggled.

'You're *diseased*,' she hissed. 'You know that? You're like a virus. You bring the world with you like shit on your shoe; I can smell it.' She inhaled sharply through her nose to demonstrate her point.

*It's not me who smells*, I thought, catching a whiff of something acrid – and oddly familiar. I went to say as much, but Maggie had already turned her back and was opening the door to leave. Sunlight rushed through the gap, momentarily blinding me.

Silently repeating my resolve – *I am done with being pushed around* – I followed, catching the door as it swung back. 'What's the matter with you?' I yelled after her. 'What happened in your life to make you such a ...'

But the words died in my mouth. All of a sudden Maggie's retreating silhouette was the very last thing on my mind.

Because someone was standing on the road outside the food store.

No, two people: one tall, one short. They were talking. The shorter person was a child: Amy. The taller person was an adult. Someone I'd never met, but whose crooked outline I knew well. Someone who stood hunched over Amy, whispering in her ear, gripping her wrist hard so she couldn't walk away. Someone with a stooped spine, wild grey hair and a pale green raincoat.

My blood went cold before my brain could process what I was looking at. A high-pitched whine started up in my ears, like the singing rim of a glass.

It was the woman in the woods.

The Pine Ridge witch.

# ALEX
## 25

The ground under my feet felt unstable, as if I were standing on the deck of a small boat.

*She's real. The witch is real.*

I took a shaky step forward. I couldn't see the witch's face, but I could see Amy's. Beneath her blunt fringe, her delicate features were pinched. She was listening intently to what the woman was saying, but her whole body was rigid, her hands clenched into fists, her eyes locked on the ground. She looked so small.

Feeling like I couldn't trust my own eyes, I blinked several times, but this time the old woman did not shimmer and disappear. I could hear her mumbling: a dry rattle, like the tumble of dead leaves.

I took another step, and another and another until I was standing close enough to hear the words.

'They come in the night,' the witch was saying. 'Listen, you'll hear them. Voices – and footsteps.' Her hair was wet, plastered to her skull as though she'd been caught in a downpour. But her raincoat – the colour of mint ice cream – was dry. It flapped in the breeze as she spoke, the lapels parting to reveal a long nightgown: blue, with little pink flowers.

'They follow the path that leads to the sky.' Her voice was raspy and urgent, as though someone had her by the neck. 'A hill of grassy green – green grass. A diamond moon, the bluest of blue skies.'

The hand clamped around Amy's wrist was skeletal. Paper-thin skin covered in liver spots. Thick discoloured nails and knuckles as gnarled as burrs on a tree.

'That's where it happened.' The witch leaned in, pressing her face right up against Amy's cheek. 'Where the birds fly. They're going north, those birds. They're going to the moon.'

My lungs, my tongue, my brain were all frozen, but somehow my body kept moving, edging closer. I reached for the woman's elbow, convinced that my hand would pass right through it … But when I touched her, she was solid. Skinny and frail, but real beyond doubt.

Very slowly, the old woman turned around.

Her face was riddled with deep lines, the skin falling over itself in tight folds, like the leaves of a Savoy cabbage. Her eyes were a milky blue, bloodshot in the corners, yellow where they should be white. They settled on me. 'You,' she croaked in her half-throttled voice. 'I know you.'

'Who the hell are you?' I said.

But the old woman didn't appear to have heard me. She was staring at a point about two inches to the right of my head, her puckered mouth hanging open.

'I said, who *are* you?'

The woman drew back her head and her chin disappeared into her neck. 'A magic trick.' Her voice was like a cheese grater against a brick wall. 'A vanishing act. Gone, just like that.'

'Amy?' I said, placing a hand gently on the girl's shoulder and looking her in the eye. 'Are you alright?'

Amy looked stunned, like she'd just emerged from a dark tunnel into bright light. 'Yes.'

'You sure?'

She nodded.

'Do you know this woman? Did she try and make you go somewhere with her?'

'Bones,' murmured the old woman. 'And a doll. Or is it a doll, then bones? I can never remember.'

I stiffened.

'Then blood.' A conversational lilt had crept into the witch's tone. 'A great wash of blood. Oh, such a shame. All over the house. All over the photograph.' She tutted and shook her head sadly. 'Things arrive, and then they take you.'

'Okay, who *is* this woman?' I turned on Amy so sharply she flinched. 'Does she live in the village? Do you know her?'

Amy said nothing, just backed away.

Spinning around, I jabbed my finger into the air just short of the old woman's chest. 'You did it, didn't you? You sent those things to me. Why?'

The woman looked innocently up at the sky.

'I've seen you,' I said. 'Why have you been creeping around outside my house?'

I paused to see if she'd respond, but she just carried on staring at the clouds.

'Did you write me a note? Did you leave it for me to

find in the farmhouse?' I watched her face closely for some kind of reaction. 'What's your name? Is it Kellerman? Renee Kellerman?'

'Oh, look,' said the woman, pointing up. 'Birds.'

A hand touched my shoulder. I turned to see Kit, talking with his phone pressed to his ear. 'Yes,' he was saying. 'It's fine, I've got her.'

*Got who?* I thought. *The witch? Or me?*

'Amy, what's going on?' said Layla, running up behind Kit. 'Are you alright?'

Other people were emerging from the greenhouses and wandering down from the meeting in the hall, staring with curiosity and concern – but not the shock I would've expected given the presence of a real-life witch. In the distance I spotted Maggie, a triumphant smirk on her face.

'We're on the road near the terrace gardens,' said Kit into the phone. 'On the corner, just opposite the food store ... No, I think she must've come through the gate this time ... Alright, no worries, I'll see you in a sec.' He hung up and turned to me. 'Alex, what's going on? We heard raised voices—'

'I don't know who this is,' I said, pointing at the old woman, 'but I've seen her hanging around the village and ... I came out of the store and saw her with Amy, and she had her hand on her like this,' I gripped Kit's wrist, hard.

I swallowed. Everyone was listening, watching, staring at me.

'So ... so, I came to see what was going on and she – the woman, I mean – was saying all this crazy stuff, and I ...'

222

Some part of me registered that I was talking too fast, but I couldn't stop; the bubble of fear had risen too high and there was no pushing it back down again.

'Look, I know it sounds insane, but there was someone in my house the other night, someone's been sending me things, and I think it might've been *her*.' I pointed again. 'And then I went up to the farmhouse, and there was a letter, and it was for me, and ...'

'Farmhouse?' Kit was frowning, his expression a mixture of pity and alarm.

Layla was staring at me as if I'd lost my mind. Bizarrely, she had her arm curled protectively around the witch's shoulders.

I pressed my fingers to my temples. *What the fuck is going on?*

Kit inhaled then let his breath out slowly. 'Alex,' he said, gently, placing a hand on the old woman's arm. 'This is Bess Hassop. She's one of our neighbours. She's not very well – are you, Bess?'

'Help,' said Bess. 'I need help.'

'That's right, you do,' said Kit, loudly. 'You like to wander, don't you? But it's alright, we'll help you. I've just called Dom, he's on his way.'

'I need help.' Bess was trembling. She was now looking a whole lot less like a witch and more like someone's grandmother: small, forlorn and in need of protection from deranged people like me.

'Alzheimer's,' Kit said to me in a low voice. 'Very severe. She doesn't know where she is half the time. Her son, Dom, he's one of the local farmers, he says it's been bad for years but the

223

wandering is relatively new. We've found her down here a few times now. She walks all the way from right over the hill.' He raised his voice again. 'Don't you, Bess?'

Bess nodded and smiled at the air in front of her.

'She's harmless, though. We just take her to the office, give her a cup of tea, call up Dom and he drives down to get her.'

'Oh god.' I covered my face. 'I'm sorry, I didn't know. I thought she was ... she said ...' I stopped. There was no explanation that would make this okay.

At the end of the path, a battered silver ute pulled up and a man got out, dressed in shorts, work boots and a paint-spattered polo shirt. Kit waved his arm in the air. The man waved back and started walking towards us.

'I *know* you,' Bess said, waving a finger at me. Her gaze was so shaky, I couldn't tell if she was looking at me or through me. Then she made a little noise, a small mournful cry, and her hands flew to her mouth. 'Sorry, sorry, sorry. No one knows where he went. No one knows. Sorry.'

'It's alright, Bess,' Kit said, kindly. 'Look, Dom's here. Let's get you home, okay?'

He put out his arm to steer Bess away, but just as he did, she spun back to me and grabbed my hand. Her grip was strong. 'There's a monster.' She pushed her face right into mine. 'Here. In the woods. A monster.'

I recoiled. Bess's breath was sour, her teeth crooked.

'I remember it all,' said Bess. 'But then ... I forget.'

'Mum?' Bess's son Dom approached and stretched out his hand as if trying to tame a dragon. He touched her gently on her shoulder. 'Mum, it's me. Come on, time to go home now.'

'Renee,' Bess said to the air in front of her. 'Where did you go?'

'Mum?'

Bess blinked. And then she stepped forward and melted into Dom's arms. He held her, patting her back. 'I'm so sorry,' he said to no one in particular.

'Don't be,' said Kit. 'No harm done.'

The weight of Dom's sadness crushed my own heart; I recognised it too sharply. I knew what it was to watch a parent disintegrate before your eyes, to have no control over their unravelling.

'Come on,' Dom said again, and Bess relented. Together, they began shuffling off down the path, back to the car.

'I'll give you a hand.' Kit looked back at me. 'Can we talk later, Alex? I'll come see you?'

Feeling too much like I was yet again being hauled into the principal's office, I didn't reply.

Layla reached out for her daughter. 'Amy, come with me please.' Without another word, she turned away from me like I was a stranger in the street, one handing out lollies from the back of a transit van.

Amy seemed reluctant to follow. She threw me a sorrowful glance and I seized the opportunity. 'I'm sorry, Amy,' I said. 'If I scared you. I made a mistake, a big one.'

Amy's gaze bounced away and landed at her feet. 'Ollie,' she said, so quietly I almost missed it. 'He's been bad, hasn't he?'

'What?' I felt my chest tighten. 'What do you mean?

'If you're bad,' Amy whispered, her eyes still on the ground, 'the monsters will get you. You have to be good, or they'll come and take you away.'

On the road behind her, just out of earshot, Layla had turned back and was glaring at me.

'No,' I shook my head. 'That's not true.'

'It *is* true,' Amy insisted, her voice rising. 'Bess told me, she *saw* them. She says that things arrive, and then they take you.'

'I know. But Bess is old. She's confused. There's absolutely nothing to be afraid of.'

'Promise?'

'I promise.'

'*Amy*,' called Layla again. 'Come *on*, please.'

Amy gave me a small nod. Her smile was as empty as mine.

# RENEE
## 26

For twenty-four hours, nothing happened. No one did anything.

'This happens all the time, Mrs Kellerman,' said the officer on the other end of the phone. 'These kids, they run away, and then they come back, and everything is fine again. I'm sure he'll walk in the door at any minute. Either that or you'll get a phone call from a parent at school, or a relative, to say that he's with them.'

Renee shook her head over and over again. She knew in her gut that wouldn't happen. She knew the way that only a mother knows that he would not walk back through the door that day, or any other day.

And she was right.

The day after the disappearance, lots of things happened at once. Police, phone calls, notepads, questions. People tramping through the house, a search continuing by torchlight.

April and Frank, their faces white, their eyes huge like the moon, *What happened, where is he?* Farm employees, the pickers, the morning team, everyone making suggestions: *Have you checked …? Might he be …? Maybe he went …?* Dom and Bess Hassop, sad heads on rubber necks, craning and peering around the door – *What can we do to help?* – their mouths falling open

227

in shock as Renee finally cracked.

'Get out,' she screamed, 'get out of this house!'

*There's something coming for me, isn't there?*

She hadn't listened. She hadn't believed him. And now he was gone.

She screamed and screamed until she had no voice left, until the people around her stopped staring and chattering and trying to solve the unsolvable, until everyone disappeared, backing away cautiously with their hands in the air, nodding insipidly as if to say, *Give her time, she'll calm down.* But Renee knew that no amount of time would erase anything, this was just who she was now. This was *all* she was.

Gradually.

Little by little.

Everyone faded away.

Until finally.

Renee was left alone.

# ALEX

## 27

After hiding my humiliation at home for a couple of days, on the day of the summer solstice party, I drove to the coast. Too afraid to let Ollie out of my sight, I pleaded with him to come along for the ride, but he point-blank refused. With Jenny once again ready and willing to look after both kids ('I do *not* need looking after,' Ollie yelled and stomped off into his room), I slipped away at lunchtime on my own.

The witch, I now knew, was not real. The mysterious grey-haired figure was just a sick old lady who kept getting lost. She'd got confused and repeated one too many scary stories to the village kids, who had taken the idea and run with it. I also knew, however, that there must be an element of truth in those stories. A boy had disappeared six years earlier. And someone had left me a message in that farmhouse.

I was haunted by that note. I was also haunted by the look Kit had given me as he'd walked poor Bess Hassop and her son back to their car, as well as the faces of the residents who'd witnessed the scene on the road with Bess. My behaviour had vindicated both Maggie's and Layla's opinions of me, and that stung.

After giving it some thought, I'd decided on two things. One – if my kids and I were going to stay at Pine Ridge, I had to be 100 per cent sure that nothing bad was going to happen to us. I had to find out who had left me that note and who was sending the packages. Until I knew the truth of those things, I wouldn't feel safe. And two – I had to prove my sanity. I was *not* crazy, and I needed everyone to know.

So, using the phone number that Mark Oppenheimer had given me, I looked up the Kellermans' home address and, as it turned out, they hadn't moved far. Just forty-five minutes' drive from Pine Ridge, right on the coast. There was a big shopping centre ten minutes from where they lived; I needed to pick up some last-minute Christmas gifts anyway, and if I just *happened* to be in the area, it made sense to drop by. Michael Kellerman's phone manner had been far from encouraging, but it wouldn't hurt to do a quick drive-by and scope the place out.

The drive to number twelve Bundeenah Close turned out to be more like an hour and ten, but only because I got stuck behind a tractor on the winding road to the coast. I drummed my fingers impatiently on the steering wheel, glaring intently at the gigantic tyres as if I could make them move faster with the power of my mind, but the tractor turned off just before I reached the highway and it was smooth sailing all the way to the comparatively bustling suburbs of the Central Coast.

Passing a sign for Newcastle, I felt a tug of nostalgia. The first time I'd driven up this way I'd been a backpacker, fresh off the plane in denim cut-offs and a halter top, dirty feet propped on the dash of a battered campervan. I'd laughed at the irony of that sign. *Look*, I'd said to my boyfriend at the time. *We're on the other side of the world and we're still going to bloody Newcastle!* The

Sydney skyline had been first impressive then disorientating – huge skyscrapers next to pure blue waterways; little green ferries sliding past the great white sails of the Opera House – but we found comfort in places like Kensington, Waterloo and Hyde Park. *Might as well still be in London*, we said. It had been surreal to find that, after flying thousands of miles across the globe, things really weren't much different than they were at home, just a hell of a lot hotter. It was strange to think how much had changed since then, as if that part of my life had all been a dream.

I turned off the highway and drove along wide roads strung with roundabouts like a beaded necklace. I passed schools, churches, small businesses with sun-faded signs, and about a thousand tradie trucks on their way to the next job. Popping up among the clusters of fibro fisherman's cottages were Instagram-ready coffee shops, organic yoga studios and brand-new houses copied straight from *The Block*, all sure signs of a once-sleepy area in a state of rapid growth. The vibe was laid-back but orderly, pretty but bland. I could see why it might appeal to someone who'd suffered a great tragedy; it was the perfect blank slate.

Bundeenah Close was a quiet cul-de-sac positioned just two blocks from the beach. I pulled up outside but kept the engine running, peering out of the window, delaying the moment I had to leave the air conditioning and step out into the soupy summer heat. Number twelve was right at the end: almost-but-not-quite beachfront. It had high fences, neat hedges and a sign on the mailbox that said *No Junk*. The house itself, from what little I could see of it over the top of the gate, was a neat brick square with a grey tiled roof and a paved driveway at the side. The bushy crown of a tall tree rose from the front yard, its brilliant green leaves dripping over the fence like water.

I switched off the engine and got out. The sun had a bite to it, but the briny ocean breeze had me breathing in deep and wishing for a beer. Gingerly, I approached the house, opening the white picket gate and closing it carefully behind me. A curvy red-brick path took me to a set of three wooden steps and a front door with a mottled glass panel. I knocked and waited.

Soon enough, I heard footsteps. A fleshy shape appeared behind the glass. The door opened, and I found myself looking at neither a twinkly-eyed gentleman nor a crooked-toothed husk. Instead, Michael Kellerman was an ordinary-looking man in a plain grey T-shirt and beige walk shorts. He was tall and broad with rough skin and closely cropped hair that might have once been blond. I guessed he'd been quite the brick shithouse back in the day, but rounded shoulders and a weary, apologetic stoop made him appear to have slowly deflated, like a cushion that over time had lost its stuffing.

He squinted at me. 'Yes?'

'Hi,' I said, aware that I was not quite projecting the warmth I'd intended. My shoulders had shot up around my ears, and for some reason I was clasping my hands like an orphan requesting more gruel. 'I hope I'm not catching you at a bad time, I'm just—'

'Are ya selling something?' Michael Kellerman's accent was pure rural Australia: thick and languorous, like he was chewing toffee.

'No. I'm actually here because we, uh, we spoke on the—'

'Ah, shit. Are you that chick who called yesterday? The journo?'

'No – well, yes, but I'm not a journalist. I just want to talk.'

There was movement from within the house, a shuffle and soft bang, like the lid of a pedal-bin swinging shut, and Kellerman shot a glance over his shoulder.

'I got your note,' I said, taking a punt that the message in the farmhouse had come from him.

He swung back to me with his lip curled. 'What? What note?'

'The note in the—'

'Look, love, I don't know what your go is, but I need you to leave.' He went to shut the door.

'Mr Kellerman, we don't know each other,' I said, pushing back, 'and I don't want to make you feel uncomfortable, but—'

'Uncomfortable? Jesus fucken Christ.' He passed a hand over his face. There was another muffled clang from inside. Michael glanced back again. 'Listen, you'd better leave or I'm calling the cops.'

'Do you think that maybe—'

'Nup.'

'—your wife might like to—'

'Sorry, love.'

'—because if she's home, then—'

The door shut in my face, and Michael Kellerman went back to being a kaleidoscopic shape behind panes of glass, disintegrating as he disappeared back into the depths of the house.

'Mr Kellerman, please.' I stood on the step for a moment, biting my lip. Then I stepped closer to the door and raised my voice. 'Mrs Kellerman? Renee? Can you hear me?' I knew she was in there; I could hear her moving around. 'Renee?'

I waited to see if any shape would return, but the house remained still.

I placed my hand on the door. The stained glass felt holy, like a confessional. 'Look,' I called, rallying the last of my courage. 'I understand that neither of you want to drag up the past. I get it. If I were in your shoes, I wouldn't want to either. But here's the thing: in a way, I kind of *am* in your shoes. Like I said yesterday, I just moved to Pine Ridge, to the ecovillage that was built on your land. I have a fourteen-year-old son, Oliver. Some odd things have been happening, things that I think only you would understand, and I was hoping you could help me make sense of them.'

No sound; no movement. Michael Kellerman wasn't coming back. I imagined him somewhere on the other side, listening patiently, hearing my sins.

'Someone has been sending us packages. And then I found out that … that you and your wife might once have received similar things? Before your son went missing?'

I paused, trying to grasp the meaning of my words, but it felt like holding a bar of soap; my understanding of events kept slipping out of my own hands. I didn't know how to explain the sense of dread that, despite all my rationalisation, was pressing against me from all sides, as oppressive as the summer heat.

'I just … I just want to know what happened. Because maybe

the same thing is happening to us, and I …' My insides were sliding around like eels in mud. *Ollie.* My home in human form. If he disappeared, I would crumble like dust. I would cease to exist. 'I can't lose my son, Mr Kellerman. Please help me.'

I waited but there was no sign of either Kellerman.

I gave up. I'd tried my best, and I needed to get back to my kids.

'Listen,' I said. 'I don't know if you can still hear me, but I'm going to leave you my details and maybe you can … Hang on a sec …'

Running to the car, I grabbed a pen and a crumpled paper bag that had sat in the passenger footwell for weeks. Smoothing the creases out as best I could, I scribbled my name and phone number on the bag. Then I folded it up with the note I'd found in the farmhouse and pushed both under the door.

'That's my number,' I shouted through the glass. 'And that's the note I mentioned. I'd love to speak to you, if only for a few minutes. I promise, I'm not a journalist. I'm a parent. Just like you.'

I waited, chewing on a hangnail. A car slid by on the road behind me. Somewhere nearby, a dog barked.

'Okay. I'll go. Sorry to have bothered you. Merry Christmas.'

I walked back to my car. Got in, cranked the air con, started the engine.

But right before I drove away, I thought I saw movement behind one of the windows. A flash of pale skin and the twitch of a blind.

# ALEX
## 28

I drove home impatiently with one eye on my phone and my earbuds connected, hoping against hope that I might hear from the Kellermans – but my phone just rattled lifelessly in the cupholder next to me, the screen frustratingly blank.

Turning off the freeway, I got back on the road that led up into the hills and put my foot down. My panic-bought haul jangled on the back seat as I hurtled around the bends and bounced over the potholes, the hollow ring of plastic packaging inspiring nothing but buyer's remorse. I'd gone way over the top, trying desperately to compensate for the last few months by purchasing half the products in a little tech store I'd found, which I knew would both please Ollie and ultimately lead to more fights.

Just before I hit the Pine Ridge turn, I spotted a small sign I hadn't noticed before. *Hassop Farm*, it said, *Next Right*.

I checked the time. It was getting late, and I needed to relieve Jenny of her babysitting duties – but ten more minutes probably wouldn't hurt.

I braked sharply and indicated right.

I found myself on a small lane edged with white reflective posts and dried brown leaves. Silver gums reached up on either side, their trunks leaning at an angle like pedestrians waiting to cross the road. A little way down was a driveway and another smaller sign. I slowed to take a look. The sign was wooden, with hand-carved lettering that read: *Hassop & Son – Pecans and Citrus since 1952.*

I turned onto a gravel track that ran through an open gap in a wooden fence. Beyond the fence were countless rows of trees stretching into the distance, towering over lush emerald grass and filtering the sunlight to a fine dusting of gold. The shade beneath them looked cool and fresh.

The track ran the full length of the orchard, stretching out in front of my car like the yellow brick road. I followed it as it curved around to the left and finished up in front of a hotchpotch of a house, a jumble of angles and levels and extensions. On closer inspection, I could see the original structure in the centre, an older brick building, had been overwhelmed by add-ons: screened-in porches, half-finished decks, precarious-looking balconies, chimneys and several sets of sliding glass doors. The effect was that of a ramshackle ranch that had looked great in the designer's head but which, like an overcooked cake, hadn't come out all that well.

Approaching the front door, I hoped that my second house call of the day would be a more pleasant experience than the first. I pressed a small yellowing button next to the doorframe and heard a chiming sound from inside the house. No ensuing footsteps, though; the house was quiet and still. I sidled up to one of the windows and pressed my face to the glass, cupping my hands around my eyes to block the stream of sunlight coming from above …

'Can I help you?' said a voice.

I jumped about a foot in the air and spun around, clutching my chest. The man standing behind me was wearing khaki shorts, a grubby polo shirt and gardening gloves, and I immediately recognised him as Bess's son, the guy who'd come to collect her from Pine Ridge the other day. He raised his eyebrows at me, in a look that said both *Hello* and *What the hell are you doing on my property?*

Still breathing hard, I gave him my very best smile. 'Hello. So sorry to bother you, my name's Alex. We met the other day, just briefly, down at Pine Ridge? When your mother was there?'

'Oh. Okay, sure. Dom Hassop. Great to meet you.' He pulled off one of his gardening gloves and offered his hand. His palm was rough and callused, but his grip was gentle.

'I was just passing by,' I said, 'and thought I'd stop in to check on Bess. You know, after ...' *After I thought she was a witch and yelled at her in public.* I tried not to wince. 'How's she doing?'

'Well, that's kind of you,' said Dom. 'You know, I was so sceptical about Pine Ridge when it first went up – all us locals were. But I've honestly never met such big-hearted people. You've all been so understanding, and so patient with Mum. It means a lot.'

He gave me a smile that didn't quite reach his sad eyes, and I noticed that under the layers of melancholy, Dom Hassop was a good-looking guy. He was a little shorter than average, with thick salt-and-pepper hair and light blue eyes. His sharp stubbled jaw and deeply etched frown lines were softened by dimples, an almost button nose and an easygoing manner that suggested he'd once been fun to be around. He had one of those faces that was both young and old, where you could see both the boy and the man. Kind of like Rob Lowe, but without the waxy Hollywood sheen.

'So she's alright?' I asked.

'Oh, yeah. I mean, she's always a bit dazed after she wanders, but other than that she seems fine.'

'That's good,' I said, when what I really wanted to say was, *I'm sorry.*

'It's confusing for her,' Dom continued. 'She often doesn't know where she is or what she's doing – like sleepwalking, I guess? And then when she comes home she's exhausted. It's a big old walk and she's no spring chook.'

I nodded. 'It's amazing she makes it all the way without hurting herself. How old is she?'

'Almost seventy-seven.'

That surprised me. I'd had her pegged as older.

'Which isn't actually that old,' said Dom, catching my expression. 'Not these days. But, you know, the body follows the mind.' He wiped his glove across his forehead then reached down into the grass and picked up a bottle of water from among lengths of timber. I noticed a toolbox, as well as an electric drill.

'You're working,' I said. 'Sorry, I can come back another time.'

'Nah, it's nothing major, just replacing a few fence posts. I was about to take a break actually. You drink tea?'

'Sure,' I said. 'Tea would be great.'

Dom led the way into the house, through the front door

239

and into a modest hallway with a bulging coat rack. It was dark inside but cosy, with a small sitting room to the right and a galley kitchen to the left. Straight ahead was a staircase that led to the first floor.

'Sorry about the mess,' he said, heading into the kitchen and flicking on the kettle. 'Between Mum and the farm, I don't always have time to clean up. I've just hired a part-time carer to start in the new year, though. It's a bit of a stretch financially but I think we've reached a point where we need it.'

I wondered if by 'we' he meant him and Bess, or perhaps him and a partner? He was definitely giving off a single vibe – not sleazy, just in the way that you know someone is on their own. The house showed no signs of a woman's touch, either. No dainty shoes or handbags left lying around, no flowers or scatter cushions. The decor was quirky and outdated – olive carpet, pastel paintwork, cracked leather sofas and lots of dark wood panelling – and the walls were mostly bare. There were pictures running up the stairs, but instead of family snapshots and wedding portraits, the frames displayed somewhat unsophisticated charcoal drawings of owls and geese in flight, suggesting nothing but the possibility that Dom enjoyed sketching in his spare time.

I followed Dom into the lino-and-formica kitchen. 'It must be tough on you,' I said. 'Doing everything on your own, I mean.'

'It can be.' He took a couple of mugs from one of the cupboards, then unscrewed the lid of a jar and picked out two teabags. 'My brother used to help out a bit before he moved up to Byron, but he doesn't get down here much anymore.' The kettle boiled and he poured hot water into the mugs. 'Milk? Sugar?'

'A little milk, please. No sugar.'

Dom made the tea and handed me a cup. 'Let's go back outside,' he said. 'It's too nice a day to stay in here.'

We went out through a different door at the far end of the kitchen, a sliding screen panel that led to a patio and barbecue area.

'Mum never used to be this bad,' Dom said, taking a seat at a trestle picnic table and gesturing for me to do the same. 'She used to be happy with a movie and some snacks and the odd stroll around the orchard. But then about a year ago she started getting restless, agitated. I'd come back and find her room empty and the front door wide open. I'd mostly find her on the farm somewhere, which seemed fine. If that's what she needed to feel independent, great. But then I started getting calls from you lot at Pine Ridge to let me know that she'd made her way over the hill ... which is, you know, not so fine.'

I sipped my tea, thinking about Bess's hand clamped around Amy's skinny wrist.

'I feel like I should lock the doors, but I don't want to be a jailer.' A sunbeam danced across Dom's face and he squinted, sending a spray of lines from the corner of his eyes out towards his temple. 'And if she can't get out, she gets even more upset, throws a tantrum. She's becoming more and more like a child as she gets older; sometimes she's just like a little girl.'

The pain on his face was hard to look at. I thought of my

own mother, how perfectly healthy she was right now, but how one day she might be struck with something similar. What would I do then? Would I finally go home? Could I care for my parents the way Dom Hassop cared for Bess? My mum, maybe. Not my father. Never him.

'You have a beautiful place here,' I said, quickly changing the subject, eager to move the conversation on. 'The orchard is spectacular.'

Dom threw a glance at the jade green of the trees behind him. 'Thanks,' he said. 'It used to be all oranges, but my grandfather planted pecans back in the seventies when the market started to shift. Now, it's mostly pecans but we still have a few good fruit trees down the back. Lemons and limes, too.' He chuckled and shook his head. 'Sorry, that's a lot of boring information you really didn't ask for.'

'No,' I said, smiling at his blush. 'It's not boring at all. I'm interested. So you've been here a while, then?'

'Yeah, it's a family business. Most of the farms round here are. I grew up here.'

I took another sip of tea and looked towards the edges of the property. I could just make out a few buildings in the distance: a couple of sheds and a large storage barn. It would've been a quiet childhood. 'I can see why the ecovillage was such a big change for you all.'

Dom laughed. 'Bloody oath. All those trucks and diggers. And, jeez, the noise. Some of the locals thought the world was ending.'

'I bet.' I hesitated, wondering whether or not I should ask.

'Did you know the previous owners?' I blurted before I could change my mind. 'The Kellermans?'

'Mike and Renee? Yeah, our families used to be pretty close. Our dads were good mates, before they passed. Cancer, both of them.'

'Oh, I'm sorry.'

'No, it's fine. Just life.' He gave me a lopsided smile, boyish and sweet. 'We all used to hang out a little, back in the day. Len Kellerman was a good bloke. Like a mentor to me, in some ways. He taught me a lot about the land. Mike and I never really got along, though.'

'Oh, really?' Michael Kellerman's jowly grey face swam into my mind; his voice rang in my ear. *Fuck off.* Yeah, that tracked. Not the kind of dude I could imagine anyone getting along with.

'Nothing dramatic,' Dom said, 'we just didn't really click. Did *you* know them?'

For a split second, I considered lying. Maybe if I fabricated a story about how I was an old friend trying to reconnect, Dom might share more of what he knew. But then I shook my head. I'd just tie myself in knots. 'No, I just moved here. I don't really know anyone. I just heard a little about what happened. I guess I'm curious.'

Dom let out his breath in a single laugh: *Ha.* 'I don't blame you. *I'm* curious, and I knew 'em.'

'So, what's the full story?'

Dom hesitated and tilted his head to one side. 'I'm not gonna end up in the papers, am I?'

I laughed. 'No, definitely not. Sorry, I'm being nosy, you don't have to answer.'

'Nah, it's okay, I'm happy to chat. Good excuse to stop work for a bit. I don't get much company up here, so …' He tapered off and rolled his eyes gently as if to say, *What a loser.* 'And there's no denying it's a strange story. Everyone round here still talks about it. It never made much sense at the time, and still doesn't. To be perfectly honest, I think that's why Mum keeps going down to Pine Ridge.'

'What do you mean?'

'Well, I think that's what she's doing. Trying to go back in time, to make sense of it.'

He paused as a russet-coloured butterfly fluttered between us, interrupting our shared line of vision. I put out my hand to see if it might hop on, but it flew away, eager to get on with its short life.

'See, Gabe was like family to her,' Dom continued. 'I mean, I liked him, he was a good kid, but Mum was really fond of him. She used to babysit him when he was little. Renee would drop him here during the day so she and Mike could both work. Mum was lonely after Dad passed, and I've always worked heaps myself, so for a few years Gabe filled the gap.' Dom gave a small mirthless laugh. 'The two of them made a pretty funny double act, actually, always chatting away. But then Mum got sick, started getting forgetful, and her temper … she became erratic, unpredictable. We stopped going over there, and they stopped coming to us, and we all just lost touch. It's a shame, but the drought was hard, and we were all busy.'

'And Gabriel? What was he like?'

Dom's face settled into a sorrowful expression. 'Ah, he was a good kid. Bit shy, bit geeky, but nice. Always on his computer – I mean, *always*. Mike gave him shit for that, but I reckon the poor kid was just misunderstood.'

He paused, and I saw how upsetting it still was for him to talk about – and he hadn't even been family, not strictly. He took a gulp of tea and swallowed thickly. 'Mum took Gabe's disappearance real hard. It sort of shattered her. And her mind was already Swiss cheese at the time, so now she can only remember little bits of it. That's what I mean by her trying to make sense of it. All the things she says … I think it really torments her.'

'So no one ever found out where Gabe went? He never turned up?'

Dom shook his head.

'What do *you* think happened?'

He sighed, blowing his breath out through loose lips. 'Oh, look, who knows? Police dropped the case, said he'd run away. Everything seemed to point that way.'

'But I heard that …'

'What?'

'Well, I think I read somewhere that the Kellermans had reported intruders shortly before? And something about their cat?'

'Yeah.' Dom took another sip of tea. 'There was definitely something going on. I have no idea what, but we went round there this one time for Gabe's birthday – that was the last time we ever saw him, actually – and someone had thrown red paint all over the house. Place looked like an abattoir.'

'And the cat?'

'Someone killed her. Left the body in a box on the porch.'

'A box?'

'Swear to god. Mum still talks about it all the time. Like I said, I think it's her way of trying to piece her fragmented memory together. To solve the mystery.'

'Like Miss Marple.'

Dom smiled sadly. 'Ah, that's a nice way to think of it.' He paused and put down his mug. 'One thing I do know is that Gabe Kellerman was scared shitless. Of what, I don't know, but I could see it in his eyes: that boy was terrified of something. Sometimes I think that maybe there was something going on in that house.'

'What do you mean?'

'Oh, look, I know I shouldn't be casting aspersions, but the cops never looked too carefully at the family. I mean, Renee was a real nice lady, but her parents were batshit, and Mike had this mean streak …' Dom stopped as if something was caught in his throat. He shook his head. 'Sorry. I've got no proof, it's just a feeling.' Sighing, he rubbed an eye with his index finger. 'Anyway, we'll probably never know. I *prefer* to believe that Gabe's still around somewhere. Maybe living it up in LA or chilling on a beach in Bali. You'd hope so, anyway.'

We both fell quiet. Over Dom's shoulder, I caught movement in the orchard. A flap of pale green material between the trees and a flick of grey hair. *The witch.* I smiled ruefully and pointed.

'I think Bess is up and about again.'

Dom turned around and followed my gaze. 'Oh, Christ.' He turned back and got to his feet. 'Sorry, I'd better go. It was nice of you to drop by – I'd invite you to come and chat with Bess herself but I'm not sure what mood she's in, and it might be better if ...'

'No, I totally understand, I have to go, too. The kids will be wondering where I am.'

'Oh, you have kids? What age?'

'Fourteen and eight months.'

'Got your hands full then, hey?'

I smiled and shrugged. 'They're not so bad.'

'I have two myself,' he said. 'Twin girls, twelve years old. They live with their mum but my world still revolves around them, you know?'

I nodded, the atmosphere inside the house suddenly making a lot more sense. I stood and passed him my empty mug. 'Thanks for the tea.'

'No, thank *you*.' Dom smiled and offered his hand. 'It was great to meet you, Alex. Really great.'

'Lovely to meet you, too.' I took his hand. 'Sorry to have distracted you from your work.'

'Don't be,' he said, maintaining eye contact for just a little longer than I would have considered normal. 'Feel free to distract me any time.'

'Oh,' I said, a little caught off guard. 'Okay. Maybe I will.' *Definitely single.* I turned away before my face got any redder.

# RENEE

## 29

The images came thick and fast. A precipice. A cliff's edge and a sheer drop. A cave. A tiny pothole under tonnes of rock.

'Eat.' April stood over Renee with a plate of cheese and crackers. 'Ren, please, you have to keep your strength up.'

Panic was a blindfold, a dirty bandage. A heart in a box buried deep in the ground.

'Renee.'

*Three days.* Gabriel had been missing for three days and no one could find him. There were no clues, no note, no explanation. No fingerprints, no broken glass, no signs of forced entry. Just a cold breeze and an empty room. He'd vanished into thin, wintery air.

On the couch, Renee twitched, startled by movement outside the window. A flash of grey. She waited but saw nothing else.

'Renee.'

Obediently, Renee reached out and took a cracker from the plate. She held it in her palm, then placed it in her mouth and chewed. It was dry and bland.

Outside, the sky was full of clouds, each one the colour of nothing. Inside, the same absence pervaded the house: all sound was muffled, all light was flat. Renee's home smelled not as it should've done, of coffee and cooking and furniture polish, but of stagnant air and unwashed skin. The whole world had lost its flavour.

Something moved again, outside, that flash of grey on the veranda. Renee turned in her seat. There was someone out there. But then, people were everywhere. For hours, Police officers had wandered in and out of the house, taking notes, talking into radios, asking the same questions they'd asked the day before and the day before that. She'd watched their faces, their expressions of resignation, the shuffle of their feet and the slump of their shoulders. She'd watched them gather the information – the lock on the door, the open window, the doctor's report, the prescription drugs, the depressed and anxious teen who had shut himself away in his room and hurt himself – and saw the verdict in their tired eyes. *A runaway. A suicide.*

She'd watched until she couldn't watch any longer. And then she'd pulled her blanket up around her shoulders and stared blankly at the floor. Second by second, minute by minute, she let the day pass around her like a stream around a rock.

'Eat.' April said again, but Renee shook her head.

Over by the back door, Michael was deep in conversation with a male officer. His arms were folded, his legs spread, and his hefty brows were knitted together in a deep frown of concentration. He nodded slowly and thoughtfully with his gaze locked firmly in the middle distance. It was an action hero's stance, a projection of calm and cooperation. But Renee could see it for what it really was. A veil. A pretence. A tightly sewn costume. To the cops, he was a capable man dealing admirably with a dreadful situation. But Renee saw his bloodshot and shadow-ringed eyes, his hollow cheeks and trembling nostrils. She saw the way his clothes hung awkwardly from his increasingly thin frame. Inside those clothes, Renee knew, deep under his sun-scarred skin, her husband was beside himself with anguish.

A part of her, the part that remembered the people they used to be, longed to go to him and stand beside him in her own costume; lean on him, weep, let him comfort her. She knew he wanted to play the stoic, the rock of the family, because that's what his father had taught him to be. Impenetrable. Impermeable. A real man. Len Kellerman's son. *That's right, officer, I have this all under control.*

Michael's mother had died when he was very young, so he'd been raised almost solely by his father, who'd belonged firmly to the 'boys don't cry' school of thought. He'd called Michael a 'sissy' and 'weak'. He'd taught his son to toughen up, play sports, eat meat, drink beer, farm the land. He'd given him 'survival skills'. What to do in the wilderness, in a fight, in a war. He'd talked constantly about 'bugging out', 'marauders' and 'level three situations'; how they would escape in the event of a total societal breakdown or a nuclear attack. But he'd never taught Michael how to cope with an emotional crisis. So now that this abyss had opened up, Michael was at a loss.

Unfortunately, he was on his own. Renee could barely breathe, let alone comfort anyone else. She sat there, fuzzy and numb, while a different officer, a woman with kind eyes and soft brown hair, repeated a string of questions. Yes, Renee nodded, her lips barely moving, Gabriel's school bag was missing. His sketchbook and some pencils. Yes, some of his clothes had gone, too. Food from the pantry. And she couldn't find her credit card, although she might've lost that. No, she wasn't in the habit of losing her bank cards. Yes, Gabe's bedroom door had been locked, as had the front door, and she'd secured the latch on the window. The latter was old though, and needed replacing. Why hadn't she put a bolt on that, too? *Stupid, stupid.*

The kind-eyed officer made a note. Renee knew what the evidence suggested. She just couldn't believe it.

Renee caught the flash of movement for a third time. Silver hair, white skin. Bess Hassop, circling the house, trying to help. *Go home, Bess*, she thought. *There's nothing you can do. What's done is done.*

A rumble of thunder from outside announced the return of the rain.

*Drip, drip, drip.*

There were more questions, all of which had been asked before. No real answers. The police were still searching the area. Yes, they'd checked the hospitals, the bus stations, the airport. Yes, they were asking questions at the school. Yes, they were looking through Gabriel's computer, laptop and phone. Yes, they'd let her know as soon as they found anything.

Renee reached out with her mind, believing with all her might that somewhere her son's skin, hair, freckles, nails and teeth all still existed. Somewhere, they still filled a space. She closed her eyes and willed herself to see, to feel, to know where exactly in the world that space was.

''Scuse me, Mrs Kellerman,' said the officer, 'but there's an elderly lady in a nightgown walking around in the rain outside.

Do you happen to know her?'

Renee nodded slowly. 'That's my neighbour,' she said. 'Ask my husband to call her son. And give her my raincoat, would you? The green one by the front door. She'll catch her death out there.'

When the detectives left, the silence returned. April, of course, decided it was her job to fill it. 'Come to church with us tomorrow,' she said, handing Renee a cup of tea. 'I think it would help.'

In the armchair opposite, Frank chewed a biscuit while Michael sipped a whisky by the window. Ebony lay at his feet, her head on her paws.

April patted her daughter's hand. 'Fine, then,' she said. 'Let's pray together. Right now. As a family.'

Renee felt rather than saw Michael stiffen. She turned in his direction but couldn't bring herself to lift her gaze. She realised that the two of them barely looked at each other anymore. Renee had learned how to skirt her vision around him, like steering a lawnmower around a tree stump.

'Count me out,' Michael said.

'Please, Michael,' April said, as though speaking to a small child. 'I think we all need it.'

Michael pushed himself off the wall and drained his glass. 'What *I* need is more alcohol.'

'I'm sure you do.' Frank's voice cut through the quiet. 'But your wife and son. What do *they* need?'

Michael turned to face him, his expression strangely still. Beside her, Renee could sense her mother backing off, conceding the stage.

'Peter, chapter five, verse eight,' said Frank from the armchair, his hands clasped loosely in his lap. 'Stay alert and of sober mind. Watch out for your great enemy, the devil. He prowls around like a roaring lion, looking for someone to devour.'

Michael's face grew dark. 'Frank—'

'Ephesians, chapter four, verse twenty-six. In your anger, do not sin.'

'I'm warning you—'

'And do not give the devil his foothold.'

'That's *enough!*' In a movement that seemed both uncontrolled and wholly deliberate, Michael sprang forward and hurled his whisky tumbler to the floor.

Renee and her parents followed the trajectory of the glass, expecting an explosion of glittering shards – but it merely bounced off the shag pile rug with a dull thunk. They all stared, first at the unbroken glass and then at Michael.

'This is my house,' Michael said, raising a single finger. 'And I won't have you speaking that way here. You can't terrorise *me*.'

'Oh, Michael, don't be so dramatic,' said April. 'No one's terrorising anyone.'

'The problem is *not* ...' Michael faltered, then started again. 'The reason ...'

And then, to Renee's shock, Michael began to weep. He hung his head and made small animal-like noises. He put a hand on the wall and folded over as if he was about to vomit. Renee shut her eyes, unable to watch.

Nobody moved.

Moving slowly, as if he'd been punched, Michael straightened up and lumbered from the room. Without opening her eyes, Renee listened to his footsteps as they shuffled down the hallway. She heard the clink of the car keys, the squeak of the front door. A few seconds later, the car started in the driveway. Four tyres crunched over gravel. And then he was gone.

Renee collapsed. With no other option left, she surrendered to her parents' hands on her back, around her shoulders, stroking her hair.

'I tried,' she managed between sobs. 'I tried so hard.'

'Shhhh,' said April. 'We all tried. We did everything we could to save him. But sometimes, evil just wins.'

Just as she had done so many times as a child, Renee cried into her mother's lap. She curled up, broke down and let her father pray to his heart's content, because the world was imploding and it all just hurt so much – and because for the past three days, everything had stopped. No more strange discoveries on the porch, no more footsteps. The prank calls, the trolling, even the rustling in the trees, suddenly it was all over, and Renee couldn't help but think that her parents might be right. That whoever, or whatever, had been creeping around in the woods had finally got what they'd been after.

# ALEX

## 30

When I arrived back at Pine Ridge, there was a buzz in the air. The gateposts had been decorated with yellow balloons and twin floral wreaths, and a handmade sign read *Happy Solstice!* Rows of white festival flags flapped on both sides of the main road, bunting had been strung between the trees, and a faint strum of guitar music lolled in the air.

I drove back to my unit slowly, the simmering disquiet in my gut contrasting with the happy hum of party preparation. After speaking to both Michael Kellerman and Dom Hassop, I still had no real answers – just more questions. Dom's words rolled around in my head like marbles. *Sometimes I think that maybe there was something going on in that house.* I kept thinking of Michael's thunderous face, the dull thumps and shuffling noises I'd heard, and the twitching curtains I'd seen as I drove away. If I'd been able to hear Mrs Kellerman moving around inside, then surely she would've been able to hear me talking about her son. So why hadn't she come to the door? *Gabe Kellerman was scared shitless.* But of what exactly?

As I passed the community hall, a figure dashed into the road and I had to brake sharply to avoid a collision.

'Alex, hi,' cried Mariko, hurrying in front of my car with

a bundle of colourful silky material in her arms. 'Sorry, can't stop!'

Paul and Simon followed, carrying a large trestle table between them. 'See you in there!' Simon said. 'Don't be late!'

At least three more people leaped into my path before I made it back to my parking spot, all carrying drink dispensers, paper plates, folding chairs and an array of musical instruments. What was the big rush? I wondered. But when I checked the time, it was almost 6pm. *Shit.* I'd told Jenny I'd be home by five.

As I got out of the car and began dragging my shopping bags from the back seat, I saw Kit standing a little way up the road, talking to a neighbour. Our eyes met before I could stop them, and my heart flipped like a Fortune Teller Fish. Ducking my head, I tried to pretend I hadn't seen him – but when I next looked up, there he was, standing right next to me with an uncertain smile on his face. 'Alex,' he said. 'Hi.'

I abandoned the bags and immediately forgot what to do with my hands. 'Hello.'

Kit appeared to have the same problem. He jammed his fingers into his pockets like a kid in the schoolyard. I felt split in two: one half of me felt nothing but mistrust, and the other half wanted to touch him so bad my hands started shaking.

'Can I help you with your …' Kit peered into my bags. 'Oh, wow. That's enough Christmas to last you the whole year.'

I eyed the bags despairingly. 'I know, I went a bit overboard.'

'Here, let me.' Kit grabbed the bags while I pulled the enormous fake tree off the back seat. Wrapping my arms around the box, I stood up and held it in front of me like a shield.

There was an awkward pause.

'I like the last-minute approach,' Kit said. 'Some people put their trees up in November. I hate that.'

'Oh, well, you know.' I tried and failed to think of a witty response. 'Better late than never.'

'Do you mean the decorations? Or me?'

I peered around the edge of the box and found Kit's eyes searching for mine.

'I know I should've come to talk to you days ago,' he said, 'but the right time never seemed to, uh, present itself. Either you were busy, or I was busy, or there were other people around. And, like, right now you have that giant tree in front of your face, so …'

I held on to the box. I wanted to come out from behind the tree; I also wanted to stay behind it. I wasn't ready to discuss what had happened between us, or the conversation I'd overheard with Layla, or the thing with Bess Hassop. I didn't want to tell him any of my own private insanity or hear him say what I knew he would: that he hadn't yet found a collaborative match for me, and that ultimately it might be best if I left Pine Ridge. And I really, *really* didn't want to ask him any questions about packing materials or digital footprints, for fear of what the answers might be. Unfortunately, the conversation seemed to be happening whether I liked it or not.

I put the tree box down on the ground. 'I'm sorry,' I said. 'It's me, I've been avoiding you and I shouldn't have. I know we've got a lot to talk about, but what happened with us' – I glanced up at my unit to check for eavesdropping children – 'it all happened a bit fast, and I didn't know how to handle it. And then there's been all this other stuff going on that I wanted to tell you about, but...' I trailed off and shrugged.

'You can tell me anything,' he said.

I studied him. 'Can I, though?'

A pause opened up between us, a great chasm of unvoiced thoughts, and I thought what a tragedy it was that we were all stuck inside our own skulls, that we could never truly know what anyone else was thinking or feeling. The loneliness of being human, the futility of trying to connect with anyone at all.

'Okay, look,' Kit said suddenly, still holding my reusable shopping bags like a hotel porter. 'I'm just going to say this quickly and then it's all out there and you can do what you like with the information. I really, *really* like you. So much that I don't know what to do with myself. I can't stop thinking about you and I have no idea why. No, sorry, I *do* know why, that's not what I ... oh god, I'm so shit at this stuff.'

Goosebumps erupted all over my skin in a way that was both wonderful and horrible. I wanted him to say more things like that, but I also needed him to stop. It wasn't what he was saying so much as the delivery: with a slightly performative edge, almost as if he was trying to replicate a scene from a movie.

'From the moment I met you,' he said, 'I've had this weird feeling that I know you, that maybe we'd met before or something? I know that sounds like a line, but it's true.'

I wanted to believe him, but instead of looking at me, he was frowning and squinting at the floor like he was concentrating on an especially tricky maths problem.

'It drove me crazy for the longest time. But I think there's just something in you that connects very deeply with something in me, like we're on the same frequency or … I can't explain it, it's just *there*. But I've never felt that with anyone else before, and I just … I just think it should be said, because if you feel—'

'Oh, look,' called Jenny from somewhere behind me. 'There's Mummy!'

I turned to find her at the top of the steps, waving and pointing with my daughter on her hip. When Kara saw me, her little face lit up, and her smile sent a chemical ripple through my heart: goosebumps of a different kind. *Oh, my girl.* My face smiled all by itself. 'Hi, baby!' I waved back and blew her a kiss. 'Mummy's home!' I'd missed her so much. I would never leave her again, not ever.

Kara's gummy grin faltered. Her chin wobbled. Then she screwed up her eyes, opened her mouth and screamed blue murder.

*Okay, maybe not never.*

I turned back to Kit. 'Sorry, I can't do this now.'

'Alex, wait—'

'I have to go.'

'Just listen—'

'Kit, stop.' I wanted so much to hear the rest of what he had to say, and I wanted every word of it to be true, but what if it wasn't? I couldn't drag my family into yet another mess. 'Please. It's just too hard.'

Kit looked away. He put my bags down and let out a slow

breath. 'It doesn't have to be,' he said, gently. 'You know that, right?'

I hesitated, studying his face, trying to read him … and then Kara screamed so loudly that we both flinched.

Shaking my head, I picked up the Christmas tree again. 'I'm sorry,' I said. 'I think it's best if we just don't.'

I trudged up the steps and returned to my kids.

'I don't understand,' said Jenny once we were back inside the unit. 'She's been good as gold all afternoon. No tears, not even a whinge.'

'Oh, she likes to save it all up for me, don't you, darling?' I bounced Kara up and down, stroked her head, tried to get her to cuddle into me, but she stiffened and bucked away from me. 'Has she had much to eat?'

'Some avocado and cottage cheese, and one of those big packets of puree. She had a whole bottle of milk right before her nap, too. And I've just changed her.'

'Perfect, thank you. She probably won't want this, then, but I'll give it a try.' I draped the cloth over my shoulder and pulled down my top, trying to encourage Kara to latch on, but she arched away and carried on screaming. 'Oh, love, come on.' I stood up again and patted her on the back. 'What's the matter, huh?' Eventually, I managed to quieten her down with a silicone spatula from the kitchen. *Teething can go fuck itself*, I thought as I watched Kara chomp miserably on the end. 'Has Ollie been okay?'

Jenny's face twitched. 'Um …'

I froze. 'Oh god, what did he do?'

'No, it's nothing he did. He's been perfectly pleasant. Lovely manners, your boy.'

I grimaced; sarcasm, surely.

'But …' Jenny's eyes drifted to Ollie's bedroom door.

'Did something happen?'

'Yes.' Jenny nodded. 'I think it's safe to say that something has definitely happened.'


'Ollie?' I tapped lightly on his door. Kara writhed in my arms, apparently confused about whether she wanted to be held or put down. 'Ollie, can I come in?'

No answer.

Jenny stood silently behind me, her brows knotted with concern.

I knocked again, then pushed the door open. Ollie was slouched at the pillow end of his bed, a miserable expression on his face. At the other end, Violet sat in a tight ball, head down with both knees pulled to her chest. She glanced up when I walked in, regarding me briefly with red-rimmed eyes before dropping her head again. Her blue hair spilled over her arms like water.

'Hey, you two,' I said warily. 'What's going on?'

Neither replied.

Jenny edged into the room behind me and stood in the corner with her arms folded.

'Violet? Does your mum know you're here?'

Violet made a little hiccuping sound and wiped her nose on the sleeve of her shirt.

Hitching Kara up on my hip, I picked my way over to the bed, trying to step on as few clothes or snack wrappers as possible. Kara squirmed again, pushing against my chest. 'Aren't you guys going to the party?'

'No,' Ollie snarled.

'Why not?'

'We're just not.'

'Go on, Oliver,' said Jenny, giving him an encouraging nod. 'Tell her what you told me.'

My gaze landed on each of them in turn. 'Okay,' I said. 'Seriously, what's happening?'

After a long pause, Jenny sighed. 'Someone has been leaving things at Violet's house. Sort of like gifts, but not very pleasant.'

My whole body went cold. 'What?'

'She found a dead possum in a box on her bed. And then a Barbie doll was left at the door. It had blue hair and was, um, mutilated in some way. I think there was a threatening note, too.'

'And Vi's mum thinks *I* did it,' Ollie said, his voice quavering. 'She think I'm some kind of psycho.'

'Layla has forbidden the two of them from seeing one another.'

'But it wasn't me, I swear it wasn't.' Ollie's face was flushed with indignation.

'Violet?' My pulse throbbed in my temples. 'Is that true?'

Violet lifted her head from her knees and nodded. Without her cool glasses and black eyeliner, she looked extremely young. 'Mum says Ollie's a bad influence. She thinks he's going to hurt me, but she's wrong.'

'She hates me,' said Ollie, turning his face away. 'Everyone does. It's just like school all over again.'

'No, honey, no one hates you.' I plopped Kara down on the floor and pushed my fingertips into the corners of my eyes. My heart ached; my head felt too full. 'This is all just a … stupid misunderstanding. Someone's idea of a joke.'

'A joke?' Violet glared at me. 'Are *you* laughing, then? Did you think it was funny when *you* got boxes?'

I went still.

'You've had them too, haven't you? Ollie told me.'

'That's what they were, right, Mum?' Ollie said. 'Those boxes you had in the kitchen the other day?'

I looked down at the floor. Kara looked up at me expectantly as if to say, *Well?* I could feel Jenny watching me too, waiting for an explanation, but I didn't know what to say or where to begin.

'You know the story, don't you?' whispered Violet. 'The witch? The one who takes kids? First the bones, then the doll, then the blood. Things arrive, and then she takes you.'

'Well, yes, but it's not—'

'She's coming, isn't she? Or *they*, the monsters or whatever the hell is in that forest. Something is coming for us. For me and Ollie. Just like it came for the kid on the farm.'

'No, Violet, there is no witch,' I said, clinging to the one solid fact I had. 'It's just a stupid story.'

'It's *not* stupid!' Violet let out a growl of frustration. 'Why doesn't anyone believe us?'

'I believe you,' said Jenny from the corner.

I turned sharply to look at her. 'What?'

'Well, I don't *not* believe them,' she said to me, spreading her hands. 'The rumours, the games the kids play – I've always wondered if there might be some truth in them. I've seen things, too; I've heard noises, things I can't explain. And, listening to these kids tonight, I can't help but think they might be right.' Her face was pinched, her eyes wide. 'What if there *is* something out there?'

I gaped at her. I wanted to admit the things *I'd* seen, the thoughts *I'd* had. But I couldn't, not in front of the kids. 'You're being ridiculous,' I managed, eventually.

'No, you're being ridiculous,' said Ollie, suddenly sitting up straight and glaring daggers at me. 'At least Jenny's listening. She's literally the only adult who ever listens, *ever*!'

I laughed; I couldn't help it. The whole conversation was ludicrous.

In one sharp movement, Violet jumped off the bed. 'It's not funny,' she said. 'It's all real, I *know* it is.' Then she pushed past me, flung open the door and ran from the room.

'Violet, wait,' I called, but she was too fast.

The door slammed. Our house seemed to hold its breath.

And then, back in the bedroom, Ollie wrapped both arms around his head and started to cry.

'Oh, love.' I went to him and, sitting on the edge of the bed, leaned across to give him a hug.

'Don't.' He jerked away from me. 'This is all *your* fault. I hate you.'

I felt like I'd been punched. 'Ollie—'

'Everywhere we go, it's fucking shit. Something always goes wrong. You said it would be different here, but it's not. It's worse than anywhere.'

I reached out again but Ollie slapped my hand away. My heart felt like it was clamped between the jaws of a vice and the handle was turning, turning, turning ...

'The only thing that made it okay was *her*,' he said, 'and now I'm not allowed to see her anymore and I just feel like ... I just feel ...'

I wiped my own eyes. It was all too much. 'What, Ollie? What do you feel?'

He looked at me with round, frightened eyes. 'I feel scared, Mum. Like something really bad is going to happen.'

Then he turned onto his side and hid his face in his pillow.


'Can I do anything to help?' said Jenny once we were back in the living room and Kara was secured in her highchair. 'Do you want me to stay?'

Suppressing a surge of irritation – *Oh, I think you've done enough* – I breathed in and out, trying to calm myself down. I shook my head. 'I can handle it.'

'Are you sure?' There was a tremor in Jenny's voice. 'I don't mean to be rude, but from what I've heard – and I've heard a *lot*; the walls are paper thin and I'm only upstairs – I'm not sure you're doing such a great job of protecting your children.'

I blinked. 'Excuse me?'

Jenny glanced down at Kara. 'I'm sorry, but I just don't see them getting the care they need right now.'

My eyes narrowed and I could feel my jaw working. 'Okay, wait a second. No offence, Jenny, but I'm not about to take parenting advice from someone who isn't even a parent, who doesn't know a thing about me or my kids.'

'I know enough,' she said, baulking at my tone. 'In fact, I think I've got to know your kids pretty well lately. And if they were mine, there's absolutely nothing I wouldn't do for them.'

'But they're *not* yours, are they?' I could feel the fury bubbling, all my pent-up anger towards every person who'd ever thought they knew better than me: all the men who thought parenting was easy, all the strangers who'd touched my pregnant belly in the supermarket, all the smug old ladies on public transport who'd informed me from a polite distance that my baby was cold, or tired, or hungry. 'They're *mine*. And I think I know what's right for them.'

Jenny swallowed. '*I* think,' she said quietly, 'that you need to listen to your children. I think you need to take them seriously. And I think you need to protect them. At any cost.'

I almost lost my righteous shit. Protect them? Take them seriously? I did literally nothing else! But as my neighbour, possibly the only friend I had left at Pine Ridge, chewed her nails and stared fearfully out of the window, the wind dropped right out of my sails.

'Because what if Ollie is right?' Jenny whispered, her tremulous words echoing my own thoughts. 'What if something bad *is* going to happen?'

# ALEX
## 31

'Put your shoes on, Ollie, let's go.'

'I'm not coming.'

'Well, after the fuss you've just made, I'm not leaving you alone, so you don't have a choice. Come on, let's go and sort this out.'

I dragged Ollie out of his room, tucked Kara into her pram and stepped into the steamy evening air, double-locking the door behind me. Jenny followed wordlessly as if we'd agreed she would now be babysitting all three of us.

Too tired to argue, I stalked ahead, wheeling the pram down the steps and along the road towards the community hall. The thought of Layla running around the solstice party telling lies about both me and Ollie was too much. I had to confront her and put things right, but I also needed to hear the truth about Violet's packages. Whoever was playing this insane game, I was going to find them. *Fuck with me all you want*, I thought, *but don't you dare fuck with my kids.*

The noise from the party increased as I got closer. Laughter, music and a steady babble of conversation spilled from the open doors of the community hall. There was a sizzling barbecue, a dance floor and strings of vibrant flowers, and along the shore of the dam each tree had been connected to the next by a line of paper lanterns. The hall itself was so thoroughly draped with leaves and lights it was impossible to tell inside from out, and a large banner had been hung across the back. Curiously, the word emblazoned across the banner was *Saturnalia*.

There were people everywhere – the entire village had turned up – and despite the fading light it was still hot. Already sweating, I pushed my way through the throng, steering my pram around deckchairs and small children, ignoring the laughter and the raised plastic cups. 'Alex!' someone cried. 'Have some summer fruit punch!'

'Come on, Ollie,' I said, reaching back to pull him along behind me. 'Keep up.'

Jenny sped up too, sticking to us like glue.

I scanned the party. Mariko was over by the barbecue, Paul was placing a bowl of salad on a long buffet table full of food, Simon was organising a photo booth with dress-up costumes. I could see the surfy mum, the Icelandic scientist, the retirees … but no Kit. And no Layla. I couldn't see Amy or Violet either. So, not the entire village, then.

In the pram, Kara gazed up at the twinkly lights, her little eyes full of dancing stars and wild adventure. I pulled the hood down and hoped beyond all hope that she might fall asleep.

'Alex,' said Shannon, appearing in front of me, a huge tray of paper party bags in her hands. 'I thought you weren't coming tonight.' She gave Ollie an uneasy smile, and he fidgeted behind me, looking as if he wanted nothing more than to die on the spot.

Jenny peered at us from over his shoulder, her face even paler than usual.

'Have you seen Layla?' I said.

'Sorry?' She leaned forward, her sequined green kaftan throwing off light like a disco ball.

'Is Layla here?' I raised my voice to be heard over the music. 'I need to speak to her.'

'Um, no.' Shannon shifted the tray awkwardly in her hands. 'She didn't come. Look, if it's okay with you I'd rather not get stuck in the middle of—'

'Sorry, Shan, I need to sort this out. It's not fair on the kids. Is she at home?'

'Yes. With Amy. But—'

'Great, thanks. Come on, Ollie.' I wheeled the pram around and pushed my way through the dance floor, heading back towards the road.

'Alex, wait.' Shannon hurried after me, still carrying the tray. 'I wouldn't just call in for a visit, not right now. Might be best to wait until she calms down. She's pretty angry.'

'Angry about what? Ollie hasn't done anything wrong, and neither have I. She's jumping to conclusions.'

Shannon looked cowed, like a kicked puppy.

Sighing, I slowed to a stop. 'Sorry. Not your fault.'

Over Shannon's shoulder, I saw that Ollie had not followed me this time. He hung back near the dance floor with Jenny, who'd placed her arm protectively around his shoulder. They both looked small, bewildered and afraid.

I pinched the bridge of my nose. *What am I doing?* 'Look,

Shan, can you please do me a favour and just explain to me what Layla thinks is going on? Just so I'm not going in there completely unprepared?'

Shannon shifted the tray again and the little paper party bags rustled softly. 'Okay, fine. But don't tell her I told you; I really don't want to get involved.' She looked over her shoulder, then leaned closer to me. 'She said Ollie was expelled from Ellenhurst High and that he was involved in the file-sharing scandal, with the pictures of the year nine girls. The one that was in the news. Is that true?'

I hesitated. 'Sort of. Suspended, though, not expelled. And he didn't take any pictures, he just had the link. Lots of kids had it, it was passed round the whole school, but Ollie was one of the few who were caught with it on their phone.'

Shannon raised an eyebrow. 'Right. Well, she also said he's some kind of dark-web YouTuber?'

I bit my lip, mortified at the thought that Layla or anyone else had watched those videos. 'That's also sort of true, but not nearly as bad as it sounds. How did she find them?'

'Facebook.'

I nodded. *Of course.*

'She said he's been harassing Violet, bringing stuff to the house and creeping them all out. I'm so sorry to be the one to tell you this, Alex, but he may have killed a possum.'

I shook my head firmly. 'Shan, it wasn't him. The same thing has been happening to us, too. I think—'

A guy next to me stumbled and bumped my shoulder, sloshing liquid all over my T-shirt. 'Oops, sorry, love,' the guy said. 'Happy solstice!'

'Listen,' said Shannon, ploughing into the pause. 'I'm sure Ollie is a good kid. I'm sure he's just going through a phase. But we're strict on online activity here for exactly these reasons. We don't want our teenagers getting mixed up with that stuff. And Layla is particularly sensitive because of what Amy went through.'

I frowned, remembering what I'd heard Layla say in Kit's office. *Amy's issues aside* ... 'Why, what *did* Amy go through?'

'You don't know?' Shannon looked stricken. 'Oh, well, it's not really my place to say.'

'Shan, come *on*.'

'Okay, but don't repeat it, because Layla doesn't want it getting around, for Amy's sake. The poor girl had a bad experience at school last year. She was walking home from band rehearsal and some older boys followed her onto the beach. She stopped to talk to them and ...' She sighed. 'The little shits assaulted her. Turned out it was part of a dares list; you know, do drugs, shave your head, have sex with someone younger, that kind of thing. Dickheads.'

'Oh my god.' I thought about Amy's skinny arms, her tiny frame. 'That's ... awful. She's so *young*.'

'Exactly. Brutal. That's why they left Sydney and came here.'

Little Amy. My heart ached just thinking about what those boys must have done to her. Suddenly her introversion, her shyness, her clinginess, Layla's smother-mothering, it all clicked into place. I gripped the handle of the pram a little harder. *If anyone ever did anything like that to my little girl, I'd ...*

My eyes fell on the tray of party bags in Shannon's hands. Something was poking out from inside one of them.

'Shannon ...' I reached out to touch one of them. 'What are these?'

'Oh.' Shannon rolled her eyes. 'These are Maggie's gifts. They're super creepy if you ask me, but what do I know. She told me to hand them out so that's what I'm doing.'

I picked one up and looked inside. I saw twigs, bound by gauze and ribbon. A head fashioned from candlewax. I snatched up another bag. And another. And another. They all contained stick dolls, exactly like the ones I'd found on my doorstep.

I plucked one of the dolls from its bag and turned it over in my hand. 'What *are* they?'

Shannon shrugged. 'Presents. Party favours, one for everyone here. Maggie does something every year; this time it's dolls, because that's apparently in keeping with the traditions of Satur ... Satay ...' She squinted over her shoulder at the banner on the back wall of the hall. 'Sa-turn-alia,' she read slowly.

'What the fuck does that mean?'

'No idea,' said Shannon. 'I think it's some kind of pagan festival? Ancient Roman, maybe? I seem to remember Maggie describing it as Christmas before the Christians got hold of it? I don't know.'

'And Maggie made all of these?' I brandished the doll.

'Yeah, she—'

'I fucking *knew* it. Where is she?'

'What?'

I wheeled around, looking for that short crop of hair, those horsey teeth. 'Where's Maggie?'

'I don't know but … Alex, what are you doing?'

Ignoring Shannon, I turned the pram around and strode away, searching the edges of the party. I remembered the collaborative living list in Kit's office, all the names and numbers and personal information displayed on the wall for anyone to see. Maggie would've had absolutely no problem finding out who I was and where I'd come from; she would've known about Ellenhurst and Ollie's YouTubing before we'd even arrived.

*You're like a virus. You bring the world with you like shit on your shoe.*

Bitch. Where the hell was she?

# RENEE

## 32

Renee stood at the bathroom mirror again, staring blankly at the image held in its frame. It was like looking at a portal to a parallel universe: a glimpse of a place where everything was the same, yet very different.

Across the hallway, Gabriel's room was exactly as he'd left it four weeks earlier. Or, rather, as the police had left it. Clothes lay in piles on the floor. Bedsheets had been stripped back and dumped in a heap at the foot of his bed. A thin layer of dust covered every surface. It was like something in a museum.

So, too, was her reflection. A stiff portrait: *Woman Holding Toothbrush.* An artist's poor impression of something that had once lived.

Renee didn't bother to inspect her appearance; her face had changed so much that it no longer felt like her own. Her skin was pallid and wrinkled, like the surface of hot milk left to cool, and her forehead had grown bold, springing forward as her hair withdrew and fell out in clumps. Her eyes were hollow, her cheekbones sharp, and her teeth felt too big for her jaw. *Hello,* she felt like saying to the spectral hag in the glass. *Just hold still while I clean those for you.*

She ran the brush around the inside of her mouth, then

leaned over and spat into the sink. When she stood up, Michael was standing behind her.

At first, he said nothing, just watched her with an unreadable expression on his face. Perhaps he, too, was wondering about the woman in the mirror, who she was and where she'd come from.

'Ren,' he said. 'We need to talk.'

It was strange, Renee thought, that while she was ageing at a rapid pace, the reverse seemed to be happening for her husband. Over the last few weeks his skin had lost its dried, flaky texture and become smooth again. His eyes were bright, and his paunch had gone. She couldn't understand it. Grief had decimated her but somehow looked good on him.

If they were still speaking, they might have talked about it. If they were still sleeping in the same bed, they might have discussed their feelings at night. If their relationship had not completely broken down within days of Gabriel's disappearance, they might each have had some insight into the other's suffering. But they had been pushed away from each other like repelling magnets: Michael to the farm, Renee to the house.

Fortunately for Michael, work was a distraction, an activity in which to get lost. But for Renee, the house was now a purposeless void. Unless April came to help, the laundry went unwashed, the carpets unvacuumed. The same minutes and hours still made up the day, but Renee had no idea where they went. She'd spent the last few weeks sitting, staring, weeping, waiting.

The police had concluded that Gabe's disappearance was not suspicious. They'd found evidence on his computer that he'd been depressed and scared. He'd been active in certain chat rooms and forums, he'd said hateful things about his family, other people, the world. His search history turned up research on religious mortification, solitary confinement and personality disorders. Doctors said his medication could have had adverse side effects.

He ran away, the detectives said. He was probably living on the streets somewhere.

But Renee's intuition was telling her something different.

Sometimes she'd walk through the forest at night, stumbling through the trees and calling for him. Sometimes she'd black out and whole days would pass without her noticing. She was rarely alone, though; visitors knocked constantly at the door. Bess Hassop, mostly. Bess was losing her mind, but she wasn't bad company. At least she listened.

April and Frank came over, too, often with members of their church. They would bring food, cook, clean the house, sit with her and pray. When they left, Renee would go to bed.

In the evenings, Michael would come home with Ebony in tow. Always the same sounds in the same sequence: the hum of the microwave, the clink of the whisky bottle, the soft *tack-tack-tack* of paws on the floor. The rustle of bedsheets being spread over the couch. Paul McCartney, playing a bittersweet tune. And then the lights would go out and the house would fall still.

'We need to talk,' Michael said again.

Renee blinked and reached for a towel. Wiping her face, she turned away from the mirror but found her reflection again in the bathroom window, that same spectral hag lurking like a ghost. She looked through the ghost and out onto the farm. It was dark outside: a small slice of moon illuminating the outline of sheds and greenhouses, shipwreck-vague in the distance.

'I sold the farm,' Michael said.

Renee inclined her head. Whatever she'd been expecting, it wasn't that.

'We're downsizing. Moving closer to the coast.'

Renee opened her mouth, then shut it again. When she'd married him, she'd known that the farm would be their life. Michael had been adamant; it'd been in the family for generations. So they took it on, and he'd worked hard, much harder than he ought to have done in her opinion. From time to time, Renee had suggested moving on, changing things up. 'We could buy an RV,' she'd said. 'Travel around Australia, see where the wind takes us.' But he'd always refused: 'Real men don't shirk their responsibilities,' he would say, and she'd known that the spirit of Len Kellerman had spoken.

Renee looked back through the window, at the dark farm, the bordering trees and all that lay beyond. 'When?' she said, not knowing whether she was asking when they were moving, or when he had sold.

'A little over a month ago,' said Michael, choosing the latter.

'But that would've been ...'

'The day of the disappearance.' Michael nodded. 'I got the call that morning. I tried to tell you – but then ...' He looked at the floor. 'With everything that happened, it didn't seem important.'

A dim memory – of Michael walking into the house,

opening the door and smiling. *I have some news.*

'It's a good opportunity, Ren. The buyers offered way above what the farm is worth. I didn't feel I could say no.'

*Buyers.* Renee looked at the taps, the bathtub and the shower, and tried to imagine someone else using them, someone else's reflection in the mirror.

The land had been bought by a cooperative, Michael explained. The entire property, all two hundred acres of it, was to be rezoned and turned into an ecovillage. The development had already secured government support and funding from the local council. And there was no rush to leave; the buyers had agreed to lease the house back to them for as long as it took for them to find a new home.

'I'm sorry I didn't tell you sooner. You were in such a state; I figured I'd just take care of it.' He had his eye on a nice little two-bedroom place by the ocean, he said. They would retire, take long walks on the beach, plant a garden. They would have space and freedom. Ebony would love it. 'We could even get that RV you always dreamed about. Do the grey nomad thing one day.'

But all Renee could think was: *four weeks.* It had only been four annihilating weeks since their son had disappeared.

'No,' she heard herself say. 'What if he comes back?'

Michael pressed his palms together and brought them to his lips. 'Ren ...'

'He won't know where we've gone.'

'Renee. He's not coming back.'

'What if he was taken? What if he's being held captive, what

279

if he escapes? He'll come straight back here, I know he will.'

Michael sighed. 'We won't go far,' he said. 'Just to the coast. It's fifty kilometres at the most.'

Renee shook her head, imagining an older version of Gabriel, exhausted and traumatised after an arduous getaway, or contrite and homesick after living on the streets, or maybe plump and healthy after 'finding himself' on a beach in Thailand, arriving back at the farm with a suitcase in his hand to find that his parents had not missed him, they had not waited, they had moved on.

'No,' she said.

'Ren, we have to. The farm … there are too many problems. It's time to go.'

Renee narrowed her eyes and went for the jugular. 'Is that what a *real man* would do? What would your father think?'

Michael went still. His arms hung limply at his sides. 'Ren, I'm sorry,' he said. 'The deal is signed. The farm is sold. We don't have a choice.'

But as Renee looked out the window at the woods, she knew he was wrong. She could still choose. Because, somewhere, her son was still out there. And so was the devil.

# ALEX

## 33

'Alex! Alex!'

Shannon was still chasing after me, but I could barely hear her over the sound of high-pitched screaming. All through the hall, children were being rounded up by their parents and taken home. *Noooo*, I heard one of them cry. *I wanna staaaaaay.* The parents crooned and bribed, threatened and promised. *It's getting late, sweetheart. Fine, one last lolly and then bed. Okay, that's it, no treats for you for the rest of the week.*

There was a ringing in my ears. *Rrriiiiing.*

'Maggie?' I yelled.

The ringing got louder.

'Maggie!'

I couldn't see her, she wasn't there. Layla wasn't there, Kit wasn't there, what the hell was going on? I couldn't think. I kept on going, pushing the pram, searching and yelling while small heads bobbed through the crowd, running, dancing, hiding.

*Rrriiiiiiiiiiiiinng.*

'*Alex.*'

I turned around. Shannon had caught up with me and was staring at me with genuine concern. 'Alex, what's got into you?'

I didn't know how to respond. 'I … need to find Maggie.'

*Rrriiiiiiiiiiinng.* 'What the *hell* is that sound?'

Shannon looked like she'd just watched my brain seep out of my ears, grow legs and walk away. 'Honey, it's your phone. Someone's calling you.'

'What?' Startled, I pressed my hand to my thigh where the pocket of my shorts was vibrating. 'Oh.' Turning my back on Shannon, I pulled out my phone and pressed it to my ear. 'Hello?'

'Alex Ives?' said a gruff voice. 'This is Michael Kellerman. Is now a good time?'

'Michael?' He sounded different. Much less harsh. Subdued. Soft, even.

'Sounds like you're busy,' he said. 'I can call back.'

'No, it's fine, I can talk. Just give me two seconds ...'

Leaving Shannon on the grass, I steered the pram away from the noise of the party and strode towards the quiet of the dam. Behind me, cheers rang out as someone turned the music up.

Stopping next to the water, I bent down to check under the hood and found Kara fast asleep with her mouth wide open and her favourite toy bunny wedged under her chin. I watched my daughter's chest, waiting for movement ... and there it was, a slight rise and an even slighter fall. Gentle, like a wish. I pulled the muslin cloth over her legs and brought the phone back to my ear.

'I'm so glad you called, Mr Kellerman, I—'

'You've had packages?' Michael's speech was slurred.

'Yes.'

'And the note?'

'I found it in the farmhouse. It was addressed to me. I thought maybe you—'

He said something but there was another loud surge from the party and I couldn't quite hear him.

'Sorry, say that again?'

I pressed the phone closer to my ear and blocked the other with my finger. I could hear music playing on the other end, a tinny guitar riff and a warm folksy voice.

'Mr Kellerman, hello?'

He made a sound, a sort of wet grunt. The clink of ice cubes hitting glass. A slurp and a swallow.

'Mr Kellerman, what does the note mean?'

'It means that she ...' He broke off and made a gulping noise like a fish out of water. 'She's ...' The next sound Michael Kellerman made was unmistakable. He was crying.

'Michael, do you think I could speak to your wife?' I said gently. 'Renee? Is she there?'

'Of course she's not here,' he snapped. 'Of *course* she isn't.'

In the background on his end, there was a muffled bang and what sounded like the scrape of a chair leg. Then the line went completely quiet, and I thought for a moment that he'd hung up.

'Hello?' I said. 'Are you still there?'

Michael cleared his throat. 'You got money, Alex?' The gruffness was back, that hard, wild edge.

My heart almost stopped. 'Sorry?'

'Money. Do you have it? Do you need it?'

I thought immediately about the Tupperware container. 'I ... I don't understand.'

'Never mind. Listen, whatever's happening to you, it's not what happened to me and Ren. Can't be.' He took two big wheezy breaths. 'And I'll tell you why. Because what happened to us … to Gabriel … was my fault. It was all my fault.'

Another great cheer erupted from the hall at my back. I ignored it, focusing instead on the violin-slide of Michael's voice. In the background, I could hear little bangs, a rattle of crockery. Then a series of metallic clicks and the sound of a door creaking. 'Go on, girl,' said Michael, softly. 'Out you go.' And then a dog barked. Once. Twice. Three times.

A dog. That's what I'd heard as I stood on his doorstep; that's what the noises had been. Not Mrs Kellerman. Just a dog.

'My fault,' he said again. 'She never knew, I never told her.'

'Michael?' Despite the warmth in the air, I felt cold. If Renee Kellerman wasn't there with her husband, then where was she?

'You'll tell her, won't you? Because I can't. You have to do it.'

With a strange feeling churning in my gut, I turned around and looked back towards the hall.

'Will you? Please, I need you to talk to her.'

Food sizzled on the grill; bodies shuffled on the dance floor. I could see Shannon in their midst with her tray, handing out stick dolls, still throwing looks my way. I saw Mariko standing with the Melburnian architect under a tree, a drink in her hand. Paul and Simon in novelty glasses, taking selfies with the feather-draped retirees. And Kit, standing just inside the bifold doors, his eyes scanning the crowd.

*Ollie.*

I couldn't see Ollie.

Or Jenny. I'd left them both near the dance floor, but they weren't there anymore.

'Michael,' I said, taking a step back towards the party. 'Where is your wife? Where is Renee?'

'What are you talking about?' Michael was back to harsh and hostile. 'She's there, isn't she? With you. At Pine Ridge.' He sighed, and the phone line popped with static. 'She never left.'

# RENEE
## 34

Renee waited under a cartoon-blue sky with her arms folded, squinting into abrasively bright sunshine while Michael packed the last of his bags into the car. A breeze blew noisily through the jacaranda tree, and then, not content with bothering the newly erupted flowers, swept down low to muss Renee's hair, or what was left of it.

She brushed the tendrils from her face, but they got caught in her fingers and came away from her head like cobwebs. The wind took them, bearing each strand away like a seed, and she ran her palms over her head, feeling the soft patch at the top where the hair was thinnest. Stress-related hair loss, her doctor had told her, was quite common after an emotionally traumatic event; even more so when coupled with menopause. *It's just temporary, the hair usually grows back.* But so far the clumps just kept on coming; the drain was always blocked, her hairbrush always full.

She shivered and rubbed her bare arms; spring had just about tipped over into summer but the heat was yet to arrive. In front of her, the car was waiting with its engine running: windows down, radio on. The sound of finger-picked guitar floated from the speakers, followed by a wistful, tremulous voice. Paul, of course. Always Paul. The song was one of Michael's favourites;

he said it was about hope. But privately Renee disagreed. It was about a broken spirit. How apt that this should be the last song they would listen to as a couple.

Shoving the boot of the car shut, Michael whistled, and Ebony came running, bounding out of the long grass at the back of the house and barrelling straight into the car without a backward glance. Michael shut the door and the dog stuck her head out of the window, her pink tongue hanging out from between her teeth. Renee waved. 'Bye, Ebs. Stay safe.'

There was a pause, a held breath of a moment during which neither husband nor wife knew what to say. The gap was filled with the distant clank and rumble of diggers. Renee glanced down towards the bottom of the hill where work on the ecovillage had already begun. The land was on its way to being unrecognisable – at some point, the farm would disappear. But for her, it would still be home.

'Are you sure about this?' said Michael for the hundredth time, his thumbs tucked into the pockets of his jeans.

Renee nodded.

'Will you be okay?'

She nodded again. 'Mine will be one of the first completed houses,' she said. 'I'll stay with my parents until it's ready. I'm told it won't take long.'

'That's not what I meant.'

'I know.' She tried to smile, but the sight of Michael was too painful. She looked at the trees instead, their branches alive with movement. She watched the clouds, racing to be first over the horizon.

287

'Come with me,' she heard him say.

She swallowed, her eyes still on the sky. 'I'll be fine. I have to stay. He might come back.' That was the main reason, but there was another. *We've been broken for such a long time. We don't belong to each other anymore.*

The music from the speakers wrapped itself around them like a ribbon, trying to bind them together. Soft guitar slides, minor chords and that haunting woodwind solo. Doleful words about a girl called Jenny, whose voice was taken by a broken heart, whose home was destroyed by poverty. Jenny Wren, who cast love aside and lost sight of life.

Michael stepped forward and reached out. His thick fingers brushed Renee's cheek.

*But the day will come*, Paul sang, *Jenny Wren will sing, when this broken world mends its foolish ways.*

'My Jenny Ren,' he said.

Renee felt her heart swell just a little. Like a sponge absorbing a small spill of milk. She opened her mouth to speak, but Michael was already turning away, his boots crunching a gentle rhythm over the gravel. And then he was gone, his car disappearing through the gate, leaving nothing but memories and a swirling cloud of dust.

Renee watched as a crane lowered a huge A-frame into place, fixing it on top of the structure like a flag on a sandcastle. The house had looked like a pile of matchsticks from the farmhouse, but close up it was much more substantial. She could see the theory of where the kitchen would be, the living room and the stairs, but couldn't envisage the end result. It looked far too big for her. What would she do with all that space?

'Hi there.'

Renee spun around, startled. A man in a hard hat was standing next to her.

'Hello,' she said.

'Could I ask you to wear one of these?' the man asked politely, holding out another hat. 'I'd hate for you to have an accident.'

'Oh,' said Renee. 'Sure.' She took the hat and put it on, grateful to have something to cover her scalp.

The man smiled at her. 'Just taking a look?' He nodded towards the timber frame.

'Sort of. That's my house.' Renee flinched. The words felt alien in her mouth. 'Or it will be when it's built.'

The man's eyes lit up. 'Is that right? Well, what a pleasure to meet you! I'm so excited to meet the buyers in person. So much of this initial stage has been handled by the agency – which is ridiculous, don't you think? I'd much rather we all get to know each other first. But it seems people are beating the doors down to get in here.' The man grinned. 'Great problem to have, though. Can't have a village with no villagers, hey?' He stretched out his hand. 'Sorry, I should've introduced myself. I'm Kit Vestey.'

Renee stuck out her hand and Kit pumped it enthusiastically. He was sweet, she thought. Impossibly young and optimistic.

'I'm so happy you've joined us,' Kit said. 'It's going to be an awesome community. And you've snagged one of the best spots. Nice big lot, great view, heaps of privacy. Plenty of room for a garden, too. Imagine a yard full of flowers and veggies against that backdrop.' He gestured grandly to the forest.

Renee shook her head. 'No flowers, I'm afraid. I end up killing everything I try to grow.'

Kit let out a good-natured laugh. 'Well, I guess we can't all be green fingered.'

They watched the crane for a moment, its huge steel arm swinging slowly back and forth over their heads. Construction workers called to each other as they stamped across the concrete slab, their banter fighting with the echo of tyres on gravel and the song lyrics stuck in Renee's head.

'Sorry,' said Kit. 'I didn't catch your name.'

'Jenny,' said Renee, her head full of music. 'My name's Jenny.'

# ALEX

## 35

I stood by the dam, my eyes still frantically raking over the party, searching for my son in the crowd. I called his phone. It rang out. I called it again, and again. No answer. He wasn't there.

And neither was Jenny.

Michael's words were stuck in my head like a radio jingle. *She lives over on the far side near the trees. Split-level. White, with a blue roof. Don't you know her?*

The more he told me, I realised that I did. But not as Renee. *Jenny.*

I couldn't wrap my head around it. Jenny had once lived in the farmhouse? She'd been Gabriel Kellerman's mother? She was Michael's wife? It didn't make sense … but of course it did. I thought about her loneliness, her fierce need for privacy. The way she'd danced around my family and me, desperately wanting to be both with and away from us. The dullness in her eyes sometimes, the downturn of her mouth, and the deep lines that I now understood had been etched not by sickness but by grief. The sheer weight of what she'd been carrying, the depths of her suffering, made me feel shaky. How had she hidden it for so long?

The past month flew through my mind. I saw our chaotic energy through Jenny's eyes. Kara's wailing, my yelling. Ollie, skinny and surly, not much younger than her son had been when he'd gone.

I imagined her life before, pictured her robust with health and purpose, standing on the veranda of the farmhouse with her hands on her hips, surveying the land. Now she spent her days looking back at her former house from the other side of the valley, watching it decay: a woman who straddled two worlds, whose broken heart had kept her tethered to the ghost of her own life. How could she stand it? Then I thought of those dust-free windowsills and swept floors, and I understood that a person with hope could withstand a world of pain.

*My son was taken.*

But had she withstood it? Or had it broken her?

*Yours will be too.*

With panic rising in my throat, I turned the pram around and hurried home.


'Ollie?' I called, unlocking the front door. 'Ollie?'

Parking the pram, I rushed down the hallway to my son's bedroom.

He wasn't there. His sheets were tangled in a ball, the blind still drawn.

'Ollie? Where are you? *Ollie!*'

I called his phone again. Straight to voicemail this time.

*Fuck!*

My brain didn't know what to do so my body took charge. It propelled me in circles around the apartment, in the hope that if I just kept looking, he'd turn up like a misplaced bunch of keys.

Stuart's voice. *Not my job to keep track of your shit.*

I looked everywhere, but the rooms remained unfilled, the beds unoccupied.

My son had vanished.

Upstairs, Jenny's unit was dark.

Heart racing, I pushed the pram along the upper road, squinting at her windows, looking for signs of life. Reaching the front door, I knocked lightly but there was no reply. Then I tried the handle and the door opened. A waft of air from inside brought Jenny's scent – roses, and a trace of geranium – but no other signs of life.

'Hello?' I wheeled the pram over the threshold. 'Jenny?'

In a small square entryway, a tulip-style stained-glass lamp cast a soft glow over polished floorboards and walls papered with a soft floral print. The rest of the house, though, felt like a void. Locking the pram into place, I tiptoed further inside. No flowers or plants, no paintings, no photographs. Jenny's unit was as empty as I imagined the last six years of her life must have felt.

'Ollie? Are you here?'

I peered around corners and nudged open doors. Both bedrooms appeared untouched, the beds neatly made. The bigger bedroom was, like the rest of the house, sparingly furnished with just a bed, a side table and an antique chest of drawers. On top of the drawers was a single photo frame, the only ornament or piece of decoration I'd seen in the whole house. I switched on the light to take a closer look. A plump and rosy-cheeked Jenny, with a man I recognised as Michael Kellerman. The boy between them had dark hair, pale skin and an awkward expression, as if he half expected the camera to launch an attack at any moment. Jenny's eyes were fixed adoringly on his face.

A hard lump grew in my throat. Blinking back tears, I replaced the frame on the drawers, switched off the light and closed the door behind me.

In the living area, Kara was stirring in the pram. *No, don't you dare wake up now, baby, please.* As quietly and gently as I could, I wheeled her around and left the unit, heading back outside to the road. Across the valley, just visible over the top of Jenny's roof, the farmhouse sat on the hill like a sugar cube. Bathed in moonlight, it seemed to be glowing.

*Listen to your children. Take them seriously.*

Kara woke up and began to whimper.

*You need to protect them. At any cost.*

The whimper turned into a full-blown cry. Letting go of the handle, I raked my hands through my hair. I had no idea what to do.

*What if something bad is going to happen?*

As I stood there, one of the farmhouse windows lit up. A flickering square of yellow, like a lantern in the dark. A flare, a distress signal.

'Alex?'

I turned my head so fast I heard my neck crack. Kit was

standing just a few yards away, his face mottled by shadow.

'Fuck,' I breathed. 'What are you doing? You nearly gave me a heart attack.'

He stepped towards me, holding up his hands as if in surrender. 'I'm sorry, I was just ... I saw you leave the party in a hurry. You seemed upset, I wanted to check on you.'

Kara wailed. I unclipped her from the pram and swung her up onto my shoulder, grateful for the reassuring weight of her in my arms.

'Is everything alright?' Kit said.

I hesitated, my gaze sliding back to the farmhouse. I could feel my pulse in every part of my body: a frantic, irregular beat.

Kit's features tightened with alarm. 'What is it? What's wrong?'

My son was in that house, I was suddenly sure of it. I had to get up there; Ollie needed me. But I couldn't take Kara on a wild chase through the forest. I pressed my hand to my forehead. *What do I do?*

'Alex, what's going on?' Kit's face was creased with concern.

I looked at him. *I'd never hurt you*, he'd said. *I would always protect you.* But the packing materials in his office, the total lack of him online ... and the flutter in my stomach that felt like butterflies but could just as easily be the ripple of red flags.

'Why are you looking at me like that?' he said. 'You're freaking me out.'

'Shush, I'm trying to decide something.' I bounced Kara up and down. I bit my lip and turned in a circle.

'What's the matter? Can I help?'

295

'That's just it,' I said, coming back around to face him. 'I don't know. Can you?'

He looked at me blankly.

'All that stuff you said earlier – how you feel about me … how do I know that it's true? How do I know if I can trust you, Kit? I mean, *really* know?'

He sighed and was quiet for a moment. 'I guess you can't,' he said at last, holding my gaze. 'But trust is about faith. I'm trying my best to earn it, but ultimately whether or not you can take that leap is up to you.'

I closed my eyes. Held my girl tight.

He was right. It was my decision to make.

So I made it.

Against the odds, I trusted him. Not because I had little choice in that particular moment, but because gut instinct told me I could – and because what was the alternative? Never put my faith in anyone ever again? I didn't want to live like that.

'Ollie is missing,' I said, opening my eyes again.

Kit's jaw went slack. 'Really? Like, *missing* missing?'

Telling him about Jenny would take too long, and instinct told me that the fewer people involved the better. 'I think I know where he is. But I need you to watch Kara for me while I find him.'

'What?'

'I won't be long. And I'll have my phone on me. Please?'

Kit stared at me. And then, almost as if she knew exactly what I needed from her, Kara lifted her head from my shoulder, yawned and reached for him. 'Oh,' he said, hesitantly reaching back. 'O-kay,'

I passed her to him, and she wrapped her arms around his neck, nuzzling into him. I smiled. *My little teammate.*

Kit patted her uncertainly on the back. 'Um,' he said. 'Alright. Yep. This is fine.'

'Thank you,' I said. 'Everything you need is down at my place. There are bottles next to the sink and a tin of formula in the kitchen, the instructions are on the back. Change her nappy, feed her, burp her, then put her straight down in her cot. She needs her bunny and a nightlight, and white noise helps. If she cries, give her a pat. I'll be back before you know it.'

I kissed my daughter and squeezed Kit's arm. In any other context, the look on his face would've been funny.

'Don't worry,' I told him. 'You've got this.'

# RENEE

## 36

'This way, Oliver, hurry.'

'Where are we going?'

'Somewhere safe.'

'But where?'

'Come on, we have to move.'

Renee slowed down, reminding herself that while she knew the path like the back of her hand, poor Oliver had no idea. At least they'd taken the easier path through the break in the trees near the greenhouses; the forest path was technically shorter, but the terrain was much trickier. This way, they'd be at the house in no time.

'Come on.' She reached back for his hand – but Oliver was dragging his feet.

'Mum keeps calling,' he said, holding up his phone.

'Don't worry about your mum. She knows you're with me.'

'I'm not worried about her,' Oliver mumbled, shoving his phone back in his pocket. 'She's obviously not worried about me. She doesn't believe me. She didn't even listen.'

'Now, that's not true. Your mum and Layla, it's not their fault they don't understand; they've never seen things like this. But I have, and I know what to do.'

As the paddock opened up and the farmhouse emerged

from behind the trees, Renee's heart rate picked up. *Home*, she thought automatically.

'What about Violet?' said Oliver. 'Maybe we should bring her with us? She got the boxes, she's in danger too, right?'

'She's already up there,' Renee said without even thinking. 'She said she'd meet us.'

'Really? She never told me—'

'All the kids know to come up here,' she lied. 'To hide, I mean. If something happens. This is the safest place. She probably assumed you already knew.'

Ollie was quiet. 'I'll call her,' he said at last. And then: '*Shit.*'

'What?' Renee turned to see Ollie staring in horror at his phone.

'It's dead,' he said. 'The battery, it's gone. I can't call her, I can't call anyone. I have to go get a ...'

He trailed off as somewhere in the distance, somebody screamed. 'What was that?'

Renee slowed right down. 'Just the party,' she murmured. But they both knew the scream hadn't come from the direction of the village.

They locked eyes.

'Let's go,' she said. 'Quickly.'


Renee held the front door open, ushered Oliver inside then shoved it closed with her hip. When she was sure the latch had clicked into place, she went straight to the cupboard by the bathroom where she kept the cleaning products. Reaching for the top shelf, she felt for the lantern and pressed the switch. Warm yellow light flooded the hallway.

'Ah, that's better,' she said, feeling pleased that she'd thought to replace the batteries.

Oliver hung back by the front door, staring uneasily at the farm tools on the wall. 'Do you have a phone charger?'

Renee didn't answer.

'I think we should go back down and find my mum,' he said. 'She might be worried after all.'

'It's alright.' Renee held the lantern out in front of her and gave him her warmest smile. 'I'm sure she'll realise where you are in due course.' Hurrying to Gabriel's room, she began removing the dustsheets. Then she tested the window, checking it was firmly locked.

Oliver watched her from the doorway, his hands stuffed into the pockets of his jeans.

When the room was ready, she beckoned him inside. 'Do try to make yourself comfortable,' she said. 'I'm sorry there are no blankets, but it's a warm night so I guess you wouldn't need them anyway. And you won't be here for long.'

Oliver shuffled forward uncertainly. 'What do you mean?'

Renee looked around the room. It was so bare, so empty. 'One way or the other, it'll all be over soon.' She went to the mattress and patted it. 'Come and sit.'

He sat. Then, as she crossed back to the door, he stood up again. 'Jenny?' he said, a tremble in his voice. 'Where are you going?'

'Don't worry, I'll be right outside,' said Renee. She left the room, closed the door and slid the bolt into place.

# ALEX
## 37

At the edge of the forest, I hesitated, listening to the distant thump of music still coming from the party. Behind me, the lights of the hall shone warm; in front, the trees huddled together, black and uninviting. On the hill, the farmhouse waited.

I pulled out my phone, tried Ollie again. No joy.

Searching for a different number, I typed a text and pressed send.

Then I rolled back my shoulders and set off.

If I'd thought the forest was creepy during the day, it was even more so at night. Every vine looked like a python, every branch a gnarled human limb. I used the torch on my phone to illuminate my path, but the vegetation closed in, obliterating the well-worn track with violent sprays of spiky leaves, lumps of rock and partially submerged roots. The ground seemed somehow animate, the surface warm and palpitant like the armoured back of a sleeping dragon.

Every step felt like a risk, but once I found the narrower track that led uphill I knew I wasn't far. The climb passed in a blur of pounding heartbeat, snatched breath and lactic acid burn. Unseen things whipped at my calves, scratching my skin and drawing blood, and my imagination ran wild, conjuring the cries and screams from my nightmares, making them seem real and loud and very close. And then, finally, I'd made it, I was in the paddock, surrounded by nothing but warm air.

I ran straight for the farmhouse, stumbling over ruts, stepping down hard into invisible holes, until I was there, under the jacaranda, on the driveway, up the steps to the veranda, at the door ...

I stopped, my fingers on the handle. Just beneath the steam-train huff of my own breath, I could hear something inside. Voices, and a faint banging.

*Ollie.*

Staring at the grain of the door, I pictured the hallway behind it. The doors, the rooms, the layout. *Go slow*, I reminded myself. *Take it easy.*

Carefully, I pushed the door open.

'Jenny?' I said. 'It's just me. It's Alex.'

She was standing outside the second bedroom on the left. Her face was flushed, her eyes were wild. Her headscarf had slipped backwards on her head to reveal thin, patchy hair.

'Come in,' she said, turning to face me. 'Shut the door.'

It was only then that I noticed she was holding an axe.

# RENEE
## 38

It took Renee a few attempts to remove the brush axe; it'd been hanging up there for so many years that the handle had somehow adhered to the display hooks. But after a few good tugs, it came loose. The handle was smooth in her hands, the bill-shaped blade heavy at one end. She stroked the blade while she waited for Alex to show up.

She took her sweet time. Renee had to listen to Oliver banging around inside Gabriel's bedroom, trying to get out, for what felt like hours before she recognised her tenant's steps on the driveway outside: dainty and hasty, always in a rush. And then she was at the door, pushing it open and peering through the gap.

'Jenny? It's just me. It's Alex.'

'Come in,' Renee said. 'Shut the door.'

Alex looked like she'd been dragged through a series of hedges – which, if she'd come up through the forest, she more or less had. There were leaves in her mousy hair and a swipe of dirt across the front of her T-shirt. Her feet were filthy, her ankles spotted with grass rash. 'What are you doing?' she whispered.

Renee said nothing. Wasn't it obvious?

From behind the bedroom door, Oliver called out. 'Mum?'

he said. 'Is that you?' The handle rattled once, twice.

'It's me, Ollie,' Alex called. 'I'm here, everything's okay.'

'Mum, what's going on? I'm sorry I didn't answer the phone. I was scared, and Jenny said she could help, she said Violet would meet us here, but then she locked me in here and it's dark and horrible and I just want to go home.' He banged on the door.

'Oh, Oliver.' Renee's heart went out to the poor boy. 'It's okay, really. This has all happened before. But it'll be different this time. This time, I know what to do.'

'No, Jenny,' said Alex, inching along the wall towards her. 'There's nothing coming. You know that, right?'

There was a long moan from outside, like the lowing of a cow.

Alex jumped.

Renee supressed a sigh. She wanted to shake her neighbour by the shoulders; how could she say that after everything that had happened, with everything that was happening right now? Wasn't Alex smarter than that? But, then again, how smart had Renee herself been? In a way, this was all *her* fault. She should've listened in the first place – to her son, to her parents. But she hadn't. Not even after Gabriel had gone.

She'd known that her son hadn't run away, but even after she'd heard the children's whispers, after she'd seen the markings in the woods, she still hadn't believed it, not really. She'd clung too tightly to the notion that it was all nonsense because it had meant that Gabriel might one day come back. But then Alex had arrived at Pine Ridge with her kids and history had begun – so clearly and so palpably – to repeat itself.

First, the dead bird. Renee had seen it in the bin the morning after Alex had moved in; the box was the same, the contents so familiar it had been like a slap to the face. Then the footsteps had started up again: that slow tread outside her window, the crunch and rustle in the trees. She'd listened with growing alarm as, downstairs, Alex had argued endlessly with her son about technology, screen time and his involvement with the dark web. Her phone had rung *constantly*. It was all exactly the same.

So then one day, while Alex and the kids were out and the unit was empty, Renee had used the opportunity to pop down and have a good look around. When she'd discovered the second box with the waxy doll inside stuffed in a kitchen cupboard, she hadn't been all that surprised. But she had been scared. *You can't stay here*, she wanted to scream. *You have to get out.* Oh, those beautiful children! She'd racked her brains trying to come up with a way to warn them without telling the whole story, to get Alex to take her kids and leave without blowing her cover. It hadn't been that hard; Alex was a predictable kind of person, she wore her heart on her sleeve, and when Renee saw her staring at the farmhouse one morning, she'd known her neighbour was beginning to make the connection. She'd left the note in the hope that Alex might be curious enough to go up there – and, lo and behold, she was. Renee had been beside herself when Alex asked her to babysit; she'd stood at the window with Kara in her arms and watched her sneak up the hill. *Clever girl.* And afterwards, when she checked, the note was definitely gone.

But then Alex surprised her by staying. *Not so clever.*

On another secret trip downstairs, Renee found traces of red on the walls, little scarlet shards stuck in the skirting board. And then Ollie came home with a bloody great scratch on his arm, and she knew for certain. It was too late. It was happening again.

This time, though, she'd been listening. This time, she was ready.

'I'm so sorry about what happened to your family, Jenny,' said Alex. 'I can't even imagine the pain. But you have to believe me, none of what is happening now is the same as what happened back then. And even if it is, how does bringing *my* son up here help?'

Renee swallowed. Inside the bedroom, Oliver was moving around, pacing the room, shifting the furniture. She heard the drag of the desk across the floorboards and knew he was positioning it under the window so he could climb up and try forcing the lock. 'I'm keeping him safe,' she said.

'But putting him in the same place, in the exact same position as Gabriel was the night he vanished – how exactly is that keeping him safe?'

Renee flinched as Oliver hammered on the door again. She opened her mouth to reply but the words got stuck in her throat: *I want to see what happens.* She *did* want to keep Oliver safe; of course she did. But she also wanted to see the thing she knew was coming, the evil her parents warned her about so many times. She wanted to face it and take it down.

From outside, there was another scream – bloodcurdling and horrifyingly close – and then a second sound, a breathless choking noise like somcone was being strangled.

Alex gasped. 'What the fuck was that?'

'I think …' Renee tightened her grip on the axe. 'I think it's coming.'

She took a step towards the front door. Through the glass panels, she could see a faint light. Slowly, the light became brighter – and she could hear a low guttural roaring, like a wild animal. She gripped the axe.

'Jenny …' Alex whispered.

Renee ignored her.

Movement. Heavy footfalls on the driveway, coming closer. The bright light flickered as a shadow passed in front of it, a black lumbering shape, climbing the porch steps …

Adrenaline coursed through Renee's veins; fear rose in her throat like blood, filling her mouth and cutting off her breath.

*This is it*, she thought as the door swung open. *It's here.*

# RENEE
## 39

Renee lifted the axe. Silhouetted in the doorway, the thing looked almost human. She held her breath as it came closer – was this what she'd slept through all those years ago? Beams of light, and the very devil at her door? – but then her eyes and brain slowly began to calibrate the picture before her.

The light was coming from a car parked on the driveway; the roar had been its engine. And the thing was familiar. She recognised the slump of its shoulders, the angle of its neck, the dangle of its arms. It was a person.

She held up the lantern. 'Michael?'

'Renee,' said her husband, stepping into the light.

His voice sent her reeling, crashing back in time, back to when the house was warm and soft and filled with furniture. She hadn't seen him in so long, *years*, and even though he was diminished in ways she couldn't begin to catalogue, he was the same man. Same ruddy skin, same green eyes, same straw-like hair.

For a moment, Renee felt foolish, and grotesque. She wanted to hide, run away, disappear right into the ground. The last time they'd seen each other, she'd had muscle tone. Curves. Hair. Not much of it – by the time they'd left the farm, her scalp had already started to show – but this would be the first time he'd seen the full extent. Now she was all hollow spaces and sharp edges, a barren place where things no longer grew. Burning with shame, she touched her head, searching for the scarf, trying to pull it back into place like a hood.

A gust of wind blew in from the open door. Twigs and branches fell on the roof in a scatter of taps, like little feet scurrying above their heads. Reaching back, Michael gently pushed the door shut. The latch clicked and the breeze died.

'I got your text,' he said, turning to Alex. His speech was slightly slurred. 'I got right in the car. Probably shouldn't have, but I did.'

Renee frowned. Michael knew her neighbour? They'd been *texting*? 'What are you talking about? What text?'

'Alex contacted me,' Michael said simply, as if that explained anything. 'She told me you were in trouble; that you were here, and you needed help.'

'I don't need help. I'm handling it.'

Michael looked at the axe. 'Clearly.'

'Someone's trying to take her son,' she insisted, pointing at Alex.

From inside the locked bedroom, there was another loud bang and the doorhandle rattled.

'It's okay, Ollie,' Alex called. 'Just hang in there, we'll be home soon.'

Michael's jaw dropped. 'Jesus Christ, Renee, you've locked him in there? What are you *doing*?'

'You don't understand,' Renee said quickly. 'Whatever or

whoever took Gabe is doing it again, playing the same sick game. They're toying with her, just like they toyed with us right before they hurt him.'

'What the fuck, Ren? What do you think this is, a movie? The stuff that happened to us back then, that was nothing to do with Gabriel. It was – something totally different.'

Renee went to set him straight, to tell him exactly what was happening, but then the air rushed from her lungs. The strange noises outside had stopped, the air was no longer full of menace. The house was just a house. Everything felt very sad and flat and bitterly real.

Another bang.

'You've gotta let that poor kid out.'

'Not until you tell me what you mean. What had nothing to do with Gabe?'

Michael sighed. Renee waited.

'What you have to understand,' said Michael, 'is that you and I led two very different lives. You lived on a thriving farm. You had family, and money. Your life was comfortable.'

*Comfortable.* Not the word Renee would've used. She thought about Ivory, covered in blood. The shadows under Gabriel's eyes. His little-big body slouching away down the lane towards the bus stop, getting smaller and smaller until finally he disappeared. Her parents. Michael's silence. His sour whisky breath.

'But me,' he said, '*I* lived in a fucking prison.'

The floor under Renee's feet shivered: a little tremor. 'I don't understand.'

Michael shifted his weight, rubbed a palm across his forehead.

'*Twenty-four seven*, Dad used to say. Remember that? *Never lets up*. Made a real song and dance about never taking a single day off. *Sucked in*, I used to think. *Your choice, mate*. Doesn't look that hard. When he died, I thought even less of him. He'd worked himself into the ground and the stress ate him from the inside out. What did he expect?'

There was a gust of wind outside and the house groaned. Renee looked up as the ceiling ticked and clicked like an old man's crooked back.

'When I took over, I set out to do things differently. Told myself it wouldn't be me in that coffin. I would live life to the full, make some bloody money. I wanted to prove that I wasn't the limp dick Dad always thought I was, that I was as good as him – as *any* of 'em. As good as Dom fucken Hassop. I wanted to show that I could do better, that I could *win*. I wanted to prove it to you, Ren.' His voice caught; his brow quivered. 'But I didn't know how.'

Renee was thrown back into the past. Questions formed on her lips. Michael had done all of those things. The farm *had* been successful. There'd been some tough times, but they'd more than survived ... hadn't they?

'I wanted to do everything myself. But I quickly realised that Dad hadn't *chosen* to work that hard; he'd had to. And the job didn't look hard because, actually, he was bloody good at it. But I wasn't. I fucked it all up. Juggled too many jobs, mismanaged the books, mishandled the drought. I fixed things too quickly, didn't play the long game.' Michael hung his head. 'And then I started defaulting on loans. The bank threatened to repossess. I felt like everyone was laughing at me, all those perfect Dom Hassops on their perfectly tended properties, making it hand over fist. Farm life made sense to them; they didn't even need to try. And your bloody father was always riding me. The place looks appalling, he'd say. You're letting the family down, your old man would be turning in his grave.' Michael laughed sardonically. 'Don't know why Dad didn't hand the farm to Hassop instead of me. Dickhead. Best pals, they were. It was like a fucken private club.'

He paused. Renee could see the swell of his shame, like a river in a rainstorm. He pressed a hand to his chest as if to stop it from cracking like a dam.

'I couldn't tell you, Ren; I couldn't tell anyone. Until one night, at the pub, I broke down and told a friend.' He lowered his gaze. 'That friend put me in touch with a couple of blokes. I'd heard of 'em, knew they were loose cannons, but I was desperate. I borrowed some cash. A lot of it. Like, a *lot*. I thought if I could just patch up the holes and get us back on top, we'd be laughing.

'But even with new machinery, bigger buildings, new advertising, we still kept sinking – and the debt kept stacking up. I missed deadline after deadline. Whatever I borrowed, the lenders asked for double back. They threatened me, said they'd make my life a living hell. *That's* what all that shit was about – the cat, the paint, the phone calls, the trolling, the ridiculous fucken Christmas angel, it was *them*. They locked on to Gabe as leverage, they told me they would murder him – and I believed them, I thought they'd kill us all. They hung around the farm during the day, just stood in the trees, watching me. They never went away.'

'I never knew any of this,' Renee breathed. 'How did I not know?'

Michael shrugged. 'I made sure you didn't. And you were so busy with Gabe.'

'Because you were never there,' she shot back.

'Being a father wasn't easy for me, Ren.'

'You never tried.'

'That's not true. I tried very hard. But Gabe … there was just no respect. No matter what I did, the kid just flat out ignored me. It drove me up the fucken wall.' A fleck of spit flew from Michael's mouth and he wiped his chin with his sleeve. 'I tried to kick his arse like my old man had kicked mine, but nothing I did made a difference. The kid just sat in his room like a king, had everything delivered to him on a silver platter. All he had to do was pull a sad face and you'd come running. And there I was, drowning in debt; spending money I didn't have, paying farmhands to help me out because my own son refused to leave his room!' Michael's mouth curled with disgust. 'Little shit never thought about anyone but himself.'

The axe swayed at Renee's side, the worn end of the handle smooth under her palm. She pictured her son's face, the crease between his eyebrows when he frowned. The time he'd sketched the dog, the time he'd made a model tractor. How he'd held them up for his father to see. *Look, Daddy.*

'It was humiliating.' Michael jabbed his finger in the air. 'He made me look weak. And I guess a part of me was jealous.

I never wanted to work on the farm. I hated the fucken place, but I wasn't allowed to slack off – and then I ended up having to run the joint, even though I was no fucken good at it.'

He took a breath and seemed to sag. The air crackled with residual rage, little particles of fury with nowhere to go.

'On Gabe's birthday, I just snapped. He wouldn't come out of his room as usual – but then in walks Dom Hassop and all *he* had to do was knock. It was like they'd planned it together. And Gabe just stood there, all innocent, making everyone feel sorry for him, and it made me so mad that I ...'

Michael's eyes went to what used to be Gabriel's bedroom door. He sucked in a big, wet breath. 'I lay awake all night, fuming. At some point, I went in there, where he was sleeping. I woke him up and took it all out on him. I told him he was lazy and selfish, that I wished he'd never been born. That I wished he'd just fuck off and leave us alone. I made him cry, and it felt good.'

He sucked in a shaky breath. 'You don't know how much I wish I could take it back. No kid deserves his father's contempt; I should know that more than anyone.'

As if Michael's words had unlocked a certain magic, Renee could suddenly see everything she'd missed back then: her husband's secrecy, his slow disintegration before her eyes. Their son, buckling under the weight of his rage. And her parents, whispering outside his door, making everything worse: *Your soul is in trouble, Gabriel. The devil has his sights on you.*

She sagged against the wall, her heart pointlessly beating in her chest. She wished it would stop and give her some peace.

'The loan sharks ...' Renee murmured. 'It was them? They took him?'

But Michael shook his head. 'No, Renee. That's just it. They didn't.'

'They must have.'

'No,' said Michael. 'Gabriel left of his own free will.'

'How could you possibly know that?'

'Because I saw him.'

Renee couldn't speak. Her mouth was dry as sand. Her jaw was clenched so tightly it hurt. She began to shiver.

'On the night he disappeared,' Michael said, 'I woke up for what I thought was no reason. My eyes just snapped open. I heard a noise outside, so I got up and looked out of the window. And he was there, on the driveway, fully dressed with a bag on his back, as if he was just off to school. He was looking at the house.' He made a small, strangled sound. 'I think he saw me. I was sure he looked right at me. And then he left. He just turned around and walked away into the dark. And I let him.'

'No.' Renee lifted a hand to touch the bolt that was currently drawn securely across the bedroom door. 'How – how did he get out? The lock on his door ...'

'The window. He must've forced the latch.'

Renee closed her eyes. 'I don't believe you,' she whispered. 'You were dreaming. Or it was someone else. Did you actually see his face?'

'It was him,' Michael barrelled over the top of her words, his voice heavy and firm. 'I was worried at first, like everyone else. But then I felt relieved. I thought about the life Gabe might be able to have if he wasn't tied to this place, to me. I thought about how miserable he'd been, how much better off he'd be. All the times I'd thought about leaving at his age but never had the guts. I thought, *Good on him*.'

Renee shook with white-hot rage. *Good on him?* 'Why … why didn't you *say* anything?'

'I couldn't! Everything had got so out of hand, and then the police were everywhere, and I wasn't thinking straight. I'm sorry, Renee. I'm so sorry.'

'No,' said Renee, breathing hard. 'You're lying. If he'd run away, he would've turned up. There would've been sightings, some kind of trace. And what about my credit card? It was never used.'

'Ren, I'm sorry.' Michael looked wrung out. 'He just didn't want to be found.'

'But, what about *your* boxes?' Renee jabbed the axe at Alex, causing her to flinch. 'The repetition, the pattern. It can't be loan sharks *again*. Doesn't that prove something?'

Ghostly pale, Alex lifted her head. 'No, I … I don't think it does,' she whispered. 'I don't think the two are connected the way you think.'

'I told you,' Michael said. 'Someone's messing with you. Someone who knows what happened.'

'No.'

'You have to come to terms with it, Ren, Gabriel chose to leave, he ran—'

'No,' Renee yelled. 'I don't accept that!'

'Why not?'

'Because I *feel* it!' She slammed a fist against her breastbone. 'Because I am his mother! Because I *know* that's not what happened to him; I know it was something else!'

She gripped the axe, pictured lifting it up and bringing it down onto Michael's head, imagined the noise it would make, the eggshell splinter of bone, the pulpy ooze of blood and brains.

'You hurt him! You hurt my son, and I will never, *ever* forgive you. But you were lying then, and you are lying now. Gabriel did not leave me. He was *taken*!'

Renee raised the axe and swung.

# ALEX
## 40

I thought she was going to kill him.

I screamed and closed my eyes, expecting to hear ... I don't know what I was expecting. What does it sound like when someone is murdered with a giant farm tool?

But then there was a bang, a dull thunk of metal on wood, and everything went quiet. I opened my eyes to see Jenny standing still in front of Michael, the blade of the axe resting on the floor. She was sobbing. He was cowering in the corner, still very much alive, his arms over his head.

'Just go,' she said through her tears. 'Please. Just leave.'

After a minute or two, he did. Edging slowly backwards, he opened the door and stepped out into the still night air. A minute later, we heard him drive away.

And then it was just us.

Jenny staggered back to the locked bedroom and sank to her knees outside the door, curling herself into a tight ball. 'I'm sorry,' she said, fresh tears running down the sides of her nose. 'I'm sorry, I'm sorry, I'm sorry.'

I shuffled close. I put my arm around her, and she laid her head on my shoulder. I held her while she sobbed and shook, and it felt like trying to hold down a boat in a storm – or maybe that was just me. My own hands were trembling, my own stomach roiling with nausea.

Into the eerie hush came a small sound. On the other side of the door, Ollie was softly tapping. 'Mum?' I heard him whisper.

'I'm here,' I replied, quietly. 'Everything's alright. We're going home now.'

Jenny lifted her head. Her teeth were chattering violently, her skin was ashen. 'I can't.' Her voice was barely audible.

'Yes, you can,' I said, as tenderly as I possibly could. 'Let's open the door and go home.'

'No. I can't.' She pulled in breath after ragged breath, and I waited quietly, knowing what she meant. She still had no answers. She couldn't move on.

In the end, I said the only thing that ever did any good. 'You're not alone,' I said. 'I'm here and I'm not leaving. Come on, we'll do this together.'

Jenny cried some more. Then she wiped her eyes and put down the axe. She looked at me; I nodded, and together we stood up.

For one heart-stopping moment when she unlocked the door, I imagined it swinging open to reveal a hole in the world where my son had been. But inch by precious inch, the room revealed itself – though not in the order I expected: the desk had been dragged over to the window, the bed pulled out from the wall, and the mattress lay half on and half off the frame. Then there he was, my boy, sitting cross-legged on the floor with his head bowed, idly tearing strips from a piece of yellowing paper.

'About time,' he said, screwing the paper into a ball and looking up. 'I really need to pee.'

With a smile so big it made my face ache, I held him and my body felt too small, too poorly designed for all the feelings contained within it. Blood and bone, I thought, were not enough. Surely we should all be made of rock, of steel, of titanium, to withstand the crushing weight of love.

Outside, the moon was high and bright, and the sky sparkled with a thick spread of stars. We walked slowly, the three of us: Ollie at my side, Jenny trailing behind. Halfway down the hill, I stopped to hold my son again, wrapping my arms all the way around his back and marvelling at how just one person can mean the whole world.

'What's going on?' he said into my hair, and a tiny, hysterical part of me wanted to laugh.

'What?' I said, squeezing him even tighter. 'You too big for hugs now?'

'No,' he said, pulling away from me with a frown. 'I mean, what's going on down there?'

I looked up at him, then turned to follow his gaze.

Down at the bottom of the hill, right in the middle of the village, was a cluster of flashing lights. The distinctive red, white and blue of an ambulance.

# ALEX
## 41

*Kara.*

Letting go of Ollie, I started running towards the forest, but he caught up and pulled me in the opposite direction. 'This way's quicker,' he said, pointing somewhere to our left.

Hurrying over the grass, we stumbled downhill, tripping over roots and fallen leaves and clumps of mud, barrelling through a break in the trees I hadn't known existed. As I sprinted past the greenhouses and onto the cycle path by the dam with my lungs screaming, a deluge of horrible images flooded my head: *she fell, choked, ingested cleaning products, stopped breathing in her sleep, Kit tried everything but couldn't revive her, I'll find her motionless, lifeless, her beautiful face covered by a blanket …*

Reaching the community hall, we found that the party had ground to a halt; the music was off, and the crowd had dispersed. Residents had gathered in small whispering groups, their faces distorted by the strobe-like lights. I spotted Kit immediately, talking to a paramedic, his expression grave. There was no sign of my daughter.

'Kara!' I called, skidding to a stop in front of Kit and grasping his arm. 'Where is she? What happened? Is she okay?' Ollie, who'd been following close behind, crashed into the back of me.

'It's alright,' said Kit calmly, placing a hand on my shoulder. 'Kara's fine, everything's fine.'

'Where is she? Oh my god, I should never have left her.' I pushed past him to the back of the ambulance, peering through the open doors, fearing the worst.

Under the flat fluorescent lights, Maggie lay on a gurney with her eyes closed, an IV tube snaking from her arm.

I spun back to Kit. 'What's going on? Where's Kara?'

'Perfectly safe,' he said. 'She's up the front, in the driver's seat.'

Running around to the cab of the ambulance, I found my daughter sitting on a female paramedic's lap, playing happily with the steering wheel.

'Oh, thank god,' I sighed, my body flushing hot with relief. 'There you are! Hello, baby!' I reached for her, expecting her to burst into tears and fall into my arms: *Oh, mama, never leave me again!* But she just batted me away, smacking her lips and pounding her fists on the steering wheel.

'Got yourself the next Ayrton Senna right here, I reckon,' said the paramedic with a smile. 'Look at her go. Does she want a job?'

Smiling weakly, I watched my daughter squeal with delight until I felt Kit's hand on my back. 'What happened?' I said, turning to face him.

'Maggie collapsed,' he said. 'It seems that she and a few others have been holding secret parties of their own in one of the old farm sheds. Taking ayahuasca at night and tripping their balls off.'

'Aya-what?'

'Ayahuasca. It's a hallucinogen. DMT, but made from plants. They brew it like a tea in the Amazon and use it for healing. It's illegal here, but somehow Maggie and her mates got hold of it. They reckon it's perfectly safe; she just overdid it this time.'

'What do you mean, overdid it?'

Kit gave a slight roll of his eyes. 'It's like a kind of therapy. Self-enlightenment, facing your demons, primal screaming, that kind of stuff. It's supposed to open up past trauma so you can work through it.'

'Sounds intense.'

'It has a purging effect too. Makes you vomit and sometimes, you know, the other thing. All very loud and messy. At some point during her trip, Maggie left the shed, wandered down to the party babbling all kinds of crazy stuff, then blacked out on the grass. Someone called triple-O.'

I pressed my hand to my mouth. I thought of the mattresses I'd seen in the shed near the farmhouse, the buckets and the plastic bottles. That strange earthy odour; the same smell in the dry goods store a couple of days later. The night noises, the bellowing. The screams we'd heard earlier. Not demons or monsters; just Maggie. I thought of her eyes, shiny and black as molasses. *Open your mind, Little Red Riding Hood.*

'Is she alright?'

Kit nodded. 'Just dehydrated. And embarrassed, probably – or she will be when she wakes up. It was quite the drama. Anyway, what happened to you? Is Ollie alright? Or should I not ask?'

323

'Maybe don't ask. But don't worry, he's fine. I'll tell you about it later.'

I glanced over my shoulder to where my son was still standing by the back of the ambulance, wan-faced and weary, with his hands in his pockets, scanning the crowd. Following his gaze, I took in the sight of the villagers, all craning their necks for the best view of Maggie. The Greatest Show on Earth. I wanted to smile – it seemed like fitting retribution for someone so self-righteous – but I couldn't. I just felt sad.

Maggie had looked so small on that gurney. Stripped of all her bluster, she was just as vulnerable as anyone else: just one more terrified human being trying to frighten other people into thinking and acting the way she did. She was no different to Jenny, writing her note and leaving it for me to find. Or Michael Kellerman, hissing vile words in his son's ear. Bess Hassop and her splintered story, her jumbled warnings. Stuart and his harmful attempts to control the world and everyone in it. Even me. I acted on my fear all the time, and most often the result was even more fear, paid forward and passed around like a sickness. I thought about how it affected the kids: Ollie and his mystery boxes, Violet's stricken face. Gabriel Kellerman and how afraid he must've been. And little Amy, whose brutal experience at the hands of those boys had—

I stopped, my skin suddenly tingling.

I studied the crowd again, paying more attention this time. I scrutinised every small group, counting heads, checking faces. Everyone was there, everyone except …

And then I saw them. Layla, Violet and Amy, standing

together outside the hall, Layla in a dressing-gown, the girls wearing pyjamas. Violet was clearly agitated, her eyes bouncing around from person to person, just like mine. When she caught sight of Ollie, her face lit up and she broke into a run, charging at him and almost knocking him down with the force of her hug. He grinned into her hair and my heart melted a little bit. But then it hardened again as I looked back at Layla. Her arm was, as usual, wrapped securely around Amy's skinny shoulders, her face tight with anxiety. My stomach lurched as I tripped over a tangle of realisations and fell into the truth – or a part of it, at least.

'Listen,' said Kit at my back. 'When this is all over and we've had some sleep, would you and the kids like to come to mine for some breakfast? I do a mean bowl of Weet-Bix.'

'Um, sure,' I said, vaguely. 'We love Weet-Bix.'

'You don't sound so sure about that.'

'No, I am – I mean, yes, that sounds good.' I glanced back over my shoulder to where Ollie stood with Violet, their heads already bowed over a phone screen. Layla watched them from behind, a dark look on her face. 'Sorry,' I said, laying my hand on Kit's shoulder. 'I just have to go do a thing, okay. Don't go anywhere, I'll be right back.'

Taking a deep breath, I walked over to Layla and Amy.

'Alex,' she said, pursing her lips as I approached. 'If you've come to talk to me about Oliver, I'm not sure now's the time.'

'I agree,' I said. 'Let's find a time to chat about it later. For now, I'd like to talk about the boxes.'

It was a leap in the dark; I wasn't a hundred per cent certain

I was right, and I certainly had no proof. But it was the best theory I had, and I was running with it.

Layla blinked. 'Like I said, I don't think it's the time or the place. If your son would like to apologise for what he did—'

'Ollie doesn't have anything to apologise for.' I looked down. 'Right, Amy?'

Amy's eyes were fixed firmly on the floor.

'What are you talking about?' Layla said.

Crouching down, I positioned myself in Amy's sightline. What was it Maggie had said at the meeting that day? *I have gifts for everyone. Although the credit should go to our beautiful Pine Ridge kids. I find their creativity so inspiring. If only we adults had even half their imagination, half their belief.*

'Amy,' I said, gently. 'I'm so sorry about what happened to you at school. It must've been awful for you.'

'Ex*cuse* me?' Layla spluttered. 'You have no right to discuss that with her, it's absolutely none—'

'None of my business, I know. And I'm sorry to have to bring it up.' I looked back at Amy. 'Amy, when did you find out that Ollie was from Ellenhurst?'

She shrugged and tucked her chin into her chest.

'Was it before we arrived at Pine Ridge?'

She nodded.

'You saw our information in Kit's office? On the board?'

Another nod.

'You check all the families, don't you? Before they arrive? You check to make sure they're safe.'

Amy seemed to shrink even further into herself.

'Listen,' I said. 'Ollie is a good kid. He just got mixed up with a bad situation. He would never, ever hurt you.'

She didn't say anything out loud, but when she looked at me I heard her question clear as a bell. *How do you know?* In all honesty, I didn't. Not for sure. But Kit had been right earlier, trust really was about faith. And it was about time I had some in my son.

'Alex, what are you *talking* about?' said Layla.

I waited. 'Amy?'

When she looked up, Amy's bottom lip was trembling. 'I'm really sorry, Mum,' she said. 'Please don't be mad with me.'

'Oh, love,' said Layla, kneeling down on the grass and holding her daughter's hands. 'Why would I be mad with you?'

'Because I made those boxes and left them for Ollie. Because I found out he was from Ellenhurst. I knew he'd been kicked out—'

'Suspended, actually,' I interjected. 'Just for the record.'

'—and then I looked on his Facebook page and there were all these weird videos, and I ... I just didn't want him here.' She looked angrily at Layla. 'You said this was a nice place, with nice kids. You said I wouldn't have to worry anymore about boys who ... did that kind of thing.'

'Amy, honey.' Layla cupped her palm to Amy's cheek. 'Why didn't you tell me?'

'Because I thought you might freak out and move us again. That's what you did after ... after what happened. You pulled me and Vi out of school and brought us here. And Vi *hates* me for it. She didn't want to come here, and she blames me, and she's been such a bitch to me. I was scared that if you moved us again, she would actually kill me. So I … tried to fix it myself.'

Layla frowned. 'By sending boxes? With dead animals inside?'

'I didn't kill them. They were already dead.'

'Oh, Amy.' Layla looked like she was all out of words.

'I think she got the mailing stuff from Kit's office,' I said, quietly. 'There are heaps of packing materials in there, and the door is never locked. Same with the doll. There's gauze and candlewax in the dry goods store; I saw Maggie getting some. Turns out she saw Amy's handiwork and decided to copy the idea for her solstice gifts. The red stuff on my wall … I don't know. Corn syrup and food colouring?'

Amy gave a small nod.

'And the symbol? The carvings on the trees in the woods? That was all you?'

Amy shook her head, her eyes wide. 'Not *all* me. The other kids do that, too. It's a game we play.'

'What about coming into my house and taking my photo frame. Was that a game, too?'

Amy stiffened and clammed up again.

'Oh my god, Ames.' Layla covered her face with her hands. 'Why would you do any of that?'

'Because she believed Bess Hassop's story,' I said.

'What story?' said Layla.

'The Pine Ridge witch. Amy thought that by sending the boxes in the right order, the witch and her monsters would come and take Ollie away, just like they took the boy on the farm.' I thought of Jenny and a lump formed in my throat. 'If Ollie was gone, then she would feel safe.'

'Wait, what?' said Layla. '*That's* where the witch story comes from? Bess Hassop? The old woman from up the road?'

I nodded.

Layla turned back to her daughter. 'And you believed it?'

'No.' Amy looked mortified. She held my gaze for a second, and then her eyes returned to the ground. 'Well, not really. I just thought you might get scared and go away. And if the witch really *did* come, then ...' She shrugged again.

'Bess said it would work, didn't she?' I said. 'Bess said it would happen.'

*Things arrive. And then they take you.*

'Amy,' said Layla, shaking her head. 'You sent *us* those things, too. You left them for your sister.'

Amy hesitated. Her chin trembled. 'I just wanted her to stop,' she whispered. 'I just wanted her to be nice.' And then she turned to her mother, wrapped her arms around her neck, and cried.

# ALEX

## 42

On paper, Christmas at Pine Ridge was perfect.

The kids and I had a tree, decorations, food and gifts; stockings and crackers and crap jokes (*Who's Santa's favourite celebrity? Beyon-sleigh!*). Our kitchen was stocked with mince pies and traditional Christmas cake and plenty of Prosecco for me, and, down at the hall, the big lunch was ready to go. The decor team had gone wild for the fake winter theme – everywhere you looked there were paper icicles, snowflakes and dustings of canned snow – and my fellow food-preppers and I had more than delivered with a huge spread of salads, cheeses, homemade preserves and plates of baked veg straight from the greenhouses. We had a seafood platter, roast chicken and ham, a Christmas cake, brandy pudding, a gigantic strawberry pavlova, freshly baked bread, locally made butter – and, of course, plenty of lentils. Poor Paul had even been roped into dressing up as Santa (with special guest Al the pug in a tiny reindeer outfit).

But in the days since the solstice party, the atmosphere had changed. Between Maggie's collapse and Amy's boxes, the village was abuzz with gossip. So far, we'd managed to keep a lid on what had happened at the farmhouse, but with everyone talking about Amy and the 'witch', it was only a matter of time before someone caught wind of it; that was just how small communities worked. So Jenny was living not only in a state of renewed grief but on a knife's edge, like a fugitive caught in a dead end. The look on her face when I'd asked about her plans for Christmas made me feel so sad, I immediately invited her to spend the morning with us – but now I was starting to think maybe it was all a bit too soon.

'Woah, thanks, Mum!' said Ollie, ripping the paper off his brand-new PlayStation 4. 'This is awesome!'

Huddled on the sofa with a cup of tea in her hands, Jenny made a brave attempt at enthusiasm, but it was obvious she was struggling.

The kids, however, were doing a great job of re-creating normality. Kara was her usual snuffly, snotty, sleep-stealing self, blissfully ignorant of everything that didn't involve food or objects small enough to stuff up her nose, and Ollie had bounced back surprisingly well. After what had happened at the farmhouse, I assumed he would never want to see Jenny again, but when I floated the idea of including her in our Christmas morning, he surprised me with some next-level maturity. 'I feel bad for her,' he said. 'I mean, she's a bit mental but I kind of get it. What happened to her kid would mess anyone up. I know she was just trying to protect me. And she doesn't have anyone else, so ...' My heart had swelled with pride.

On the floor by the tree, Ollie was unwrapping another gift. 'A VR headset?' he yelled. 'Oh my god, Mum, you're the actual *best*!'

I glanced anxiously at Jenny. *You okay?* I mouthed.

She nodded but her smile was tight, her eyes dull. My own were probably no brighter. There was a knot of unease in my chest that I couldn't shake, as if Jenny's heart had shattered up there in the farmhouse, and a shard of it had become lodged in mine.

I should've been happy. Everything had been explained – the packages, the noises, the note, the symbols – but I still felt restless. Certain aspects of Michael's story had hit uncomfortably close to home, and I'd found myself reflecting a little too deeply on my own father's rage. The bag I'd kept packed under my bed, the page I'd ripped from my favourite book. My own grand escape plans.

And then there was Bess. I kept hearing her rasping voice. *They come in the night. Listen, you'll hear them. Voices and footsteps. They follow the path that leads to the sky. A hill of grassy green, green grass, a diamond moon, and the bluest of blue skies. That's where it happened. Where the birds fly. They're going north, those birds. They're going to the moon.*

Dom's voice, too. *I think there was something going on in that house.*

The more I thought about the whole twisted mess, the less sense it made.

'Can we set it up now, Mum?' Ollie waved the headset at me. 'Please?'

I glanced again at Jenny. 'I don't know if there's enough time, mate. We'll be heading down to the hall soon. Why don't you go change your clothes and we'll take a look after lunch?'

Just as he was making a big show of rolling his eyes – *Ugh,*

*Mum, you're killing me* – there was a knock at the door. I opened it to find Kit on the doorstep.

'I won't stay long, I'm sure you're busy. I just wanted to drop this off.' Shyly, he produced something from behind his back and passed it to me. It was wrapped in brown paper and tied with a piece of string.

'Oh, now that's not fair,' I said. 'I haven't got you anything.'

'I wasn't expecting anything. And don't get excited, it's really not much. Open it.'

Inside was a piece of wood whittled crudely into the shape of a figure standing on a paddleboard. 'It's a bit lumpy,' he said. 'I'm still learning. But I found the wood down by the dam and thought of you.'

'It's lovely,' I said, genuinely touched. 'Thank you. And while we're on that, thank you for taking care of my girl the other night. You really came through for me and I haven't yet had an opportunity to tell you how much that means.'

'You're welcome. And actually, speaking of opportunities, I was hoping I could tell *you* something.' Kit cleared his throat and threw a nervous glance into the unit behind me. 'In private?'

'Oh. Sure.' I stepped outside and pulled the door closed behind me. 'What's up?'

'I just, um ...' Kit chewed his lip for a moment. 'I was thinking about what you said the other night about trust? And I need to be completely honest with you. But you have to promise you won't tell anyone.'

'Are you a spy?' I said, with a half-smile.

'What?'

'I googled you. There's literally nothing about you online, so naturally I assumed you're with the CIA.'

I expected him to laugh, but instead his expression became even more serious. 'Definitely not a spy. But this is kind of about that.' He lowered his voice and shifted his weight awkwardly from one foot to the other. 'Remember I told you I don't speak to my folks anymore?'

I nodded, confused.

'Well, there are lots of reasons for that, but the main one is that, um ...' Kit ran a hand over his face. 'Okay, I'm just going to say it. My father is the CEO of one of the largest food production corporations in the world.' He spread his arms and let out a big sigh as if he'd just relieved himself of a huge and heavy burden.

I blinked. 'Right,' I said. 'Okay.'

'His company profits massively from deforestation,' Kit explained, as if his meaning should be obvious. 'They buy palm oil illegally, they exploit their workers.'

I shook my head. 'Sorry, I still don't get it.'

Kit paused and looked down at his feet. 'Kit Vestey isn't my real name,' he muttered.

My mouth fell open. '*What?*'

'It's Chris. Chris Langella.'

'Huh?'

'Langella? As in the guy who owns all the fast food chains?'

'You own fast food chains?'

'No, not me. My father.' His words suddenly tumbled out at rapid-fire speed. 'It's a long story, one I'll tell you another time.

But the short version is that my family are not good people, and I was an unhappy kid. Fortunately, after the thing with the bridge, I discovered activism and found a new family, friends who accepted me – but I was too ashamed to tell them about Dad, so I lied about my name. I panicked and used the surname of some kid I'd vaguely known at school. And after a while it got too late to come clean, so I changed it legally.

'It wasn't such a big deal until I got serious about this place and then I realised that no one could ever know. I'd poured my trust fund into Pine Ridge; if the media found out, we'd never hear the end of it. The community would write me off as a spoiled rich kid spending Daddy's dirty money. That's why I'm not online. I don't do social media, I removed myself from data collection sites. I'm not totally off-grid, obviously; I still have email and stuff, it's just my personal info isn't available anymore, so I don't come up in search results.'

He stopped and blushed like a kid who'd just been caught shoplifting. 'I don't date much, either. After so many years of being careful, I'm not great at putting myself out there. So, yeah. I'm sorry if that's made things weird. And I'd understand if you don't want to take things any further.'

I stared at him. It was like putting on a pair of glasses after a lifetime of blurry vision. All the discomfort, the effort, the pretence I'd picked up on, it all fell away and for the first time I could see him clearly.

'Here's *my* thing,' I said, taking a step towards him, closing the gap. 'I've run away from people my whole life. It's basically my go-to solution to every problem. I've made a lot of mistakes and I've been hurt a lot; it's just easier to keep moving. But some day I'd like to stop. Get quiet. Be still.' I reached out and brushed his hand with my fingers. 'I think maybe I could do that with you.'

A lopsided smile crept across Kit's face. 'You want to be … still … with me?'

My heart was a moth stuck in a jar. 'Well, not all the time, obviously. Sometimes I'd like to be very *un*still with you; really quite active, in fact. But yeah, on the whole, you make me feel like stillness might be an option for me.'

There was a beat: a moment so loaded I was scared it might crush me.

Kit smiled. He took my hand. We moved towards each other …

'Mum!' Ollie yelled from inside the unit. 'Have you seen my green hoodie?'

We both froze. Kit laughed, and the moment fizzled.

'Well, that was predictable,' I said, grinning sheepishly. 'My kids are professional mood wreckers. You'll get used to it.'

'I can't wait.' Kit gave my hand a squeeze. 'Guess I'd better go. But I'll see you at lunch?'

'You will.'

'And maybe a few more times after that?'

'If you're lucky.'

He let go of my hand and set off down the steps, his fingers leaving traces on my skin like vapour trails in the sky.

Back in the living room, Jenny was sitting on the floor with Kara, helping her stack some coloured blocks in a pile. She smiled knowingly at me as I came in. 'How's Kit?'

'Fine.' I couldn't stop the smile from spreading over my face.

'I bet he is.'

I turned away to hide my blush. 'Did you find your jumper, Ollie?' I called. 'It's in the hamper, but please don't wear it to lunch, it hasn't been washed since the night of the ...' *Farmhouse*, I was going to say, but I stopped myself just in time. 'Solstice party.'

'Got it,' Ollie said, coming out of the laundry with the hoodie balled up in his hands. 'Looks fine to me.' Bringing it over to show me, he shook it out and a crumpled piece of paper dropped out of the pocket.

It landed on the rug near Jenny's knee. She reached out to pick it up for him, glancing down as she did – and then she stopped. 'What is this?' she murmured.

'Oh, yuck, sorry, Jenny,' I said, assuming it was an old tissue. 'Here, give it to me, I'll throw it away.'

But Jenny didn't move. She unfolded the paper and spread it out. 'This ... this is Gabriel's.' Her face had gone an alarming shade of white.

'What?' I went to stand next to her, but she was holding the paper at such an angle that I couldn't see what was on it. 'What do you mean? What is it?'

'It's a drawing,' she said, quietly. 'One of Gabe's.' She looked up at Ollie, her mouth slack. 'Where did you get it?'

Ollie shrugged. 'Your old place. I picked it up while I was, uh ...' He cleared his throat and his cheeks flushed pink. 'While I was in that room. When I was trying to get out.'

There was an uncomfortable silence while the elephant in the room lumbered slowly around us.

'I moved the desk so I could get up to the window,' he added, 'and I found it on the floor. I guess it must've fallen behind.'

Jenny pressed her fingers to her lips, her eyes still locked on the drawing. Her chin trembled.

'Did I do something wrong?' Ollie said. 'I'm sorry. I don't even remember putting it in my pocket. I was just looking at it. There wasn't much to do in there ... I guess I just thought it was good.'

'It is,' Jenny whispered, a tear sliding down her nose. 'Oh, it's very good. He was such a talented artist.'

'Can I see?' I bent down to take a closer look.

Jenny turned the piece of paper over to show me. It was a charcoal drawing of a goose. It had a long neck and a black head with a little white stripe like a chinstrap. Its enormous wings were outstretched, each feather rendered in careful detail, and its legs were tucked up beneath its body. I stared at it, my scalp tingling.

'He loved to draw animals,' Jenny explained. 'Birds were his favourite. Birds in flight.'

The tingle became a full body shiver, and my breath caught in my throat.

'What is it?' said Jenny, turning sharply to me.

*Birds in flight. Owls and geese.*

'Mum?' said Ollie. 'Are you okay?'

*A flock, all of them going up, up, up.*

Shaking my head, I took the piece of paper from Jenny's hands. I felt numb, like all the blood in my body had just evaporated. Because Bess's rambling story suddenly made sense.

'This picture ...' I said, forcing my lips to move. 'I think I've seen it before.'

# ALEX
## 43

The Hassop farm was eerily quiet when Jenny and I arrived. No rumble from the nearby road, no distant whir of machinery. Even the cicadas had fallen quiet for once. I imagined them hiding under fat green leaves, like dogs under a bed.

I drove slowly through the orchard, struck once again by its beauty, the light streaming and flickering through the constantly moving leaves, the grass below so intricately dappled it resembled the glittering surface of a lake. But I also noticed things I hadn't seen last time. Tumbledown barns just visible through the citrus trees. A large lily-laden pond with a pontoon made of planks and plastic barrels. A scarecrow in a far corner with a bucket for a head, black rags dangling from its wooden-cross body. I leaned forward in my seat, gripping the wheel, scouring the property for anything else I might've missed.

In the passenger seat beside me, Jenny sat stiff and pale, her eyes fixed on the higgledy-piggledy house at the end of the track. I hadn't wanted her to come. I'd told her I was just going to run a quick Christmas errand, check on Bess, see how she was doing – but it was too late, she'd already seen my face and wouldn't take no for an answer. 'I'm sure Layla wouldn't mind watching Kara for twenty minutes,' she said firmly. And Layla, eager to make amends, hadn't minded one bit.

When we reached the house, I parked up next to the silver ute I recognised as Dom's, but, unlike last time, there was no sign of the man himself. There was no sign of anyone at all.

Killing the engine, I got out and studied the house, shielding my eyes from the fierce summer sun. Paint-drip shadows trickled from the windowsills and wide eaves, turning the facade into one long, mournful face. Without any discussion, Jenny and I began to walk towards the front door together, our footsteps quiet on the soft ground.

The door was unlocked, the inner panel standing ajar. 'Hello,' I called through the screen. 'Dom? Anyone home?'

Just as I'd done before, I pressed the bell and listened to the chiming music echo through the building. I pressed it again. When still no one came, I pulled open the screen door, held it for Jenny, then followed her inside.

In the hallway, I stopped. There was the coat rack. The sitting room and the galley kitchen. The cracked sofas and the dark wood panelling. My eyes travelled to the staircase.

'Jenny,' I said, nudging her. 'Look.'

When she saw the diagonal line of picture frames, she frowned. When she realised what they held, she took a small step forward. 'The pictures,' she said, her voice little more than shaped breath. 'They're ...'

Birds. All different species. Flocks in V formation. Individuals with their wings spread wide. Necks all straining in the same direction, beaks pointing up. *They're going north, those birds. They're going to the moon.*

'I don't understand,' Jenny murmured. She stepped closer, right up to the wall. 'Gabe was so private about his drawing. He hardly ever showed anything to anyone.'

'Weren't they friends?' I said. 'Dom told me Gabriel and Bess were close.'

'A long time ago, maybe, but ...' She shook her head. 'I just don't understand.'

Neither did I.

Bess's scratchy voice came back to me in scraps. *A path that leads to the sky. A hill of grassy green. A diamond moon and the bluest of blue.* That, according to her, was the place where 'it' happened. At the time, I'd assumed she was describing the Kellerman farmhouse, but ... I turned to look out the nearest window and saw green grass and a blue sky.

'Stay here,' I said to Jenny. 'I'm going to look around.'

Outside, I scanned the property, trying to determine the farm's boundaries.

A paved path around the side of the house led to a patch of dirt that housed an ancient air-con unit, a water tank and a sagging clothesline. On a patch of unmown grass, a few wooden planks had been stacked against the back wall.

Stretching away into the distance was the old citrus orchard, and I could see three weather-worn wooden huts. I jogged over to take a look, but they were just disused outhouses, probably for the farmhands back in the day.

The barns I'd glimpsed driving through the orchard were

bigger than they looked but no more interesting. I had a peek inside one and found wooden beams, old trailers, concrete bricks, coils of hosepipe, a few fence posts.

No hills, though. No grassy paths, no diamond moons. And still no sign of Dom.

I'd almost walked in a complete circle before I noticed the workshop – at least, that's what I assumed it was. Just a nondescript fibro structure with a rotting timber lean-to and a corrugated roof, half hidden behind yet more trees. But when I got up close, I glimpsed lace curtains behind the cobwebby windows.

Inside, garden tools sat on old shelves warped by damp. Junk had been stacked in piles. In the far corner, though, I found something curious. A wooden plank had been laid across two plastic barrels to look like a table. The plank held a set of teacups, a teapot, two delicate side plates and three tiny teaspoons, each with a decorative handle. Two sad-looking plastic garden chairs faced one another over a mouldy offcut of carpet.

I frowned. Were Pine Ridge kids sneaking up here and playing house? But then I found a crumpled piece of paper on the floor, with squares of dirt-clogged sticky tape on each corner. *Bess's house*, it said, the words drawn shakily in purple crayon. *Please knock.*

With a heavy heart, I trailed my fingers over Bess Hassop's imaginary world. In one corner, a small storage box had been made up with towels to look like a bed, and a ragged teddy bear sat in a bucket with a sponge and a rubber duck. Beneath the bucket was a vintage suitcase, powder pink under all the dirt, with the words *Bess's Secret Things* written in shaky cursive on the outside.

Bending down, I moved the bucket aside and pulled the suitcase towards me. Unclipping the clasps, I lifted the lid. Inside was a broken music box, a few hair clips, a perfectly spherical stone and a bright green feather. And, right at the bottom of the case, I found a thick sketchbook, the pages bloated with moisture.

I dug it out. Thumbing through the damp-rippled pages, I found pencil drawings. Fruit, rocks, flowers. The desiccated skeletons of leaves, the whorled cross-section of a cabbage. A mossy nest cradling four smooth eggs. And birds, lots and lots of them. Cockatoos, swans, galahs, parrots. Same style as the ones in the Hassop house.

My eyes swam. This book had belonged to Gabriel.

I turned page after page. Some were missing, leaving ragged tears where the paper had been torn out. At about the halfway mark, the tone of the sketches began to change. Nature images became portraits. A girl reading a book. A child holding a toy rabbit. A smiling woman who bore a resemblance to Jenny, her long hair falling in her eyes. Other pictures were chilling. In one, a slithering black creature with horns and a forked tail crawled through an open window, all glistening sinewy limbs and outstretched claws. In another, Michael Kellerman hung from a butcher's hook, gutted like a fish.

Towards the end, the mood changed again. The drawings became softer, more peaceful. Bess Hassop with an angel's halo. Dom standing by a tractor, gazing into the distance: a catalogue model's pose. And then Gabriel began inserting himself into the pictures. Standing with Dom by an apple tree, helping Bess to bake a pie. The three of them smiling in front of the Hassop home, the various extensions of the house all lovingly laid out behind them in soft charcoal.

I was reminded again of my obsession with the childhood storybook. In the absence of any artistic talent, though, I'd simply torn out the pictures and pored over them in secret, inhaling the fantasy, wishing it to life.

Then it hit me.

*Holy shit.*

*Holy fucking shit.*

He'd come here. Gabriel *had* run away, but he hadn't gone far.

*This* was his fantasy, his ideal family, his dream life. This was where he felt safe. He'd packed a bag, left his house in the middle of the night and …

*There's a monster in the woods.*

I turned towards the door.

The air around me seemed to shift, like a change in barometric pressure.

And then I heard a scream.

# RENEE

## 44

Alone at the foot of the stairs, Renee stared at the birds. She pressed her fingertips to the frames. The lightest of strokes, the most delicate of shading. Tiny, feathery pieces of her son's heart, trapped behind glass. How had they come to land here in this dark, drab place?

It had been years since she'd been inside the Hassop house. It was starkly familiar, of course. Same old smell, chicken stock and dish soap. Same old fixtures and fittings. But there was no life anymore, no light.

She bit a nail, wondering where Alex was.

Slowly, she became aware of a faint clicking, dripping sound. A leaky tap? Stepping to her left, she peered into the kitchen. It was still and empty.

The noise continued. It was coming from somewhere behind her. She turned around and—

Her body spasmed.

Bess was standing by the fireplace in a long nightgown, clicking her tongue against the roof of her mouth. Her thin grey hair quivered at her temples.

'Christ alive, Bess.' Renee pressed her hand to her heart. 'You gave me a shock.'

Bess just gave her a blank look, her mouth quivering, her jaw slightly misaligned. Her skin was papery and powdery like the wings of a moth.

'It's me. Renee. You do remember me, don't you?'

Bess clicked her tongue once more. 'You look nothing like Renee,' she said. 'I remember her very well. She's gone now. Where did she go?'

Renee felt awful. Over the last six years she'd been careful to avoid all contact with the Hassops; she'd seen them occasionally but made sure they hadn't seen her. She'd had no interest in maintaining any connection between her two worlds. But clearly that had been a mistake. 'I didn't go anywhere. I've been here all along.'

'Ah. Just like her boy.'

Renee frowned. 'What?'

'What?' Bess repeated. Her eyes narrowed, then widened as if she'd just thought of something surprising. 'He's around here somewhere. Always chooses the best hiding places, I can never find him!' Her puckered lips spread into a smile and she wagged her finger. 'He finds me, though. Every time.'

Renee felt the chill in every part of her body. 'What are you talking about?'

'He should've told her.'

'Who?'

'Should've told her he was here.'

'Gabe was here? When?'

'Should've said something. It's wrong to wander off. You might hurt yourself.'

Renee edged forward. 'Do you know something, Bess? Did

you see something the night he went missing?'

Bess's crepe-paper eyelids fluttered. 'It was the bones,' she said. 'The bones came first. A gift, but nothing wanted. Next, a doll: a likeness, a promise. And the blood marks the choice. It finds a face, and then you know.'

Renee stifled a screech of frustration. *Not this again*. 'Bess? Bess, look at me.' She walked right up to the old woman and stared into her pearly eyes. 'The drawings on the wall, the ones on the stairs. Why do you have them? Did Gabriel give them to you?'

'Help,' said Bess. 'I need help. That's what he said, I remember it clearly.'

'Who said that?'

'I remember voices in the night ...'

Under Renee's breastbone there was a feeling of both expansion and restriction, like her organs were being replaced by a steadily inflating balloon. 'When? When was this?'

'... and footsteps, soft and slow on a carpet of green, on the grassy path that goes up to the blue sky and the diamond moon and the place where the birds fly north. That's where it happened.' Bess winced as if she'd been hit. 'A noise. No, two noises, one after the other. First quiet, then loud. Oh, there was so much blood.'

Renee felt as if her heart had stopped. Bess knew. She *knew*. Something had happened ... But Bess's eyes were vacant, she was barely even there. The panic began to swell and Renee's throat became tight. 'Stop this, Bess. Please, stop and *think*.'

Bess became agitated. 'I didn't know what to do,' she said, shaking her hands as if trying to free herself of something. 'I didn't know how to help.'

'You have to remember.' Renee was yelling now, barely able to restrain herself from grabbing the old woman and shaking her hard. '*Remember*, Bess.'

'I remember all of it – only then I forget. The rules, though; I won't forget those. Bones, doll, blood. Listen to me carefully, repeat after me: bones, doll, blood. That's how it goes. Things arrive, and then … a magic trick. Here one minute, gone the next. No one knows where he went.'

'*You* know, Bess. I know you do.'

'No one knows.'

'Just fucking *tell me*!' Renee's fury spilled over. Wild with frustration, she raised her arm and drew back her hand.

'No one except the birds.' Bess pointed at something behind Renee. 'They know. They saw everything.'

Renee stopped. Lowered her hand. Slowly, she turned back to the picture frames. And then she saw it.

The stairs.

They were an olive colour. A literal carpet of green.

Renee's eyes travelled up, following the line of birds to the top of the staircase. Hanging from a ceiling painted a pastel shade of blue was a delicate cut-glass light shade, a glittering orb. *A grassy path. A diamond moon. And a blue sky.*

'It wasn't his fault,' whispered Bess. 'It couldn't be stopped. Things arrive, and then they take you.'

Somehow managing to put one foot in front of the other, Renee moved towards the staircase as if she was being pulled.

Behind her, a soft click. The front door opened.

'Excuse me,' said a voice. 'Who are you, and what are you

doing in my house?'

Renee turned. Dom Hassop was standing in the doorway.

'It wasn't his fault,' Bess repeated faintly.

Dom's eyes widened. 'Renee Kellerman?' he breathed. 'Is that you?'

'What did you do?' The words spilled from Renee's mouth before the thought had even formed.

Dom's face went white. 'What?'

'Where is he?' Renee had never experienced anything like it. Feelings she never knew existed coursed through her body, undoing every joint and crushing every bone until she was sure she would crumble like dust. 'What did you do to him?' *Blood. There was so much blood.* 'I know you did something.'

Dom's mouth hung open but no words came out.

Reaching for the banister, Renee put one foot on the first step.

'Stop. Renee, please.'

Another step. Another. Higher and higher.

'It was an accident.'

His words were like four bullets in her back. They ripped through her skin, freezing her in place.

'He just appeared in the middle of the night. I don't even know how; I woke up and he was just there.' Dom's frantic, trembling voice was on the move, coming closer, climbing the stairs behind her. 'He was standing at the foot of the bed, just this tall whispering shadow. I thought … I was half-asleep and I thought I was being attacked.'

Renee dug deep. With renewed ferocity, she continued to climb, her eyes on the sky. When she reached the first floor, she scrutinised the walls, the floor.

'I hadn't been sleeping well,' Dom said. 'I was taking pills. I wasn't thinking, wasn't in my right mind. I saw him and I ... reacted. With everything that was going on with Rachel and the kids – and then all that stuff at your place, the intruders and vandalism, and Mum banging on about the Devil all the time – I was rattled. Paranoid. I kept a cricket bat under the bed, and when he came in, I ...'

The landing was dark. Dom's bedroom door was ajar; Renee could see one of his shirts lying discarded on the bed. The room was rustic but neat. Threadbare blankets and thin pillows. A freestanding robe. A used mug on a side table made of wooden pallets.

Renee gripped the doorframe. There was a spot on the carpet, a stain near the wall. A dark mark that had been scrubbed over and over again. Mud? Ink? Coffee? Something else?

'Help.' Bess's voice rose from the living room like embers from a fire. 'I need help.'

'I didn't realise what I'd done until it was over.' Dom was close now. He'd reached the topmost step, teeth chattering, speech cracked and broken. 'He was on the floor. He had his shoes on, a hoodie, a backpack. It didn't look like him, but it was. I didn't understand, I didn't know what to do.'

Renee hadn't yet seen grief, not properly; the image had never been clear. She'd expected something bloody and brutal, like roadkill or a slaughterhouse. But when she learned the truth of her son's death, the image she saw was the blackest of skies. Grief, it turned out, was a vacuum with no air to breathe or scatter light. Grief was an astronaut falling at speed while appearing to remain still.

Suddenly, Dom was right behind her. 'Please, Renee, you have to believe me.' He grabbed her wrist and yanked her arm, trying to make her stop, make her listen. 'I swear, it was an accident. I can't go to jail. My girls, my beautiful girls ...'

Renee's teeth rattled in her jaw as he clawed at her shoulders, his face red, his eyes round, his lips white. She looked up and their eyes locked. She saw right into his core, saw what he'd done, the secret he'd lived with, the things he'd kept hidden. She imagined her son's final breath, the last things he ever felt, ever thought, ever knew – and the agony of it demolished her.

'*Murderer,*' she spat, and twisted away from him. But Dom threw an arm around her neck and dragged her back. 'No, no, no, Renee, please, I'm sorry, I'm so sorry—'

It happened too quick. When she reached for the banister, it wasn't where she thought it was. She tumbled forward into the stairwell; Dom came with her, and they both slammed into the wall. Renee tried to free her arms but couldn't move fast enough. She felt her feet leave the floor and, tasting blood and panic, she lashed out, trying to hang on to something, anything ...

The world was a blur, and her body was on fire. She crashed into things; her hip – *bang* – her head – *smash* – then her fingers got crushed and her knee popped. Pain exploded in her leg, and Dom was still with her, his breath in her face, his teeth against her skull, his bones grinding into hers, and then—

*Crack.*

She stopped falling.

She tried to move but, oh god, *the pain.*

Her lungs burned.

Her bones screamed.

And then the floor beneath her fell away and she couldn't feel anything at all.

When Renee opened her eyes, she was flying. Hovering over a mirror, looking at her reflection. But when she moved, the reflection did not.

Everywhere around her, shadows were moving, shifting and swirling like ink in water. The darkness was alive – and *full* somehow, as if she was seeing not the absence of light but the other side of it.

Suddenly, a rush of movement: the sound of pounding feet, and a breath sucked in like a bow drawn slowly across a string. In the mirror below, Renee noticed a second reflection, a wretched lump huddled in a corner on the floor. And a third, frail and dressed in white, lingering in the next room. But – she turned her head left and right – she was alone.

And then she realised what was happening.

Floating calmly in the air above her own inert body, she watched as Alex came running, throwing herself to the ground and calling Renee's name. She checked for a pulse, then straightened up and frantically patted her pockets. Unable to find what she was looking for, she called to the shape on the floor.

'Dom! I can't find my phone, I need yours.'

Dom was catatonic. There was a cut above his left eyebrow

and his lip was bleeding. He was holding a small black rectangle tightly in both hands. When he didn't stir, Alex lunged at him and tried to grab it.

With one sharp shove, Dom pushed Alex away. Fear rose from him like smoke, the black tendrils reaching up to Renee and twisting around her limbs like cats' tails.

'Quick, Dom, please,' Alex was shouting. 'She could die.'

Indeed, mused Renee, there seemed to be something pooling under her corporeal head, thick and sticky like tar.

Dom didn't move. Renee could see his thoughts jumping off him like fleas. If the paramedics came, the police would follow. If they did not, she would die. Another life lost, another senseless accident. Another loop in the endless cycle of lies and fear.

'*Dom!*' Alex yelled again.

His hand twitched. His head fell back against the wall. His shoulders sagged and somehow he looked smaller. And then Dom Hassop did what he hadn't done before. He lifted the phone and made the call; broke the cycle and sealed his fate.

As he did, Renee saw a light.

*Gabriel.*

He was there, in the room, by her side, holding a lantern. Dark hair, blue eyes, full lips, gapped teeth.

*It's you*, she said. *Oh, it's you.*

Her brilliant, beautiful boy: a multitude of layers and ages, a nesting doll of a human. A thousand different incarnations, each more miraculous than the last.

Leaning forward, he took her hand. *Everything's alright. They'll be here soon. All you have to do is hang on.*

*I missed you, Gabe. Oh, I missed you so much.*

She reached for him and the lantern shone brighter ... but then Gabriel began to fade. His fingers started to slip from her grasp.

*No*, she said, clinging to him. *Don't leave me.*

He shook his head. *I'm right here.*

And even though Renee was broken in ways she'd never imagined possible, her son's smile sent a strange flood of feeling through her body, a warm peaceful glow that filled every last part of her and made her feel as if everything might really be alright. She would never stop loving him. She would never not miss him. But finally – *finally* – she could stop looking for him.

As the glow from the lantern became blinding, a snarl of emotions unspooled inside her, releasing a flurry of images. She saw death as a dragon-shaped nightlight, a torch in a tent. Birthday candles reflected in a tiny pair of eyes. A rainbow found in the fine spray of a garden hose.

*Everything's alright.*

Life, on the other hand, was a painful flash of ultraviolet, a huge ball of flame, and cirrus clouds hanging in a silver sky.

*Just hang on.*

Life was faraway beams of gold pushing through bright green leaves, warming the ground, making magic.

*I'm right here.*

Some things, she realised as the brightness consumed her, would never end. But perhaps others – cautiously, tentatively – would begin.

At last, Renee felt ready. She let go, and moved towards her own light.

# EPILOGUE

## SIX WEEKS LATER

The hall was full. Every seat had been taken, and all eyes were on me.

Public speaking had never been high on my list of favourite things; it made my palms sweat and my legs shake. But, after weeks of careful planning, I had somehow managed to deliver the best part of a solo presentation to a packed room without passing out or throwing up or saying anything too stupid, which felt like a very special kind of progress. *Almost there*, I told myself. *A couple more minutes and it'll all be over.*

Adjusting my grip on the microphone, I took a shaky breath and glanced down at my notes. 'So to summarise, the main objectives will be to maximise the capacity of working parents, ensure the safety of the kids and help facilitate their learning and development. The construction and business plans, including cost breakdown, are all laid out as explained in the proposal pack and, um ...' I double-checked the whiteboard to make sure I'd covered everything. 'That's it. I think I'm done.'

Beside me, Kit rose from his chair. 'Thank you, Alex. And well done, that was really fantastic. Now, if—'

'Actually, sorry, just one last thing.' Folding my notes and tucking them under my arm, I looked out at the circle of expectant faces. The view was much less intimidating now that

Maggie had moved on. Kit had initially tried to talk her into staying but she'd insisted the village had become too crowded. She'd apparently found another one on the Sunshine Coast, one that aligned more with her 'spiritual priorities'. Kit had since admitted that it was probably for the best.

'Look, I know we have a lot of projects on the go here and a lot of big decisions to make, but I really believe we could do something amazing here. We'd not only be making life easier for our families, but it would also strengthen us as a community *and* bring in extra income from the wider area. And as a qualified childcare practitioner, I promise I will do absolutely everything I can to make sure this facility succeeds. Because' – I looked across the circle to where Layla was grinning encouragingly and giving me a massive thumbs-up – 'it really does take a village. Okay, *now* I'm done.' I handed the mic to Kit and sat down.

Grinning, Kit took my place at the front of the room. 'Alright, let's put it to the group. Does anyone have any objections to the Pine Ridge day care centre?'

My heart pushed its way up into my throat.

'Any questions?'

I closed my eyes, unable to look.

'All those in favour?'

There was a rustle of movement. I held my breath.

Kit laughed. 'It's okay, Alex, you can look now.'

I opened my eyes. Every single person in the room had raised their arm, and every palm was open. A unanimous yes.

'Congratulations,' said Kit, looping an arm around my shoulders as we strolled home along the dam. 'You did brilliantly.'

'I can't believe it,' I said for the eleventh time. 'I didn't expect *everyone* to say yes.'

'Well, I never had a doubt.'

'Not even when I had that massive meltdown and said I couldn't do it?'

'Not even then. You're incredible, Alex. You don't give yourself enough credit.'

Above us, the blistering summer sun beat down as the wind whipped the blue gums into a hissing frenzy. The air felt heavy with humidity but the land was dry for lack of rain, and while the evergreens were hanging on to their leaves, the grassy hills were bleached to a dull matchstick yellow. It wasn't hard to imagine the whole lot going up in smoke (living in the middle of an Australian forest, as it turned out, brought with it a whole new set of concerns once bushfire season rolled around), but our action plans were in place and our evacuation drill well practised, so all we could do was hope we never had to use them.

Squeezing Kit's waist, I smiled up at him. His face was as comforting to me as a map, his features like road signs pointing the way; I couldn't imagine ever getting tired of looking at them.

'And now the real fun starts,' he said. 'Do you still need a hand going over the insurance and licensing?'

I shook my head. 'I think I've figured it out. And you've got enough on your plate anyway. Any word on the Hassop farm?'

Kit's smile faltered and he looked uncertain. 'Dom had his lawyer call me this morning. The place is ours if we want it.'

'Oh. Well, that's good news, I guess?'

'It is,' Kit nodded slowly. 'I spoke to the bank and I think we can make it work. The potential for expansion is exciting and there's a lot we could do with the orchard. It's just ... I don't know, it all feels so uncomfortable – and still too soon, don't you think? He ought to hang on to it a while longer, just in case. I mean, the trial hasn't even started yet.'

I knew exactly what he meant. Any discussion of obtaining the Hassop farm seemed somehow distasteful, as if even engaging with Dom's offer to sell was tantamount to picking over the tragedy for meat. It also seemed extremely presumptuous, given that Dom had not yet been proven guilty of anything. But I'd been there on Christmas Day; I'd seen it with my own eyes. I'd watched, confused and horrified, as the police arrived with the paramedics and Dom gave himself up, describing the night of Gabriel Kellerman's disappearance in tense, breathless bursts as if he was trapped under something heavy. I'd never seen a man so pulverised by his own words, so broken by his own regret. It didn't take a polygraph to know he was telling the truth – or a lawyer to confirm that he might face a lengthy sentence. And, even if by some miracle Dom was acquitted, I couldn't see him wanting to stick around on the farm. Not now.

I exhaled heavily, as if I could expel the thought from my body along with my breath. All that pain and loss; all those damaged lives.

'I'd like to speak to him in person,' said Kit, 'but apparently he's not accepting visitors at the moment.'

'At least Bess seems to be doing okay,' I said, quietly. 'She seems happier away from the farm. Less agitated. And she likes the water views, so that's something.'

Kit smiled thinly. 'Silver linings.'

When I'd visited the Blue Bay Aged Care Home, I found Bess sitting peacefully in a chair by the window, and I was told by the staff that she spent most of her time there, alternately napping and gazing contentedly out at the waves, for which her body was likely thanking her. No more hobbling through the forest for those old knees. I was also told that she could really 'spin a yarn', which sent a prickle up my spine – but as she could no longer wander, there was probably no harm in that.

'Speaking of silver linings,' I said, trying to rescue the mood, 'I'll be putting in a lot of extra hours at the office now that my proposal has the green light. Probably a few late nights too.'

'Late nights, huh? Well, that's a shame. Not a lot of room in that office.'

'No. We'll really be, ah, on top of each other.'

'Sounds awful.'

'If only there were some advantage to that.'

'I can't think of anything.'

'Nope.'

We made it about another three metres before Kit spun me around and pulled me into a deep kiss. 'Can we stop pretending now?' he said, his hands in my hair. 'Because I can actually think of a *lot* of benefits to that scenario.'


A little while later, after Kit and I had managed to disentangle ourselves, I set off for home, leaving him to continue on the cycle path back to his place. As I reached the steps that led to our unit, I saw Ollie coming from the opposite direction, slouching along the road in his new school uniform, shirt untucked, arm slung casually around the shoulders of his first ever girlfriend. I watched, smiling, as Violet gestured in the direction of her house and they stopped to say goodbye; he whispered something in her ear, she laughed and pressed her forehead to his. Caught in a patch of sunlight, the two of them seemed to glow like they were made of different stuff than the rest of us.

Not wanting to break their spell, I waited until she'd gone then called out when Ollie was close enough to hear me. 'Hey,' I said. 'How was school?'

'Fine.'

'What did you do?'

'Um … designed our own website.'

'Really? Sounds very advanced. When I was at school, I designed leaflets. With a pencil.'

'That's because you went to school in the Cretaceous period.'

'True enough.'

Side by side, we climbed the steps.

'Did you know,' Ollie said when we got to the top, 'that there's a college down the road that does software development and programming?'

'No, I didn't know that.'

'They do IT security, too.'

'Huh. Sounds interesting. And when you say down the road, you mean …?'

'The coast.' He caught my look. 'It's not that far. I could drive.'

My heart contracted. He was right. In a few weeks, he would turn fifteen; L plates would follow the year after. So much potential for adventure – and disaster. 'Why don't we get through this first term of school and then maybe we'll discuss future plans, okay?'

Shrugging, he pushed open the front door and disappeared inside.

I lingered on the doorstep, feeling a strange mix of pride and melancholy. I wondered what kind of man my son might turn out to be. He'd been through such a big change over the past twelve months; our relationship had felt for so long like yet another bad break-up – *Let's just call it quits, shall we? There's no point in trying to make this work* – but now it felt like we might be on the mend after all.

I still had that twitchy feeling of powerlessness, though. In a way, things were easier with Kara; her needs were comparatively simple, the solutions more obvious. But with Ollie, each year that passed had me feeling less and less sure what to do with him, or *for* him. How could I make sure he didn't end up like my dad? Or Stuart? Or poor Gabriel Kellerman? What could I do to save him from the abyss? The answer, I knew, was not much. I could no longer carry him around with me strapped to my chest, couldn't swaddle him or breastfeed him or put him in a cot that he couldn't climb out of. Pretty soon I wouldn't be able to control any part of his life at all. But I could be less afraid. I could keep talking to him. Stop running. Be close and have faith.

Easier said than done, of course, but I would try.

I nudged open the door and sighed happily as the cool of the house hit me like a cold shower, soothing my flushed skin. Ollie was making toast in the kitchen while Kara pushed a fire truck back and forth over the living room rug, her brow creased adorably with fierce concentration.

'Hey, baby girl,' I said, crossing the room and bending down to kiss her peachy cheek. 'What are you doing by yourself?' I looked around. 'Where's—'

Down the hall, the toilet flushed and Jenny emerged from the bathroom with her arm in a sling. 'Oh, Alex, you're home.' She limped towards me, her eyes wide. 'How did it go?'

'Oh yeah, sorry, I forgot,' said Ollie, his mouth full of toast. 'How was the presentation?'

'Amazing.' I beamed. 'A full house of yes votes. We got it.'

Jenny squealed.

'Good on ya, Mum,' Ollie said, reaching over to give me a high five.

'I *knew* you could do it!' Jenny pumped her free fist in the air, then winced. 'Ouch. I keep forgetting I still can't do things like that.'

'Yikes,' I said. 'Have you been alright looking after Kara? Sorry, I didn't think—'

'Oh, shush, I'm not that infirm. I can cope for forty minutes.'

'How's the head?'

'Not too bad.' Jenny touched her headscarf. 'I'm using the cream and the scar now feels less raised, so that's a good sign.'

'And how are you going otherwise?'

She made a face. 'Ribs are still sore, but my shoulder's getting there. The doctor said the sling can come off next week, so …'

'No,' I said. 'I meant, um, everything else.'

Jenny's face dropped a little. 'Oh, you know. One day at a time.' She gave me a thin smile. 'But I'm going to visit my parents tomorrow, so I must be feeling stronger, right?'

I smiled. 'Right.'

'Oh, and I have something exciting to show you.' Hobbling to the kitchen bench, she picked up a stack of papers and handed them to me.

'What's this?' I said, taking them.

'The final Tiny House designs,' Jenny said, proudly. 'They just came through today.' She unfolded one of the pages and spread it out on the benchtop. 'Isn't it beautiful?'

'Oh, Jenny.' I peered at the plans. 'It really is.'

'See how it's long enough to have a bedroom downstairs as well as up in the loft? That way it'll still be comfortable when I can no longer handle ladders and limited head space. And the dining area – look, there's more than enough room for a table.'

'It's stunning,' I said, leafing through the rest of the paperwork.

'Come outside and let me show you again where it's going in.' Moving carefully but quickly to the door, she held it open for me and beckoned excitedly.

'Ollie,' I said, following her. 'Keep an eye on Kara for five minutes?'

'Sure,' came Ollie's reply. 'In exchange for the whole top floor when Jenny moves out.'

'Enough with that, it's not going to happen.'

'It's happening.'

'It's not.'

'Love you, Mum.'

'Stop trying to butter me up.'


'So, we'll level the earth out here, look.' Jenny swept her outstretched arm across the far side of the garden. 'The front door will face that way, and the kitchen windows will look out onto the forest. See?' She pointed at the designs in my hands.

'It'll be lovely, Jenny,' I said, holding on to the papers as they flapped lightly in the wind. 'Just perfect.'

She studied me, detecting the note of unease in my voice. 'What's wrong?'

'Nothing, it's just … are you absolutely sure you want to stay? *I* want you to, of course, but after everything that's happened, wouldn't you rather a change of scenery? Get away from everything and just start over?'

Jenny gave me a small smile. 'I thought about it. But eventually I realised that all that stuff I'd want to be leaving behind would just come with me anyway, so what's the point? I love this land, it's part of who I am. I love this community. And as for the scenery … well, it'll all change sooner or later, won't it?'

I nodded. The construction plans for stage two of Pine Ridge were already in motion and within the year new houses would start appearing on the other side of the valley, too.

'What about you,' she said. 'Are *you* sure?'

I looked at her. 'What do you mean?'

'Well, I understand how much of an adjustment it must be for your family, collaborating with me, sharing the land. And it must feel scary to be putting all your savings into buying me out. Maybe you're having second thoughts?'

'No, definitely not, I'm all in.' A gust of wind blew through my hair and I pushed the strands back with one hand. 'And using our savings to secure homes for both me *and* you is really not that scary.'

In fact, it felt the very opposite of scary – more like appropriate, given how Jenny had lost her home in the first place. I'd done a little digging and my former neighbour's story had checked out: Stuart was indeed wanted by the police for money laundering. Which meant that, in a karmic kind of way, that money belonged to Jenny. Or Renee, anyway. Criminals had taken her money and she'd lost her house, but because I'd taken money from criminals, she now had a new one: a place she'd designed herself, a home she loved. I couldn't think of a better use for it. And if Stuart ever came looking for me, or the cash, he would find a different woman: one with friends and a mind of her own. I thought about my Tupperware container, now sitting in the pantry instead of under the laundry sink, crammed full of cookies instead of banknotes, and it made me smile.

As I did, the wind came at me again, this time tugging hard at the building designs and blowing them right out of my hand. 'Oh!' I gasped as three sheets of paper flew into the air and took off towards the trees like a flock of doves. 'Oh, no!'

'Quick, catch them,' cried Jenny, and I chased after them, trying unsuccessfully to grab them as each sheet whirled and spun away from me as if playing a game. They cartwheeled into the woods and danced among the trees before finally coming to a stop, one on the path, one in a puddle and one flat against the rough trunk of a gigantic red cedar.

Panting hard, I snatched the papers off the ground before they could escape again, brushing off the dirt and smoothing out the creases as best I could. A clump of mud was stuck to the corner of one and I used the hem of my shirt to wipe it away, revealing the village logo. *Pine Ridge. Create the life you want.*

I stopped and took a moment to breathe. The forest was cool and sheltered from the breeze. Bellbirds tinkled like wind chimes, kookaburras cackled, and from somewhere deep in the undergrowth I could hear the chatter of running water. Above, the sun flashed through the gaps in the canopy and cast a shimmering pattern of light and shade on the gravelly ground.

As all around me nature did its thing, I thought about how much had happened since my arrival at Pine Ridge. The different experiences and interpretations, all mixed up together. The scattered pieces of the puzzle, and the way in which those pieces had been shoved together to make something new. The spiderweb of rumour, the snowball of gossip. The scary story in the deep, dark woods, and the light that always found a way in.

*Create the life you want.*

For the first time, I felt as though the life *I* wanted might finally be within reach. Or maybe it had always been there, just waiting for me to find it.

Either way, it was time to go home.

Clutching the runaway papers to my chest, I walked out of the forest and back to my family.

# Author's Note

Thank you so much for reading *The Shadow House*. I hope with all my heart that you enjoyed it. If you'd like to reach out and tell me what you think, please do drop me a line. I was blown away by the messages I received after the release of my first novel, *The Safe Place*, and the response to my author's note was especially moving. So, with that in mind, I'd like to tell you a bit about how *this* book came to be.

Second books, like second albums and second children, are notoriously difficult, and this one was no exception; in fact, for a while I was completely petrified. I'd poured everything into my first book: what if I had nothing left to give? My publishers were waiting for a follow-up, but what if I couldn't deliver? What if I couldn't come up with an idea that worked? But then, as the readers of my first author's note will already know, I am a bit of a worrier.

While suffering from post-natal anxiety following the birth of my second child, I worried all the time. I was trapped in a hamster wheel of fear – but fear of what, specifically, I couldn't have said. I was so sleep deprived that everything seemed imbued with dread and menace. *Nothing could be worse than this*, I remember thinking one particularly awful night.

But then I had a conversation with a friend, a single mum, who told me she was going through a rough patch with her fourteen-year-old son. 'I love him so much,' she said, 'but he's changed. He used to be my best friend; now it's like he's possessed or something. We clash all the time. I just don't know how to connect with him anymore.' I thought about my own beautiful little boy, and my astonishing baby girl, trying to imagine a time when they no longer wanted to play with me, or even talk to me. *Ah*, I thought, my heart shuddering. *That's what could be worse: sleep deprivation* and *a teenager.* Suddenly, I had the tiniest seed of a workable idea, or a character, at least: a woman who has to free herself from her own issues while also juggling a baby and a teenage son.

Shortly after that, I listened to a podcast about screen addiction, and it made me want to throw away all our devices. I heard about dark-web mystery boxes, a real-life trend from 2017, and it totally freaked me out. I read about a Melbourne family whose lives were shattered when police raided their home one day and arrested their twenty-three-year-old son, who, it transpired, had spent four years in his bedroom building child exploitation websites. His parents just thought he'd been gaming. *Okay, yep*, I said to myself. *That's much, much worse.*

And then, in February of 2020, Covid reared its ugly head and gave 'worse' a whole new meaning. I won't describe it for you; you were there. It was awful. Everyone was scared. Life as we knew it was basically cancelled. *Erase, and start again.*

Locked down in my house, I tried to be productive. *What a great opportunity*, I thought, assuming I'd have plenty of time on my hands to write. But, in addition to rising case numbers, the news was full of climate change and shocking acts of racism.

Then my family and I lost someone very dear to us, and I couldn't get back to the UK to be with them. Between fear of the future, grief, isolation and homeschooling, time seemed to bend and shrink. The kids climbed the walls. The same day repeated itself over and over. And when I did get time to write, the words felt ... wrong. I'd managed to turn my idea into a first draft, but for some reason it wasn't working and I couldn't fix it, no matter how hard I tried. Deadlines loomed, and panic set in.

But, amid all the bad stuff, there was also some good. Lots of people read my first book, and many of them wrote to me to tell me how much they liked it. My sister announced she was pregnant. Despite the painful separation from my family in England, we found ways of staying connected. My kids and husband made me feel very loved, and we all survived both homeschooling and the sudden increase of screen use. We bought a fire pit, swam in the ocean and discovered new bushwalks. My daughter started sleeping through the night. My sister had her baby. My mind was blown by good books, my heart was warmed by the kindness of friends – and, by some happy accident, I discovered an ecovillage down the road: a joyful community of people trying to find new ways to live.

Meanwhile, I was still wrestling with that crappy first draft. One day, after an exceptionally maddening few hours at my desk, I went outside. I wanted to scream – *I can't make it WORK, it's IMPOSSIBLE, this is a NIGHTMARE* – but, fearing judgement from the neighbours, I stomped to the end of the garden instead. I set up a chair under the orange tree, sat down and looked up at the branches. Through tears of frustration, I watched the leaves dance in the wind and tried to breathe. The sun winked at me from above, and down near my foot a bird pecked at the ground. My muscles began to relax. And, as they did, I realised that it *was* a nightmare. The worst *had* happened, on both a large and a small scale. A pandemic had swallowed the world; my manuscript did not work. BUT. I was living through it. The sun was still shining, the trees were still growing. Good things were still occurring all around me.

And then something clicked. A new story. New characters. New hope. They seemed to fall on me like rain.

Obviously, my problems were not all magically solved in that one moment, but things did get a lot better from then on. I ran inside, back to my manuscript, and I printed it out. I cut it up, laid the scenes on the floor and moved them around like a jigsaw puzzle. I kept a few, but threw most out. I realised that, in order to move forward, I had to let go of what I thought I knew and allow myself to see things differently. *Erase, and start again.*

The story I eventually came up with, the story you've just finished reading, is of course about fear. How could it not be? But it's also about looking up. Letting go. It's about hope. Because, if 2020 and this book have taught me anything, it's that things can and do get worse, but they also get better – sometimes at the exact same time. (Case in point: as I write these words in July 2021, Greater Sydney is back in lockdown, back to homeschooling. But my novel is now finished, and this morning I saw dolphins at the beach. So there you go.)

Things will get better.

We can move on.

And things that seem impossible are very often not.

If you're a bit of a worrier like me, you might find those things difficult to remember. I know I will. But hey – we can try.

And, in the meantime, we always have books.

# Acknowledgements

My deepest love and gratitude to the following people, the Dream Team, without whose help, support, knowledge and expertise I would be lost. Working with you all is an absolute pleasure and one of the greatest honours of my life. Thank you to:

Tara Wynne and Hillary Jacobson, my guardian-angel agents, friends and first readers. What would I do without you? No, don't answer that, it doesn't bear thinking about.

All the wonderful folk at Curtis Brown Australia and ICM Partners.

Martin Hughes: publisher, editor, anchor. Steadiest of hands and safest of nets. Thank you for raising me up and never, ever letting me fall.

Keiran, Ruby, Laura, Grace, Rosie, Lauren, Kevin and the whole Affirm Press team: you're all dead set legends. I adore you.

Catherine Richards, for whose endless encouragement and razor-sharp editing skills I am forever grateful. Thank you for believing in me.

Nettie, Joe, Steve and the wider team at Minotaur, who always go the extra mile.

My insanely gifted copyeditor, Nikki Lusk. (Authors, if you ever get the chance to work with this woman, jump at it. She is incredible.)

Katie Greenstreet at C+W. Eve Hall at Hodder and Stoughton.

I'd also like to thank the people and places who have directly influenced the creation of the characters and settings in this story:

Sarah Carr, whose emotional honesty sparked the very first idea for this book.

Justin Wiggins, my brother from another mother, who first brought dark-web mystery boxes to my attention.

Sheree Downes, my sis-in-law, for answering my questions about high-school kids.

Louise Dominello and everyone at S&P Dominello Flower Growers in Peats Ridge, New South Wales, who very kindly allowed me to spend a day observing their work and asking questions about farm life.

Lyndall Parris and all the residents of the beautiful and genuinely idyllic Narara Ecovillage, New South Wales. Without you, I wouldn't have a setting. Thank you for being so warm and generous with your time.

The stunning Pecan Lady Orchard in Somersby, New South Wales, whose farm stay provided a peaceful writing retreat and whose trees supplied unexpected and timely inspiration.

Orion at Truth & Power in Avoca Beach, New South Wales, with whom I spent a fascinating afternoon talking about healing, shamanism and ayahuasca, back when this book was about something else entirely. (Unfortunately, I couldn't make that particular draft work, but I have kept some of the smaller details and, who knows, maybe shamanism will make an appearance in another book one day.)

Thank you to my beloved author friends, my writing 'village', whose support means the absolute world. There are so many of you, but extra big hugs to:

My Central Coast writers group, retreat team and book coven: Donna Cameron, Adrienne Ferreira, Lisa Kenway – and Hannah Gierhart, whose help and insight around the fifth-draft mark was utterly invaluable.

My Zoom writers' group, who are hands down one of the best things to come out of 2020: Ashley Kalagian-Blunt, Rob McDonald, Petronella McGovern and Josh Pomare.

Kate Mildenhall, whose boundless generosity and wisdom made a whole lot of difference to my second draft.

And Christian White, whose friendship and pep talks I just couldn't do without.

Finally, a huge and heartfelt shout out to my family and friends near and far, especially those I haven't seen for a very long time. Special thanks to:

My mum, Heather, and stepdad Charlie, Grandma Jo, my dad, Robert, stepmum, Liz, sisters, Jessie and Lotte, and the whole extended UK crew for all the regular check-ins and support from the other side of the world. Covid has been, and continues to be, tough for us all, and there are no words for how much I miss you … but when the reunion finally comes, the celebrations will be epic.

Adam Lollback, for loaning me your office space when I so desperately needed it, and Jackie, for all the tequila. Candice Boyd, for listening to me talk through those first few ideas.

Lucy, my sestra, my whisp. Elsie, for all the smiles.

My kids – *always* my kids – Daisy and Jack. You are my inspiration. I love you. Please never get too big for snuggles.

And, last but never least, my husband, Matt. Without your constant positivity and willingness to brainstorm plot ideas with me, I would probably still be crying on the couch. Thank you for being the kindest and best co-parent and co-pilot a girl could wish for.